The Reluctant Prophet

By

Susan Davis Sandberg

To
My son Eric
For being the first one
to support my dream

Chapter 1

The sound was slight, a mere cracking of a few dry twigs. The dog's eyes opened and his head came up. His ears came erect. He turned his head toward the sound. His muscles tensed as he rose slowly to his feet.

He was a large dog, ninety pounds of solid muscle beneath a short wavy coat of hair rough as wire. The hackles between his shoulders rose slightly as he stood motionless in the dark living room. The blinds had been tilted earlier to soften the rays of the setting sun and had not been reopened when the moon took over the lighting of the countryside.

The expanse of window at the front of the house gave credence to the overworked phase picture window for when the blinds were raised, the view was spectacular. This was not uncommon in the first cities on the peninsula north of San Francisco. Half the houses boasted a fantastic view of the bay and the harbor to the east; the other half overlooked the tree shrouded hills huddled around Mount Tamalpais to the west. On the other side of the mountain lay the vast expanse of the world's largest ocean.

This could not be seen from the house which perched on the western side of a medium-sized hill, its footing rooted in solid rock. It was a house of modest size, not large considering the local realtor's evaluation at an even three million.

There were but six rooms inside. The large bulky furniture fit comfortably. Old furniture. Hand carved dining room chairs. Ornate glass windowed bookcases. Deep cushioned couches upholstered in tapestry. Twin leather recliners. Large tables of polished wood serving as resting places for books and magazines about dogs and hunting. It was a house unafraid to be a home in a beautiful town of tree-lined streets barely two lanes wide that wound up and down hillocks, past houses whose faces were hidden behind a veil of carefully planted shrubbery. The road from the freeway to the town's center was split by a stream which snaked its way under a small family owned lumber mill and then veered left and wound around homes tucked beneath its tree lined banks shaded from the sun and sheltered from the noise of the world save for the gurgling of the brook. For a moment now and then the princes in the world of commerce could again live like the frog on top of the lily pad.

Two million was the going rate for that experience.

Inside the house, the only sound was the soft snore of the older of the two female dogs lying on the soft pads in their crates. Both the doors to their crates were locked. Only the door to the male's crate was left ajar.

Haze Spader, whose feet had crushed the dry twigs, stood outside beneath the bedroom window. He pulled down his black ski mask. Haze knew about the dogs. In fact, he counted on them.

His brother Clay was head mechanic in a garage that specialized in foreign cars so he didn't personally know anything about the lady; but, he pointed out Mrs. Locke's gardener, a gnarled, bent old man, a regular at the Beer Joint. Clay told his brother that if he got a few pints into the old man, he'd run off at the mouth about the dogs.

Haze had returned the next night when his brother wasn't around and sought out the old man, fed him a line about being asked to bid a job for Mrs. Locke and he'd heard she had some big dogs on the place. He ordered two whiskeys.

"That she has," the old man said eyeing Haze suspiciously. Haze pushed one of the glasses toward the old man and told the bartender to leave the bottle.

"How many?" Haze asked downing his drink in one swallow.

"Three," the old man quipped. He pulled the shot glass toward himself and fingered it for a brief moment before lifting it to his lips.

"What does she want with three dogs?" Haze asked refilling his glass and the old man's.

"She says she takes them hunting," the old man drawled, "but I don't believe it. I ain't never seen no game anywheres. But lots of show ribbons. I think she wants people to be afraid of them so's they'll leave her place alone. That's what I think."

Haze hesitated asking for more elaboration. Fortunately, he didn't need to ask about the security system. There was a small metal blue and white sign attached to the perimeter fencing warning would be thieves that the Marquis Security Company guarded the property. Haze knew their reputation. He counted on them doing their job as well. It was important to the Ciccone Family that it looked as if Mrs. Locke had been killed when she surprised a burglar.

Haze veered to more mundane matters. Were the dogs destructive? Did they mess with you when you were working? Did they ever attack anyone?"

The gardener took a long time with the first question. It seems that the youngest, Babe, as a pup took a liking to the jasmine vine climbing up the bedroom side of the house and she destroyed several main branches before Mrs. Locke gave up trying to discourage the pup with various commercial sprays and put a fence around the vine. While Mrs. Locke had generally limited the puppy's access to the patio and the garden behind the house, still the gardener talked about how he had to replace dozens of plants the pup had pulled from the soft earth. Confining the dogs to the grassy front area didn't lighten the gardener's load. While there was plenty of shade beneath the ash tree at the bedroom corner of the house and soft grasses beneath the three birches at the other side, still on hot days, Stoney, the big male, dug deep holes in the lawn and laid in them.

Haze asked why she didn't lock them up. He said that he knew lots of Lab owners who'd built kennels so their dogs wouldn't wreck the place.

"Labs don't like being left alone," Haze remarked with some authority. "So they do all kinds of digging when their owners are gone."

The gardener had grinned triumphantly. "Well, these is worse," he explained. "They's Chessies. And what Labs don't like, Chessies don't like double. They's hardheaded sons of bitches. And strong as bulls. Don't know that a bit of wire would hold them in."

"So she never locks them up?" Haze queried. He'd finally gotten around to his real question.

"Sure," the gardener said. "She crates 'em. That's what she calls it. She's got these little boxes like the airlines use to ship dogs across the country. And she puts them in them at night. She says they like it."

"Do you believe her?" Haze asked, not because he wanted the old man's opinion but because he'd find out more about the woman of the house and where the dogs were at night. He'd just as soon not have to shoot a dog. He'd do it, but he'd rather not.

The old man reached for his glass, and Haze poured another shot of whiskey into it. He waited while the gnarled hand held it to the waiting lips and the head tipped back. The old man set the glass down on the counter and asked Haze what they were talking about.

"Dogs," Haze said.

The man nodded. "Oh, yeah, I remember. No, I don't believe it, but what do I know? She's the one with all the ribbons. And the dogs mind her real quick. You never saw dogs that mind like hers. She says 'Here!' to that big male of hers and the damn dog runs to her as if his tail was on fire. He can be clear across the yard and he'll spin around and run straight toward her."

"What happens if she's gone and you're in the yard with them?"

"Never happens," the old man said slurring his words. "She never leaves them alone outside."

"Never?"

"Nope. If she goes away, she locks them in the house."

"In their crates?"

"Nope. They's loose. She says they keep out the burglars."

"But she's got a security system!" Haze protested. Haze wanted to bite his tongue. The words had escaped unbidden. It only happened because he'd let his guard down. The old man didn't seem to think the question odd.

"She only uses it at night when she locks up the dogs or when she leaves town."

Now, standing at the side of the house, under the ash, in the shadows cast by the fully leafed tree, Haze stared at the stairway leading to the deck. The moonlight glistened on the steps still wet from the sprinkler. He would be fully exposed for as long as it took to reach the deck and turn the corner.

He reached behind him and pulled out his gun. Just the feel of it in his hand pumped him up. There was a big paycheck attached to this one. Easy. In and out. He stuck the gun back in his belt as he reviewed his plan one more time.

When he reached the door, he would cut the glass and then put the cutters back in the bag next to an odd assortment of tools, none of which were his. The bag was to be left behind to bolster the illusion that entry had been made by a professional who was subsequently scared off by the barking dogs. He was certain the dogs would bark after he shot their mistress.

The gun would be left at the scene. It'd been provided by the Ciccone Family that hired him. It couldn't be traced.

His car would be found abandoned a mile and a half away. It had been stolen earlier.

The bottom stair creaked under the weight of his foot. He paused and gazed sideways at the open bedroom window.

Damn woman, he mused silently. Why didn't she use her air conditioner like everyone else?

He held his breath. He hadn't figured on the window being open. His heart pounded.

Inside the house, the dog lifted its head as a faint breeze rustled the leaves on the Italian Ash and carried the scent of Jasmine mingled with the scent of a man through the bedroom into the hallway where the dog now stood. A soft rumble, no louder than the purr of a tiny kitten, but more full-bodied and deeper, reverberated in the throat of the big dog. Had the man's ears been as keen as the dog's, he would have recognized the seriousness of the warning.

The breeze carried the man's fear to the dog. The dog believed the man had heard him. He had no way of knowing that the man was afraid of the open window and the mere possibility of a dog—any dog—leaping through it.

The quickness of the man up the stairs sent the dog scrambling toward the kitchen which extended along the entire back of the house.

As the man hit the top stair; the dog was standing on his hind feet, poised in midair, his back feet solidly planted on the polished brick floor, his front feet tucked back by his chest. While small poodles and terriers dance on their hind feet readily, the bulk and weight of the larger breeds makes this a difficult feat. The dog had learned early in life that his front feet were never to touch his mistress's burnished wood counter top. His curiosity kept his standing muscles well-toned and he stood motionless watching the man who was staring at the garden behind the brick retaining wall.

From the gardener's description Haze Spader had expected a well-ordered formal garden with hard rock paths that would yield no footprints. Instead he was looking at what appeared to be a field of wild flowers and grasses. The large olive tree was the only item in the gardener's description he recognized. The moonlight filtered between its slender leathery leaves and fell on a tangled mass of plants. Where were the pale yellow columbine, the daisy-like feverfew, the red sweet williams, the buttercups, the daisies? Where the hell were the masses of California poppies? He didn't know that the poppies sleep at night by pulling their bright orange petals back into budlike position until the dawn urges them to awaken and stretch out. He didn't know that those flowers that remained open grayed under the pale moonlight. What he did know, however, was that he couldn't go up the hill without signing his name with every step.

When the man didn't move, the dog dropped down on all fours. There was no click from his neatly trimmed nails as his thick pads hit the brick. He watched the man turn and a growl formed deep in his chest.

The man peered through the window and looked straight at the dog. The moonlight filtering through the branches of the olive tree coupled with the dead grass coat color of the massive male Chesapeake Bay retriever made him invisible. This was partly caused by the fact that Haze Spader was expecting to see a smaller dog which was the result of him not being able to picture a seventy-year-old woman with a large dog and partly because the oak cabinets behind the dog were the same color as the dog himself.

Haze Spader, satisfied that the kitchen was empty, moved swiftly along the wall to the door. The dog followed his movement and stood motionless as the cutter sliced through the glass and a circular piece of glass was removed.

The rumble from the dog's throat grew louder. Haze Spader heard it, but he didn't care. He wanted the dogs to make noise. He didn't, however, know that one of the dogs was loose. Or that it was standing on the other side of the door. If he had, he would not have reached through the hole with his gloved hand.

The dog cocked his head as the hand snaked through the hole and fingers gripped the handle of the dead bolt, turned it and pulled it back with a soft snap.

The sleeping dogs turned over, brushing their short claws against their crates. It was a normal nighttime sound just like the leaves rustling in the breeze outside the open bedroom window. In the distance a dog howled and the small yap of a terrier answered the mournful call. Harriet Locke stirred but didn't waken.

Spader turned the knob and pushed. The knob rattled lightly but the door didn't yield.

Again his hand snaked through the round opening. It dropped to the lock button on the knob and twisted it open.

The pain that hit Spader was sudden and sharp and without precedent. His howl of agony swept through the house like a clap of thunder startling both sleeping dogs into a frenzy of barking and catapulting the athletic seventy-year-old from her bed. She landed on her feet and went for her rifle.

There was no fumbling for shells. The gun was loaded.

As she released the safety and swung the barrel upward with the ease of one not only used to handling a weapon but familiar with doing so safely, she heard loud cursing intermingled with glass shattering on the brick floor.

Spader had yanked his hand away with enough force to send his arm crashing into the glass above the circular cut, breaking out the remaining square of glass and cracking the wood frame above it that separated the small panes from one another. His wrist, already on fire with pain from the deep puncture wounds, thrown upwards, felt the rigid glass pierce his sleeve, his skin and his muscle as effectively as the slash of a knife. He reached behind his back with his left hand and grabbed his gun. At this range he couldn't miss.

First the dog, then the damned owner.

Fury brought his foot up and slammed it against the closed door with such force that the wood frame splintered and the door banged against the back wall.

The dog who'd released the man's arm immediately after biting it, had watched the hand withdraw through the hole. Stoney had not been taught to attack. He was a retriever. He'd been trained to fetch birds, and his mouth was so soft that not only were the birds delivered table ready, the cripples were brought in alive. Stoney could carry a fledgling robin in his mouth without hurting it. More than once his mistress had returned a wayward baby bird to its nest to take its first flight another day.

Chesapeake Bay Retrievers, however, are not only instinctive retrievers, but also instinctively protective. Powerful, strong-willed and intelligent, a Chessie's loyalty, once won, knows few equals in dogdom. Stoney was a champion master hunter. He epitomized the best the breed had to offer. And Harriet loved him with a passion that she had not even felt for her children. That love had been returned. He'd allowed her to channel his natural talent and they'd been a noteworthy team in competition both in the breed ring and in hunting tests.

A piece of falling glass hit Stoney's leg, cutting it. He didn't even flinch. The man was still at the door. He had not left yet.

He saw the man's hand move behind him and reappear with a gun. Stoney knew it was a gun. It smelled different than the shotguns and rifles he was used to but it was a gun. Guns didn't scare Stoney. They went off and birds fell.

So, Stoney didn't growl because the man held a gun. He growled because the man was still on the patio. The man was still threatening to enter the house unbidden.

Stoney's ears heard Harriet release the safety on her rifle. He didn't look back. The quarry was never behind him. Stoney's muscles tensed in anticipation.

As the door flew open, Stoney leaped backwards landing lightly on his thick pads, his eyes fixed on the man, his ears erect, and his muscles taut. He half sat, waiting to be released.

Harriet Locke, the gun to her shoulder, stepped into the open doorway. Her finger on the trigger, she had planned a warning shot through the window beside the kitchen door. In front of her sat Stoney, waiting. Beyond the dog, framed by the moonlight behind him, in the open doorway, stood a man whose hair was covered by a black knit cap. One arm hung limply by his side; the other was rapidly being raised. The gun barrel glinted in the moonlight.

Spader's attention was directed for a second by a flutter of white behind the dog. The woman's nightgown swirled lightly around her legs as she moved into the doorway, the rifle at eye level. The dog was between the two, half-crouched, almost sitting, ready to spring.

Spader's brief glance told him there was a rifle leveled at him. Experience told him that the woman would hesitate. Only two people could look a man in the eye and shoot without a reflective pause: a soldier who'd been in combat or a professional killer. The woman was neither.

The dog, however, was another matter. He was like a coiled snake ready to strike. The rattles had already been shaken. The warning growl was unmistakable.

The dog would be first. He was the most dangerous.

Spader was wrong.

The woman was the more dangerous.

The blast from the rifle hit Spader's forehead before his finger pulled the trigger of his gun.

The dog never broke.

He knew the rules of hunting.

The woman knew the rules of war.

Chapter 2

Later Harriet would try to envision just what prompted her to act as she did; but, try as she might, she wouldn't be able to conjure up either a vision of the future, even in the shape of a kaleidoscope of images, nor any sound inside her head forming intelligible words of command. She couldn't even remember focusing on the dead body on the floor. In fact, after the shot hit and the man crumpled to the floor, she didn't even remember watching him fall.

Instead her mind busied itself with numbers. A bank trust officer, her days had been filled with spread sheets spewed out each morning filled with numbers, numbers of shares bought and sold, numbers of dollars those shares represented, gains and losses, dividends, interest, contributions, disbursements and transaction totals. Her life was circumscribed by numbers.

She knew, for example, that she could dress in two and a half minutes in jeans and a sweatshirt. One of those minutes was spent putting on shoes with laces. Dressing for work took twenty-seven minutes.

Her mind calculated the distance the police station was from her house. They would have been called by the alarm company at the same moment her phone ceased ringing without being answered. It had rung six times, she knew.

The first ring had startled her. Had she not had both hands on the rifle, she would have picked it up without thinking. Never careless with a gun, Harriet took two steps toward the kitchen counter and laid the rifle flat on its clean tile surface.

The second ring jarred her again like a thunderclap expected with a lightning flash but startling nonetheless.

It must have been then, she told herself later, that she made the decision. She didn't remember making it; but, the urgency with which she moved after she cautiously laid down the rifle pinpointed the moment her movements accelerated. All she remembered thinking was that she had to get the dogs out before the police arrived. She couldn't remember when the thought was birthed but it grew to adulthood in a matter of seconds.

On the third ring of the phone she was in the laundry room off the kitchen, slipping her feet into the one pair of walking shoes she owned without laces. She scooped up an armful of clothes from the top of the dryer. There was no time to dress. Minutes were too precious.

She grabbed her purse and her car keys from their place just inside the back door. Stoney, who had remained motionless per Harriet's command to stay, watched as she opened both crates and made both of the female dogs sit immediately upon exiting their nighttime dens. The three remained steadfast as Harriet hurried to the front door. As she opened it, she called them to come. Her voice was firm. Still, each dog hesitated drawn by the smell of gun powder in the air and the bloody body of a stranger in the kitchen. Then Stoney whirled around and sped toward the door. Both the younger ones followed.

Harriet ran down the stairs and across the sloping hillside toward the garage on the lower level of the acreage. She fleetingly thought of the spectacle she must be running across her yard in the moonlight in her filmy nightgown with three large dogs running after her. She pushed the remote in her hand and hoped the garage door would peel up despite her distance and angle. Evidently the garage door opener didn't care from whence the signal came, for the metal door was completely rolled up by the time Harriet and the dogs reached the gate at the base of the hill.

Loading normally took only a few minutes. There was a pattern. Each of the girls went into their own crate through the rear hatch; Stoney rode in a crate that faced the side door.

However, as Harriet entered the garage, a flash of blue light through the trees told her the police were already at the far end of the street. They were faster than she had anticipated. Quickly, she opened the door to the driver's side and shouted at the dogs to get in. Confused, they danced back toward the rear hatch.

Harriet was surprised at how quickly she calculated the odds. It would take longer for her to get her dogs to break their pattern than for her to load them up as usual. She sprinted for the rear hatch and both dogs, relieved at their crate doors being opened, leaped inside. By the time they'd turned to face the door and lay down, the hatch was slammed down. The crates were never latched.

Stoney was sitting in the driver's seat when she slid in beside him. He scrambled into the back and laid in front of his crate as Harriet turned the key in the ignition.

As she eased the car out of the garage, she saw the blue lights slowing down as the patrol car drove along the front of her property looking for the entrance to the house.

Harriet took a deep breath to still the flutter of her heart. Her one hand clicked the garage door remote while the other turned the van left. It was the way she always went. The dogs put their heads down on their paws. The route out of town was familiar. Later, when the van approached their destination would be time enough to rise and guess what the day had in store.

The faint smell of gun powder wafting back toward their noses was an aphrodisiac to these retrievers. It boded well.

As the garage door slowly rolled down, Harriet, still operating on automatic pilot, turned on her lights and drove down the street. When the blue flashing lights hit the corner and turned, she pulled over to the right and stopped.

Her brain began a search for a reasonable explanation as to why she was in her van leaving the house. The truth was she was overwhelmed by a fear that her dogs would be taken from her, that a mistake would happen and she would lose them.

As the patrol car approached, she rolled down her window. The patrol car slowed and before Harriet could utter a word, the driver of the police unit asked her if there was a path that led to the back to the house.

Harriet answered automatically, "Go around the far side of the garage and take the steps to the patio. It's the way everyone goes."

"Thank you," the officer said, then added politely, "Please move on now."

"Yes, Sir," Harriet replied taking her foot from the brake and rolling forward.

Chapter 3

The police were still at Harriet Locke's house when her granddaughter, Aleta arrived. Conan Lloyd, her current boyfriend, a fellow lawyer at Waltham, Geyser, Schonecker and Hill, had reluctantly agreed to drive her from her San Francisco apartment; but, they had argued the entire way.

"This is so stupid," he said for the third time, glancing over at the auburn-haired beauty he planned to marry someday.

"She shot a man. No matter how this comes out, you don't want to get involved."

"She's my grandmother," Aleta countered for the third time. She liked this handsome man she was currently sharing her life with. They hadn't argued like this before. Their lives had evolved into a sharing of social events aimed, they hoped, at helping each climb the corporate ladder.

"Hey, I'm as much in favor of supporting a family member as anyone; but, well, she's old enough to know how the corporate world works."

"She wants me to represent her. I don't see a problem."

"We're corporate lawyers," Conan argued. "All we know about criminal law is what we learned in school."

"She shot a man breaking into her house armed with a gun," Aleta retorted. "How hard can that be?"

"That itself is an anathema—a gun-toting grandmother. Our corporate clients won't deal well with that image."

Aleta reared back in her seat. Her brown eyes blazed. "You knew she and I hunted over our dogs."

Conan was cool in his response. "When you were a kid, yes. When your grandfather was alive. I thought you and your grandmother went along to keep him company."

"You've never been in a duck blind in the middle of a freezing rainstorm, have you?" Aleta asked. "One doesn't go there to be company. One goes there to shoot ducks!"

"Well, I'd go light on your hunting escapades at social events," Conan returned. "Men still consider duck hunting a man's game. Besides you don't look like a woman who'd do that."

"I look like my grandmother!" Aleta shot back. Her fists clenched as she tried to rein in her anger. He couldn't mean what he was saying. He was not himself. When he was short of sleep, he was always cranky. And he'd only had about two and a half hours.

She'd met plenty of women competing in Hunt Tests, women who were expert shots and hunted in all kinds of weather, women like her grandmother who at seventy was lean and sinewy, yet feminine. Like her grandmother, they moved with the surefooted grace of a gazelle. As a teenager, she'd admired these women and their confident approach to a sport most women shied away from.

Her mother couldn't understand her penchant to follow in her grandmother's footsteps and was only slightly mollified when Aleta decided to study law like her dad. Her mother had forgiven Aleta completely when she hooked up with Conan. Finally, in her eyes, her daughter was on a proper path. She could handle a daughter who was career-oriented, but not one who liked to hunt.

Her grandmother's second love had been dog showing and, with her mother's blessing, Aleta entered the junior showmanship competition. Her mother couldn't fathom Aleta's interest in dogs, nor did she understand, when in her teens, Aleta's focus turned to competing in equestrian events; however, while her mother took no pride in Aleta's natural talent with animals, she did appreciate the fact that Aleta excelled scholastically and developed into a long-legged beauty who wore the expensive dresses her mother bought her with a casual style that enhanced the beauty of not only the dress but its wearer.

Conan had first spotted her at a party welcoming the new additions to his firm and quietly begun his pursuit of her. They were talking about moving in together; but now, with this snag, Conan was glad they hadn't, Aleta obviously needed some careful coaching.

As he drove in front of the Mill Valley house he looked at the broad expanse of lawn and in the moonlight could tell that the area around the house perched high on the hill was professionally landscaped and cared for by a gardener. The house itself was a redwood and stone ranch with a huge window overlooking the hills.

"Wow," he breathed. "This is worth a fortune in today's market!"

"Do you want to come in with me?" Aleta asked.

Conan shook his head. He didn't want to be any more involved. "I'll wait here. I need to catch up on sleep. You may have an excuse not to go to work tomorrow, but I don't."

Aleta walked away disappointed. She decided that Conan needed a real introduction to her grandmother and, after this was over, she'd be sure he got it. She couldn't believe he didn't want to see the inside of the house she'd talked so much about he'd deemed it her second home, especially as she said she wanted one just like it someday. Still, this wasn't the best time. He was just using his head.

Something her grandmother had said over the phone bothered her terribly. "Someone is trying to kill me. Go to the house and see if you come to the same conclusion."

Chapter 4

Ed Ornstein was waiting for her at the front door. His dark penetrating eyes might have made him ominous were it not for his rotund frame and his short stature. It was difficult for Aleta to be afraid of a man whose eyes were level with hers.

Once inside she noticed he was balding and his dark eyes carried a twinkle. She liked him instantly.

"I was waiting for you," he said, his voice pleasant, his accent from New York he told her later. "The police gotta respect my license; but, I need a family person to verify that I'm workin' for your gramma. She's somethin', huh?"

Aleta grinned. "Yes, she is."

"Emma liked her right off."

"Emma, your wife?"

"Was."

Aleta raised a brow.

"Named my dog after her. Somehow I needed to have someone named Emma to talk with."

"What kind of dog?"

"Lab."

"Lab's like everybody."

"Not Emma. She tells me who to work for and who not to."

"And you listen to her?"

"Sure. She ain't never wrong," Ed said. "Let's go back where the activity is. You up for this?"

"The body still there?"

"Yeah. The coroner's here, but he ain't done yet."

"We allowed?"

"Your grandmother didn't want me to miss anything."

"Why is she worried?"

"She didn't say."

"She told me she thinks someone is trying to kill her," Aleta said.

"Then I guess we better look at things real good."

The man in charge, once he was told who Aleta was, blocked her from the area where the body lay and demanded to know where her grandmother was. Aleta gave Ed a slight nod and then sat down.

"Your men told her to leave," she said calmly.

Astounded by the improbability of this, the captain's double chin shook as he stuttered. "What the hell are you talking about?"

"Ask them," Aleta said.

Fletcher turned around and barked orders. Several men dispatched themselves to hunt for the two officers first on the scene and Ed Ornstein slipped quickly through the kitchen door and positioned himself in the doorway leading to the laundry room. He noticed a pair of white slippers sitting there with what looked like splatters of blood on them. A couple of socks lay on the floor. They were marked and folded.

So, the laundry had been sorted, but not put away, he reasoned. She'd taken it with her which means she had left in her nightgown.

He turned his attention to the body on the brick floor. The victim's right glove was torn and beneath the tear he saw bloody flesh. He couldn't see the wound; but, he could guess it was made by her dog.

Ed saw the two guns lying on the counter each encased in plastic. He lifted a tiny camera to his eye and snapped a series of pictures with high speed film. The camera shutter made a sound as soft as the flutter of a butterfly wing. No one noticed as angry words from the living room had captured the attention of those near the body.

The coroner directed the loading of the body and Ed shrunk back into the laundry room as the men moved about.

His tape recorder was switched on. It didn't record much. Just some speculative chatter. The big question appeared to be why the woman had fled.

As the body was being removed, the coroner inquired. "Has Animal Control got the dog?"

"What dog?" came the response.

"The man was bitten," the coroner said. "The dog has to be put down."

Ed held his breath, glad his recorder was on.

"I thought they held it in quarantine for several weeks to see if it's got rabies," one of the men remarked.

"No need. The man's dead," the coroner replied. "I'll sign the order tonight. The dog's dangerous."

Chapter 5

Harriet Locke, Atherton Investment Bank's prestigious Vice President and Trust Officer, had spent the night at her desk at the bank with almost every member of the Trust Division under her wing. She had called them at home on her cell, having each of their home numbers stored in her memory.

After all were present in the conference room, the earlier arrivals guzzling coffee and eating packaged donuts and sweet rolls until all had arrived, Harriet addressed the sleepy-eyed group with the shocking statement. "I killed a man tonight."

The gasps elicited an inner feeling of satisfaction in their leader. She had them. She went on, "My private investigator verified that the burglary was a subterfuge. I was the target."

"But who?" Jeff Cole blurted out. "And why?"

Harriet noted that of all her crew, he seemed the least affected by the odd hour. Of course, his lanky frame, slightly stooped because he was too tall in his estimation belied his efforts to appear well dressed. His tight curly hair added to the illusion of youth.

"It has to be the Tontine Trust."

A loud gasp from Douglas Lim drew eyes to his shocked face.

"But it is doing well," he stated with as much emotion as anyone had seen him display. An experienced bank officer with impeccable credentials, he was instantly believed.

"J.G. wants Sprattley…," Harriet began.

"That prick!" Jeff Cole burst out. "If he comes in, I'll be the first one downsized."

Considering his height, his choice of word elicited a few snickers.

"Hey," Neil Willis countered grinning, "it's the brothers that's the first to go. You all knows that!"

"Cut the crap!" Jeff shot back. "You'll be the last, especially with your college background. Sprattley will fire me first to prove no racism."

"He will not keep any of us except Melissa," Lim remarked sagely, "Where is Melissa, by the way?"

"I don't have her home number memorized," Harriet said evenly. No one believed her.

Janis Thai timidly raised a hand. "Are we in trouble?" Her voice was as small and timid as she.

Wendy Oshiro leaned over and patted her hand. "Just listen," she whispered.

"Down to the reason you're all here," Harriet announced. The room was instantly quiet.

"We are going to move the Tontine Trust."

Gasps were heard from everyone. That was a momentous task, one that would take weeks, even months. The paperwork involved in moving an ordinary trust was heavy but the Tontine held hard assets: Gems, gold, coins and art work, some of it on loan to galleries. It also had vast real estate holdings.

"Where's the Tontine going?" Jeff asked, his legs sprawled out under the table.

"Signet Bank in Willow Glen, Illinois."

"Do they know this?" Lim asked not meaning his query as a joke. Reactive giggles were evoked by his question. The nervousness among those gathered was rising.

Harriet smiled. "They do."

"When did all this come about?" Neil asked pointedly. "And when were you going to tell us?"

"Originally I had planned to set up a new bank to handle the Tontine and bring all of you over to help me run it; however, that's not a good plan."

"Why not?" Neil asked. "We have the education and the experience to do it. It sounds like a fine plan to me."

Murmurs of approval told Harriet she had a consensus for her original plan.

A part of her wanted to go with it. It was a good idea. She was sure of it. Up until a few hours ago she would have thought nothing could persuade her to deviate from her chosen path to her alternate plan.

She looked at all the eager faces of her friends hoping that she would wave a magic wand and save their careers. If the Tontine went, so would they. It would be a slow erosion as one by one they were peeled off and discarded like sunburned skin. The bank would remain, but they would no longer be a part of it.

"Let me tell you a story," Harriet began and she told them about fleeing with her dogs simply because she sensed that something was going to go awry, then she paused and let everyone assure her she had had nothing to fear.

When all had had their say, Harriet pulled out a tape recorder, set it in the center of the table and played the brief conversation between the police officer and the coroner.

The room went silent.

"That is why we are here tonight," Harriet said. "I have another feeling. No vision. No voices. Just a feeling. I don't know what the danger is. All I know is that the action to take is to move the Tontine Trust as fast as possible."

The murmurs of assent began slowly; but, as Harriet watched, heads began to nod. These people trusted her. She couldn't believe she was asking for such a leap of faith. She knew she was vulnerable at this moment. If anyone of the group naysaid her plan, she knew she'd fold and crawl away.

"We can do this," Lim said finally, "but why are we here tonight?"

Harriet swallowed hard. "Because you have to do it without me. Because someone is trying to kill me, and I must leave this place."

The assent was verbalized around the room, as if by agreeing to the transfer, they were voting to save their leader's life.

"Tonight," Harriet went on, "you will prepare papers for my signature. In the morning I will disappear.

"Won't J.G. try to stop us?" Neil asked, his scowl enhanced by the darkness of his skin.

"Yes," Harriet said, "which is why we sign the papers that need the signature of Atherton Bank officers tonight while we all have jobs."

"He could still fire us," Jeff put in. Experience had taught the lanky six footer that when it came to homosexuality, there was little wiggle room in an employer's eyes.

The room was again quiet. They needed answers, assurances that their worst fear wouldn't be realized.

Harriet's silence lasted over a minute. Later, some of her cohorts would say she was praying. Others would claim she was simply thinking. She broke the silence with an odd question aimed at Jeff. "How are your hands?"

Jeff looked down at his hands and sputtered, "They're fine."

"Can they sign documents?"

Puzzled, Jeff stuttered out a yes.

"But not forever, right?" Harriet queried. "Tonight just might be the last straw, right?"

Suddenly, Jeff smiled. "My surgery."

He looked around. "I need to take a couple weeks off for carpal tunnel surgery."

"He can't go now," Lim wailed. "I need him."

"Which is precisely why now is perfect," Harriet said. "With a man out, it'll be much harder to legitimately downsize the group. It will give you all breathing room."

"Where do we start?" Lim asked.

"Jeff, you start with my two favorite properties that parcel in Marin County and the acreage in the hills near Dublin. Those are the two pieces J.G. has been hammering at me to sell."

"Do you think that they are the reason...?" Jeff began to say. He stopped and shook his head, thus dismissing his own thought. "No, of course not. People don't kill to get their hands on property. They just offer more money."

Harriet went on, "Neil, take over the transfer of the property in the Midwest. It's important that that be done as soon as possible."

"The trust has many properties," Lim said. "Why these first?"

"They are of personal interest to the Tontine members. The others are investments."

She turned to the two operations officers. "Wendy, you and Janet inventory the coins and prepare them for shipping."

"We need an outside appraiser before we ship," Wendy Oshiro said. "I know one who will come anytime I ask. He is a relative."

"Do it!" Harriet said. "Have him come immediately."

Chubby Valerie quietly ventured an inquiry as to what she was to do. Harriet had her slated to fill in. Doug, however, recognized her cry to be assigned a special task, so he answered quickly, "The mutual funds, of course. They must be transferred immediately."

Harriet, at first, kicked herself for her insensitivity to Valerie's need, but then realized that because Valerie's need had been recognized by Doug and answered, the power had been transferred from her to him. She decided to put her stamp of approval on the transfer of power.

"Doug, just see I get whatever papers I need to sign before seven. I need to be gone before anyone arrives."

And with that the group scattered.

Harriet went to her office and dialed Aleta's home number. As she waited for her granddaughter to answer, she became edgy. She rose and went to the door and looked out into the large area of cubicles divided by half walls. The activity was lively; the chatter, pleasant; the aura, exciting. Coffee was perking at both stations and cans of soda were periodically banging to the bottom of the vending machine. Adrenaline and caffeine would get them through the night and the early morning hours.

She heard Aleta's voice emerge from the speaker phone and picked up the receiver.

"Aleta, I need you to do something for me," Harriet said without preamble.

Sleepily, Aleta murmured, "I just got back. Can't it wait until morning?"

"I won't be seeing you in the morning."

Aleta's eyes opened. "You can't not come! You promised."

"I promised a statement."

"I need one that will stand up in court."

"I move hundreds of thousands of dollars a day on my signature. It should stand up in court."

"You need reliable witnesses."

"Would bank officers count?"

"You're supposed to come here before you go to work, besides I thought you weren't going to work. Does Ed Ornstein know you're going to work?"

"Is your friend there?"

"Conan? No, of course not. He doesn't live here. You know that!"

"You told him when I was coming, didn't you?"

"He asked," Aleta replied.

"Why did he ask?"

"He wants this mess to be over as soon as possible."

"Aleta, listen to the tape I'm going to play."

The tape played for less than thirty seconds. Aleta gasped her horror at the end.

"No!" she shouted. "I won't let them. I'll fight them! Stoney's not dangerous!"

"Well, except to murderers," Harriet chuckled. Suddenly, she sobered, "Aleta, listen to me. Conan will betray you. I don't know how, but it will happen not once but twice."

"Are you a prophet now?"

"Not exactly. I just sense things. And my gut tells me that your career will destruct unless you leave now."

"Grams, I'm on the fast track up the corporate ladder," Aleta said. "I can't believe anything is going to push me off it."

"The price may be too high," Harriet warned. "Would you, at least, ask for a leave of absence to take care of family business? I need legal representation in Illinois."

"Grams, I'm not licensed to practice in Illinois. And why do you need a lawyer in Illinois?"

"Tontine business," she replied succinctly and Aleta knew better than to ask for details. Her grandmother went on, "You'll be working with an Illinois attorney who isn't a specialist in corporate law."

"Laws vary from state to state."

"He's a quick study."

"Well," Aleta said thoughtfully, flattered by the offer, "Just maybe it could work that is, if he's a tax lawyer."

"Try children's advocate," Harriet said, smiling inwardly. Her friend Martha Cook had told her he was single after Harriet mentioned that she didn't like Aleta's current boyfriend.

Harriet could tell Aleta was tantalized.

"I could ask," Aleta said. "It would broaden my experience and that might work for me in the long run."

"I'll book the flight," Harriet said as if the matter were settled.

Aleta couldn't be pushed. "I said I'd ask."

"My statement will be waiting for you at the bank. Ask for Doug Lim."

"That's across the Bay!" Aleta complained.

"I'll messenger it to your office then," Harriet said. "Ed Ornstein will contact you at your office. Have your suitcase with you."

"Grams, I didn't say…," Aleta began. The phone went dead.

Aleta stared at the receiver and with a scold in her voice said, "I said I'd ask."

She rolled over to go back to sleep; but, all she could think about was what to pack. Eventually, she got up and packed her bag, then fell back in bed and slept until her alarm went off.

She'd just emerged from the shower when the doorbell rang. She ran to the door and looked through the peephole. She threw open the door.

"Conan! What a surprise! You wouldn't guess…," Her words trailed off as she saw that he wasn't alone.

"Captain Fletcher," she remarked. "What brings you here?"

"May we come in?" Conan asked, stepping forward, a smile plastered on his face.

"No, you may not," Aleta said coolly. "I'm not dressed."

And with that she closed the door.

Conan rapped loudly. "Come on, Aleta. Be reasonable."

"Come back with a warrant," Aleta shouted.

She heard Conan say, "We can wait in the lobby downstairs."

Aleta sighed with relief and went back to dressing for the day. She didn't know exactly when the remembrance occurred.

He will betray you twice Grams had said.

Chapter 6

The law offices of Waltham, Geyser, Schonecker and Hill were on the sixth floor. Aleta Locke exited the elevator and carried her suitcase to her cubicle and tucked it in a corner behind the file cabinet. She moved her wastebasket in front of the case and felt guilty immediately afterward.

She sat down at her desk and looked over the day's work. Why had she picked corporate law? The excitement was in criminal law. Of course, so was dealing with the worst of human kind.

Her father was a tax lawyer and spent too much time in her estimation in audit sessions with the IRS. Wills, and trusts involved too much death and hoarding as if what one left to one's heirs would truly enhance their lives. Human rights and environmental law brought too much deep heartache. Same with child advocacy. She was a corporate lawyer by default.

She didn't hate it. She sometimes tired of it, but she didn't hate it. That would be too emotional a term for corporate law.

Only this morning, she wasn't sure she wanted to be a corporate lawyer.

The phone on her desk rang and roused her from her reverie. It was Ed Ornstein.

"Your grandmother booked us on the twelve o'clock nonstop to Chicago's O'Hare. I have to see to Emma so I guess I'll see you on the plane."

"See to Emma? You're taking your dog?"

"Mrs. Locke said we'd be going to dog shows. Emma will like that."

"You can't take unentered dogs onto the show grounds," Aleta said.

"Told her I wouldn't go without Emma. She said you'd work it out."

"Me?"

"Yeah, she said since you'd be showing dogs you could probably put her in with some of them. Emma gets along real well with other dogs. Ain't never been a dog that didn't like her. Some dogs are like that."

"I'm not going to show dogs. I'm going there to do legal work."

"That's just your cover story."

"Which? Showing dogs or the legal work?"

"Both."

"What am I going there to do, exactly?"

"Find out who's trying to kill your grams."

After she hung up, Aleta could think of several quips. She was a bit dismayed that she, a lawyer, had found herself at a loss for words.

My you are a clever one, Grams, she thought. You know how to play me.

She chuckled. You always did. That's why we never fought. You always gave me time to work the idea until it was mine. And you're doing it again. You knew I'd want to do this myself. You knew I'd figure cops would bungle the investigation just like Fletcher did last night.

Her computer screen signaled that she had mail. She logged on.

"You asked for the time off yet?"

There was no signature. She guessed it was Grams.

She picked up the phone and called Jethro Waltham's secretary. When she identified herself, the woman said, "You're late for your appointment."

"What appointment?"

"I emailed you this morning."

"I didn't get it."

"You replied."

"When?"

"Quarter to nine."

"I wasn't at my desk until nine," Aleta said. She didn't like the feeling she was getting. "I'll be right there."

Why would the senior partner want to see me first thing in the morning, she asked herself? She drew a blank.

When she was ushered into Jethro Waltham's office, she found he was not alone. Another senior partner was there as was Conan Lloyd.

The opening greeting was awkward. Aleta knew she'd been the topic of discussion. She decided not to wait but opened with her request. "I'd like to take some personal time to deal with some family business."

"How much time?" Jethro Waltham asked, glancing knowingly at Conan Lloyd.

"Couple of months," Aleta said.

"Months?!" Waltham choked. "I was thinking you might need a couple of days to get your grandmother to come to her senses."

Aleta glanced at Conan Lloyd. He looked equally taken aback. He'd probably suggested that she'd need the morning.

Aleta spoke calmly although the attack on her grandmother had left her seething inside. "What you may not know, Gentleman, is that my grandmother is the Vice President of the Atherton Investment Bank of Oakland. She makes critical decisions correctly every day of her life. She wouldn't still hold that title if she'd lost her senses in crisis situations."

Waltham cleared his throat. "Are you telling us that the Harriet Locke is your grandmother?"

Aleta nodded. "I don't think Conan had all his facts in place when he took my place at the meeting this morning."

Conan burst in to defend himself.

"I was just looking out for your interest and the interests of this firm. We aren't versed in criminal law. You are still a member of this firm. What you do reflects on all of us."

Mr. Waltham took over after scowling Conan into silence. "Mr. Lloyd came to your apartment with a police officer this morning and was rudely turned away. When you embarrass a member of this firm, you embarrass us all."

"My grandmother changed her plans."

"You could have let the gentlemen in and explained."

"I wasn't dressed. Have you no sense of decency either?" Aleta shot back.

Jethro Waltham scowled at Conan Lloyd who bit his lip and studied his shoes.

Aleta continued, "Grams is messengering her statement in."

Waltham smiled. "So then it's all settled."

"Yes," Aleta said. "I guess it is. I won't be needing that leave of absence after all."

Waltham rose and offered his hand. "No hard feelings. This was a touchy situation. We had to be sure you hadn't crossed the line."

Aleta shook his hand. "I'm actually grateful this exchange occurred."

Conan looked up hopefully. This was going to come out okay. He rubbed his hands together. "I guess it's time to get back to work."

He started for the door, a small smile on his face.

Aleta smiled at him. "I guess you'd better. You've already wasted enough time in here. What I'm about to say next doesn't really concern you. Actually none of this matter was any of your business."

"Miss Locke," Jethro Waltham said. "He was only trying to keep you from making a mistake."

"Do you know what section of the bank my grandmother works in?"

Jethro smiled knowingly,

"Yes, as a matter of fact, I do. The trust department."

"Well, you could use a bit of that around here, Gentlemen. It's because you can't trust me that I'm moving on."

Conan gasped, "You're quitting?"

Aleta chuckled. "First thing you've had right all day."

On Aleta's way out, Waltham's secretary stopped her. "A messenger left this for you."

So much for a dramatic exit, she thought as she opened the large envelope. She smiled when she saw the note.

"Good news?" the secretary asked.

"As usual my grandmother has taken care of everything." Aleta replied walking away.

Conan rushed after her. "Why did you quit? Just because you're mad at me; that's no reason to quit."

Aleta tucked the envelope in her purse, picked up her suitcase and walked to the elevator.

Conan rushed after her. "Where are you going? When will I see you? We need to talk."

"Goodbye, Conan," Aleta said stepping into the elevator.

"I don't understand you at all," Conan spouted.

"That's the second correct thing you've said today," Aleta commented softly as the elevator doors closed.

Aleta called her mother from the airport and told her she was sending her the keys to her car and her apartment.

"Not you too!" her mother complained. "First your grandmother and now you."

"I will need you to send me some good new suits, something bright. All I've got are stodgy old corporate-type lawyer suits. And maybe a dress or two in case I'm asked out."

"What's happening?" her mother pried, her tone more curious than critical.

"I've got a new job, Mom and if I'm good it could lead to bigger things. But I need to look sharp and you know me and clothes."

"I'll get right on it," her mother said.

"What about Jayline? Doesn't she have some big social affair coming up?"

"Jayline can help," her mother said. "She loves shopping as much as you hate it."

"Glad you had one daughter that took after you."

"You're no bother. Really. I love to be needed."

"Thanks, Mom. I owe you."

"How about a grandchild?"

"With or without marriage?"

"Aleta!"

When Aleta joined Ed Ornstein on the plane, she was smiling. The smile stayed on her face as she asked about Emma.

"Emma's fine," he replied. "You quit didn't you?"

"Yep," she replied. "Now tell me who we're supposed to be investigating."

"You like to have a handle on things in advance, don't you?"

"Yep!" she said grinning.

"Okay, here goes," Ed stated. "There's five ladies in the Tontine. Some of them's married, some ain't. All of 'em got dogs they take to shows. Mrs. Locke said that's how they met, but there's more than that that holds them together only she didn't tell me what."

"Does she suspect any of them?"

"Nope. She says that anybody can get as much money as they want once a year. That's the way they set it up. To protect themselves."

"From others?"

"Take the Scottie lady. Beatrice is a sucker for men. She'd tied the knot three times. She's got a live-in boyfriend that a couple of the ladies is sure he wants to con her outta her share and then take off.”

The Lab lady Julia, she's got seven kids. She's the one who put in the most rules.”

“Why?”

“Seems her husband was a gambler long time ago. He got himself righteous, only her eldest son took up where his dad left off.”

“So her son's in debt now?”

“Big time,” Ed replied. “Then there's the Doxie lady. Her husband's in a wheelchair. An accident.”

“That must have meant a lot of medical bills.”

“Trust took care of all of it.”

“How rich is this trust?”

“Really, really rich,” Ed said.

“But my grandmother works so hard,” Aleta protested.

“Which is why the Trust is so big. She's good at her job.”

“Who's the last one?”

“Evelyn. She has three Golden Retrievers she considers her kids. You guessed it. She ain't married. But she's got a greedy nephew who's trying to pry money out of her. He's probably our prime suspect.”

“How would killing my grandmother help any of them?”

“Near as I can figure, the death of your grandmother puts the power in the hand of two others.”

“Which two?”

“Marge and Beatrice.”

“So why are we going after Evelyn's nephew?”

“Because she's the one that told Harriet there's trouble brewing. She says bad things are happening.”

“I need to read the trust document to really understand what's going on.”

Ed reached down and opened the briefcase lying under the seat in front of him. “That's why your grandma sent this along.”

"Do you know where Grams is?"

"On the move," Ed replied succinctly.

"Alone?"

"Didn't ask."

"How will we know she's okay?"

"She's gonna call every day, so she'll call tomorrow."

Ed's cell, however, rang within five minutes of their deplaning at Chicago's O'Hare airport. Ed was on his way to pick up Emma, so he handed the phone to Aleta.

"Take care of things," he said as he rushed away.

"Grams, how are…"

"Aleta," Harriet interrupted, "there's trouble at Evelyn's."

"Did she call?"

"No."

"Then how…? Never mind, you had a feeling."

"How fast can you get there? I have such a bad feeling."

"Is there anyone you can call? We're over an hour away."

"I can't reach Marge or Julia. Beatrice's boyfriend is not someone I'd trust with a message."

"There must be someone!" Aleta said.

And, suddenly, Harriet knew who.

Chapter 7

Willow Glen's Police Chief Tom Milani had company in his office and had told his staff he was not to be disturbed thus when he was buzzed, he was surprised. His "company" Arborville Police Chief Lyle West grinned. His former boss had about as much control as he did over his own crew. Neither ran his unit with an iron fist and interruptions were expected. Not even the sharing of coffee and homemade chocolate chip cookies was sacred.

Milani punched on the speaker phone. It would be police business. His wife used his cell.

"Martha Cook on the line," the dispatcher said. "She said it's an emergency."

Lyle West raised an eyebrow. Martha Cook lived in his town.

"Tom Milani here," Tom said with the proper tone of seriousness. Martha Cook's requests were always extraordinary, but never ones to be taken lightly.

"You're using the speaker phone, aren't you," the thin crackling voice of one of the area's oldest residents accused. "So who's with you?"

Lyle smiled as he acknowledged his presence in Tom's office.

"Good!" Mrs. Cook cackled. "Two is better than one. I got a call from Harriet Locke that Evelyn Barnes is in trouble. I want you two boys to hightail it over there and take care of things."

"I'll send a unit right over there," Tom said, winking at Lyle. Both knew she expected them to go personally.

"You'll do no such thing!" Martha Cook countered. Age hadn't lightened her manner any. "Are you boys dressed?"

The question took Tom by complete surprise, but Lyle who'd had more dealings with Martha Cook replied, "Yes, we are in uniform."

"Use your chief cars the ones with the lettering on the side," Martha enjoined. "I want you to scare the bejabbers out of anyone messing with my friend Harriet's friend."

"An address would be nice," Tom suggested quietly.

"Doesn't Lyle know her?"

Lyle's brows shot up. "Why would I know her?"

"She has show dogs."

"Labs?"

"Harriet said they were Goldens. And she's got too many; but, don't you dare cite her," Martha Cook went on. Old age hadn't made her any less querulous. "A lawyer and private investigator have just landed at O'Hare but it'll take them over an hour to get there. Keep her and her dogs safe until they arrive. Are you boys still munching on cookies?"

Tom swallowed his mouthful and took a sip of coffee to clear his throat.

"Tom is," Lyle chuckled. "He needs to keep up his strength."

"Hustle, boys!" Martha barked. "I'll expect a full report."

The two police chief cars rolled to a stop in front of 532 Alder Drive, Chief Milani having gotten the address from one of his officers who then preceded him to the house and was waiting in front for instructions. The officer's patrol car was blocking a beat-up station wagon in the back of which there was a crate with a dog in it.

"What's going on?" the unkempt, unshaven man hollered at Milani as soon as the stocky chief opened his car door. "Whatever it is I ain't a part of it. Your man won't move his car."

Lyle West, trim and on the short side of medium didn't generally impress anyone until he spoke, which is why he was able to get a good look inside the car before saying, "Check inside, Tom. I'll take care of this."

Tom Milani, a short barrel of a man whose love for his wife's cooking defeated every diet he tried, signaled the waiting officer to accompany him.

Blocking the doorway to the modest single story house was a sloppily dressed man of considerable height and weight. Beside him stood a petite brunette with penciled-in arched eyebrows and bright red lip gloss spread over lips that were collagen-enhanced.

"Whatcha want?" the big man spit out. "Nobody's done nothing wrong. Your man needs to move his car."

"Is this the home of Evelyn Barnes?" Tom asked.

"Was."

"She deceased?" Tom pressed, his ears picking up screeching from inside. Behind him Milani heard West asking the driver of the station wagon for his license.

The busty brunette spoke up.

"May as well be dead. She's gone loony tunes. Louie is her nearest family, so we gotta do what's right. We got a space for her over to Vollers'."

Milani raised a brow. Vollers Health Care Center was the most expensive private sanitarium in the area.

The brunette caught the look and hastened to explain, "She's got insurance what will cover it. We was just taking care of disposing of her dogs when your guy shows up and blocks the buyer in. He's ready to go so can you get him to move his car?"

"We received a report," Milani said calmly. "Officer, please check out their identification while I talk with Mrs. Barnes."

"Won't do you no good!" the brunette declared as Milani entered the house. "It's them damn dogs. The neighbors been complaining. We told them we were taking care of it. And that's what we're doing. Jesus! You can't do something like that overnight."

"Where are the dogs?" Milani asked looking around the living room where every piece of furniture was covered with a throw and there were several dog beds lying empty.

"Outside in the dog kennel where they're supposed to be," Mayette Barnes said, answering Chief Milani's questions while showing the officer her driver's license. "They don't like it none. Barked all night."

Chief Lyle West entered the house with a dirty Golden at the end of a makeshift leash.

Louie Barnes suddenly came alive. "Whatcha doing with that dog? That man paid good money for it."

"He changed his mind."

"Why?"

"Didn't want to go to jail for receiving stolen property," West said calmly. "And I suggest you give him his money back or you'll wind up arrested for theft."

"Who the hell are you? And where do you get off saying this dog ain't mine?"

Milani grinned, "Chief West would you care to explain the facts to the man?"

Louie blustered, "Chief?" He turned to Milani and said, "I thought you was Chief."

"Today is a two-for-one day," Milani replied.

"Jesus, Louie! I told you we should a waited. You go tell that man he can come back for the dog on Monday after you get power of attorney."

"No," Lyle West said. "You go and give the man back his money and tell him this dog is not for sale."

"Who's gonna take care of it?"

"Your aunt hired someone. The woman will be here within the hour," West said. "Mrs. Barnes made arrangements to fly a handler in from California."

Louie's expression underwent a radical change from belligerence to outright shock. "She hired help? Damn!

Where the hell did she get the money? She said she was flat broke until September."

Mayette broke in. "That just proves she's nuts. Who hires someone from that far away to take care of dogs?"

"I said 'handle', not 'take care of'. Evidently, your aunt hired someone to handle her dogs in the show ring."

Mayette understood only half of what was being said but it was enough to know that someone was coming to take away the money that should be coming to them as Evelyn Barnes' closest kin. She tried one last ploy.

"Her doing that just proves she's nuts. Go in and talk to her. You'll see I'm right," Mayette declared. "And we ain't paying for no fancy dog sitter from California."

A car pulled in next to Chief Milani's car, effectively blocking it.

Milani saw it and said, "What the hell?"

West turned and laughed. "It's Martha's favorite attorney."

"Yeah, but he's blocking my car."

"I'll bet he got marching orders too. You know Martha."

The man who popped out of the car was the least impressive man of the lot. Only five feet seven with big ears that stood out from his head and a bulbous nose separating clear blue close-set eyes he strode up to the sweaty man in the dirty tee shirt standing at the back of his station wagon, paused a moment, spoke to the man and then walked up the cracked cement walk to the house where both chiefs noticed that the driver of the wagon was unloading the dog crate.

"How'd he know?" Milani asked.

"Martha never picks run of the mill people," West replied.

Smiling, Stanley Praetzel handed a business card to Louie and one to Mayette. "I'm Evelyn Barnes' attorney."

Louie shoved the card back into the short man's hand. "She don't need no lawyer."

"The presence of two police chiefs tells me she does."

"They ain't here 'cause she done anything," Louie declared.

"So, you're the problem?"

Louie stepped back. "Me? No. I ain't done nothing. These guys is here because of the dogs."

Praetzel grinned. It was a nice grin. It crinkled the lines near his eyes and they twinkled. "A dog barks and police chiefs from two towns come running. I have got to meet this dog."

"Here she is," West said, standing back so the newcomer could see the dog. "Her name's Carmel."

"She looks dirty," Praetzel observed. "Is the most important call you got today was that a dog needed a bath?"

"I was just about to explain to Mr. Barnes here why he couldn't sell this dog to that man out there," Lyle West said.

"Go right ahead. You've got a law degree. You passed the bar. My guess is you're right."

Louie's face again registered shock. This time Mayette's did too.

"A lawyer?" Louie burst out. "He didn't say he was no lawyer. He said he as a police chief. Isn't that against the law?"

Praetzel grinned. "Not when he is. So tell me Chief, why can't he sell the dog?"

"He doesn't own it."

"I'm her nephew," Louie declared, suddenly getting his mind back to his right to his aunts' property, being her nearest kin as Mayette was fond of reminding him. "She's gone schizo and I'm in charge."

"You can't sign her name without power of attorney."

"I'm getting that," Louie declared.

"Which is why I'm here," Stanley Praetzel said. "Evelyn Barnes has already designated who has power of attorney should she need someone to care for her."

"I'm her closest relative," Louie said. "Who else she gonna pick?"

"Harriet Aleta Locke."

"Never heard of her."

"You will," Praetzel said.

"I ain't paying you!" Louie declared. "I'll take you to court."

Praetzel's eyes narrowed. All warmth left his manner. "You aren't expected to pay for me anymore than you are expected to pay for Mrs. Barnes medical bills."

"She's got health insurance," Louis stated flatly. "But I know she ain't got no lawyer insurance."

Praetzel smiled, but it was cold. "As a matter of fact she does. And that same so-called insurance bailed you out back in '99 when you didn't have the $300,000 to replace the tanks at your three gas stations. And that same insurance is going to put your three kids through college. If I were you, I wouldn't get greedy."

The last statement fired up Louie's ire.

"I ain't greedy. All I want is what's mine. She made me pay back half of that money. Said it was a loan. She only give me half. I'm her nearest relative, for God's sake. She's loaded. She should share."

"Where is Mrs. Barnes?" Praetzel asked.

"She's out back talking to the oak tree," Mayette said, then added, "She's certifiable. We only been seeing to her care. That's all."

"I thought she was in the bedroom," Milani said.

"Yeah, she was. Then he shows up with that damn dog and she stops all that yelling. Didn't you notice? I seen her sneak outside," Mayette said sourly. "I done told her to stay in the bedroom and watch the TV. She said it weren't in English but it were. She said she couldn't understand the words and she wanted her baby back and that was the last straw. She was making no sense. That's when I left the room."

"Let me take her her baby," West said, leading the young dog away.

He found Evelyn leaning against the oak tree. Milani and Praetzel came to the door.

"We've bonded," Evelyn said. "The tree spirit and my spirit are communicating."

West looked over at the kennel. There was only one run. He guessed immediately it was meant to hold Topaz when the bitches were in season. These were house dogs. No wonder they barked all night.

The grass was soggy underfoot. West guessed that the sprinkler had been forgotten overnight.

"The tree likes it here," Evelyn announced. "But it doesn't like the dogs peeing on it."

"Only the male lifts his leg and wets the trunk," West said, "but you've locked up the girls too."

Evelyn turned and looked at the dogs in the kennel and announced, "They all have penises."

"What else do they have?"

Evelyn looked over at the kennel. "It's pretty isn't it? The way the colors melt into one another. All those golden bushes waving in the wind."

Chief Milani approached the pair. "What do you think?"

"That we should listen to the trees," Evelyn said. "They are a part of the whole. Their spirits will speak to us if we listen."

Milani queried West with a look.

"What else do you see?" West asked.

"Besides the gnomes?"

"You see gnomes? As in elves?" Milani asked. "Where?"

"Sitting in the tree over the golden bushes."

West's cell phone went off.

Evelyn shied away. "Why are you banging on that pan?" she yelled.

As Milani led the frightened woman away, West answered his phone. He was rarely called because he could count on one hand the people who had his number and one of them was in the yard with him.

"Chief West, my name's Harriet Locke," said the strong raspy voice of a woman. "Is Evelyn okay?"

"Where'd you get this number?" West asked, too surprised to answer her simple question.

"Martha Cook, of course."

"She doesn't give out...," West began. Milani glanced over, his expression a question.

"This is an emergency. Tell me, how is Evelyn? She's not dead, is she?"

"No, but I can't talk about her..."

"For Pete's sake, Chief, I thought my calling you on your cell which Martha says almost no one has the number for would be enough. Didn't Stanley Praetzel tell you I have power of attorney to dictate Evelyn's medical treatment?"

"Well, yes, he did, but...," West started and suddenly realized that her knowledge of Praetzel practically guaranteed her identity.

"So, ask me," the raspy voice demanded.

"Ask you what?"

"Well, I won't know what to tell you to do until you tell me which options you're considering."

Milani left Evelyn leaning against the trunk of the oak and came over and whispered, "Who is it?"

"I think Martha has a twin."

"I heard that!" the voice snapped. "She's over twenty years older than I am."

"I was referring to your authoritative style," West countered smoothly. "What position do you hold in your firm?"

"I'm Vice President of Atherton Investment Bank."

"I've heard of that bank."

"No you haven't," Harriet snapped. "We aren't located in the Midwest."

"I know. You're in Oakland, California."

"No one's heard of us."

"I have."

"My, my, my…," the voice said fading into a new softness.

Lyle West grinned and Tom knew he'd taken charge.

"Tell me, what medical problems does Mrs. Barnes have?" Chief West asked.

"She has high blood pressure. Don't tell me she had a heart attack." The voice was suddenly rife with concern.

"No, but she's hallucinating. Can you explain that?"

"Well, she's not psychotic."

"How do you know that?"

"She's a depressive. Doesn't fit. There's some other explanation."

"Could she have ingested drugs to get high?"

"Not on purpose," Harriet said. "Hospitalize her. Do drug tests. Don't overlook any that cause hallucinations."

"That was our plan," West said.

"Thank goodness!" Harriet sighed.

"You sound surprised. Why?"

"Because you didn't infer that I was being paranoid."

"Martha Cook would never have put you through if you were."

Harriet switched to her other concern.

"Are the dogs okay? There are four—Topaz, Lady Jane, Tess and Carmel."

"I just rescued Carmel from a prospective buyer."

A gasp told West that his action was correct.

"Evelyn would never sell her baby."

Chapter 8

Chief Lyle West went to the Tri City hospital with Evelyn Barnes. He declared the room off-limits to all but hospital personnel and posted one of his men at the door. He hired an off-duty nurse to sit with Evelyn. He wanted someone who would recognize non-staff visitors as well as be a comforting companion for a woman having frightening nightmares along with her hallucinating episodes.

Georgina Johnson was young enough to handle two shifts and eager for the extra pay. Chief West always paid triple and that made Georgina pay close attention to his orders.

For an hour after the ambulance left, Chief Tom Milani and his forensic man, Hawkins Monroe searched and gathered while Louie and Mayette Barnes sat on the edge of the couch alternating between nervous twitching and angry outbursts.

Stanley Praetzel watched the interplay between the two faces with amusement. What appeared to be a waste of time for a busy lawyer wasn't. This was the most prestigious account he'd yet to handle and it appeared to be fascinatingly complex. Each member of the group was involved in a world about which he knew nothing. Another reason for hanging around was that Harriet Locke insisted he be at the house when her granddaughter arrived. She'd called him twice to check on what was being done and he was glad he had been personally present. She was not the kind of woman who would have been satisfied with a secondhand report.

He sat on the chair opposite the couple and began to ask casual questions. He had only been given enough information to make his one grandstanding speech. He began by inquiring about their children Louie III, Damon and Lynn and their college plans for them. Mayette expanded on Louie's succinct replies, having been quicker than her husband in assessing the possible kingpin role this homely little man might play.

As far as Mayette was concerned, Louie's arguments were too generic and Louie's sisters might well squeeze themselves under his umbrella. Mayette didn't want to share.

"Louie's got plans of his own," Mayette offered at the first lull in the conversation. "He just needs some seed money."

"What about his gas stations?" Praetzel asked.

"They ain't doing good."

Praetzel was familiar with the three stations, all sporting the name "Louie's". They were poorly run, poorly maintained and barely eking out a fair share of the market. Their locations were prime. Louie had to be working at not making them flourish.

"I mean what about selling one to generate seed money?" Stanley ventured.

"I still got a big loan on them."

"Pay off the loan and use the rest."

"There won't be no rest," Louie spat back. "I had to borrow for medical expenses. Last bill was over twenty grand all outta my pocket."

"You don't carry medical?" Pretzel queried a twinge of surprise in his tone.

"Don't cover elective stuff," Louie growled.

Stanley Praetzel looked over at Mayette. "And your wife deserved the best."

"Yeah," Mayette butted in smiling. "That's what I told him. You gotta treat your body well. You know, I could give you my doc's name."

Praetzel's surprise was obvious.

Mayette plowed on. "I'd do both the nose and the ears at the same time. I did two operations at once the second time. You save a bundle."

While this conversation was taking place, Hawk started carrying plastic baggies to his car. It being a warm day, Hawk chose not to close the door to facilitate his trips.

A car drove into the driveway and parked and an attractive auburn-haired woman emerged. Hawk was immediately taken with her. Well over six feet and single, he struggled to walk with his back straight. He had developed a habit of slouching when his height put him a head above his classmates. The nickname had evolved not from his last name but rather from his stooped shoulders and large beak of a nose.

Aleta walked in as Mayette was finishing her spiel.

All turned and Mayette decided to drive her point home. "Mr. Praetzel, it ain't nothing to be ashamed of. All kinds fix what's not too good in their looks."

"I don't...," Stanley began trying to ease off the embarrassing subject.

But Mayette wasn't about to let go. A convert to the miracles of plastic surgery she pushed on. "Let's ask her." She turned toward Aleta. "Don't you think he should get a nose job?"

Aleta looked squarely into Stanley Praetzel's eyes and asked bluntly, "Does your nose work?"

Stanley, taken aback, replied with a nod.

"Then don't touch it."

Mayette thrust a second question into the fray. "What about them ears?"

Again Aleta looked at Stanley.

This time he grinned and replied quickly, "They work fine."

"But he'd be so much handsomer!" Mayette insisted completely oblivious to the lawyer's discomfiture.

"His face has character. I like it," Aleta said as she moved toward the kitchen. "The ears are part of the package."

"I thought you was a dog show person," Mayette spit out, guessing who she was. "Dog show people are all about good looks."

"You're wrong," Aleta retorted. "We're all about dogs being healthy and fitting what they were bred to do. If a Retriever is missing too many teeth he can't grip a slippery duck softly. It will slide out of his mouth if he tries."

"I thought you were going to say they should have long noses," Stanley quipped.

"That too," Aleta said as she leaned over the kitchen sink and peered through the window.

"My stars! What are all the dogs doing in one run?"

"Aunt Evelyn's only got one," Mayette explained testily.

"It's filthy," Aleta said with disgust. "And the water bucket is tipped over."

"They do that," Mayette said. "Always jumping around."

"Ed, where's my suitcase. I've got to change."

"All done," Hawk announced exiting from the kitchen and hoping for a word with this stunning redhead.

But, peeling off her jacket, Aleta headed into the bedroom. "Never mind the suitcase. I'll find something of Evelyn's."

She unbuttoned her blouse as she entered the bedroom and slipped it off one shoulder so quickly, Tom Milani didn't have time to warn her of his presence.

She spotted him immediately, "Who are you? And why aren't you in the living room with everyone else? And why didn't you announce your presence when I arrived instead of lurking about in the bedroom? You'd better be the plumber fixing the toilet."

Taken aback by Aleta's last comment, Tom looked down at his uniform. "Do I look like a plumber?"

"You look like someone who should be in charge out there." Aleta blustered pulling her shirt back up over her shoulders.

"I apologize," Tom said calmly. He exited the bedroom muttering, "Next time West stays behind."

"So you're not West," Aleta said holding her blouse closed with her hand.

"Tom Milani," the chief said, turning. "You must be Miss Locke."

Aleta's cell phone rang. She motioned the chief to wait. "Yes Grams," she said. "I'm here."

She listened for a few minutes replying to queries with a yes and then closed her phone and directed her message to Chief Milani. "Grams says Evelyn is still in danger."

"She's under guard at the hospital," Milani assured her.

Louis Barnes sprang from the couch. "Whatcha mean she's under guard? You mean nobody can see her?"

"Correct!" Milani said. "Nobody. Not even her family."

"You can't do that. It's illegal," Louie blustered.

Stanley Praetzel spoke quietly. "No it's not. They call it protective custody."

"Well, we'll just see about that," Louis stormed. He grabbed his wife's hand and stomped out the door, half dragging the lightweight brunette.

"Hey, Louie, calm down," Mayette whispered stumbling to a run. "They're done looking."

Ed, whose head was buried in the trunk of their rental car, overheard the relief in her voice.

Thus shortly afterward, Hawk left the house with the canisters of tea and coffee and the bag of sugar cubes, all suggested hiding places for hallucinogens.

Milani left satisfied.

Stanley Praetzel hung back and as Aleta was flying out the back door, he said, "We need to talk."

Ed stood next to Stanley Praetzel and grinned. "She's a looker, huh?"

"Yeah," Stanley breathed. "That she is."

"Smart as a whip, too," Ed added. "You like dogs?"

"I guess. I never had one."

"Ever had a cat? Snake? Mouse? Hamster? Goldfish?"

"I have a wall aquarium in my office," Stanley said. "I like fish."

"What kind you got?"

"Do you know about fish?"

"I own a pet store."

Praetzel didn't hide his surprise. "I was told you were a private detective."

"I like animals. This way I can keep lots of them."

"But you sell them."

"Some got sold signs on their cages. That's so they don't disappear while I'm gone on business. When I'm there, they're free."

"Does Aleta know this?"

"Her grandmother does. That's where she interviewed me. She's a cool lady. Emma liked her right off. Betty did too, but Mrs. Locke, she wasn't too comfortable with Betty."

"Who's Betty?"

"My boa constrictor. She's about seven feet long. They make good pets if you keep them fed. The kids love to come into the store and pet her."

Stanley's cell rang. It was Harriet Locke.

"Aleta's outside washing the dogs. Louie and his wife had crammed them into the kennel. They're a mess... Yes, I guess she could use help, but, I don't know anything... yes, it would... yes, he's here..."

Stanley plunked the phone into Ed's hand and took off his coat and tie, rolled up his sleeves, and opened the back door.

"Mrs. Locke," Ed said, "are you matchmaking?"

"Is he nice?"

"Yeah, he is. He don't know a thing about dogs. Or even cats. He's a fish lover."

"I hear he's sharp."

"He is. He's a good choice."

"I warned Milani; but, I'm not sure he understands that the danger to Evelyn is still lurking."

"From where?"

"It's so vague. But, I'm feeling a stronger uneasiness. That's why I called again."

Chapter 9

Evelyn's phone rang and Ed Ornstein picked up the receiver and announced his name. The caller said politely, "I was calling Evelyn. I guess I have the wrong number."

"Evelyn's in the hospital," Ed announced bluntly. The caller's reaction would tell him volumes.

"She can't be! What happened? Who's taking care of her dogs? Louie, if any harm comes to her or those dogs, you'll be sorry." In one breathe the caller had gone from shock to curiosity to threatening.

Ed knew she was a friend, so he told her the truth. "She's under police protection. Louie's not here. And Aleta is washing the dogs."

"Harriet's Aleta?"

"Yes, I'm her friend."

"I didn't know she was bringing her boyfriend."

Ed chuckled, "Do I sound young enough to be that? I haven't had such a nice compliment in years."

"Is Aleta going to show Evelyn's dogs this weekend?"

"I don't know."

"Tell her to bring them here right now. I need them clean if I'm going to hire a handler."

"They're all wet."

"There are dog cloths in the garage and Evelyn's van has enough crates," Beatrice said. "Can one of you help me wash them?"

"Sure, I can," Ed said. He liked the sound of this woman's voice.

A very wet Stanley Praetzel helped Aleta rub the dogs partly dry and then had Aleta follow his car in the van to Beatrice's house situated on a tree lined street across from the golf course.

It was a pretty house set back on a spacious town lot immaculately landscaped. The house was painted pale green with white trim acting as a backdrop to the masses of fuzzy blue ageratum, the bright golden clusters of marigolds surrounding the red and pink roses behind which tall yellow delphiniums were in full bloom. Purple heather, zinnias, dahlias, and asters were mixed in for color and contrast.

While the lawn and the hedges were professionally maintained, Ed knew the flowers bespoke the woman's fond hand.

As they turned into the driveway, a tall, gray-haired, distinguished appearing man emerged from the house followed by a short, slightly plump woman with light blonde curls who was obviously trying to placate the man.

"These them?" the gray-haired, snappily dressed man growled. Ed hated his handsome leanness.

Quickly, Ed opened the van door and moved toward the man, his hand extended. "Name's Ed Ornstein. I brought over Evelyn's dogs."

The man ignored Ed, turned and addressed the woman behind him directly, "Beatrice, since Evelyn's not going, there's no reason for you to go."

Beatrice looked distressed. That his angry tone upset was obvious.

"Evelyn was hoping to win this weekend. The judges have always put up her dogs," Beatrice said plaintively. She was horribly embarrassed that this altercation was occurring in front of strangers.

"So what? She won't be there to see it, so it won't matter."

Aleta stepped out of the car. Even in Evelyn's old tee shirt and jeans, mud splattered from her dog washing ordeal, the young woman was quite beautiful.

"She needs to take me," Aleta said. "I don't know the area or the show grounds and I need to do things right."

"Who're you?"

Beatrice replied quickly,

"I told you. She's Harriet's granddaughter."

"She's older than I pictured," the man muttered.

"Grams' is much older than Beatrice. My father is your age, Mr. Pacheco," Aleta said, having remembered everything in her grandmother's notes.

"Name's Bill," he responded with newfound cordiality.

"I'm Evelyn's new dog handler. I'm showing her dogs."

"You're too pretty and too young to be a pro."

"Really? Guess you haven't been to many dog shows," Aleta quipped. "Guess we better get to it, Beatrice. I appreciate your offer to help, Bill. We've got four dogs and it's getting late."

"Help? Me?" Bill sputtered. "I don't much care for dogs."

"Must be hard living with four then," Aleta noted. "Still we could use your help."

"I'm … I'm … going out. Beatrice knows I don't like this hobby of hers, so I never participate. Soon we're going to be traveling full-time."

After the dogs were washed, Beatrice set out a plate of sandwiches and cups of hot coffee, announcing that she's baked a cake that day, adding that Evelyn loved her chocolate cake.

"Goodness knows I don't need it," Beatrice said depreciatingly.

"Well, I do," Ed put in patting his tummy, "If I stave my fat cells they complain and who needs complaining fat cells."

Beatrice and Aleta both chuckled. Then Aleta eyed him suspiciously.

"What?" Ed asked catching her look. "What's wrong?"

"Your speech."

"What's wrong with it?"

"Before it lacked the fluency and correctness it now has," Aleta observed.

"So, I'm trying to impress a lady. I shouldn't talk as if I just crawled out of the gutter."

"How come I got the gutter stuff?"

"I was testing. Then I couldn't stop so I decided to hang with it, that is, until I heard Beatrice's voice on the telephone."

Beatrice flushed lightly as she cut the cake and offered Ed a big slice. "So you were married?"

"To Emma."

"Your dog?"

"Emma's named after my wife. She's just as sweet too."

He cut a piece of cake with his fork and put it in his mouth.

Aleta noticed that Beatrice held her breath while Ed slowly savored the chocolaty goodness.

"Well," he said after two bites, "Emma could bake and I loved her cooking, but this is better than any cake I've ever tasted."

Aleta saw Beatrice relax. Why was this man's opinion so important?

"You been married?" he asked.

Beatrice nodded. "Three times."

"Good men?"

"Yes."

"So what went wrong?"

"We liked different things. You've heard the adage 'opposites attract'. Well, it's true, but if some changes don't happen afterward you fight all the time. Each of you keeps pulling the other in a direction he or she doesn't want to go."

"Well, Bill is sure an opposite."

"He's working at trying to please me."

"The hell he is!" Ed blurted out. "He's trying to make you into someone you aren't. And, worse than that, he doesn't treat you like the lady you are."

"I'm not so perfect," Beatrice demurred.

"Ladies aren't always perfect," Ed observed. "But they have style and grace. You have those qualities. Bill is not a gentleman."

"What qualities define a gentleman?"

"Consideration for others, I guess," Ed said. "Now show me your house."

Aleta cleared the table while Beatrice took Ed on a tour of her home. They didn't miss her until they were standing in the living room and Ed pointed to the painting over the fireplace and commented that it didn't fit in.

"Bill said it was better than the one I had up there. More class, he said."

"This entire house is decorated with artistry," Ed said. "I can pick out everything Bill added."

"You can't!"

"Want to bet?"

"Sure. What'll we bet?"

"If I win, you owe me a dinner. If you win, I owe you one."

Go for it," Beatrice said excitedly.

"The clock in the dining room. It's…"

"Garish," Aleta finished entering the room.

"We have a bet," Ed announced.

"I'm a witness. Big stakes here."

"That black and gold chest in the hall," Ed went on.

"Bill said it made the entry striking."

"Oh, it's showy, but not pleasant. You are a pleasant lady not a showy one."

"He says I could be," Evelyn commented. "What else?"

"Every black and red outfit in your closet," Ed grinned. "Bet you thought I'd miss those."

Ed won the bet. Arrangements were made for him to come over and help with bathing and grooming the Scotties, a long involved process which would take most of the next day. The Goldens would come with him as they always did when Evelyn helped Beatrice get her Scotties ready. Goldens could be done a day or two earlier. Scotties had to be done as close to show time as possible.

When Aleta and Ed left that evening, Aleta worried aloud that Ed needed to meet the rest of the group and to uncover whatever plot against Evelyn still existed.

"I'm working on that," he said.

"By flirting with Beatrice?"

"Beatrice is Evelyn's best friend. She'll know whatever it was Evelyn suspected."

"So you're just getting close to her to pump her for information."

"Never would I do that! That would hurt her."

"You're not serious about her?" Aleta questioned. She glanced at the rotund little man with a sparse crop of gray covering the bald pate and the wrinkles of age around his eyes and saw the wrinkles crowd together as he smiled.

"She's gonna be the next Mrs. Ornstein with the best pre-nup you can write," he announced.

Aleta gasped. "You want me to write a pre-nup? You just met!"

"I've been looking for a long time. No one since Emma has made my heart beat so fast."

"She's got a boyfriend."

"A con man!" Ed declared. Rancor coated his words. "And my guess is he's behind all that's happening."

"You mean the attack on Grams?"

"Well, maybe not that. Maybe he's not the mastermind; but he's involved."

"Are you sure you're thinking with your head and not your…"

"Heart…? Yes, I'm sure."

"I need to go to the bank early to inventory the arriving assets. Grams wants me to call her with the count."

"Is Stanley going to be there?"

"Why, yes."

"Be nice to him," Ed counseled. "Even homely men have hearts."

"He's not homely!" Aleta declared. "Just different looking. And he has a great smile."

"Just be nice."

"I'll be me."

"Guess that'll have to do," Ed sighed.

"What's that mean?" Aleta charged.

But Ed knew better than to answer.

Twelve hours earlier, back in California, the Trust department of the Atherton Investment Bank was a beehive of activity. As morning approached Doug Lim and Jeff Cole sequestered themselves to discuss what to do about Melissa Bolton who was sleeping with Dennis Rimmel, Roger Sprattley's chief assistant. Sprattley was a VP on equal footing with Harriet Locke. J.G. Garding, the Bank President planned to move Sprattley into a newly created position as head of the two trust divisions. That would force Harriet Locke into retiring.

In preparation for the takeover, Sprattley had studied the terms of the Tontine. A lawyer familiar with estates and trusts, he admired the near-perfection of the document. And he appreciated fully the vast wealth that Harriet Locke had amassed in that fund. Harriet Locke had a golden thumb when it came to investing. While Sprattley knew he couldn't match her, he knew he could keep the trust profitable.

Doug Lim and Jeff Cole had heard enough rumors to sense that Sprattley was looking to take over their division. He would block the transfer of the Tontine assets if he were aware of them. The night had not been long enough. They needed another day and night to transfer enough assets to assure that it would be considered a fait accompli.

If no one tipped Sprattley off, he wouldn't ask what was happening. This morning's computer run would reflect all business transacted the previous day. What had been started early this morning until closing today would be reflected on Friday's run. By the time those sheets were delivered, if and when the changes were noticed, a second full night of activity would have been completed and perhaps even half a morning.

It was decided to move Melissa into Jeff's private office when he left, set his regular work in front of her and have Doug Lim check on her frequently.

Neil Willis was called in and agreed to the plan.

"Sprattley won't object if you move Melissa into Jeff's spot instead of me," Willis said. "But you'd better talk to Valerie. We need her to be part of the plan."

Valerie was brought in along with Janis Thai and Wendy Oshiro. All understood the need for secrecy. Janis and Wendy would feel the most pressure as other administrative trust officers asked them to complete transactions. Still, it was a good plan.

Sprattley entered the bank early. He noted a flurry of activity in the vault area. That the vault was open was an anomaly. It took three officers to open it.

He investigated. Doug Lim explained that Harriet Locke had made arrangements to dispose of the gems the day before and had planned to be here early with the appraiser to oversee the inventory. She'd asked him to fill in.

Lim showed Sprattley the paperwork authorizing the appraisal.

"Who bought the gems?" Sprattley asked.

"Signet Bank in Willow Glen, Illinois. Trustee for the M&W Development Company Trust," Lim replied.

"M&W Development Company? Never heard of them."

"Owned by Martha and Wayne Cook. Cook Construction. Headquarters are in Des Plaines, Illinois. M&W Development is an offshoot," Doug reported.

"Have we been paid?"

"Before the final appraisal?"

Sprattley stammered that he didn't need to be reminded of procedure.

"Well, good riddance," Sprattley said. "I wish we could get rid of more. I hate hard assets."

"She also sold the coins. We have another appraiser coming a little later. The same trust bought those."

"What we really need is to get rid of the art."

"We have a buyer for one of the paintings. We will be shipping that today as well."

"To the same trust?"

"No, to a gentleman named Ed Ornstein from San Jose."

And as Harriet Locke had predicted, that sale snuffed the smoldering fire of suspicion ready to burst into flame in Sprattley's mind. Satisfied, Sprattley hurried into J.G. Garding's office just as Jeff Cole entered.

He frowned at the curly haired man and the look told Jeff to back off; but, Jeff had to be first so he pushed past Sprattley and without any preamble, announced, "I'm going out on Worker's Comp today. My surgery's this afternoon. Mrs. Locke did the paperwork this morning. I'm having both hands done at the same time so I can come back to work sooner."

"How long will you be out?" J.G. Garding asked coolly.

"A month."

"There may be some changes in a month," Sprattley put in.

"Not for me there won't be," Jeff shot back. "Read your rules."

J.G. hastened to amend Sprattley's statement. "What he meant to tell you was that some shuffling of responsibilities will occur if Harriet decides to retire. You will, of course, come back at your present level as Trust Officer."

Jeff acknowledged his satisfaction with a nod then continued, "I have to be at the hospital early for blood work; but, I'll be here long enough to show Melissa the ropes."

"Who chose Melissa to fill in?" J.G. Garding charged. That was his call to make.

"Doug Lim. He thought he'd give each of the three ATO's a chance to take over my accounts and see which one is best suited to take over for me. Me, I'd have just put Neil in the spot. He's already Trust Officer material. And he's connected."

His two superiors reacted—J.G. by stroking his fat jowls and Sprattley by peering down his long nose through his pince-nez glasses. Neither said anything for a moment. Then J.G. Garding cleared his throat and said, "Give us a call when you're ready to come back."

Jeff left the bank afterward. He assured Lim that neither Sprattley nor Garding would check on his surgery. "Hell, they didn't even ask the hospital," he said.

When are you going in?"

"Tuesday. I'm getting the blood work done today. So I'll see you tonight."

On his way out, he leaned over and whispered in Willis' ear that he told Sprattley and Garding that he was connected and that made them sweat.

"I wonder why?" Neil mused.

Shortly before five, Roger Sprattley passed Doug Lim's office and stepped in. "What's keeping everyone so busy?"

Doug checked his watch.

"Jeff carries a heavy load. So does Harriet. But, you're right. It's time to go home. I'll take care of it."

"How'd Melissa do?"

"I'd like to try Neil Willis in that spot tomorrow."

"That bad, huh?"

"She made errors on every trade. Some were simple ones," Lim stated, closing the folder on his desk and putting it on top of the stack on his desk. "I need to try someone else. I haven't time to give her the necessary supervision."

"I was thinking of moving Dennis Rimmel over to help out," Sprattley said.

"Are you considering him for Jeff's spot?" Lim queried. "Jeff's coming back in a month."

"None of us knows whether Harriet Locke will return. I need another experienced man in this division," Sprattley said.

"You are correct. We do need more experience over here," Lim responded. "Perhaps Neil can work with him."

"I'd prefer you do it."

"As you wish," Lim said politely. The man had picked up the reins. Maybe he wasn't officially in charge; but, with Harriet gone, he was the highest ranking officer. He needed to call Harriet. She hadn't expected Sprattley to move so fast.

Darn, he thought, all I had to do was say Melissa was wonderful.

Lim took a select few folders and put them in his file cabinet and locked the cabinet with the push of a button.

"How soon could he be free to join us? I'm sure Monday is a little soon; but maybe by afternoon?"

Lim hoped Sprattley wouldn't realize he was trying to delay Rimmel's joining his division.

But Sprattley sensed something was going on.

"He'll be here tomorrow morning," he stated flatly.

"What about his trust accounts?" Lim inquired respectfully.

"I'll take care of those," Sprattley said. "You need help now."

Lim recognized defeat. "I will greatly appreciate his presence."

With that he set his chair in place, looked around once and walked out of his office, waiting for Sprattley to exit before locking it.

He moved quietly from desk to desk.

"Time to go home," he said to everyone. "Thank you for your help. You worked hard today to pick up the extra load and I appreciate it."

Neil said, "If you sign this, I'll take care of it first thing in the morning."

Lim frowned slightly. Didn't Neil realize that Sprattley was dogging him.

True to form, Sprattley asked, "What is it?"

"A bid on a second painting in the vault," Neil said. Lim smiled. Neil was sharp. Too bad his term was to be so short-lived. He wished he could get him promoted to Trust Officer before he left. He wondered if there was a way. He had to call Harriet.

"If we accept it, we can ship the canvas out tomorrow."

"Is it a good bid?"

"I asked three appraisers," Neil said. "I only got a verbal, but all three said they would send their appraisal in writing. It would be worth getting them. The bid is over the appraised value."

"How'd that happen?" Sprattley asked.

"The buyer took our delay in accepting their offer as an indication that we had another bidder and the man increased his bid."

"Will he go higher?"

"We could lose him."

"What would Harriet do?" Sprattley spit out and then bit his lip.

"She always said the surest way to make no profit is to try for too much profit."

"She was a risk taker."

"Her risk was buying this painting. Its sale will bring the Tontine a hefty profit."

"I'll sign the papers," Sprattley said. "Who's the buyer?"

"Someone named Praetzel."

Lim slipped Valerie a note. On it was the number 630. She put away her work and passed the note to Neil. He took the note and went to operations and had them FAX the acceptance of the bid to Stanley Praetzel. He slipped the note to Wendy Oshiro who shared it with Janis Thai. Shortly afterward the vault was closed and all the trust personnel left the building.

Back at their desks at 6:30 PM. every member of Harriet's group except Melissa Bolton immediately set to work. Transferring property could not be done by computer any more than transferring diamonds. There were pages of signatures for each transaction. Harriet had spent her time signing the required paperwork in blank. Now the paperwork needed completing, the transactions checked and cosigned by a bank officer. Lim elected to go with two additional signatures.

When the call came up from the guard downstairs that Roger Sprattley was on his way up, the vault was closed and everyone collected the paperwork on their desk and gathered in Harriet's conference room, located behind her office.

Tensely the group sat on the plush chairs, a mess of paperwork on the polished oak table in front of them.

"Are these walls sound proof?" Neil asked.

"Not really," Doug said. "That's why Harriet chose to have her own office be the closest one."

He flicked a switch and the TV monitor came on. Sprattley was in Harriet's office. Behind him was the night janitor, a black man named Josiah Washington, who had evidently been called to open the locked door.

"We want to use the conference room," Sprattley said.

"I ain't got a key," Washington said.

"You clean the conference room don't you?" Sprattley's tone was sharp and accusatory.

"When I'se to do it, Mrs. Locke puts the key on the desk."

"Maybe it's in her drawer," a new voice said. Dennis Rimmel entered the field of the camera's vision.

"Dunno 'bout that. I don't look in drawers," Washington said.

In the conference room, the group held its collective breath.

"No keys," Rimmel announced. "There must be a master somewhere."

Again the group in the conference room froze in silence.

"No time for that." Sprattley announced. "Garding's here with the clients. Grab today's computer printout and let's go."

"Where?

"We'll use my conference room. It's not as nice, but it will have to do. We need to open the vault and get the Tontine rules and regs."

Lim looked at Wendy Oshiro in the closest thing to panic his bland face ever registered.

"In vault," Wendy whispered. The men had left the office. Since no one inside the conference room could hear them, Wendy knew they couldn't hear her.

"What do they want with the Tontine docs?" Neil asked.

The vault made no noise as it was opened. The copy machine, however, did.

"They're copying the Tontine charter?" Jeff questioned, more as a supposition than a query.

"They'd have to do it at night," Lim said. "The charter is not to be copied."

"They're making many copies," Wendy said. "I can hear it collating them."

Silence followed the collating. The assumption was made that the invading group had gone to the other conference room.

"What's going on?" Neil whispered.

"I don't like this," Lim said.

The turn of a key in the lock startled the group. Rather than turn to the monitor behind them, as one man they looked at the door which opened cautiously.

"It's okay, guys," Neil said. "It's Josiah. Hey, thanks, man. You saved our hides."

"Thank you," Doug Lim added.

"What's happening out there?" Neil asked.

"You wanna hear?" Washington asked.

"Yeah, man. That'd rock."

"Is the vault still open?" Lim asked.

Washington shook his head.

"Guess we can't pull anything else out until they leave," Lim announced. "Let's finish what we've got. And Neil…"

Neil turned.

"Don't get caught."

Thirty minutes later Neil was back. He opened the door and said, "Josiah gave me the key. He said he don't want it found on him."

He slid it across to Lim. "They'll expect you to have one."

"I can't have two."

"Give it to Jeff," Neil said, "in case they confiscate yours."

"Why would they do that?" Lim asked.

"The men who arrived with Garding are Roy and Big Mike Ciccone. I left my recorder behind the books in the bookcase in Sprattley's office. I got nervous when someone mentioned coffee, so I split."

"Ray and Big Mike Ciccone are from Nevada," Jeff said. "Why are they interested in the Tontine Trust?"

Neil smiled knowingly. That question he could answer. "They're fascinated with its size and the variety of assets it holds."

"Why?"

"I think they plan to launder money through it."

"Harriet would never allow that," Lim said. "No wonder she was attacked.

"But why pick the Tontine?"

"The reason they want to use the Tontine Trust is because it's a player and into every kind of asset," Neil explained.

"What'll happen tomorrow when they discover the Tontine Trust has moved?" Jeff put in.

"What can they do?" Valerie asked quietly. "I mean besides fire us all."

"Let me call Mrs. Locke," Lim said.

While the staff went back to work, Lim retired to a corner and updated Harriet on the plans of the bank management. As he talked, he began smiling. One by one, the members of the group put down their pens and waited. Something good was happening. The tension permeating the conference room like early morning fog off the Bay slowly dissipated.

"What did she say?" Jeff asked.

"That we are to do as much as we can. When we are told to stop, we do so."

"What about our working all night?"

"She said Garding has no idea how much work is involved in a Trust transfer."

"Sprattley will," Jeff commented.

"But he won't know who or how. The property work could have been done during the day. Wendy needs to process the work first thing in the morning; however, before the computer runs hit the desk. And Wendy, we'll buy you as much time as we can. Janis, process the stock transfers first. Valerie, do the T-bills and bonds. Roll over the CD's."

"Don't we want to cash those?"

"No. We might get stopped before we get the money moved. We can roll the CD's over several days early and then transfer them later."

"Why not transfer them now?"

"Because that would send up red flags. Garding has friends in those banks. We do those last if we can hang in there that long."

"I sold most of the mutual funds yesterday. Won't that do the same thing?"

"The Tontine is always making huge withdrawals and buys. That won't alert anyone," Lim said.

"The sale will hit the books today. What do I do with the money?"

"Wire it to M&W Development Company."

"All if it?"

"Yes, evidently the Tontine is going to build something."

"So it'll be a purchase."

"Mrs. Locke said the instructions for the wire transfer are in the top drawer as well as a blank authorization. She thought she might need to get the money out that way."

"There'll be a complete downsizing of this department," Jeff said.

"They can't fire us all, can they?" Valerie asked. "We have other accounts."

"Mrs. Locke said she was planning to retire," Lim said.

"Oh," moaned the group.

"But she's going to call in some favors," Lim added.

Lim's smile made Neil rush in, "Favors that will help us?"

"She's going to put her retirement contingent on Garding approving the promotions on his desk: Valerie and Neil to Trust Officers, Jeff to Assistant VP and me to VP."

"They'll never do it!" Jeff said. "They'll get rid of her some other way."

"She says she can get at least three of these approved."

"I guess that means I'm out!" Neil said bitterly.

"You are the one promotion she practically guaranteed."

"Yeah?" Neil said. "So I get it. Two months down the road they begin to reshuffle the work load and soon after that I'm out the door."

"Maybe. But at least you leave as a Trust Officer."

"There is that," Neil conceded.

"She doesn't think that's going to happen. Just make sure you don't authorize any shady deals. Pass them off to Sprattley or Rimmel or anyone but one of this group."

The next morning by the time Aleta and Ed had showered, dressed and fed the dogs, the first of the assets had already begun to arrive at Signet Bank.

The first call, Aleta answered was from Guy Stevens, President of Signet Bank, telling Aleta that the assets were arriving. The second was from Stanley Praetzel arranging to pick her up. The third was from her grandmother.

"Did you call Dad?" Aleta asked immediately. "He needs to know you're okay."

"Yes, I told him I was at Golden Glen Kennels training the dogs."

"He's worried about you being safe."

"I know," Harriet assured her granddaughter. "I assured him I was. I told him I was parked in the back and that my brand new wonderfully comfortable RV couldn't be seen from the road. Now can I tell you why I called?"

"Yes, of course. Go ahead," Aleta said. "But I hope you aren't having any more visions. I'm not sure I can sell another one."

"I got a call this morning from Doug Lim at Atherton…"

"Yes, I know who he is. Signet Bank just called. The assets are coming in. Stanley is going to pick me up and we're high-tailing it over there."

Harriet pressed past the obvious. "Garding, Sprattley and Rimmel met last night with the Ciccone Family. They plan to use the Tontine to launder money."

"They can't do that!" Aleta protested. "You can stop them, can't you?"

"I'm resigning this morning to give Doug Lim as much time as possible. I'm resigning with the caveat that all my people get the promotion due them."

"He won't honor that," Aleta shot back.

"Oh, he will. He wants me gone," Harriet said. "But I need you and Stanley to look and see if there is any legal basis by which Garding could halt and even reverse the transfer."

"Okay. We'll do the inventory just so the bank can legally accept the assets coming in. Then we'll study the Tontine document."

Harriet uttered a dispassionate murmur of assent, and then her voice grew strong. "First you will take care of Marge Tobias. She's in trouble."

"What kind of trouble?"

"I don't know. But it's bad. She was crying so hard she made no sense. I told her you'd be right over."

"What?"

"Take Ed with you."

"He's working on the Evelyn problem. Your gut still says that's important, doesn't it?" Aleta charged.

"Yes."

"Stanley and I will go to Marge's on our way to the bank."

"Just remember while logging the assets is important, I need all the members of the Tontine alive and capable of decision making at the annual meeting in three weeks. You have my power of attorney. Use it!"

Marge Tobias' house was a modest brick home with a lovely garden full of flowers on each side of the walkway. Climbing roses adorned the arched trellis over the path to the front door.

The approach of the two lawyers was heralded by the excited yips of the four Dachshunds pawing at the door. Marge opened it before they reached the bell and ushered them into a spotless kitchen where Nathan was sitting in his wheelchair nibbling on a fresh baked cinnamon roll. The curtains were a fresh lemon yellow, the glasses on the open shelves sparkled and soft music was playing.

"Smells good," Aleta said. "Cardamom seed rolls?"

The stocky fifty-five year old woman with dull brown hair and a muddy complexion smiled and Aleta was warmed by the genuineness of it. She's as pleasant as her house, Aleta thought.

"Nathan and I were hoping you'd be able to come. Here, sit. Have a roll. Can I pour you some coffee?"

Aleta greeted the four dogs who were standing on their hind legs trying not to paw at her legs and not succeeding. Marge introduced them as one would children of which one was proud.

"The red one is Rufus; Lisa is the boar; Katy is her daughter and Anya is six months. Rufus is my special. Lisa just finished, Katy is in obedience and Anya is entered in her first show tomorrow only I don't think I can go. Nathan usually holds the ones I'm not in the ring with and he's having trouble with his hands now."

It was then Aleta looked up from patting the dogs. She saw Nathan's gray curly hair, patches of which were missing as if it had been pulled out, and the strong chin. She also saw the jaundiced skin and the drawn look of a man who'd lost too much weight. The cinnamon roll dropped from Nathan's hand hitting the table before it rolled over the edge and landed on the floor. Marge scooped it up swiftly as the Doxies dove for the crumbs.

"A little sugar won't hurt them," she commented, "but too much could make them sick." She dropped the bits of bun in the sink, then turned her attention to setting out cups and saucers for her guests.

"Are you well?" Aleta asked the wheelchair-bound man. His blue eyes met hers and she knew he wasn't. "He's in pain," Aleta blurted out.

Marge's head shot up.

"Nathan, why didn't you tell me? What can I do for you?"

"Just a cramp, Marge. It'll pass," Nathan responded thorough gritted teeth.

Marge relaxed and explained,

"He's had this flu for several weeks and he just can't seem to shake it. He rarely keeps anything down. And he has lots of cramping."

"You dropped your cup," Stanley observed quietly, then asked, "Did your hand go numb?"

"How did you know?" Nathan questioned, perplexed.

"I've seen such symptoms before," Stanley said. "You need to go to the hospital right away."

"My son's a doctor-to-be," Marge hastened to explain. "We talked to him and he thinks with rest Nathan will shake this."

Stanley's voice was soft. "He hasn't seen him recently, has he?"

Marge hesitated. "Well, no. But that's because interns keep long hours."

"The Tontine will pay the bill," Stanley said. "Aleta and I both have the power to say that."

"I hate to rack up a hospital bill without cause," Marge said. "What will the others think?"

Stanley's voice stayed even, but firm. "Aleta, call 911. Get an ambulance over here now."

Aleta picked up the phone.

"Is that really necessary?" Marge asked, her voice trembling. "I mean, is he really that sick and I didn't see it?"

"You've been with him day and night. He's been getting slowly worse and he's seen the worry in your eyes. Tell her, Nathan. Tell her about the other symptoms. The headaches, the dizzy spells, the burning sensation in your hands and feet. Stop me when I'm wrong."

Nathan was mute. Marge's jaw dropped and the color drained from her face.

"All that? And you didn't say anything?"

"You called Harriet," Aleta said. "You must've had some clue."

Marge broke down in tears. "I didn't call her. She said she had this feeling something was terribly wrong and I started bawling because that's how I was feeling."

"Well, you were both right," Stanley said, taking charge again. "I need to ride in the ambulance with Nathan. Aleta, you follow with Marge."

Aleta wasn't used to taking orders, but it was Marge who objected first. "I should ride with him."

"This is important," Stanley declared in a kind, but firm, voice. "I have an idea what's making him sick. I can make a better case than you to get the hospital to run the necessary tests."

Aleta had to agree this made sense. Marge was on the verge of collapse. She put her arms around Marge's shoulders and said, "You know yourself that a man's lawyer has more clout than his distraught wife when it comes to influencing a doctor."

The approaching siren sent the dogs into a sudden frenzy.

Aleta grabbed the puppy. "Let me help you put them away."

Marge took the second biscuit from Nathan's plate and urged the dogs to come get a treat. Rufus was the last to give up his stand by the door; but, even he couldn't resist not getting another bit of biscuit. Aleta closed the sliding glass door behind the little red dog and watched Marge give each a bit of the cinnamon roll.

In the ambulance, Praetzel leaned over and whispered to Nathan, "Until now, did you suspect you were being poisoned?"

Nathan's countenance underwent a series of changes ranging from surprise to resignation. The secret was out. And his worse fear was sitting on his chest.

"Those biscuits?" Nathan asked sadly.

"No," Stanley replied. "She fed them to the dogs."

The frown between the brows smoothed out as Nathan relaxed. "Yeah, she'd never hurt the dogs."

"You take any pills like vitamins or herbs?"

"The doctor prescribed something."

"After you're settled, I'll go back and fetch it."

"Marge keeps them in an old prescription bottle with her name on it. She couldn't get the cap off my new prescription bottle so she put the pills in an old bottle of hers. We keep my pills in an old bottle of hers because I'm supposed to take them with food. We didn't bother to mark the label because Marge keeps hers in the medicine cabinet. I'm sure she never mixed them up."

Stanley patted Nathan lightly on the shoulder. "So am I… Tell me, did you come down with the flu before or after you switched to pills in Marge's old bottle?"

"I don't know."

"Think, Nathan. This is critical."

"She didn't mix them up," Nathan repeated.

"Just answer the question."

"Tell me why."

"Only after you answer. My thinking could influence your answer otherwise."

Nathan began to think back aloud. "Let's see it had to be after we renewed the prescription the last time because I was still opening the bottle each time and Marge complained that old people didn't need childproof caps but easy-to-open caps for weak fingers and I told her…"

The paramedic interrupted. "We're coming up to the hospital."

"Tell the driver to slow down," Stanley said.

"What?" the paramedic blustered. "I can't do that."

"Just do it!" Praetzel ordered and the paramedic told the driver to slow down.

"What's wrong?"

"Just slow down, damn it!"

The ambulance slowed and Praetzel leaned over and urged Nathan to continue.

"You said Marge complained about the cap on the prescription bottle."

"Yeah, she did and I told her that as long as I was around she didn't need to worry; but, you know Marge. Well, no, I guess you don't, but, if you did, you'd know she hates to depend on anyone for anything, so one day after I opened the bottle she dumped all the pills into an old prescription bottle of hers that had a big cap and she threw my bottle out. I told her to fish it out of the garbage because the prescription number was on it so she did. She washed off the label and stuck it in the drawer and then she threw the bottle out. She was sure mad at that bottle. Good thing too because it was after that that I got sick and pretty soon I couldn't have opened the bottle even if I wanted to."

Praetzel turned to the paramedic. "The driver can speed up now."

"Hell, I'm not giving a new order," the man said. "We're almost there."

Nathan lifted his head and touched Praetzel on the arm. "You think the medicine left in the old bottle mixed with my pills and made me sick?"

"No. I think someone was trying to kill your wife; not you."

Nathan's head fell back. "Marge?"

"The bottle had her name on it."

"But who?"

"I think I know who's behind it, but what I don't know is who visits your house regularly that has some connection to the Tontine Trust."

"All the women in that trust come over, except Harriet who lives in California; but, never in a million years would it be one of them. Never!"

"What about Bill Pacheco or one of the other men?"

"You don't suspect one of them?" he asked incredulously. "They'd have no reason to hurt Marge."

"Does Bill come over?"

"Once when Beatrice dropped a cake off for Marge for her bake sale, Bill stopped in for two minutes. He couldn't wait to leave. The man has no manners."

"What about Louis Barnes?"

"Evelyn's nephew? A real jerk. Marge insists we go to his gas station because of Evelyn so I see him there, but only there."

"What about Jason Danielson?"

"Yeah, he comes over a lot. He's a friend."

The ambulance stopped, the door opened and Nathan's gurney was quickly ushered in through the emergency entrance.

Stanley Praetzel charged in behind the gurney and stopped the first nurse he spotted.

"I need to see the doctor in charge," he said.

"That would be me," a voice behind him said.

"Why aren't you in there with Nathan?" Stanley Praetzel charged recognizing the voice of Dr. Wayne Cook.

He turned to face the lean muscular man five years his senior. The doctor's smile was pleasant and the eyes twinkled as he spoke, "My interns are in there. Aleta said you had diagnosed him. I always knew you were smart but when did you find time to study medicine?"

"Aleta called?"

"She's a take-charge kind of gal, isn't she?"

"Like your grandmother, only younger."

"So what's going on with Nathan?"

"Arsenic poisoning is my guess. And he's entering the last stages."

"And you know this how?"

"I had a case once involving arsenic poisoning."

"It could be something else," Dr. Cook said.

"It's a place to start," Stanley said.

"Well, considering Evelyn's condition, I would be on surer footing if it were Marge and not her husband."

"His pills were in Marge's bottle," Praetzel said then eyed him curiously. "How much do you know?"

"M&W Development Company, you know, the company that the Tontine is pouring hundreds of thousands of dollars into today," Wayne Cook replied. "I'm the 'W'."

"I should have known."

"You would have the minute you reached the bank. Guy Stevens is pretty proud of his new connection with my grandmother."

"Who's going to run this new company? You aren't giving up your free clinic, are you?"

"Not on your life!"

"Your grandmother's in her nineties and isn't she still running Cook Construction?"

"You'd think she'd just turned seventy. Nothing like a new venture in business to get her fired up," Wayne commented. "I think she'd holding out until one of the twins is old enough to take over."

"When will that be?"

"Sometimes after they finish fourth grade."

"That long, huh?"

"Maybe longer since Alex wants to be a golfer like his mother and Chris wants to be a doctor like me. And neither wants to do any math at all!" Wayne said. He turned toward the examining room. "Now it's time to go in and knock out all the theories my interns have come up with and look like a brilliant diagnostician."

"Nathan may have clued them in."

"They'd have asked who you were and... well... you know."

"Yeah, lawyers are not doctors, so they wouldn't even have considered the possibility," Stanley rejoined. "Remind me to always ask for an old doctor."

"Unless you want a good doctor. Then ask for me."

Jason and Julia Danielson arrived in time to join Marge for Dr. Cook's confirmation that Nathan was suffering arsenic poisoning. He told them he'd called Chief West which was required by law when someone was poisoned. He told them West was going to supervise the forensic team to find out what the source was.

Marge asked when she could see her husband.

"That's not going to be possible," Dr. Cook said kindly. "Chief West placed him in protective custody. No visitors."

"But surely I can be with him," Marge pressed. "I'm his wife."

"That will depend on Chief West," Dr. Cook said. "I know this is difficult for you; but you were his sole source of food."

"Surely, you don't think...," Marge gasped. "I would never... Oh, God. Does Nathan think...? Oh God... Oh, my God..."

She sank to a nearby chair, buried her head in her hands and sobbed as if her heart was breaking. Julia sat down beside her and put her arms around her. Soon the two heads were bowed in prayer, the words mingled in with sobs from both women.

Jason asked Dr. Cook what was going to be done. He knew the women would want to know.

Dr. Cook told him that after the gastric lavage which Marge couldn't be present for anyway, Nathan would be on a regime of Dimercaprol for two to three days while they monitored the arsenic level in the urine.

He then explained that if the Dimercaprol bound enough of the arsenic, there was a second drug that would be given.

"If it doesn't?" Jason asked.

"Kidney dialysis to remove both the Dimercaprol and the arsenic," Dr. Cook said. "Meanwhile we will treat him symptomatically. Rehydrate him. Keep lungs clear. Treat the anemia and address the obvious liver damage."

"What are his chances?" Jason asked.

"The body can actually develop a tolerance for arsenic, so he had an even chance of surviving right now."

Marge gulped hard and wiped her eyes.

"When will you know?"

"It'll be a while," Dr. Cook said. "If you want to wait, I'll give you an update in a couple of hours."

"I'll wait," Marge said.

"We'll wait with her," Julia added.

Marge smiled weakly and then started. "Julia, what did you do to your hair?"

"Like it?" Julia asked. "I used a redder rinse."

In the car on the way to the bank, Aleta commented, "It's hard to believe that a woman so petite and with such a figure can be the mother of seven. And those red highlights were better than a facelift. I hope I look as good at her age."

"Is that important?" Stanley asked.

"Appearance is always important," Aleta tossed back.

"So you like handsome men?"

Aleta laughed. "What woman doesn't?"

She glanced over at him and saw the somber expression. She read it as disapproval.

"Hey, give me a break here," she snapped. "What man doesn't like to meet a pretty woman? It's the way of things."

Stanley became more morose until Aleta added, "It's just a good thing everyone has a different idea of beauty."

Stanley felt hope come alive in his heart. "Is your father handsome?"

"As handsome as they come. My ex-boyfriend looked a lot like him. I think maybe that was the attraction."

"Why did you break up?"

"He betrayed me. Grams predicted he would."

Stanley almost smiled. Grandmothers who didn't take to boyfriends often predicted dire outcomes.

He decided that it would be prudent to talk business. "I thought that after our stint at the bank we could repair to my office and go over the Tontine Trust's legal docs again as your grandmother asked. Then I thought we might have dinner."

"I know this is going to sound terrible, but can I take a rain check on dinner? I'm going to be showing dogs tomorrow and I think we're leaving tonight. But we can have a working lunch at your office. I like Chinese."

Stanley brightened. "I know a great take-out place."

When they arrived at Signet Bank, Guy Stevens rushed out to greet them. "We are all set up in the conference room. I asked for extra police protection today and Chief Milani sent over three men. With my regular security guards that gives us five. Will that be enough?"

"Not too many people know about the transfer," Aleta observed, "so that should be plenty."

"I wouldn't be too sure. A man flew out from San Francisco, said he was a friend of yours. I put him in the Vice President's office. He gave me his card."

Guy Stevens nervously wrung his hands. "He said he was from Hamilton, Schmidt etc., a law firm."

Aleta took the card. "Conan Lloyd! What's he doing here?

She looked around and spotted the handsome profile of her ex-boyfriend. "He shouldn't be here!"

"Do you want me to have him escorted out?" Guy Stevens asked.

"No, I'll take care of it," Aleta said walking toward the office.

Stanley trailed her uncertainly.

Aleta threw open the door and stormed into the room. Her eyes blazed as she demanded to know who had given him her location.

Conan smiled engagingly and Stanley saw the statuesque profile and his heart sank. Here was the model for Michelangelo's David. Good Lord, how would he ever be able to match that.

"Your mother told me," Conan replied. "She was devastated that you'd quit the firm on a lark and flown out here."

"She was not!" Aleta declared. "She was thrilled about buying me a new wardrobe."

Conan amended his statement, "Well, she told me where you were, so that says something, doesn't it?"

"It says she likes you," Aleta said.

"I thought we could talk," Conan said. "You ran out so fast. You were so upset about your grandmother and I know you thought I wasn't there for you; but, I was. Look, the firm even gave me time off to straighten this out. They said you can have as much time as you need. They want you back. So you see I'm the bearer of good news. The whole affair was nightmarish and people don't always react as one expects when confronted with such an event. Mr. Waltham realizes he may have been less understanding than he should have been."

His voice trailed off as Aleta's anger seemed to be unabated by anything he was saying.

"You have no business here," Aleta declared. "I want you to leave. I have work to do."

Conan Lloyd stepped toward Stanley and introduced himself. Stanley could feel the eyes of an appraiser on him but he smiled as he shook the man's hand.

"Stanley Praetzel," he said smiling politely. "A fellow lawyer. Mostly child advocacy."

He saw Lloyd relax even more. Aleta didn't like that kind of law. Had he been a tax lawyer like her father he would have something to worry about.

Stanley knew he'd been set aside as a flawed gem. It wasn't the first time.

"Stanley and I have a ton of work," Aleta said. "So I have no time to talk."

"Surely, Stanley will excuse you for the day to spend time with your finance who's flown..."

Aleta cut in, "Ex-fiancé. And I don't excuse myself. We have a job to do."

"Well, can't he start without you, so we can talk for an hour or so?"

"No, he can't," Aleta said firmly. "We need to do this together."

"How about lunch then. I'll pick you up anytime you say."

"Stanley and I have planned a working lunch at his office."

Stanley was aghast at the honesty of this woman. She didn't play games. Boy, was she a gem. No wonder Dr. Cook was so happily married. He'd found such a woman. Cook's grandmother was such a woman. He never had to second guess her. She, too, spoke her mind.

"A working lunch?" Conan scoffed. "That's a farce."

"We have documents to go over. I like to eat when I read," Aleta said coldly.

"Documents?" Conan sneered. "Not etchings? Well, at least, he's original. You can tell me all about it at dinner. I'll pick you up at seven."

"No way," Aleta said. "I already turned down Stanley's invitation because…"

"Well, this is different. I've flown two thousand miles to be with you. I deserve some consideration."

"Well, you're not getting any. I didn't ask you to come. I have things to do. Bottom line: I'm too busy to rehash what happened yesterday morning."

"Then I'll see you tomorrow," Conan said. "And we can start over."

"I'm showing dogs tomorrow," Aleta said. "I do not like to communicate about anything but dogs when I'm at a show."

"How many are you showing?"

"Two, possibly four."

"And you're in the ring how long? Five minutes?"

"You have no idea what goes on, so just stay away from me when I'm showing."

"Is Stanley going to be there?"

"I imagine he is."

"Then I will be too."

"Suit yourself," Aleta said. "Now, leave." Conan looked askance at his ex-girlfriend, "You're not yourself. You've never acted like this before."

"I haven't changed," Aleta said. "You just never noticed. Now, go, or I'll have you escorted out."

"You wouldn't dare!" Conan challenged.

Stanley smiled inwardly. That was something even he knew not to say to a woman, let alone a redhead.

"Guard," Aleta called, motioning to the security guard. "This gentleman is slightly addled. Will you show him to the exit?"

Conan Lloyd gathered himself and stormed through the door and out the bank.

Aleta grinned at Stanley. "Do you think he'll be mad enough not to bother us again?"

Stanley smiled. "You have no idea what a prize you are. He doesn't know it; but, he's learning. He'll be back. His ego won't let him do otherwise."

"You don't like him, do you?"

"Whoever likes their rival?"

"Rival?" Aleta queried, puzzled.

Stanley decided that an honest woman deserved an honest answer. "Yes. I'd like to court you too."

Aleta blushed.

At twelve thirty, Aleta received a call from Harriet. "J.G. has stopped the transfer. I think he plans to recall the assets in route."

Aleta told Stanley what her grandmother was saying. He rushed outside and found Guy Stevens.

"Can you shut down the phone system?"

"You mean put on the automatic messaging system?"

"Yes," Stanley said. "Millions are at stake. Can you do it?"

"Yes. I can. You want to tell me what's going on?"

"Do it first."

"We sometimes close for lunch from twelve to one," Stephens said. He told the receptionist to close the board.

"Make it twelve to two," Stanley said.

The receptionist looked at the bank president. He nodded his approval.

"Why are we doing this?" he asked Stanley as they walked away.

"Do you have a cell?"

"Yes, I do."

"Turn it off."

As the two reentered the conference room, Stanley explained. "According to Harriet Locke, J.G. Garding has stopped the transfer of assets."

"Can he do that?"

"Aleta and I are going to study the documents when we're finished here. My guess is that we may wind up in court. What's important right now is for you to receive as many assets as possible before Atherton's attorneys notify you to stop receiving them. They may or may not have a legal basis for making that request, but…"

Aleta interposed, "But while you may not receive any more transfers, all those you have received in good faith stay here. To force their return will require a court injunction."

"Aren't you two playing fast and loose with the law?"

"That's that J.G. Garding is doing," Aleta said. "My guess is that Harriet's resignation from the bank allowed him to take over as trustee of the trust."

"Why did she resign?"

"To give her people guaranteed employment until they got their feet under them," Aleta said. "She is counting on Stanley and me to counter their moves and eventually win the game."

"What happens to the owners of the Trust?"

"Their money is safe. Atherton bank just wants to control it," Aleta explained. "They only need three votes out of the five to force the return of the funds."

"We can match any offer they make," Guy Stephens said.

"You can only offer money. The Ciccone Family is involved and they have other less pleasant incentives at their disposal."

"What assets are still due?" Stanley asked abruptly.

"The coins are due to arrive at one," Stephens said. "My God! I forgot about the stocks. They were being transferred by computer."

"Have they been accepted?"

"She was still checking the transfers in case there were any numerical errors."

"Assume there are none," Aleta said. "Grams said I had her power of attorney and I know her crew would have double checked everything."

"Banks don't operate that way."

"They do today," Stanley said. "Garding may be counting on your following protocol. He's going to be so busy putting his finger in the dike at his end he won't pay much attention to what's been sent. All we need is for your acceptance to precede his notice to cease."

The ring of the phone startled them all.

"We need to move now!" Aleta said.

"What do you want me to do?" Guy Stevens asked.

"Are you computer literate?"

Guy Stevens nodded. This always surprised the younger generation, but with a son majoring in computer science, he had studied to keep up.

"Take the whole incoming report and send it back with a blanket acceptance."

Stephens fingers flew over the keyboard. Stanley watched him scroll down the list to the end and type in "All above accepted as presented." It was an unusual transmission and Janis Thai's heart almost stopped when she saw the list being sent back. She scrolled down to the end and saw the note. She punched the printer button and the printer spewed out the pages of stock data.

A second transmission arrived at Atherton as the printer was copying the first. Janis hoped it was the bonds. They hadn't been sent until 9:30 AM Pacific time. The CD's were the last to go and the last of those went out a little after ten. It was their transmission that alerted the bank officers that the Tontine was in the process of transferring.

The list of CD's was incomplete. Janis has sent those from other banks before notifying Atherton's commercial department. Within minutes Garding was notified and he stormed into administrations and asked for a copy of the transfer order signed by all the trust principals. When none could be unearthed, the transfer was stopped.

Stevens concluded his email acceptances with the partial list of CD's.

He sat back. "Now all we need is for UPS to deliver the coins and the US Post Office to deliver the property papers."

"They aren't here?" Stanley asked. His dismay was obvious. "Anyway we can speed things up?"

Stevens chuckled. "Speed up the US post office?"

Aleta began pacing. "Is there any other way we can work this? I wish I knew more about trusts."

"Call your grandmother," Stanley suggested. "She orchestrated this. I can't believe she didn't foresee this."

Harriet answered on the first ring.

"So where are we?" she said.

"We don't know what to do about the property transfer. If it's not recorded, Garding could stop it at his end."

"I have a friend at the County Recorders office. She owes me," Harriet said.

"If the property's not recorded with Signet Bank as trustee before the order to cease activity, it could fall into the category of assets not transferred," Aleta told her.

"Let me handle it. Where'll you be?"

"Stanley and I were planning on going over the trust document at his office where it's quiet."

Suddenly Harriet gasped. "Don't go there today."

"Why not?"

"I sense danger."

"Grams, aren't these feelings of yours a little whacky?"

"All I know, Aleta dear, is that they've been good ones so far. Trust me. And know this, I'm not happy about being able to prophesy danger. It's uncomfortable and scary; but, please just do as I ask because it's me that's asking."

"Okay, okay!" Aleta said impatiently. "I guess we can go over the agreement somewhere else."

When she hung up, Stanley grinned. "I guess I don't get to show off my fish."

"Your fish?"

Stevens butted in, "He has this amazing aquarium. It covers one whole wall of his office."

"It's expanded since you were last there," Stanley said. "It now covers two."

"Tropical fish?" Aleta asked.

"Goldfish," Stanley replied.

Aleta's jaw dropped. "You want me to come over and look at a bowl of goldfish?"

"Aquarium," Stanley corrected. "And yes, they're neat. They even have names."

"Do they do anything?"

"You mean besides swim around gracefully and add beauty to my office and help me think?"

"I have an aquarium in my office," Stevens offered. "If you need fish to think."

"I need my fish!" Stanley declared.

Aleta laughed, "Not some stranger's?"

Stanley frowned, "Don't mess with what I need to think."

"Then let's go to your office."

"Your grandmother warned us."

"Do you do everything your grandmother says?"

"You promised."

"That's before I knew how important fish were for your brain to function."

"You're making fun of me."

"We've been warned," Aleta said. "We can call the police if we see anyone suspicious hanging around."

"I guess we'll be fine if we're cautious," Stanley agreed.

Chapter 10

Lou Zalkan parked his rental car in the parking garage behind the business plaza and, brief case in hand, walked across the brick pathway leading through the tiny park past the small fountain spilling water over a series of large rocks into a pool of clear water in which several large goldfish could be seen swimming in lazy serenity. He skirted the benches lined up around the fern-bordered pool and headed for the boutiques lined up on a tree-shaded street above which were various offices.

He found a small brass sign hanging suspended to one side of an oak entry door leading to the law office of Stanley Davis Praetzel, Esq. The light from the glass panels beside the door lit the second sign in the lobby pointing to the elevator behind the stairway.

His footsteps were unheard on the thick carpet and he was halfway up the stairs when he heard a woman answer the phone and say, "No, he's not in right now. May I take a message?"

Carefully, he backed down the stairs, and as he did so a patrol car rolled up in front of the door, and through the glass panel, Lou saw a cop get out of the squad and head straight toward him.

He ran toward the back and scooted into the open elevator. He punched no buttons so the elevator remained on the first level.

A few minutes later he heard talking in the office above. He caught a few snatches of the conversation, enough to know the place was going to be watched by the police. He quietly slipped out the door. Once in the street he walked briskly to the end, crossed and came back. He matched the window of the law office with its counterpart across the street.

The woman in the office had her back to him when he entered. His blow on her head rendered her instantly unconscious. He locked the door, taped the woman's hands, mouth and eyes with duct tape he found in the drawer and then stuffed her in the closet.

He strode over to the window and looked through the blinds at the street below. The door to the law office opened. First the cop came out, and then a plump, gray-haired woman whom he realized at once wasn't his target.

Lou didn't personally know the Ciccone Family but evidently his boss owed Big Mike a favor and Lou had been commissioned to do it. He wasn't local so he'd flown in with a small carry on. The briefcase with the weapon disassembled inside had been passed to him as he left the airport.

He was average height with thinning brown hair and ordinary features. His suit hung well on his thin frame and considering what he paid for it, it should have.

He opened the case on the desk and began to assemble the gun. While he hadn't personally tested the sight, he assumed it was accurate enough to do the job. It always was.

He wondered as he waited how good the source was. How could Big Mike Ciccone know what time the lawyer and the girl were going to return to an office in Illinois.

The patrol car remained in place in front of the lawyer's door. That meant the lawyer and the girl were coming back to the office soon. He rolled the soft leather office chair near the window and waited.

Chapter 11

Stanley Praetzel and Aleta Locke strolled down the brick walkway next to the pool of water sparkling in the bright sunshine. Oak trees shaded the walkway and the warmth of the air was pleasant rather than stifling.

They walked slowly and Stanley pointed out his fish. "That one's Milani and West is over there. Wayne is that big one. His grandmother's back in my office."

"You named a fish 'Martha'?" Aleta gasped. She hadn't been in town long; but she'd been here long enough. Martha Cook didn't seem the kind that one named a fish after.

"She picked out her namesake herself. She liked its tail."

The light banter eased the tension a bit. They had tried to keep their minds on the task before them at the bank, but they kept worrying about Nathan Tobias who was fighting for his life and Evelyn Barnes who was struggling to regain her sanity. With two Tontine families in dire medical need, both lawyers realized that if the trust funds were frozen by the court, the group might swing toward returning the trust back to Atherton in San Francisco to free up funds to take care of their friends.

As they walked along, Aleta asked, "Can't we take out any money and set it aside in an account for medical emergencies?"

"The Tontine Trust doesn't work that way," Stanley replied. "But we can prepay the hospital. Wayne Cook can give us a ballpark estimate."

"How are we going to do that?"

"With this," Stanley said pulling a checkbook from his pocket.

"What's that?"

"A checkbook. Guy Stevens recognized your legal right to write checks on Tontine Funds so he coded these checks as soon as the first money arrived," Stanley said.

"I thought the money was wired to M&W Development Company," Aleta said. "We have to do this right, you know."

"Wayne Cook bought a painting from the Trust yesterday. He gave me the check. I deposited that money into the Trust account at Signet Bank."

"Was the painting worth enough to make a dent in the hospital bills?"

"How about half a million?"

Aleta tried not to look aghast at the amount, but she failed. "I had no idea."

"What? That the Cooks were that rich or that the trust was?"

Aleta flushed. "Both I guess. I mean I half guessed that there was more money in the Trust than I imagined; but, you are surprising me. The CD's I was worrying about are small potatoes."

"Harriet invested heavily in art and property," Stanley said. "She was in for the long haul."

As the two left the park, Aleta muttered, "What's he doing here?"

"You mean the cop?"

"No. Conan Lloyd," Aleta said sourly.

As they approached, Conan walked toward them with a paper shopping bag in hand. A cop appeared from inside the store and intercepted him.

"It's alright," Aleta said. "He's someone I know."

The cop stepped away and Conan approached, annoyance riding on his furrowed brow. "You're late." He held up the bag. "I bought us lunch only now it's cold."

In the upstairs window, Lou Zalkan peered through his telescopic sight. It would be so easy to do it now. He kept the red- headed woman in his sight. If she turned to go, he'd take his shot.

"You said you were going to eat lunch here," Conan charged.

"We are, Conan. But you aren't invited." Aleta's voice was firm but not harsh. "In fact, I remember uninviting you from the rest of my day."

Conan grabbed Aleta's arm. "I need to talk to you. It's important."

Aleta pulled her arm from his grasp.

Conan apologized immediately and the bluster disappeared from his manner. "We need to talk about us. Surely this new friend of yours is gentleman enough to allow us a few minutes to straighten out our misunderstanding."

He looked at Stanley. "Can't your business wait half an hour?"

"No," Stanley replied. "It can't."

"Are you telling me you're the kind of man who puts business before personal relationships?" Conan charged.

Stanley answered calmly, "Yes, I do."

He ushered Aleta into the lobby. They entered the elevator without Conan.

"Where's your secretary?" Aleta asked when she stepped out of the elevator.

"I sent her home."

"Why?"

Stanley hesitated before confessing that he'd taken her grandmother's warning seriously and that he didn't want his secretary in harm's way.

"So you don't think my grandmother's nuts?"

"I have a friend who has psychic ability and I've learned not to discount her predictions."

"My grandmother's not a psychic!" Aleta declared. "She just has gut feelings about danger. I think it's a result of her close brush with death. She's always had good instincts. Nothing that she's predicted can't be explained by some prior knowledge that things weren't right with her friends. Her reason and intuition took over."

"So that's why you agreed to come see my fish?" Stanley said. "Well, come see them."

The two stepped into Stanley's large office with two walls with huge built-in fish aquariums.

Aleta felt as if she'd stepped into another world. The bottom of the aquariums glistened with colored coral and the seaweed fronds waved gently as if in a breeze as the gentle motion of the swimming Koi moved the water. There were rock caves, overhangs and tunnels as well as fences of seaweed for the fish to hide behind. The tank layout was almost as interesting as the fish.

"Which one's Martha?" Aleta asked.

"She's in the new tank," Stanley said moving to the right. "Guess."

Aleta moved to the right and stopped in front of the tank and watched the fish looking for the one with a tail that was somehow unique.

Across the street Lou Zalkan waited until Aleta was stationary before firing the first shot.

The bullet penetrated the window glass, sailed along the top of Aleta's skull and kept going straight through the aquarium glass, shattering it.

Lou Zalkan took a fraction of a second to readjust his aim. The sight was off.

That moment cost him his shot. Whereas when he pulled the trigger, Aleta was in the crosshairs, the cascading water shoved a fish in her face and she jerked her head away.

The bullet missed her but penetrated the belly of the fish. The sudden movement caused her to slip on the wet rug and sit on the floor suddenly. The dead fish fell in her lap as the water pouring from the aquarium slowed to a trickle.

Stanley saw Aleta sit down hard and his first thought was that she was alive and out of danger. His attention was drawn to his fish, one of which was lying between them gasping for air and flopping helplessly. He reached for it quickly.

The third bullet nipped his ear.

He ran with the fish to the other tank with no heed to the fact that the gunman was obviously still shooting. His brain told him a moving target wouldn't be hit. His heart had insisted he save his fish, so his brain had given in and provided a rationalization for his foolhardiness.

Thus, Stanley no sooner had one fish in the tank than he scrambled across the floor after a second one. Aleta meanwhile, stunned by the jarring she'd received when the water pushed her backwards, noticed that the fish in her lap was dead. Dead and bloody.

Her skirt moved. A fish was flopping between her thighs trying to breathe. She picked it up and scampered to her feet and raced to the tank and dropped it in. She saw blood swirling around it.

"It's bleeding," she cried.

Stanley looked over as he dumped in another fish. "It's you that's bleeding, Aleta. Sit down."

"Me?" Aleta said bewildered. "Where?"

"Your head."

"So's your ear," she said pushing past him to grab another fish. "Get that fish!"

Stanley, his love for his fish driving reason back again, went after the last fish. It had stopped flopping and Stanley watched it hopefully as he slid it into the water.

Aleta put her arm on his shoulder and watched with him. He assumed she was being sympathetic until she staggered slightly.

The gills of the comatose fish began to move and within a minute he was swimming.

The two embraced in celebration.

"Don't mean to interrupt anything," came the familiar voice of Chief Milani, "but are you two okay?"

"His ear's bleeding," Aleta responded.

"She's hurt," Stanley said.

"A fish is dead," Aleta said. "It hit me in the face when the tank broke. I think it got shot."

"I just have a regular ambulance coming," Milani said, swallowing a chuckle. He looked at the fish on the floor. "It's dead alright."

"Tell me it's not Martha," Aleta pleaded.

"It's not Martha," Milani said.

"You're just saying that."

"I think it's Stanley's mother."

"Oh, my gosh, I killed his mother's namesake," Aleta wailed.

"She'll get over it," Milani said. "Although her son may not."

Aleta turned to Stanley, tears forming beneath her eyelids. "Oh, Stanley, I'm so sorry."

Stanley couldn't believe that a woman he'd just met could understand how dear his fish were to him.

Milani cut to the chase. "Who knew you were going to be here this afternoon?"

"No one," Aleta said.

"Who was that man that was waiting for you?"

"Oh, him. Conan Lloyd. My ex-boyfriend."

"What was he doing here?"

"He wanted to get back together," Aleta said.

Milani eyed Stanley surreptitiously. The man was remarkably calm.

Milani pressed on. "Who else?"

"I told my grandmother and she warned me not to come."

"And you came anyway?" Milani asked, a touch of disapproval in his tone even though he knew about the warning. Stanley had called him.

"Stanley can't think without his fish," Aleta offered lamely.

"Anyone else?"

"Guy Stevens," Aleta said, and then switched back to her ex-boyfriend, "but Conan hasn't any reason to want me dead."

"Then he talked to someone who does."

Chapter 12

While Aleta and Stanley were being cared for by Dr. Cook in the Tri City Hospital emergency ward, across the country in J.G. Garding's office in the Trust Department of Atherton Investment Bank, a high-level conference was taking place. Every lawyer in the bank had been called upon to study the section of the Tontine document dealing with Trustee transfer.

They all came to the same conclusion that Aleta and Stanley arrived at the first ten minutes in Aleta's hospital room. Harriet Locke had the power to transfer the assets as designated controller of the Trust and Vice President of Atherton Investment Bank.

That she had garnered the signatures of other bank officers on each transfer document meant it would be difficult to win a court case based on malfeasance on the part of a single bank officer. The Bank needed to take another route. It was laid out clearly. If three of the five principals objected to the transfer, then it could be voided and the assets returned.

Later, alone in his office, Garding and Sprattley called in Dennis Rimmel and gave him his marching orders. It was decided that Melissa Bolton would accompany him. She had been promoted to Trust Officer in a brief ceremony that morning along with everyone Harriet had put up. Garding and Sprattley had decided to comply with all Harriet's recommendations to cement her resignation.

Rimmel had questioned Melissa's inclusion in so important a task and was told she was his "golden girl" and now was the time for her to shine.

"We need a member of Harriet's staff on this junket," Garding said. "Harriet has been holding a tight leash on the money. Let them know we will not. Pepper them with attention and gifts at the Bank's expense. Let them know we value them as customers. Suggest creative investments that they could enjoy themselves."

"Like what?" Rimmel asked.

"Art in their homes instead of in our vault. Houses built on the land they own instead of letting the land remain undeveloped," Sprattley said. "They've got large pieces of property near Willow Glen and Arborville where they all live that they could use to build themselves estates reflective of their wealth."

J.G. turned to his VP, "We could probably get them to sell the land in California our friends want to develop. They won't care what happens in California."

"Harriet Locke will," Sprattley put in.

"She won't be around to resist much longer."

Sprattley frowned. "I don't like the implication of what you're saying."

"We aren't the only ones who studied the Tontine legals," Garding commented. "Ray Ciccone studied them too. He thinks that we need Harriet and her granddaughter out of the picture."

"Why her granddaughter?" Rimmel asked as he tried to grasp the cool attitude his superiors had acquired.

"Harriet gave her granddaughter power of attorney. Aleta can act on Harriet's behalf," Sprattley explained. "The Tontine Trust allows people with power of attorney to vote if one of the principals can't, so taking out Harriet won't accomplish anything if we let her granddaughter live."

Rimmel felt the cold reason shutting out all emotion. Money had been raised to the position of supreme deity to be served above all else. Slowly Rimmel's conscience began shriveling up. Since he hadn't used it much since succumbing to Melissa's wiles, he hardly noticed that its strength was waning.

Sprattley leaned forward and looked past the pince-nez glasses perched on his long thin nose, "We need signed affidavits from at least three of the principals. And no one's going to ask what tactics you use to persuade the ladies to return their Trust to Atherton. Just remember who we are all now working with."

Rimmel paled as he stuttered, "How far can I take the tactics?"

"To the limit."

"What if I'm arrested?"

"We don't mind that," J.G. said. "Just as long as you won't lose in court."

"Won't that look bad?"

"We'll claim you were harassed by our opponents."

Sprattley spoke up. "Did we mention a sizeable bonus if you pull this off?"

Rimmel's eyes lit up. He'd been wanting to move his family up into the posh Piedmont area in the Oakland Hills. This was his chance to dump Melissa and surprise his wife into believing that he'd been secretly squirreling away money to make a move up in class possible. She'd began to notice money disappearing as Melissa got more and more demanding. He could cut Melissa off on the trip where no one would notice her anger.

Garding was about to offer another money incentive when he caught the pleased look on Rimmel's face. There'd be no need. The younger man saw this trip as a way out of something. He wondered what.

Dennis Rimmel and Melissa Bolton were in the air by four o'clock. At ten o'clock, they were met at O'Hare by Conan Lloyd, who'd been called by his boss Jethro Waltham and urged to cooperate. Conan wasn't quite certain why he was supposed to get involved but he guessed it was one exec doing a favor for another. Besides all he had to do was meet these two and tell them where four people were. He'd been given the list of names. He surmised that a little networking wouldn't hurt his career.

When the two bank officers deplaned, Conan eyed the voluptuous, dark-eyed Melissa with interest. He suggested a late supper at one of the better restaurants in Chicago.

Conan was quick to relate to these two Bay Area professionals. He found it pleasant to again be in the company of people of his own ilk. Dennis and Melissa were both too hyped up to sleep.

The three found it easy to chat about inconsequential matters on the trip into downtown Chicago. The restaurant Conan had selected was one of Chicago's finest. When the tossed spinach-apple salad was placed in front of the diners after the chilled consommé had been removed, the talk turned to the business that brought the Atherton Investment Bank officers over two thousand miles.

"We need to contact all four of the women as soon as possible," Dennis said placing his wine to one side after a small sip.

"One you can't get near," Conan responded. "Evelyn Barnes is in the hospital under police protection. No visitors."

"What about the others?"

"Nathan Tobias is in the hospital too. His wife Marge is spending hours alone in the waiting room downstairs. He's under police custody too. Seems someone is trying to kill these ladies."

"No!" Rimmel shouted, then toned down his voice. "They can't. We need them alive!"

"So far, thanks to Aleta, they are," Conan said with a touch of pride.

Melissa frowned, "Aleta Locke?"

"Yes."

"Does she have access?"

"If she does, she's not using it. She's too busy playing love nest with another lawyer, a real hick."

"What about Beatrice Johnson and Julia Danielson?"

"They'll be at the dog show all day tomorrow."

"Dog show," Melissa sputtered. "I hate dogs."

"Well, you better not say that around these women. They're all dotty over their dogs. Didn't you know that what binds the Tontine group together is their hobby of showing dogs?"

"Well, at least we'll be on even footing with Aleta," Rimmel commented.

"No, you won't."

"Does she have a show dog?"

"Worse."

"What's worse?"

"She's a handler."

Melissa burst in. "She washes dogs?"

"Handles," Conan corrected. She shows dogs in the ring. She's showing some of their dogs tomorrow. In the dog show world, handlers are revered."

"Unless they lose," Melissa said and the two men realized she at least understood competition.

Talk was suspended while the plates of Beef Wellington were slipped in front of each diner. Potatoes Parmesan were nestled beside the green peas and onions. Soft fresh baked biscuits were placed on the table in a covered basket and wine glasses were filled.

Eating took the next quarter hour and the subject of the dog show was put aside. They would not return to it. None of the three had ever seen a dog show.

Rimmel who owned a Lab Golden cross was a bit excited at the prospect. He was curious which pure bred type his dog took after.

When he thought of his dog, he thought of his wife. He left Melissa at her hotel room door telling her that this was strictly a business trip. Any allusion to their previous liaison would cost her job. Suddenly he realized he'd outgrown her.

It was a rough letdown for Melissa who tugged at his tie as she shoved her door open with her foot and cooed at him to join her for a nightcap. He yanked back his tie and bid her goodnight through pursed lips.

What had he seen in her, he wondered. The money he'd be getting could move him up in the world. She wouldn't fit where he was going. She'd begun hinting that they make their arrangement permanent. He thought about sharing her tiny apartment with her and choked on the idea.

Satisfied that he'd shed himself of her, he went to his room and made plans for the next day. She'd do what he asked, he knew. She couldn't afford to lose her job.

Melissa, however, seething from their rejection made her own plans, strangely enough, not against her ex-lover as one would expect, but to outshine him in the eyes of his boss. Her ultimate revenge would be to cost him his promotion to assistant VP.

Two thousand miles away, another person was plotting his revenge with the same seething anger coursing through his veins. Clay Spader, a hit man, occasionally employed by the Ciccone Family, insisted that he be the one to take out Harriet Locke. His other brother, Fogg, wanted to come along; but, Clay insisted it needed to be a one-on-one deal to mean anything and so Fogg, being younger, had stepped back.

A tap had been placed on Robert Locke's phone. Eventually Harriet had called her son and at his prodding, told him exactly where she was.

Clay had driven to the Redwood City area, found a motel and surreptitiously investigated every side road around the training grounds. He had parked his truck on the road running along the backside of the acreage and walked through the field and up a small hill and dropped to the ground the minute he'd reached the top. Down below, barely twenty yards away Harriet Locke stood fully exposed.

He cursed himself for not having thought to bring his gun with him. He snuck back to his truck to retrieve it; but, by the time he returned, the woman was at her trailer. It was then he noticed that she was carrying a rifle.

He remembered that she'd beat his brother to the draw and her single shot had been dead center. He sank back on his heels and considered his options.

A night assault would be best he figured. He liked the idea of using darkness as a shield.

I need to separate her from that gun, he decided. There's no way I want her armed.

He studied her big RV parked by itself toward the rear of the property. The house, the kennels and the other trailers were all clustered beyond the series of training ponds. She had isolated herself, perhaps believing that the hill he'd climbed protected her from view of the road. She was right. If he hadn't spent time scouting the area, he wouldn't have found her. It did help, he was ready to admit, to have her assure her son she was well hidden.

No one would notice if he snuck up on her at night.

He noticed a trash barrel sitting near the RV and he had an idea. A fire in that barrel would bring her outside with a fire extinguisher. If she stayed inside, she'd die of smoke inhalation before anyone in the distant group of campers spotted the fire.

It was fool proof.

Harriet was restless. The day's heat was still rising from the ground. She hooked special individual cooling fans onto the wire fronts of the crates housing Babe and Keeper and walked outside with Stoney and sat down in her lounge chair. Stoney laid at her feet.

Her mind refused to relax. It regurgitated the events of the day for a second and third rumination. Aleta had almost been killed. That bothered her the most. Stanley had assured her that she was safely bedded down in the hospital. She wished she could keep her precious granddaughter there, but she didn't know how. Robert would never forgive her if she were the reason his eldest daughter was killed. More than that, she'd never forgive herself. She had had no idea when she sent her to Illinois that she would become a mob target. Ed, whom she'd sent along to guard her, had expected only local smalltime bad guys.

Now it was more important than ever that the Tontine be broken up and the money divided into trusts that would fund each Tontine member's dream.

I have to go there now, she resolved. The annual meeting of the Tontine will be too late.

I could start now, she thought. I can't sleep anyway.

Her better judgment, however, won out and she resolved to leave early in the morning after giving the dogs a good workout so they'd sleep peacefully through the first day of travel. Driving through the mountains would be taxing enough in an RV without worrying about the dogs needing to be exercised. The morning would be soon enough.

As she looked at the stars above, she felt relaxed.

I'll sleep out here, she decided. Only not on this chair. I'll wake up too stiff and I have a lot of driving to do.

She went inside the trailer and dragged the mattress from the bed. She would have it laid down on the ground, except that soft skittering in the grass reminded her she might wind up sharing her bed with unwanted critters.

Stoney will keep them away, she thought at first. But it didn't take long for her to remember that dogs don't react to snakes which she couldn't count on to be dormant with the ground still so warm.

I need to be off the ground, she told herself.

She shoved the heavy wooden picnic table next to the RV. Next she dragged the mattress out of the RV, climbed up on the table with it and pushed it on top of the roof. Still uneasy, Harriet went into the RV and fetched her rifle and shells and climbed onto the roof. Stoney joined her, and laid down next to her.

"Don't push me over the edge," she chided softly, "or you'll get no breakfast."

Stoney rolled over on his back and waited for his nightly belly rub.

"You keep watch," she said as she rubbed his soft belly and let her fingers run over his curly coat. After the rub he nestled down beside her.

Clay Spader came up over the rise of the hill a hundred yards from the trailer, a gasoline can in his right hand, his rifle slung over his shoulder and a tied bundle of brush in his left hand. He had no idea how much trash was in that big can next to the RV, but now that wouldn't matter. He brought his own fodder for the fire. The dry brush would take the fire right up the wall of the RV.

He was upwind whenever the air stirred now and then, so no breeze alerted Stoney of his presence. The crack of a single twig, however, brought the big dog's ears up. The large head followed at the snap of a second twig.

The rustle of the small rodents scampering about at night, Stoney recognized. The twig was a big one snapped by a heavier footfall.

His eyes and nose failed him.

The tiny crackle of the dry grass, the rustle of the bundle of twigs and the heavy breathing of a man struggling up a slope however told the dog exactly where the stranger was.

His nose continually sniffed the air but it was his eyes that seconded what his ears had told him. In the faint moonlight he saw a man creeping toward the trailer.

Slowly the big dog rose to his feet. His hackles rose with his body. The dead grass color of his coat blended perfectly with the dry field behind him.

Stoney growled deep in his throat. Any animal other than a human would have heard it and veered off. But neither the creeping man nor the sleeping woman heard it.

Stoney took a small step forward and Harriet felt his foot against her thigh. She reached over to move it and her hand touched his leg. The leg was horizontal.

She left her dream midway through and mentally fought her way to consciousness. By the time she opened her eyes, Stoney's growl was loud enough to be heard.

The man inching his way toward the RV heard it and he stopped. The growl was instantly swallowed.

In the silence, Harriet reached under her mattress and extracted her gun. Two shells lay unwrapped beside it. She grabbed them too as she looked in the direction Stoney was staring. She could see nothing.

Clay had lowered himself to peer under the RV and see if he could see the dog who'd growled.

He stood for almost a minute telling himself that if the dog was outside, he'd have rushed him. Still he hovered close to the ground searching every nearby bush.

On top of the RV Harriet had shoved the two shells into the breach. She didn't snap the gun closed because she didn't want whoever was out there to know either where she was or that she was armed.

She assumed that it was just one person; but it could be more.

As she lay there, Harriet wondered if she could kill again. There had to be another way to stave off the threat. She decided she was a good enough shot to wing the man. This time she'd let the Sheriff do his job.

Satisfied with her plan, Harriet drew herself into a kneeling position and snapped her gun closed. She fired the gun into the air knowing that the people at the house would call the Sheriff.

The bark of the rifle spurred Clay into running the last ten yards.

Harriet rose into a standing position as she watched him thrust the bundle of twigs into the trash can next to her RV. She smelled the gasoline and knew immediately what the man intended to do.

The gasoline can had been filled to the brim and not capped. Clay had moved so fast the last few yards that the gas slushed out of the can and splashed on his jeans and shirt sleeves. He didn't care. So he smelled of gas. It would go away. If it didn't, he'd toss the clothes.

Harriet was looking down at the man when he lifted the gasoline can. Her shot went straight through the can. Gas spurted through the holes onto the brush.

Clay dropped the can and backed away. The hand in his pocket grasped his lighter.

"Put your hands in the air!" Harriet yelled.

Clay looked up and saw an old woman in a flimsy white gown standing on top of the RV. The glint of the rifle barrel told him she had him in her sights.

He thrust his hands in the air. "Don't shoot!"

The right hand was slowly raised over his head, the lighter buried in his closed fist. He shrugged his left shoulder and the rifle sling slipped down his arm. He caught the rifle in his left hand and fell to the ground and rolled over.

This time Harriet hesitated before shooting. She absolutely didn't want to kill another man. On top of that she felt as if someone was physically staying her hand. It was just a feeling but it was a strange one. She prided herself on her decisiveness and here she was hesitating.

Perplexed, she kept the man in her sights trying to focus on his shoulder or arm. Suddenly the man's right hand came up. Harriet sighted down the barrel, caught the hand at the peak of its arc and fired.

The round hit the hand a millisecond after Clay had flipped the lighter switch and caused a flame to burst forth. The penetration of the bullet and the resulting shock of pain was eclipsed by the sudden burst of flame that encased the hand and sped down the sleeve across the shoulders and down both legs.

Clay's scream of agony could be heard a quarter of a mile away. He scrambled to his feet as Harriet yelled at him to roll over. He began to run toward the pond, the surface of which glimmered in the faint moonlight, his body engulfed in flame. His running made the fire soar into the air in his wake yet never left his body. He ran at full speed toward the pond and relief.

Harriet's shouts to drop down and roll fell on deaf ears. He was too close to stop. The pond would stop the searing heat that was eating away his clothes, curling and blackening his skin. The pond would stop the pain, the excruciating pain. He reached the edge of it and fell forward. He sank an inch into the muddy water and the fire danced unabated on his back. He lifted his head and howled that he could not bear it.

"Let me die!" he screeched.

"Roll!" Harriet screamed.

This time he listened and rolled. The fire was out by the time the Sheriff arrived.

The fire department arrived soon afterward by which time Harriet had already backed up the RV. The mattress had fallen off the top and wound up bringing the conflagration to the picnic table; but, Harriet's quick reaction had saved her vehicle.

Stoney was safe inside with her, and when she stopped, she hugged him.

The rest of the night she spent wrapped in a blanket to counter the shaking the shock had brought on. She couldn't stop.

And she didn't understand why this affected her more than the last time. She hadn't shot a man dead this time. But what happened to him was worse. Maybe that was it. Fire was her biggest nightmare.

Her mind refused to reason. Her thinking was muddled. She welcomed the feel of strong arms around her shoulder along with the soft head of her big brown dog in her lap. Eventually, without realizing it her eyes closed and her head dropped. She was laid gently on the couch in her RV and Stoney slept on the floor beside her.

Chapter 13

The sheriff hung around until the Fire Chief confirmed Mrs. Locke's story.

"It was arson alright," he said. "And he meant to do it. It wasn't just a prank because he brought the stuff with him to make sure the RV would go up."

"Attempted murder?' Sheriff Sparks asked.

"Sleeping on the roof," the Fire Chief mused aloud. "Not your ordinary lady, is she?"

"Ron Maxwell says she's quite the shot," Sheriff Sparks said.

"Well, the bastard deserved what he got," the Fire Chief retorted. "If he survives, Sheriff, you got him for arson as well. Any judge in these parts will throw the book at him."

Ron Maxwell, a hefty man, deeply tanned, who owned the training grounds, emerged from Harriet's RV and joined the two men.

"Can she leave in the morning?" he asked.

"What's her hurry?" Sheriff Sparks questioned.

"She's scared," Maxwell responded. "The problem is she's going to be in no condition to drive; but she's a stubborn lady, so she'll go whether she should or not."

"She got family?" Sparks inquired.

"Yeah. She even gave me the number to call if anything happened to her."

He shoved his hand in his pocket and handed the card to the sheriff with a sheepish grin,

"Never got around to taping it anywhere, he admitted.

"You been wearing those same jeans for a week?" the Fire Chief asked. "Those are the ones that should've gone up in smoke."

"I washed them."

"With the care in the pocket?"

"Forgot it was there."

Sheriff Sparks shone his sight on the card. "I can still read the number. Looks like a cell."

Aleta's phone was answered by Stanley Praetzel who, when the sheriff identified himself, got straight to the point, "What's happened to Harriet.

"I need to talk with Aleta Locke."

"I'm Harriet Locke's attorney," Stanley said. "Answer my question."

"She's asleep so I can't ask her if you are or you're not."

"So's her granddaughter," Stanley replied, throwing up the same brick wall.

"Someone tried to kill her," The sheriff announced boldly, hoping to shock the men into compliance. "I need information."

"Aleta was shot in the head last night," Stanley responded coolly. "I'm not disturbing her."

"Mrs. Locke is in no condition to travel and we need to get hold of a member of her family and have them…"

"Is Ron Maxwell there?"

The sheriff mumbled a yeah and handed the phone to Ron. "Says he's Mrs. Locke's lawyer. He could be. He's a tough son of a bitch."

The conversation was almost completely one-sided as Ron related in detail what had taken place that night. He wound up with his worry that Harriet was determined to travel to Illinois, and he felt she was too shaken up to travel.

"Could she handle a plane ride?" Stanley asked.

"She wouldn't leave her dogs."

"Not even with you?" The surprise in his query was a compliment.

"Stoney saved her life tonight by alerting her to danger," Ron replied. "She owes him."

It was then a deal was struck. Stanley hired Ron to drive Harriet to Illinois at a thousand dollars a day.

"Is she that rich?" Ron asked.

"I am," Stanley replied.

Aleta woke at the tail end of the conversation. "What are you?" she asked half awake.

"Ready for a day at the dog show," he replied.

"How does my head look?"

"Like a reverse Mohawk," Stanley replied, handing her a mirror.

Aleta stared at the part made by the bullet. "It's horrible! Is it permanent? Tell me it's not permanent. I'm going to be like those old men who comb their hair across their head to cover their bald spot. I'm too young to do that. I guess I could shave it all off and go bald," she rattled on at top speed. "Or live with a hat on my head. Ugh! I hate hats. A wig's like a hat. Why couldn't he hit a little lower. Then I'd have just a little round hole..."

"And be dead," Stanley interjected. "Are you always so irrational when you're upset?"

"I'm not irrational. I'm just exploring options."

"Like a hole in your brain?"

"It's an option."

"I think the part is distinctive," Stanley said.

"You like it?"

"You said my nose had character," Stanley said. "That didn't mean you liked it, just that it was what it was. You have a battle scar. Don't be ashamed of it."

Aleta's smile was small. "Well in a large class of dogs that all look alike, I'll stand out."

"You don't get away with that!" Stanley shot back. "You'd have stood out anyway."

"I was just trying to be positive."

"The positive is that you weren't killed."

"Yeah, there's that."

"Milani brought me the morning news. We made the front page."

"Us?"

"My office did actually. But we were mentioned. That is my ear and your head were mentioned."

"That's right. Your ear. How is your ear?"

"A mess. The bullet did a number on it."

Aleta chuckled. "Be positive. You're still alive."

"But I'm lopsided."

"And I'm bald."

"You ready to go the Fairgrounds. I had Ed bring your clothes. They're in Beatrice's trailer."

"I think we should see how Evelyn is before we go," Aleta said. "People will ask."

"It's no visitors, remember?"

"We aren't visitors. We're her lawyers."

On the far side of Willow Glen in the house across from the golf course, Evelyn's nephew and niece were hard at work spiking the oranges in the fruit basket with mescaline.

"She'll gag after the first bite," Pacheco had warned.

Mayette had tossed her head. "She gulps her pills with her orange juice. She's never gonna taste it."

"She won't have any pills."

"We're gonna stick some in the basket."

"The police will find them and confiscate them," Pacheco said.

"So what?" Mayette retorted.

Bill's smile of understanding emerged gradually. "The pills will be un-tampered vitamins, right? And once the cops remove them, they won't think about checking the fruit."

"She's gotta be delusional for that court hearing on Monday," Louis said. "Two oranges a day'll do it."

"How can you be sure she'll eat the oranges?"

"She's a health nut," Mayette responded. "She gotta have fresh orange juice every day. No bottled stuff for her!"

"Okay!" Bill said after injecting the last orange and sticking it under the cellophane wrap. "Get this over to the hospital and leave it at the desk."

"Me?" Louis protested. "I thought I'd use a delivery service."

"Don't take a chance on it not getting there just the way it was packed."

Louis and Mayette Barnes were pulling out of Beatrice Johnson's drive when Jason Danielson Jr.'s beat-up jalopy drove up. He waved at the two as they drove away. Their presence told him Bill was up. No RV in the drive told him Bill was alone.

"It's Saturday morning," Bill complained as he opened the door. "What's with this group? Can't you guys do anything on your own?"

"The Ciccones are gonna call you," Jason said as soon as he was inside.

"The Ciccone family from Vegas?"

"That's the ones."

"How do you know them?"

"They're holding my markers."

"Peanuts!" Bill scoffed. "Your bookie is just trying to scare you."

"It was them! The guy said his name was Mike Ciccone."

"Big Mike?" Pacheco scoffed. "He doesn't bother with lowlifes that are into him for a couple grand."

"Try a hundred big ones."

"No one would let you run up that kind of tab. You ain't a good risk."

"They want something," Jason Junior said nervously. Bill wondered fleetingly how this man ever won at poker. He was so transparent.

"Spill it," Bill urged.

"They want the Tontine Trust to stay at the Bank of California."

"I didn't know it wasn't," Bill pondered aloud. "Sit down. Want coffee?"

"Yeah, sure," Junior said sitting at the kitchen table and grabbing a sweet roll from the plate. Beatrice always left fresh rolls for Bill when she left for a dog show. Bill accepted her offering as his due.

"Well, Harriet Locke is trying to transfer the Trust out here."

"Why does that matter? Your mother will still get her yearly windfall and you'll be able to pay them off."

"She'll never give me that much."

"Don't tell me they want you to kill her so you can pay them out of your inheritance?" Bill ventured. "I guess it could be that much. They must know. That's why they let you run the tab."

"No," Jason declared. "They want the opposite. They want us not to harm any of them. The bank is sending reps out here to get all them ladies to sign some papers. We're supposed to see that they do and that nothing bad happens to any of them, except Aleta."

"Aleta?"

"She's acting for her grandmother and so she's for the transfer. She's gonna be taken out. We aren't to stop that."

"No problem there."

"How's that?"

"Haven't you been listening to the radio?" Pacheco asked. "They hit her yesterday and we didn't know nothing."

"Yesterday?"

"The shootout downtown."

"That was her?"

"Yeah, only they missed," Pacheco said. "But the guy who missed has to complete the contract. That's how it works."

"Good," Jason Junior declared vehemently. "I ain't into murdering nobody myself."

Bill's mind snapped back to the first thing Junior had said, "Why are they calling me?"

"To tell you to listen to me, I guess."

"You told them I was helping you?"

"They wanted to know why Nathan Tobias was sick."

Bill gasped in horror. "And you told them?"

"I thought they knew."

"But they didn't, did they?"

"Mike scared me. He wanted to know who was messing with the ladies in the Trust. And I told him that I needed the Trust to break up to get the money to pay him back and he pushed and pushed so I told him everything."

"Shit!" Bill exploded. "Shit!"

"They ain't mad at you," Junior hurried to assure the man across the table. "Leastways not yet."

"What's so damned important about this trust anyway?" Bill said.

When the phone rang, Bill's question was answered.

"I had no idea," he stammered, his mind racing as a new plan was beginning to form.

He finished with assurances that he was totally on board.

When he hung up, Junior saw his hand tremble slightly.

"It seems our ladies have a really big secret," Pacheco said picking up his coffee mug with two hands.

He glanced at Jason Junior and saw him staring at his hands.

"You hold out for anything?" Pacheco asked.

"Yeah, I got a deal."

"What'd they give you?"

"Time to get the money."

"But they're charging you interest, right?"

"Yeah. But they're letting me keep going. And I know I can win that back and more." Jason Junior declared, his enthusiasm for the game rising.

"I got a sure one for you," Bill said with a slight sneer.

"What?"

"Great odds! A thousand to one," Bill teased. "But it's a sucker bet."

"Hey, I got ten bucks," Junior said. He dug out a bill and plunked it on the table.

"You wanna bet the ten bucks and you don't know what the bet is."

"Tell me."

"I'm betting you can't resist betting for ten minutes."

"At a thousand to one?"

Pacheco nodded.

"You're on."

"Double or nothing you can't last twenty minutes," Pacheco said.

"You're on!" Junior said.

"You lost!" Pacheco said.

"You suckered me."

"I said I would. Gamblers are dumb. The odds are against them."

"Well, you ain't so smart," Junior retorted, "sitting here and letting that new guy romance your woman right under your nose."

"They just went to a dog show."

"Yeah. Right."

In another part of town, Melissa had risen early and walked to a nearby convenience store where she bought half a dozen energy bars, a pack of razor blades and a bottle of sleeping pills.

During the next hour she slit open the back flap of the wrappers, pressed the tiny pills underneath the chocolate coating of the bar and then squeezed the back flaps back together. The first two attempts were failures. By the third one, you had to look hard to tell that the seal on the back had been tampered with.

It was a crude scheme, not meant to injure, just take the sharp edge off Aleta's alertness and rob her of the competitive edge Melissa assumed she needed in the dog show ring as much as in any other sport.

She stuffed four bars in her purse. She needed to appear as if she'd brought extras to share. Dennis had assured them both that Aleta would be easy to spot.

"That auburn mane of hers is a thing of beauty," he'd bragged. "And she has the face to match.

Dr. Wayne Cook was an early visitor to Aleta's room.

"I'm joining you for lunch," he announced. "My grandmother roped me into carrying her picnic baskets. She told the ladies she was providing lunch."

"Dog showing is pretty hectic," Aleta apologized. "During break the judges eat, but the handlers get the next dog ready."

"Well, at least half the group will be done, right? And half of the others are just spectators, so they'll want to eat, right?"

"Of course," Aleta stammered. "I just didn't want to appear rude. I don't eat on dog show days."

"Nothing?"

"My stomach is tied up in knots. I eat afterward."

"We'll save you some in the fridge," Dr. Cook offered.

"We'd like to visit Nathan and Evelyn," Aleta said. "May we?"

"West has put restrictions on both," Cook said.

"We're Evelyn's lawyers," Stanley said, "and she has a court date Monday."

Cook nodded. "You can visit Evelyn."

"Nathan too," Stanley said.

"Are you his lawyers too?"

"Sorta," Aleta said. "Family lawyers."

"Close enough," Dr. Cook grinned. "Nathan needs visitors. He's pretty lonely."

"Marge didn't poison him," Stanley put in.

"I believe you. Talk West into lifting the ban on her. She's going to worry herself sick if she's kept from Nathan one more day. West will be at the dog show."

Aleta scowled. "What's he doing there?"

"Showing his dogs," Cook said. "He wins a lot I hear."

"He's got crimes to investigate," Aleta charged. "He shouldn't be gallivanting around at dog shows."

"My you are all fired up," Dr. Cook said with quiet understanding.

"I got shot. I expect results!" Aleta stormed.

Dr. Cook decided she needed to know his friends were doing their jobs. "He and Milani figure whoever shot you will try again."

"I'm bait?" Aleta questioned angrily. "Without my permission."

"I'll keep you here if you want," Dr. Cook said. "The ladies will accept that as a good reason not to show up."

"I don't want an excuse," Aleta railed. "I want to be safe."

"Stay here and you'll be safe," Dr. Cook responded, keeping his tone level. "It's your choice."

Aleta's face crumpled in defeat.

"I can't stay here. I've got dogs to show."

"West said you'd make that choice."

Unexpectedly, Aleta exploded. "I'm not predictable. That's one thing I'm not!"

"That's what I told him," Cook grinned. "But he said you were a dog show person first and a redhead second."

"What's that mean?"

"It means he was right and I was wrong. And I have a redheaded wife, too."

Aleta switched to a new topic. "Is Evelyn well enough to go to the show with us?"

"You think that's wise?"

"We'll monitor her eating and drinking," Aleta promised. "We'll get the others to help."

"If she can interact as a rational person, I have a good shot at winning the competency hearing on Monday," Stanley explained.

"You have my permission. You'll need hers."

Lou Zalkan had changed out of his usual business attire to a navy blue polo shirt and slacks. He couldn't bring himself to don jeans.

The Ciccones had a new source that assured them Aleta Locke would be active and obvious. He had but to choose his time.

She would be easy to spot. He remembered having her in his sights coming up the street. Long, slender legs, a body to match, flowing, auburn hair. She was stunning.

He planned to take his time scouting out the place. It was a two day show. There would come one good chance, one safe chance in that time span. He'd chosen his weapon carefully. A gun was too bulky and he was wearing close-fitting clothes to allay suspicion. A knife while easy to hide made a bloody mess and Lou Zalkan abhorred a messy killing. The garrote, on the other hand, was merely a small coil of thin rope. That killed quietly, swiftly and without bloodshed.

What Lou Zalkan didn't know was that the Ciccone Family had insisted on sending in a second hitter. And, Alfonso Mariana didn't work alone. He had a young couple with the unlikely nicknames of Shark and Sugar which they'd obviously given to each other. Shark was anything but shark-like in character, and Mariana assumed that Sugar gave him that nickname to give stature to his weak chin, small dark eyes and pronounced overbite.

Sugar was currently seven months pregnant as a result of which she was generally overlooked as dangerous. But while the two worked as a pair, it was Sugar's ring that carried the lethal venom that took out its victim in two hours after injection.

Mariana was their backup and he was in disguise with a gray wig, steel rimmed glasses and a brace on one leg which was visible because he wore shorts. His knife was inside the cane he carried ostensibly to ease the pressure put on the leg in the brace when he walked.

As Aleta and Stanley exited the elevator with Evelyn in tow, Marge met them, questions pouring nonstop from her mouth. Aleta brushed aside her queries.

"We're going to stop at your house to get your video camera and lots of film."

"Whatever for?"

"Why to tape the dog show. Nathan gave us specific instructions."

"Can't someone else…"

"Nathan wants you to come tonight and supply the commentary."

"You mean I'm going to be allowed to sit with him?"

"All night if you want," Aleta said, "and wouldn't it be great to have a video of the day to share?"

"Yes, yes, it would; but suppose something should happen to Nathan and I'm not here?"

"The Cooks are supplying lunch," Aleta said. "So you'll be eating with his doctor."

Marge smiled. There was a light in her eyes.

The nurse at the desk stopped the group. "Aren't you Mrs. Barnes in Room 407?" she asked.

"It's okay…," Aleta began.

The nurse held up a large basket of fruit, "These were hand-delivered this morning. They're for you."

"Oooh!" Evelyn said. "How nice!"

Marge took the basket.

"I can even make myself fresh orange juice for breakfast," Evelyn said.

"That you can," Aleta responded. "These oranges are juice oranges."

Chapter 14

All dog show sites have a unique character. The Lake County site was no exception. But to Stanley who had never been to a dog show this one would forever be the gold standard against which all others would be judged.

Illinois was part of the Corn Belt known worldwide for the flatness of the land. Geographers visited just to marvel at the broad seemingly unending expanse of fields whose only undulation came from the wind swaying the stalks of ripening wheat. Perhaps it was because the state lacked hills that what few had spilled over from Wisconsin were so prized. - Lake County had snatched, from the state replete with them, a few small ponds and creeks as well. One of these was located in the middle of the fairgrounds and currently served to divide the RV parking from the rings. A wide wooden bridge connected the two. Uniformed policemen were stationed at the bridge and exit of the single lane road snaking through the woods alongside the creek and ending at the bridge. It was via this road that Stanley drove his car.

In the seat beside him Aleta was studying the judging schedule.

"Both Goldens and Scotties show at eight," Aleta said. "Beatrice was going to show your bitch special. Won't that be too close?"

Stanley drove over the bridge into the RV section where lined on two sides of an imaginary road were rows of

RV's and trailers. To the side of the entrance to each RV were rows of metal wire exercise pens in which various dogs were housed. Most RV's had canopies that rolled out to offer shade. Mesh screens were attached to the end of the canopies and extended over the dog pens. They were held in place variously.

Stanley glanced to his left just before turning to cross the bridge and saw that at the top of the grassy slope leading from the tree-shaded creek were the flags with ring numbers on them. He could just make out the ropes of the nearest rings.

To his far left were the vendors situated between the main gate and the ring area. To the right of the flat area of rings loomed the first of the barn-like metal buildings that normally housed exhibits, but today housed three indoor rings and the superintendent's table.

Stanley's quick survey of the layout along with the guards at the bridge told him that Chief West had neatly made the RV area sacrosanct. Inside the perimeter they would be safe.

Stanley drove over the bridge. Ed and Jason waved him to his parking spot.

Evelyn answered Aleta, "There are four German Shorthairs and eight Brittanys in the ring before Goldens go in. That should take thirty minutes. Dogs are before bitches. There are thirteen class dogs. So Carmel won't show until nine."

"Unless there are a lot of absentees."

When Evelyn did a quick rundown of why that wouldn't happen in this case, Stanley was delighted with her obvious mental acuity. He had only to make sure her nephew didn't slip her any more mescaline and she would win in court on Monday.

When they got out of the car, Evelyn told Marge to put the basket on the table. "I know Mrs. Cook sent it to me," Evelyn said, "because she thought I'd be unhappy about missing the show."

"Was there a card?" Marge asked.

"No, but it's just like her not to take credit for a nice gesture."

Aleta didn't hear the exchange, having already entered Beatrice's trailer to change.

The three women chatted for a few minutes before Evelyn reached under the cellophane covering the fruit basket and took out the four oranges.

"I'm going to make fresh orange juice," she said.

When Evelyn entered Beatrice's trailer, she found Beatrice, hairbrush in hand studying Aleta who was seated on a stool.

"What's wrong?"

"Her head hurts," Beatrice said.

"I can show my own dogs."

"You don't understand," Beatrice said. "It's okay so long as I don't brush her hair."

"Well then don't brush it."

"It's a tangled mess," Aleta complained.

"Isn't that the style?" Evelyn asked heading for the bedroom.

"Let's ask Julia," Beatrice said.

While Ed and Stanley helped Jason set up the awnings over the pens, Beatrice and Julia discussed Aleta's injury.

"It looks pretty raw," Julia said sympathetically.

"I'm not sure how it'll handle the sun," Aleta said. "But I can't touch it."

"There's only one solution," Julia said sadly. "Cut it. If we cut it short, it has enough body to handle that short tousled look."

Seeing Aleta's distressed look, she added, "You won't have to wash it or brush it for several days at least."

"Do it!" Aleta decided. "I need to be ready in less than an hour."

"Julia's very good with scissors," Beatrice said. "That's what comes of doing family haircuts."

The haircutting was moved outside so Julia would have room to move around. While the men began moving the dogs from their crates into their pens, Julia began the haircut. Marge dressed in brown slacks with a matching blouse, came out of Julia's trailer with the video camera in her hand exclaiming excitedly how much Nathan was going to enjoy this video.

Aleta managed a weak smile. "It's necessity, not choice."

Stanley whispered something in Beatrice's ear after which she carefully gathered the long locks of auburn hair, holding them in her hand until Stanley emerged from the trailer with a plastic bag.

"What are these for?" Beatrice asked as she dropped the locks in the bag.

"I just want them," Stanley said.

Julia and Beatrice exchanged knowing winks. Aleta was too busy watching her hair being butchered via the hand mirror in her hand to notice what Stanley was doing.

"It's going to work," Beatrice said encouragingly.

Aleta frowned in consternation. "It's such a departure from my style. It's not a good style for a lawyer. It looks frivolous."

"I think it's… it's youthful and carefree and cute," Evelyn said.

"I don't want cute or youthful or carefree," Aleta moaned. "I want professional."

"Too late," Evelyn observed with a wry smile.

"I like it," Beatrice declared. She looked over at Stanley who was observing the procedure with interest. "What do you think, Stanley?"

"It goes with my nose," Stanley responded, a tiny smile trying to emerge.

"What's that mean?"

"It's different. It has character."

No one saw Conan Lloyd come over the bridge until he spoke. "What the hell did you do to your hair? It looks awful!"

Aleta burst into tears. Stanley and Ed jumped up and escorted the taller man back to the bridge.

"What are you doing?" Conan sputtered, pulling back. The anger of the two men gave them the strength to push him down the path despite his protests.

"You see this bridge," Stanley said. "You cross it again and I'll have you arrested."

Conan pulled himself to his full height. "You have no right!"

A police officer stepped out from the shade of a tree. "Is he one of them?"

"Yes," Ed said. "He's one."

"One of whom?" Conan spit out.

"Those on our list of people to keep away from Aleta."

Conan gasped. "You can't do that!"

"Aleta was shot in the head last night," Stanley said. "I was shot in the ear. You're our number one suspect, so, yes, we can."

Conan's shock was honest.

"Shot? She was shot? What's she doing here? Is this for real? Why isn't she in the hospital?"

"She has dogs to show," Stanley said. "You just steer clear of her."

"I didn't hurt her. I wouldn't do that. And I don't view you as a threat. Good God, man, you wouldn't interest her. You're just a small town hick."

"Well, Mr. Lloyd, this small town hick knows better than to say such a hurtful thing to a woman."

"It's the truth. Aleta values the truth."

"It's your version, and you hurt her. A gentleman doesn't do that."

Stanley and Ed turned and walked away. Ed put his hand on Stanley's shoulder and said, "Have you ever met this Pacheco guy I'm up against?"

"Another Greek God?"

"Yep!"

When they turned, they saw two men talking with Aleta, and they hurried over, worried.

"It's different, I'll grant you that," the shorter man said and both men recognized the voice of Chief West who was nattily attired in tan slacks with a brown coat and red and brown patterned tie.

"It's got flair," the taller man declared.

As Stanley approached, West turned and said, "Here's the man whose opinion you should be asking."

"He says it's like his nose," Aleta remarked.

Both men laughed.

"You better be laughing at my remark and not my nose," Stanley quipped.

"Your reasoning escapes me," West said. A chief, who had passed the bar, West prided himself on his ability to follow a lawyer's thinking. It was his ability to anticipate a defense lawyer's tactics that set him head and shoulders above most small town chiefs.

"It doesn't escape me," Stanley rejoined and smiled. "But Aleta knows what I mean."

West turned and raised a brow in query.

Aleta swallowed her discomfiture to prove that she could see Stanley's logic. Why this was important she couldn't have explained however.

"He means that while not a thing of beauty according to today's standards, it does the job intended and therefore is acceptable."

"Go on," West urged, fascinated.

"Stanley likes long hair, but he understands that my long hair was hurting me. My short hair doesn't please him, but he can accept it because it's part of the me that was changed by the bullet."

"Wow!" West breathed. "A pair of lawyer-philosophers. Remind me never to let you get on the defense side of a case I'm dead set on winning."

"We aren't in practice together," Aleta announced a bit stiffly. "I'm a corporate lawyer. Stanley is a child's advocate."

"Yesterday you had long hair," West countered. "Today you have short."

His reasoning was clear. An awkward silence followed until Evelyn broke it.

"How about a piece of fruit? I'm going to make some fresh orange juice in a little bit."

"No need, Evelyn," Beatrice said. "I made some yesterday."

Ed said, "I'll get it."

Beatrice followed him inside. Ed spotted the four oranges lined up on the counter. "Where'd those come from?"

"Evelyn took them out of her fruit basket. She's a nut for fresh orange juice," Beatrice said. "They're Valencia's. The skins are too thin for peeling. I guess somehow Martha Cook found out that Evelyn liked her oranges as juice."

"Hmm," Ed murmured.

Ed poured the first glass for Evelyn who drank half of it down in one gulp and then went back to putting the finishing touches on Topaz who was standing on the grooming table. She turned to Tom Wilson who was eating a fresh pear and asked him his opinion.

Stanley was worried because while he found her questions to be specific and relevant, she was wearing a slip over her dress.

"Like your apron," Tom chuckled as he left.

"Don't you even be thinking what you're thinking," Evelyn quipped. "Slips make good aprons. Hair falls right off them."

"They're a little sexy, don't you think?" Tom shot back.

"At my age, I'll use anything that helps!"

"See you in the ring, Evelyn," Tom said smiling. "Good luck!"

Stanley found himself holding the video camera as the group came alive with last minute perpetrations for going to the Dachshund ring. Ordinarily, there wouldn't be such a flutter, but Marge was without her car which held all her equipment and so she had to borrow. And Beatrice was worried about leaving Evelyn, and Nathan, who usually let the dogs ride on his lap in the wheelchair, wasn't there to transport them.

Ed stayed behind to help Evelyn and watch the campsite. Julia and Jason each carried a dog. Leashes were borrowed and the group set off for the ring. Marge videotaped the procession.

When Anya was set on the grass on the other side of the bridge, she scratched her neck, shook her head and rolled in an effort to remove her collar. Being unsuccessful at that, she next attempted to pull the leash from Aleta's hand.

Aleta gave the pup a few tiny pops with the lead and Anya, eventually, decided that her rebellion was hurting only her. She settled down. This person on the end of the leash was more determined than she.

Anya was the only one in her puppy class, but the judge went over her carefully knowing he would see this young one in winners. Aleta could tell he liked what he saw.

Marge captured every moment on tape. Anya went back into the winner's class and won the points to the delight of the group who clapped loudly. Her first two points!

Anya, however, wasn't done winning. She took Best of Variety and because the Winners Dog took Best Opposite Sex and earned three points, Anya's points were increased and she thus earned her first major.

Outside the ring, the group went wild and Stanley caught it all on tape. The photographer was called and time was forgotten by all but Stanley who kept an eye on his watch.

"I've never been so glad in my life that the judge didn't like red dogs," Marge said on the way back to the camp.

A dark-haired voluptuous woman dressed in a suit approached the group. "I'm looking for Aleta Locke," she said.

Melissa had been told to check the Dachshund ring first. Dennis was going to check out the Goldens. Marge happily pointed to the two women walking fast toward the bridge.

"Up ahead," she said, "the one with the wild boar bitch."

Melissa had no idea what she meant. Both were walking Dachshunds, but when she looked at the back of the two she decided she didn't need to ask. One of the women had long reddish brown hair; the other didn't. She hurried to catch up; but they crossed the bridge and disappeared into the row of RV's.

Marge caught up to Melissa. "You can catch her at the Golden ring," she said.

Melissa nodded and walked back toward the rings. At least she knew who to look for. She hesitated near the bridge and the saw both women returning with one Golden Retriever.

Behind them at a slower pace were several others, one of whom was a man with a video camera. He was walking backwards taping the slower women, each of whom had Goldens on the end of their leads.

Melissa fell in with the two women in front just as the one with the long hair said, "I haven't had a thing all morning. I'm starved."

"Hi," Melissa said. "I have a couple power bars with me. You want one?"

"No thank you," Aleta replied. "I never eat when I'm showing."

"I like to eat," Julia said, "especially breakfast and it's a long time until lunch on an empty stomach."

Julia looked over the power bars in Melissa's open hand and took one. "This is my favorite. Thank you."

She took a large bite and noticed a small bitter piece. Her next bite was smaller. It tasted just fine. Her third bite was okay too, so she finished the bar. On the last bite she tasted the same bitter taste as before. She held it in her mouth a moment. To spit it out would not only be rude but revolting to everyone nearby. Reluctantly, she swallowed it.

Tom Wilson took Winners Dog, handed the dog off to his assistant to water and cool down, and hurried to the French Bulldog ring inside the building.

By the time he got back to the Golden ring, Aleta was in the ring with Carmel. He watched her form. She was not only lovely to look at; she was as graceful as her dog. The young bitch wasn't yet fully mature but Aleta brought out her smooth clean movement and her puppy-like joy at being in the ring. The dog seemed captivated by Aleta and Tom couldn't put his finger on why. He hoped Evelyn would show her veteran as usual. He wanted the breed with his Winner's Dog. He hoped to persuade his owners to let him handle him as a special once he finished. He needed this win. His reputation was on the line every time he stepped into the ring, especially under a judge that didn't owe him a favor and perhaps owed someone else one. His clients had to feel that he made no mistakes handling their dog. They expected wins for their money.

Judges understood that shows depended on handlers to bring a string of dogs on circuits all year long. Being a judge that catered to handlers had its drawbacks. The breeders kept score and didn't enter as often under those judges or, if they did enter, they hired a handler and the handler judge wound up with a ring full of handlers which meant a ring full of powerful people. Consequently, the dog show ring was not as political in the classes as it was in the Breed. Everyone wanted new dogs showing up in the ring. They were the lifeblood of the sport.

Still, Tom worried. There were times he wanted the win more than others.

That Aleta won the points didn't surprise him. She'd shown the young bitch beautifully.

Tom Wilson congratulated Aleta as she emerged from the ring. His assistant handed him the lead of his winner's dog and he changed armbands.

Aleta handed Evelyn Carmel's leash and turned around and sailed back into the ring with Topaz who was entered in Veterans and Tom Wilson moaned inwardly. He took his charge back into the crowd and got him to focus. Goldens were people pleasers and his dog was no exception.

The specials began lining up and Tom saw armbands hurriedly switched and he knew Evelyn had recognized Aleta's talent even as he had and she'd put aside her affinity for showing Topaz herself. He saw a Scotty breeder on Evelyn's bitch special and he wondered at the choice. The woman was in bright yellow which worked well with the little black Scotties but was a poor choice for a Golden. Evelyn was on Carmel.

Tom began to perspire and he realized that the sun was rapidly making the day a hot one, maybe even a record breaker. In such heat older dogs, like Topaz, wilted.

Aleta exited the ring, and the champions and winners filed in. Aleta took her place at the end of the line after a quick drink of bottled water and a light spray of water on Topaz's face and tongue. While Topaz had been alert and active in Veterans, to win the Breed he had to act young. Aleta sensed she'd need a miracle. Then one happened. One of the bitch specials was in season. Topaz, a stud of some experience, forgot the heat and came up on his feet. This bitch had to be won over.

The muscles in his shoulders hardened as he leaned toward the wonderful smell. His ears rose, and his attention was riveted forward. When the judge stood back to survey the group, the male specials in front of the in-season bitch seemed to lack the striking pose of the Veteran Dog at the end of the line. He'd always liked Evelyn's dogs, and this old one of hers was a prize animal in his estimation.

Carefully he went over each champion and moved them. It was a superior group. Any one of them would be a good choice. When he finished, he moved Topaz and the Winners Dog to the front and compared them. With the bitch at the back of the line, the winner's dog faded slightly. Tom teased him back. The heat was bearing down on dogs and handlers.

The bare spot on Aleta's head was burning and it itched. She shook her head hoping the movement of hair would relieve the uncomfortable sensation. Topaz saw the movement out of the corner of his eye, and he came alive just as the judge's eye hit him one last time. He was resplendent with his coat glimmering in the bright sunlight.

"Breed," the judge said pointing to Topaz. "Best of Winners," he said pointing to Tom's dog. Tess, with Beatrice handling her, took the other prize, Best Opposite Sex.

Out of consideration for the older dog, Topaz's photo was taken first, followed by one of Tom Wilson and his dog. As they passed in the ring, Tom asked her to wait for him.

Together they walked back to the RV campsite and Tom asked her for a favor.

"I have this Bulldog bitch in American Bred and I have a conflict. I have two Afghan Hounds to show for a client of long standing. I explained this but the owner doesn't want one of my assistants. He watched you in the ring with Carmel and he's decided you're the one he wants to handle Maggie. She's the only one in her class," Tom went on. "Don't tell me why he got this notion in his head that the judge would like the dog better if he saw her twice; but, hey it's his dog. He may have to learn some things the hard way."

"Bet he's seen a Bred-By win after being alone in its class," Aleta ventured, "and jumped to the wrong conclusion."

"Anyway, can you do it for me?"

The tone was respectful and his manner warmed Aleta. No residual animosity over her beating him. No condescension. She liked this man.

"When do Bulldogs go in?" she asked.

"Ten. Same time as the Labs."

"The Danielson's are handling their own dogs," Aleta said. "Sure. I'll do it if you'll teach me how to get a Bulldog onto the ramp."

"After you put Topaz away, come over."

Back at the Golden ring, Melissa had joined Dennis Rimmel at ringside.

"Did you see that woman leave earlier?" she asked. It was a rhetorical question meant to introduce her brag. "Well, that was Aleta Locke and she left because I slipped her some sleeping pills in a power bar."

"You did what?" Rimmel gasped.

"To slow her down so she wouldn't win, you know, and be the hero of the day."

Alfonso Mariana, who was standing at ringside watching the photography session, heard the name Aleta and moved closer. When he heard what she'd done, he cursed silently. He was about to open his cell phone, when Rimmel asked her how she knew the woman was Aleta. Alfonso slipped his phone back into his pocket.

"I asked and was told she was the one with the wild boar, as if either of them had a pig on the leash."

"So you could have been wrong."

Melissa's voice rose. "I wasn't wrong."

Dennis hushed her up and pressed for more information.

"She had reddish hair," Melissa said in a defiant tone.

Meanwhile the photographer finished up and Beatrice turned to Evelyn and asked, "Who's going to show Julia's dog? She shouldn't go back out in the sun after heat stroke."

"I can't," Evelyn said. "I've done all I can do today. I'm still weak. I think hospitals do more harm than good sometimes."

"It's hot in this sun," Beatrice said. "And I think I've run about as much as I can today. Thank goodness I can walk with the Scotties."

"And be in the shade," Evelyn added. "Guess Aleta will have to take Mint in. Jason probably won't leave Julia."

Outside the ring, both Mariana and Rimmel were flipping through their catalogs looking for the Lab listing. By now both had figured out the catalogs were the key to finding people.

When Rimmel found a dog in the catalog called Peppermint, he figured that was the Mint the ladies were referring to. Owners were Julia and Jason Danielson.

"You slipped your damn med concoction to the wrong person. You gave it to Julia Danielson!" Rimmel fumed. "Talk about stupid mistakes. This is the worst!"

"I'm sorry," Melissa said contritely, "but it was only a sleeping pill. She'll probably just think it was the heat like the ladies said."

"I don't care. You stay clear of me. Understand?"

"I was only trying to help."

"Well, don't help!" Rimmel snarled. "You're too dumb to be any real help."

His words stung Melissa into silence. Her anger built into a determination to prove him wrong. It was not a dumb move. She just mixed up on the target.

Alfonso drifted away, but not until he decided that Melissa was a screw-up that would have to be dealt with. She wouldn't stop now. She was angry. Angry people do crazy things.

On the other hand, because angry people do crazy things, he might be able to use her.

Accordingly, Mariana approached her after Rimmel stormed off.

"He had no right to say that," he said.

Melissa turned, startled and ashamed that anyone had heard the words. She faced an average looking man with a brace on one leg. He limped toward her leaning on his cane to support the leg with the brace. She liked his steel rim glasses. It made him look scholarly.

"Look," Alfonso Mariana went on smoothly, "I didn't hear anything but the last sentence, but he was way out of line."

Melissa felt herself relaxing. It might shake Dennis up to see her with someone else.

"He was downright mean," she said. "And he had no reason to be. Everyone goofs up now and then."

"You are so right," Mariana soothed. "Let me treat you to a glass of ice tea. We can sit over there on that bench in the shade and talk."

"Sure. Sure." Melissa agreed falling in step with the stranger. She hoped Dennis was watching.

When Beatrice and Evelyn returned to their campsite, Aleta was nowhere around. Julian told them he'd called Dr. Cook about Julia and had been told to keep Julia quiet and out of the sun.

"Julia's going to want to show Mint," Evelyn said. "You need to tell her she can't."

"Julia's asleep," Jason responded. "It's weird. She never sleeps during a show."

"Is Dr. Cook coming?"

"He'll be here with his grandmother at eleven thirty, but he said to call him if she got any new symptoms," Jason reported. "I'll just have to scratch the dogs.

"Don't do that," Evelyn said. "Beatrice and I can watch her for you. Remember Marge is supposed to film your dogs in the ring for Nathan."

Chief Lyle West saw the three gathered with worried frowns when he came out to take Morgan for a walk. He walked over and asked about Julia.

"Sound asleep," Julian said. "It's like she was drugged. And you know what she said to me on the way down here?"

West's interest was obvious, so Jason went on. "It was kinda a dumb remark and well it has nothing to do with what happened. I mean, how could eating an energy bar cause sunstroke?"

West's interest increased.

"Where'd she get the energy bar?" he asked and his manner was no longer casual.

"I don't know. Some woman."

"Any of you see her?"

All the heads shook.

"Aleta was with Julia," Evelyn offered. "Maybe she saw the woman."

Ed Ornstein and Stanley joined the group.

"Where's Aleta?" West asked the man.

Stanley answered. "At Tom Wilson's rig. She's so excited. He asked her to show a Bulldog."

"Then she can't help show the Labs," Evelyn said. "Jason, I guess you'll have to take Mint in."

"Mint's on the shy side. She doesn't show well for me. She needs a woman handler."

"Not me," Beatrice said. "I'd fade halfway through the class."

"Sorry, I'm not up to it," Evelyn said. "I'm really sorry."

"Lauren will do it," Lyle West said, referring to his redheaded wife. "She loves to show."

"Haven't seen her all morning," Beatrice commented.

Lyle smiled sheepishly. "Morning sickness. She's feeling pretty good now. That's why we brought two specials. She likes to compete against me."

"And she wins sometimes too, doesn't she?"

"She could take the points with Mint," Lyle said. "She loves that little girl."

The group perked up.

"I'm up for a glass of orange juice," Evelyn said.

"We're out," Ed said.

"There are four oranges on the counter," Evelyn said. "Just cut them and squeeze them. They're juice oranges.

Marge handed the camera to Stanley. "Go photograph Aleta learning how to show a Bulldog."

Before he left, West issued a new order, "Until further notice, no one eats or drinks anything that wasn't brought by one of you."

Ed paused in the doorway of the RV.

"Mrs. Cook's bringing lunch," Beatrice said.

West grinned. "And I'm invited. Of course, Mrs. Cook's offering will be above reproach."

Ed entered the RV. The fruit basket had been sent by Mrs. Cook. He went to the counter and cut open the first orange. Emma got up from the couch and joined him.

"Boy, you got some nose," Ed said. "Okay, you get a slice."

Stanley arrived at Tom Wilson's trailer as Aleta was shaking the hand of a tubby little man with a bald pate. His dark eyes were merry as Stanley shot him as he approached.

When the man saw the camera he looked perturbed. Stanley quickly explained that he was shooting a private video for a man in the hospital whose dogs Aleta showed earlier.

The little man relaxed, smiled and extended his hand, "George Sciretta."

"Stanley Praetzel," came the reply. "I'm really here to film Aleta learning how to handle a Bulldog."

"You don't know how?" the little man asked Aleta. His face reflected his worry.

"Well, I wouldn't let that worry you," Tom said smoothly. "She hadn't handled a Dachshund before today and she took the points and the breed, and with a puppy."

"But that doesn't mean I can win every time," Aleta said quickly.

"But, you're having a good day," the little man said.

"I seem to be," Aleta agreed. "Let's hope it keeps up. But Tom said there's a lot of competition."

"But I cut that down by entering her in American Bred," George Sciretta declared.

Aleta looked at Tom. It was his client.

"Well, we'll see if that works for us or against us," Tom replied. "It may well turn out to have been a very wise move."

Aleta liked his answer. She could learn a lot from this man.

In the woods on the other side of the creek, Lou Zalkan watched Aleta practicing with the Bulldog. The practice session was a short one but at least he knew where she was headed. He fingered the thin rope in his pocket.

Outside the RV, Evelyn was getting impatient. She was thirsty.

"You know men in the kitchen," Marge observed. "They act as if they've been dropped on an alien planet."

"Have a peach," Beatrice said. "I had one earlier. They're perfectly ripe and juicy."

"I'm so wed to orange juice," Evelyn commented. "I forget about options."

Beatrice handed her a peach and Evelyn took a bite. She leaned over as the juice spilled down the front of her dress.

Beatrice rushed into the RV for a washcloth. She took it and held it under the cold water. Only then did she notice that there was an orange slice on the floor.

"Emma won't touch it," Ed said. "She loves oranges."

"So maybe she doesn't like Valencia's."

"There isn't a fruit Emma doesn't like."

"Try another orange. Maybe that one was going rotten."

"Bring me the fruit basket," Ed said.

"There's not much left."

"I need to test my theory," Ed said.

"What theory?"

"That someone monkeyed with just the oranges because they knew how Evelyn was about orange juice."

"Mrs. Cook?"

"Someone could have written her name on the card."

"There was no card."

"Then how…?"

"Evelyn said only a few people knew she was in the hospital."

"What about her nephew?"

"No way. He never even remembers her birthday," Beatrice commented.

"But he knows she likes orange juice in the morning."

"So do all of us."

Ed looked at her with a question in his eyes.

"I'll get the basket," Beatrice said. "I'll tell them I'm going to add some more fruit."

Ed took a peach and cut a slice and put it on the floor. Emma slurped it right up and looked at Ed and wagged her tail. He tried an apple slice next. Same reaction. Then a pear was put down. Emma snatched it out of Ed's hand.

He cut a slice out of a second orange and Emma backed away when he put it on the floor.

Just to test if perhaps she was too full of fruit, Ed dropped a couple grapes on the floor. Emma gobbled up two of them. The third had rolled next to the orange slice. She pawed it so it rolled away and then ate it.

Ed put the four oranges and the two slices in a plastic bag and marked it. He put the plastic bag in a paper bag and took it to the cop standing at the corner of the RV and told him what he suspected and why.

"Can't it wait?" the cop asked. "The chief and his wife are getting ready to show their dogs. He only wants to be interrupted for an emergency."

"Call Captain Milani then," Ed said. "He's not busy."

"I can't go over my chief's head."

"Then you take it to the forensic lab."

"I can't. Chief West said I wasn't to leave this area even if the world came to an end."

Ed shook his head. "This isn't gonna get done, huh?"

"It will when the chief comes back," the cop said. "You said you had all the oranges gathered up, so there's no danger right now, is there?"

"Can you watch the bag?"

"Sorry."

Ed turned to find Beatrice telling the three women and Jason what Ed suspected. Aleta and Stanley joined the group in time to hear most of it.

"That's pretty vague bit of fact to go on," Stanley put in.

"A dog's nose is forty times sharper than a human's," Aleta said.

"My Scotties won't let me put their pills in food," Beatrice said. "They turn their noses up it when I try."

"My Lab'll swallow anything," Jason said.

"Not our Doxies," Marge put in. "But it seems to me when a Lab says no to a treat; it's got to be bad."

"Jason, I'm sorry I didn't know about Julia when I took on the Bulldog. Can you show Mint? I can come back for the Breed and show Drummer."

"Lauren West is going to show her," Jason said. "I'm taking Possom into Breed, so if you'll take Drummer I'd appreciate it. If Mint wins, Beatrice will take her into Breed. Lauren's got her own Special.

Aleta looked at Beatrice, "I thought you were worn out."

"There are six specials," Beatrice said. "And Lauren will be showing her girl who's Mint's mother. Mint's not mature enough to take it from her mother. And no one can beat Lauren when she shows except for her husband. Reality is reality. I just need to run around with her once, maybe twice."

"Well, I'll be there in time to take in Drummer," Aleta promised.

But that didn't happen.

Lyle West arrived with his dog and his wife's in time to see his wife go into the winner's class with Mint and take the points.

Marge recorded every moment.

When Lauren came out of the ring, everyone's eyes looked across the several rings to the corner ring where the Bulldogs were being shown.

"Is Aleta here?" Lauren asked, giving Beatrice Mint's lead. "Who's going to show Drummer?"

"I am," said a smooth voice. The group turned to face Tom Wilson. "I arranged this, you know. I've been dying to take on West here."

"You two both have to beat me!" Lauren said gaily.

As they filed into the ring, Lyle whispered, "What's happening in the Bulldog ring?"

"She's winning," Tom grinned. "Now aren't you glad you're up against me and not her?"

Tom had assigned one of his assistants to stand outside the ring and help. Aleta won her class; she sat outside the ring with Maggie who put her big head in Aleta's lap. A cool coat wrapped around Maggie kept her from overheating. By the time the young Bulldog returned to the ring for the winner's class, Maggie was rested and cool.

Tom had sent word via the assistant that he'd take in Drummer and Aleta relaxed. It was nice to sit under the shade of the large oak just outside the ring with Stanley beside her. They watched the open class without speaking. Stanley understood without her telling him that it would be rude to critique the dogs in the ring aloud.

She whispered a suggestion.

"Just pick your favorites and figure out why you like them. Later, we'll talk."

"You'll remember?"

"When you look at them, think about their original purpose which was to grab a bull by its nose. Their jaws had to be strong enough to hang on but their bite was meant to be viselike rather than to tear away the flesh like a tiger. The bull would toss his head to rid himself of the dog so they had to have thick short necks and a strong front assemblage to survive being shaken so violently."

"I like these guys," Stanley said.

A voice from behind them said, "There you are I've been looking all over for you."

Dismayed, Aleta turned. She bent her forefinger and motioned him to come closer. He saw the dog with its head in her lap and remarked, "What an ugly dog!"

"She's really quite beautiful," Aleta whispered. "And she's got a great temperament which is more than I can say for you. Now go away."

"Promise you'll have lunch with me so we can talk. I owe you all sorts of apologies."

"I don't eat until I'm done showing."

"Dinner then."

"No," Aleta hissed. "Now, go."

Conan didn't budge. Stanley stood up and signaled a man standing toward the back. The man moved forward and showed his badge.

"I have to ask you to come with me," the officer said politely.

"Whatever for?"

"Disturbing the peace if you don't come quietly."

Stanley gripped Conan's arm. "Let's move back and I'll explain why I can have you arrested."

Shocked, Conan allowed Stanley and the police officer to guide him away.

"I want to see Aleta," he protested as soon as they were on the other side of a small maintenance building. "I know she was attacked last night but I had nothing to do with that."

"Besides Aleta's grandmother in California," Stanley said, "you were the only one who knew we were spending the afternoon in my office."

"You're implying something that is unthinkable," Conan spot back. "If you think I'm going to back off so you can have a free ride, you don't know me."

Stanley's response was calm. "If you love Aleta, you will not hang around her. She's the target of some very bad men. They know you. Your presence will signal where she is.

"And yours won't?"

"I know a lot of people. I'm in and out of groups. You only know one."

"That's not true!" Conan argued, driven to drive this toad's arguments back down his throat. I had dinner last night with two bank officers form the Bay Area. And they're here at the show."

"Two Atherton Bank officers?"

Conan nodded, "So you see your argument is…"

Stanley interrupted as if pursuing the veracity of Conan's declaration. "How on earth did you ever connect with them?"

"My boss told me to meet their plane," Conan said. "He also wants me to persuade Aleta to come back to the firm."

"Even if she doesn't want to?"

"She doesn't know what she wants."

"And you do?"

"I know what's good for her."

"And you want to do what's good for her, right?"

"Of course."

"Then leave now and I'll ask her to speak with you after the show is over."

"Why not now? She's sitting there doing nothing but petting that dumb dog."

"She's getting herself and the dog ready to go back into the ring."

"What for? She's already got one blue ribbon. It's a pretty silly prize if you ask me."

Stanley decided this man was not going to be appealed to on any rational basis, so he gave up that line and switched to the bizarre.

"It's not silly. The more blue ribbons she gathers, the closer she'll be to turning professional."

"She's a lawyer."

"How much fun is that?" Stanley quipped. "It's more fun to go to dog shows. What a way to make a living."

"Are you crazy? You can't make a living going to dog shows."

"A good handler makes more than most lawyers," Stanley said with a straight face. He could see the man squirm under the possibility.

"I'm surprised she didn't insist you two get a dog when you were living together in San Francisco."

"We never… she wouldn't… but once I propose things will be different."

"Well, you'll get your chance, but not now," Stanley said firmly. He sighed. He hated to use a cannon but buckshot wasn't going to deter this jerk.

"Officer, escort this man to the Willow Glen Police Station. Tell Chief Milani he knows something about his attempted homicide investigation."

"This is bogus and you know it!" Conan declared.

"If he speaks to anyone, arrest him. He's being used to finger Aleta," Stanley said.

"You won't get away with this," Conan declared.

"If you go quietly, the officer won't cuff you," Stanley said. "One word and the cuffs go on. Make no mistake, I was shot too and I'm serious about this."

Stanley watched him walk meekly away with the police officer. Lawyers didn't resist arrest. They saved their arguments for court.

Stanley joined Aleta shortly afterward.

"Is he gone?"

"For the day," Stanley replied.

"How'd you manage that?"

"I had to pull out the big guns."

"What did you do?"

"Let's just say he's on his way to police headquarters to be questioned."

"Didn't Milani do that already?"

"New information. New questions need to be asked," Stanley said. "I called and gave Milani a heads up."

"Why not have West do it?"

"He's busy protecting us and…"

Aleta smiled. "And showing dogs. You really do understand this world."

"I'm beginning to."

"Did you say you wanted to get a dog?"

"I like this one."

"So do I," Aleta said. "A Bulldog would make a great pet."

"Can't we show it?"

"A show puppy will cost more."

"But none of your friends here are Bulldog breeders so you'll fit right into the group."

"That's weird reasoning."

"Yep." Stanley smiled. "It is, but you understand it, don't you?"

Aleta stood up. "Time for me to get ready."

Stanley saw the light in her eyes. Her mood was again gay and free. Maggie bounced a little on the end of the leash as if expecting a play time.

Chapter 15

Alfonso Mariana watched the man being led off the show grounds. He wasn't in cuffs but the cop had hold of his arm. He was being escorted.

So there were police here, he concluded.

He stayed where he was and watched the auburn-haired woman showing the black Lab. She was slender and lithe and ran around the ring with the grace of a leaping ballerina. The dog kept pace without breaking stride. That she won didn't surprise him.

He watched the flurry outside the ring when she emerged and developed an unexpected gnawing sensation in his gut that maybe the redhead wasn't Aleta Locke.

As the people switched dogs he heard someone say, "Aleta is supposed to show Drummer." More discussion followed, but he missed most of it as people bent down to spray various faces and paws. When the group filed back into the ring, he saw the redhead go in with a new dog , a brown dog a little shorter than the two black males.

That must be Drummer, he thought.

When she spied a stocky older woman in yellow take in Mint, the gnawing sensation faded and he nodded at Shark and Sugar and confirmed the target.

Marge, pursuant not only to Nathan's instructions but also to a request from Chief West, panned the crowd of onlookers. It was unexpected, so she caught both Shark and Sugar standing arm in arm watching the ring, but Alfonso

Mariana managed to duck behind a larger, taller, blonde man as the camera swung in his direction. The mustached blonde unfolded a chair and bent over to speak to his companion, an elderly lady, as he was settling into the chair and Alfonso was caught on tape.

Alfonso saw the men with the two black Labs each watching every move the other made. The judge went over each dog carefully and Alfonso could see no fault in either animal.

They're twins, he thought. He wasn't far from wrong. Lyle West was showing his dog, Morgan, against that dog's son, Drummer. The dogs were matched in style and soundness. It would come down to which handler made no errors.

Alfonso was surprised at how quiet it was around this ring. He heard distant chatter, but the spectators watching this competition were practically holding their breath.

At the ring tucked in the corner, Stanley was watching with rapt attention as Aleta moved Maggie. He marveled at the ease with which she did that. She's only just learned the nuances an hour ago.

When Aleta moved Maggie, Stanley smiled. Maggie had such a weird gait; but then so did all the winners. The skin on the back rolled from side to side and the rear legs waddled. From his seat on the grass, he saw them between the widely-spaced front legs plunked solidly on the ground. The jowls jiggled and while Stanley would not have called Maggie's movement good, but liked it better than the other two.

All of the handlers knelt beside their dogs and lifted their heads. Aleta stood in front of Maggie who looked up at her. The sun beat down on Aleta's head and her wound began to burn from the heat and she shook her head. Her hair, which wasn't sprayed for fear of getting spray in the wound, was soft and, had there been a wind, it would have blown askew. Aleta didn't dare put her hand on her head. She shook it to hopefully interrupt the pain signals flooding her brain.

Maggie stared at the wildly flying hair and woofed. The judge, who had been looking down the line, looked back at Maggie who woofed at him. It was a soft woof; but, the judge was momentarily caught in this display of emotion from the normally placid bulldogs and he took a second look at Maggie.

Maggie won the purple ribbon and her first major points. George Sciretta screeched his joy from outside the ring and people leaned over and congratulated him.

Maggie filed in at the end of the line when the Breed competition began.

Stanley could see the unadulterated joy on Aleta's face mixed with just a hint of bewilderment. It was an unexpected win.

His eyes never left her for a moment which is why he didn't see Lou Zalkan slide into the back row of spectators.

Lou saw the bandaged ear of Stanley Praetzel and knew he was the man with Aleta Praetzel in the office. He was the lawyer. The light weight rope in his pocket wouldn't do both, besides men were stronger, and angry men stronger yet. To do Aleta, on the other hand, would only take him a minute. This ring was near the women's restroom. Lou was an opportunist. Still the restroom was too public and too busy.

He decided he'd wait for an opportunity near the woods. A plan was even forming in his mind as to how to make it happen.

He relaxed and let his brain look at his plan from every angle as he watched the show. It was a simple plan. He couldn't see any downside.

Meanwhile, over at the Lab ring, the judge had moved Lauren and her chocolate bitch up next to the two black males. He left them for a moment while he went back and compared the winner's dog and winner's bitch and considered both for the Breed. It would be a major for either one but neither deserved to beat the three at the front of the line. Maybe someday, but not today.

He walked back up the line and studied each dog's expression as he walked backward. The chocolate bitch had a gorgeous head, the judge thought, but if he gave her the breed, he still had to choose between the two males. Then he studied Drummer's expression. Again a magnificent head. These dogs had to be related.

Finally, the judge moved on to Morgan. Lyle was smiling at his dog. This always made Morgan's tail wag just a bit faster. Morgan cocked his head and raised one brow to render that quizzical look that Lab owners prize. He took the Breed. Lauren took Best Opposite with her bitch and Tom and Drummer were handed the large green rosette designating a Judge's Award of Merit. Mint took Best of Winners to Beatrice's surprise.

The photographer came and dogs and owners gathered around the entrance to wait their turn. After Tom was photographed, Lyle insisted he remain and be photographed a second time with Morgan and him. Lauren stood watching her back to the spectators. Her dog lay at her feet.

Outside the ring Shark and Sugar stood face to face and quietly talked as Sugar turned her ring so its stone was on the palm side of her hand. She flipped open the latch. If the sun had penetrated the shadow formed by the two heads close together, it would have glistened on the tiny pins inside the ring that were coated with the venom from one of South America's deadliest vipers.

Theirs was a variation of the two-man pickpocket con only these two didn't pick a pocket. They killed people.

Sugar was actually pregnant. Her thin, flimsy dress didn't hide fake padding. It was worn because the day was hot and she wanted to be cool. Smug fitting Capri's were too hot. Sugar wanted air on her legs. She wore the briefest of underwear. She was purposely dressed to look frumpy. People would remember her dress more than they would her face. They'd remember her stringy dishwater blonde hair and her husband's worn leather jacket and faded jeans, long dark hair and unshaven face but not the color of his eyes which weren't brown any more than his dark hair was dark.

Alfonso Mariana had spotted them picking pockets on a crowded subway platform in New York and had recruited them to do more lucrative work.

Mariana stood near a group of people gathering for the next event and watched his protégés at work.

What he didn't know was that Melissa Bolton, Rimmel's ex-girlfriend, had an agenda that would conflict with his.

Melissa had replaced her doctored power bars with unadulterated fresh ones and planned to insist they be tested. She planned to acknowledge that she had given the bar to Julia but claim she had no idea it had been tampered with.

The only way she could pull this off was to go back to the show and act innocent.

Dennis Rimmel spotted her and stood on the far side of the ring fuming. What did she think she was doing? He knew she had some seemingly rational explanation for defying his order, some grand scheme that would restore her to his good graces, some scheme he was certain would make the mess worse.

He had to reach her and stop her. But he had to be discreet which is why he moved casually.

Lyle West took Tom Wilson over to where Martha Cook was sitting and introduced them. Tom shook her proffered hand gently.

"I couldn't tell the difference between the dogs," she commented. "Both they and you were quite magnificent!"

Never let it be said that cool professionals don't blush. These two did. Martha had a power that rode on each word she uttered.

"So, tell me, Mr. Wilson, why did Lyle want you in his picture?"

"His dog is the sire of mine, Ma'am," Tom replied easily.

"So you're that good?"

"What?"

"I'm sure he has photos of the two dogs; so it must be beating you that crowned his day today."

Lyle grinned. "He's the best in the business."

"I expected the judge to put up Lauren with all that male testosterone floating around in the ring."

"He almost did," Lyle responded.

Tom joined in. "I would have."

Mrs. Cook smiled, "My, you are a gracious loser. Tell me, why are you here? You two acted like this was your first encounter in the ring."

"It was," Tom said. "And I met my match."

"I would guess that it would go the other way the next time, hence the photograph," Martha cackled and the men chuckled with her.

"I was hoping to see Aleta here," Martha added.

"She's showing my Bulldog," Tom said.

"You had a conflict?"

Tom raised a brow. "How did you know?"

"This is a business. In business there are conflicts."

Lyle stepped in, "Mrs. Cook runs Cook Construction."

Martha smiled. "I tried to get my grandson to take over, but all he wanted to do was be a doctor. There's no explaining the weird choices men make."

"You have free medical care for life," Wayne put in.

"As if I need it," Martha quipped. "Now, Wayne, take me to the Bulldog ring so I can watch Harriet's granddaughter. And, Lyle, get Lauren to head straight back with your dogs."

"Why?"

Wayne helped his grandmother to her feet.

"There's danger close by. Wayne do you know where the Bulldogs are?"

Tom looked at Lyle slightly bewildered. The old lady had been making sense. Lyle, however, was hanging on every word.

"I'm going that way," Tom said. "Let me show you."

The three took off and Lauren came over and handed Lyle her dog's lead.

"No," he said. "You take them back."

"Not until after Mint's photo," Lauren said. "Give me one more minute and then you can go back to being a cop."

Marge was still filming. This was all part of the experience she and Nathan would have shared. He wouldn't have wheeled away to watch Aleta. He'd have stayed here to watch the tail end of the Lab competition.

She'd caught the entire conversation between Martha Cook and the two men and she knew Nathan would enjoy that.

Martha's warning had chilled her; but, when she looked around by panning the crowd, she couldn't see any immediate danger.

Maybe it was elsewhere, she thought, like in the bathroom which was why Lyle wanted Lauren to go straight back to camp. Lauren reached Jason as a dark-haired woman pushed her way through the people and dogs still waiting to be photographed. It wasn't that there were a lot of people but everyone had more than one dog at his feet. Jason had three. The leads were tangled.

As they worked to separate them, Melissa saw her opportunity to congratulate Jason. Sugar saw her opportunity to approach as well.

"I wanted to ask you…," Sugar began as she moved toward Lauren.

Melissa sized up the pregnant woman with a glance and decided she was not worth anyone's time, so she pushed in between her and Lauren just as Sugar stumbled on cue. Melissa's arm shot out toward Jason as she overpowered Sugar's timid query with a loud congratulation.

Sugar, whose plan had not taken such rudeness into account, could stop neither her fall, which Shark was there to catch, nor her reaching hand, which Shark was not prepared to handle. Her hand gripped Melissa's arm by mistake. Sugar pulled it away quickly.

Melissa turned and snarled at the young pregnant woman, "You scratched me!"

"Sorry," The pregnant woman murmured and she and her husband hurried off.

Lyle West watched them leave. They were heading straight toward the exit at a fast pace. That made no sense to him. Why would a stumble cause anyone to run?

Pickpockets! He concluded and signaled his man to stop them. He went over to Jason to ask him to check his pockets.

Melissa was still complaining, "She scratched me. I don't know what she used; but, it hurts like a bee sting."

Chief West told Jason he thought a pair of pickpockets was at work in the area. Jason slapped his hand on his rear pocket.

"Wallet's still there," he said happily. "They were a strange pair though."

West waited for Lauren to finish. He only half heard Melissa's rapid fire conversation; but, he understood she was a representative from Atherton Bank who'd come here to persuade the members of the Tontine not to switch banks.

"You have to talk to my wife about that," Jason said, taking Mint's leash from Lauren.

"Where is your wife?" Melissa asked with apparent innocence.

"She's sick," Jason said. "You can't talk to her now."

"Are you parked near the other members of the group? Maybe I can join you and talk to them."

"No, you can't," Lyle West broke in. Martha had said there was danger, and he was going to draw a tight, protective circle around the group that was the target.

"Who the hell are you?" Melissa charged.

Dennis, who was approaching, couldn't think of how to shut Melissa up. He decided it would be prudent to back away and so he stopped.

"He's the Chief of Police," Jason said coolly. He didn't like this woman.

Melissa was startled but she regrouped quickly. "Oh, I'm sorry. You don't know who I am. I'm his wife's banker and there's my boss, Mr. Rimmel."

West turned and Dennis had no choice but to put on a good front. He extended his hand to Jason and introduced himself telling Jason to call him by his first name. He nodded at West not certain if one shook hands with a police chief, even one dressed in civilian clothes.

Lauren came out of the ring and Lyle handed her the leashes and told her to make no stops but to go straight back to the camp.

Melissa frowned as Lauren took off. "Why does Aleta get to go to the camp and not us?" she asked querulously.

Lyle noticed that Melissa's eyes were fastened on Lauren.

"That's my wife, Lauren," Lyle said watching her face closely. The surprise was quickly hidden, but he saw it. "Why did you think she was Aleta Locke?"

"So you do know her," Melissa came back.

"I didn't say I didn't."

"Point her out to me."

"Why?"

"Because she's my competition."

"It would seem to me you would have asked what she looked like."

"I did. They said she had long reddish hair."

"Interesting," West commented.

Melissa rubbed her arm and Dennis looked down at it. "My God!" he gasped. "Your arm's turning purple."

It was indeed turning purple and swelling as well.

Melissa followed his gaze and paled. "What's happening?"

"You need to go to the hospital," West said signaling a young woman standing nearby. "Call an ambulance and accompany this lady to the hospital. Don't leave her."

The young police officer spoke into her radio set.

"My car would be faster," Rimmel said, pulling Melissa with him.

"The ambulance is at the gate," the officer said. "And it's not wise for her to move."

Rimmel stopped when he saw the paramedics approaching at a trot with a stretcher.

"I'm not lying on that to be some freak show!" Melissa declared moving forward.

The young woman cop moved faster and, looking Melissa in the eye, told her to lie down.

"Why should I do it your way?" Melissa argued her dignity at stake.

"You have a nose bleed," the young officer said. "You'll ruin your outfit."

Melissa put her hands to her nose and it came away bloody.

"Dennis, your handkerchief," Melissa said.

"Lay down," he said, pulling it from his pocket.

Melissa did as she was told.

Chief West, meanwhile, approached the young couple and said to the two officers guarding them, "Cuff them."

Shark protested. "What'd we do?"

West ignored him and told his officers they were to be taken straight to Milani for questioning.

As the woman was being cuffed he noticed the large ring on her finger. The officers led the two away when West told them to halt. All four turned and surreptitiously the woman slipped the ring from her finger and let it drop on the ground. She stepped on it with her heel.

"When you get to Willow Glen have Hawk examine the ring she's wearing." The two officers nodded and moved away.

West called the officers to hold up again. He caught up to them and asked for an evidence bag. One of the officers reached in his pocket and handed it to his chief who went around behind the woman.

"The ring's gone!" he exclaimed. "She dropped it."

He ordered his men to hold them while he looked for it. Slowly he backtracked.

West figured he'd never find it without help. He whistled sharply and Morgan who'd been trotting calmly beside Lauren heard him. The big black dog spun around and leaped away. The lead slipped from Lauren's grasp. Morgan raced toward Lyle, avoiding everyone in his path who leaped to stop him assuming he was a loose dog.

He rushed right up to Lyle and sat, waiting.

"Good boy," Lyle said with genuine warmth. "Now let's find the ladies ring."

Shark smirked and winked at Sugar. She nodded almost imperceptibly. This was a show dog and a Lab. Had it been a bloodhound they would possibly have a reason to worry.

Lyle led Morgan over to Sugar and had him sniff her hand. Sugar pulled away, disgusted.

"Find the ring," Lyle said unsnapping the leash from his collar.

Morgan recognized the word find. He'd often been asked to find keys after one of the children had taken them to play with and left them somewhere in the house or yard.

Morgan moved quickly in the direction the woman had travelled. He went scarcely ten feet when he stopped and began to dig in the grass with his front paws.

West quickly pulled Morgan back by his collar and studied the spot where the dog had begun digging. He took a pencil from his pocket and moved the dirt with it. He heard metal hit metal and using his pencil pried the ring from the ground and slipped it into the plastic bag.

He approached the woman, "You care to tell me what poison you used?"

"I didn't use no poison," Sugar said vehemently. "And that ain't my ring."

"Take your choice," West said. "Either attempted murder or murder."

"How about I tell you what and you let us go?"

"Read them their rights," Lyle said coolly.

The office did as bid. Lyle stood there eyeing the two. They'd been arrested before.

That they'd hit the bank person was an error. They were aiming for Lauren. They had the same description Melissa had—long red hair.

"Take them to Milani," West said. "He's questioning their partner."

"Mariana?" Sugar gasped before Shark could hiss at her to keep her mouth shut. She'd practically confessed with that last statement.

"He's not talking so far," West said. He saw relief on both faces. So there was someone else on the show grounds. And he was targeting Lauren. He was torn. If he could get them to release the name of the poison, he could possibly save someone's life.

He borrowed one of his officer's radios and radioed his men.

"Who's closest to Lauren?" he asked. "She's approaching the bridge."

Two men responded.

"She's a target right now because she has long red hair. Go get her and guard her."

The two in handcuffs exchanged puzzled glances. West caught the look and with an icy coldness said, "You targeted the wrong woman. You almost killed my wife."

"So no one's in custody?" Shark quipped. "You was playing with our minds."

"Actually, we have someone in custody," West said. "Obviously, there's more than one player in this field."

"Must be Lou," Sugar said. That her husband was talking encouraged her to comment.

"Whatever," West remarked with no apparent interest. His tone belied his intense concern. He had two more hit men on the loose and he was running short on personnel.

West radioed his men. "Do you have Lauren?"

When he received an affirmative response, he said, "Keep everyone in camp until I get there."

One of the cops said, "Ed Ornstein wants to send something to the lab. He says it's important."

"Put him on," West said.

Ed came right to the point. "We think the oranges have been tampered with. They need to be tested."

"Anyone eat one and get sick," West asked, briefly wondering if he was wrong about the cause for Melissa's illness.

"Nobody," Ed said. "But Emma won't touch the orange slice."

Fortunately, Ed was talking to a fellow Lab owner.

"I haven't the man power to send someone to you," West said. If you could bring the oranges to me I'll send them to Hawk along with the ring."

"Be right there," Ed said.

West ignored the two standing in handcuffs waiting while he gave orders to his officers. People began to spot the arrest in progress and made a wide circle.

"Gently lead the group from the Bulldog ring back to the RV area," West ordered. "And I mean gently. If any of you gives Mrs. Cook a heart attack, you'll be looking for work in Alaska."

The two standing beside the handcuffed couple smirked. The entire station knew their chief had a strange bond with the ancient matriarch. They knew it wasn't her money. West was from a wealthy family himself and his father, once his son passed the bar exam, not only allowed him to follow his dream of being a cop but even supported him.

West didn't move the suspects out of the public eye, not because he had a faint hope that they would make eye contact with their companion, but because, out in the open, less could happen.

Ed trotted all the way up the slope from the creek area to the level field where the rings were. By the time he reached West, he was red-faced and puffing hard.

He held out the bag and Lyle took it and gave it to one of his men.

"What do you know about poisons," he asked.

Ed smiled. "Mostly just about snakebite."

"But you've got a boa,"

"They aren't poisonous," Ed said, "But people come in with snakes all the time to have me sell them. I don't sell nothing what's poisonous."

"The victim's arm swelled up and turned purple," West said.

"Cobra, most likely," Ed said. "Only we ain't got any of them here. Never heard of a rattlesnake or water moccasin doing that. Has to be a viper."

When Ed said the word "viper", Sugar started. It was a small twitch but the officer who had hold of her arm noticed it.

"Viper," he said confidently.

Ed went on. "If it's a viper, your victim could be dead in two hours unless they inject some antitoxin. Is she bleeding from the nose or mouth?"

West nodded.

"She's hemorrhaging. She hasn't a lot of time."

"You're sure?"

"Ask if she's vomiting blood," Ed said. "If she is, I'm sure."

West was put through to the hospital.

Chapter 16

Most of the group managed to gather around the Bulldog ring during the Best of Breed competition and witnessed the judge signal Aleta to move to the head of the line with her little bitch.

"The Breed?" Beatrice whispered to Marge.

Marge nodded.

Evelyn whispered. "I thought she had an American Bred. Did she take on a Special?"

Tom Wilson leaned over, "Same dog."

In the ring, Aleta moved past the other dogs thinking, this can't be what I'm thinking it is. She looked over Maggie's head at the dog being moved behind her. Her first reaction was what a magnificent animal.

She shook her head as if to shake away the notion that she couldn't possibly win and looked at the happy face of the dog in front of her. Maggie's panting was a little heavier. Aleta looked behind her while the judge was at the other end of the line and Tom's assistant thrust a spray bottle of water in her hand.

She bent over and sprayed the open mouth and Maggie closed her mouth and licked around it with her tongue.

She leaned over and whispered,

"Too much garlicky liver makes one thirsty, huh, old girl. You're a good girl Maggie. A pretty, pretty girl."

The judge, who had walked backwards down the line, reached the dog behind Maggie.

"You be good, Maggie, and I'll get you a date with him."

The judge heard her and laughed. "Me or the dog?"

"Both," Aleta shot back. "You first, then the dog."

As the judge took a step back to look at Maggie one last time, Aleta felt perspiration running down her face. The wound was now thoroughly sunburned and it burned. Aleta tossed her head and Maggie again seeing the hair flying around Aleta's head perked up just as the judge's eyes rested on her face. Curiosity and interest were reflected in her gaze as before.

Without another second of hesitation he pointed to Maggie and said, "Breed," then to the dog behind her and said, "Best Opposite."

The handlers in the ring broke out of line and crowded around to congratulate Aleta. A cheer went up from her friends on the outside.

Mrs. Cook sat while Aleta and Maggie were being photographed. Wayne answered his cell and enlisted Stanley's help meeting the caterer at the gate and helping them get through the cordon of police guarding the RV area.

"I don't want to leave Aleta," Stanley said.

"Hey, she's got as many friends here as my grandmother does. She'll be fine."

Stanley looked at Aleta accepting congratulations and the little rotund owner and Tom Wilson hovering nearby and decided he was pretty superfluous right now.

"Let's go," Stanley said.

"You still like her?" Wayne asked as they left the group and took out toward the road the RV's had travelled on earlier.

"The catering truck won't get through there," Stanley said.

"That's why we're needed," Wayne said. "So you do still like her, huh?"

"Yep," was all Stanley could manage to get out. Like was too light a word to describe his feelings. Love was even too inadequate. He found Aleta fascinating, stimulating, engaging, exciting and unpredictable. Her mind was sharp, her wit quick and her humor pleasant. She was also stubborn, willful, volatile, easily riled and capable of great fury.

"Does she remind you of anyone?"

"Your grandmother."

"I think we've had this conversation before," Wayne said. "Don't let her go."

"It's not up to me."

"Of course it's up to you," Wayne said. "These redheads are not easily wooed; but they're worth it."

Stanley couldn't believe he actually spoke the next words that came out of his mouth. "I'm not attractive, you know.

Wayne's laugh was honest and hearty. Tears came to his eyes, and when Stanley scowled at him he apologized, "I'm sorry. You're talking about a woman I heard whisper 'pretty, pretty girl' to a bulldog!"

Stanley was smiling when he retorted, "You're comparing me to a bulldog?"

"Hey, some people like bulldogs."

"But Poodles prefer other poodles.

"Sometimes," Wayne said as he left Stanley to rush toward the cops telling the truck it had to leave.

"Call Chief West. Tell him his lunch has arrived."

The cop let the truck through.

"Why did I come along?" Stanley asked.

"To keep me company," Wayne said. "And so I could pump you about your romance for my wife."

"Your wife?"

"Once you're married, you'll understand," Wayne grinned. "I can't wait."

"That's hardly a positive statement," Stanley quipped. "You can't wait to tackle a patient with a deadly disease either."

"Or deliver a baby," Wayne countered. Stanley let him have the last word. He was feeling pleasantly stimulated.

Back at the Bulldog ring, Aleta looked at Maggie after the photo session. The dog was hot and getting hotter.

"I need to put her away," she told Tom Wilson.

"I can get one of my assistants to do that," Tom said. "We need to talk with Mr. Sciretta together."

"He's your client," Aleta said. "Of course, you'll take Maggie into Group."

"I have a Frenchie that took the Breed. And Mr. Sciretta isn't going to want anyone but you. Do you have a dog in that group?"

"One in Sporting. One in Hound. That's it," Aleta replied. "If he wants me, I'll take her in; but, it's up to you."

"Walk along the woods by the creek. It's cooler there," Tom said. He put his hand on George's shoulder and they followed her a few steps as Tom began to tell George what his options were.

After a few steps Tom and George stopped and began their conversation in earnest. Tom explained that he was showing another client's dog in the Group and he could tell the man didn't understand that by electing Aleta he was taking the choice out of Tom's hand. He didn't know how to explain to such a neophyte, drunk with his first victory, that politics dictated group placements over half the time and, if one of his assistants was on the dog, it would be as if he were on it.

George Sciretta understood the politics all too well. He hadn't come up with Tom Wilson's name without researching the man.

"But you won't be taking her in, right?" George asked. "You'll be with the French Bulldog."

"Yes, but politically if my assistant's on the dog, the judge will know he's one of mine."

"But the judge'll look at whose leash is in your hand and he'll figure he knows how you're voting."

By the time the discussion had reached this point, Tom knew which way it was going. He looked down the slope at

Aleta and Maggie. Aleta had taken a spray bottle with her and stopped in the shade and sprayed Maggie's face.

Aleta looked back. "She's too hot," she called. 'Okay if I get her feet wet?"

Tom nodded. He saw Aleta dive into the woods with the dog and began to run toward her. The creek was deep and Bulldogs don't swim.

But Aleta didn't make it more than a few feet into the woods before Lou Zalkan stepped out from behind a tree and slipped a rope around her neck. His was a quick practiced movement and Aleta was caught completely unprepared.

The noose tightened so quickly that the scream she'd started in her throat was reduced to a gurgle by the loss of air. Her hands went to her throat to loosen the tightening noose. She stomped her foot hard and it glanced off his shoe and hit the ground. She tried to wriggle around to knee him in the groin but his grip was too tight.

She let go of the rope and dug her fingers into his eyes. Simultaneously, Maggie opened her big mouth, clamped it on the attacker's calf and let her teeth sink in to the bone.

Lou howled in agony as he let go of the rope. Aleta collapsed to the ground and lay still.

Maggie shook the leg. Tendons and muscles ripped apart at the force of her heaves. Howls of agony could be heard in every ring. Showing was suspended by the sound. Police and onlookers rushed to the sound. West spoke into his radio and the melee was halted by a cordon of police which allowed only certain officers to proceed into the woods.

Lou thought to shake the dog off, but she clung to his leg with the tenacity of a leech. He beat on her face with his fist, but it was Aleta's whispered, "Come Maggie" that got her to let go.

Tom, who had assumed Aleta was going to swim Maggie, was the first to reach her. He was in time to see Lou Zalkan disappearing into the wood.

Shocked, he guessed what happened when he saw Aleta lying on the ground.

"Don't talk," he counseled softly as he quickly knelt beside her. "Help is coming."

He looked up and saw the man limping away as fast as he could. He rose hesitantly. He could catch him if he tried. The cops were coming; but, he knew the man would escape if he didn't give chase. Then the man looked back. The rage Tom saw in the man's face told him not to follow. He knelt down beside Aleta again.

"Maggie...," Aleta whispered.

"She's okay.'

"She bit him," Aleta rasped. "Take your handkerchief and wipe off her teeth."

He pulled out his handkerchief.

"I can wash her face faster and better," he said.

"First preserve the guy's DNA," Aleta whispered, "then wash Maggie off."

Tom handed her the handkerchief when he was done and Aleta folded it and stuffed it into her pocket.

Aleta stumbled to the creek's edge after Tom and Maggie.

"I'm a mess," she murmured. Her voice was soft because her throat still hurt.

Tom looked up from the shallow spot he'd found to stand Maggie in. Aleta noticed he was standing in the water with his shoes on.

"Water feels good," he said. "And Maggie thinks we're rewarding her."

"As well we should be," Aleta declared, her voice still raspy. "She saved my life."

"If you don't stop talking, you're going to lose your voice," Tom warned.

Both turned at the crash of heavy footsteps.

"Police!" shouted two baritone voices at once.

"Here we are," Tom said.

One cop pushed back the last bush branch and wound up at the water's edge with two handlers.

"The attacker went that way," Tom said.

"Maggie bit the man who attacked Aleta," Tom said. "He's limping badly."

"You okay?" one cop asked as his partner took off.

"Yes," Tom said. "Go!"

The second cop took off.

West was the next to arrive and Tom brought him up to speed. West called in a single officer by name and was about to order him to look for the rope when he was stopped by the appearance of a second man with him. The tall hunched over man held a case in his hand.

"Hawk!" West exclaimed. "Why aren't you back at the lab working on my stuff?"

"My assistant can test for known substances," Hawk said. "As soon as I heard about this hot bed of crime I rushed right over. You need me here more."

"The perp probably dropped his rope."

"And that's all you were going to look for, right?"

"Well, it's important."

"Well, I'll get you more," Hawk promised. "Too bad you washed the dog."

Aleta took a handkerchief from her pocket, "Not until after we'd cleaned her teeth."

"Good girl!" Hawk exclaimed. "You're hired."

A voice interrupted. "Hired?"

"Stanley! What are you doing here?" West said. "This is a crime scene."

"I came from the bridge. Dr. Cook is with me."

"First let me get some photos of that neck," Hawk said.

"And take some scrapings from under my nails. I scratched his face," Aleta added, her voice still hoarse. "I didn't see him but I scratched him."

Hawk worked fast but Dr. Cook grew impatient, "She's not a corpse, you know. You can't have her all day."

Dr. Cook moved in and examined her briefly. "That cut on your head is in bad shape. No more sun for you, young lady."

"No more anything," West said. "You're done for the day as are Lauren and Julia. There's one more perp on the grounds."

"Lauren?" Aleta questioned.

"They're looking for someone with long reddish hair. That's why Lauren was attacked."

Aleta gasped, and West hastened to assure her Lauren was fine. "They got one of the bank officers by mistake."

"But this guy came after me!" Aleta pointed out, her voice not allowing her to say more.

"He knew what you looked like. According to the bank officer, they had a vague description. I'm assuming the attackers weren't any better informed," West said. "Reddish hair, nice figure. Lauren will be pleased when I tell her that."

A cop poked his head in.

"Hate to bother you, Chief, but the dog owner is out here and I think he'll have a stroke if we don't tell him if his dog's okay."

"Dog's fine," West said. "She's just getting a cool bathe."

Within minutes, Tom and Aleta emerged from the woods with Maggie in tow. A camera clicked and West knew they would make the front page of tomorrow's Tri City Register. In the crowd of people slowly gathering was Alfonso Mariana.

Finally, he knew what Aleta Locke looked like.

Lou Zalkan was found hiding in the creek under a bush, waiting for the officers to abandon their search of the area. Even though he was well hidden his leg continued to bleed and one of the officers spotted the blood in the water and hauled him out.

Chapter 17

Consternation for Aleta's wellbeing rose to new heights. West explained the situation and the need for the subsequent confinement of these women.

All agreed that no one new was to enter the camp.

It was then that West received a call from the officer at the bridge telling him that two men insisted on coming into camp.

"Who are they?" West asked.

He turned to the group and said, "Bill Pacheco and Junior Danielson."

It was Jason who decided. "Say no. Julia is still asleep and I don't need him asking for money right now."

"Say no to Bill, too," Beatrice said. "He won't like what I'm wearing."

West kept his face sober as he told his officer that the two were not to be let through. The area was off limits to all strangers.

"But those are my parents!" Jason Junior protested. "I need to talk to my mother. It's a matter or life or death."

The officer passed along the information and West said he'd be right there.

Aleta, meanwhile, had disappeared into Beatrice's RV and changed clothes. She emerged in jeans and a polo shirt and said, "I'm hungry."

Thus the luncheon party got underway.

Marge was the first to mention the afternoon show schedule.

"I can take Anya in," she announced. "Maybe Stanley or Jason can photograph me in the ring with her. Nathan would enjoy that."

As she was talking, Jason took over the camera. Marge went on. "I really didn't expect her to place in group, but…"

"I did," Aleta said. "She's quite lovely."

Marge faltered, "But you can't show her."

"You can win with her," Aleta started but her voice gave out and she reached for her water bottle and took a long drink.

Beatrice picked up the theme. "You can do it, Marge. And wouldn't a Group placing be icing on the cake?"

Marge looked down at her outfit. "I'm not dressed right."

Beatrice grinned. "I thought you'd never ask. I've got just the thing. And you can help me show my Scotties."

Evelyn came over later and took Aleta's hand. Stanley was sitting beside her. She put her hand on his as well.

"You two have saved my life," she said. "And you showed Topaz to perfection. I've had a good day. Tom said he'd take Topaz into the group if I want. I wanted to see what you thought."

"Tom's good," Aleta whispered. "But no."

Stanley sucked in air loudly. "No?"

"I'm showing him."

"But West said…"

"West will be next to her in the ring," Evelyn put in.

"See," Aleta whispered. "Good protection."

"You just want to beat Lyle West!" Stanley exclaimed.

Aleta grinned. That was part of it, but the biggest reason is that she didn't want to be sidelined. Her reason told her that the one man that knew what she looked like was in the hospital. And he wasn't talking. West had speculated that he was the man who'd shot her the day before. She believed him.

She decided while people were replacing her that she probably had only one more safe shot in the ring. She chose Topaz. She would have had a hard time choosing between him and Maggie, but Tom had taken that decision out of her hands. But the Sporting Group was last. The crowd would have thinned by then and a stranger would be more noticeable.

West had the name Sandy Ruiz had spit out. Mariana. He was running it through the police computer banks.

"I'm calling your grandmother," Stanley said.

"Don't," Aleta whispered. "Ask Martha."

Stanley was confused for a minute, and then he realized that if Martha forbade it, Aleta would listen. He went over and sat next to the ninety-year-old woman and before he said anything she observed aloud, "Such a day! What a lot of decisions were made. I'm seeing everyone at their best."

Curious, Stanley pursued the last statement. "I would have thought you'd have been horrified by the bad things that happened."

"Bad things happen all the time. It isn't often one sees people rising to meet the challenge such unfortunate events give birth to."

"So, share," Stanley said as Aleta joined them to listen.

"Take Beatrice," Martha said and both young people looked at her in bewilderment. She was the last person that came to mind.

Martha laughed. "Hers was the quietest confrontation of them all."

"You mean her turning Bill away?"

"It was the way she did it," Martha said. "What a reason! I loved it! It spoke volumes."

Martha took their quiet as assent and went on.

"And Jason," she said, "putting his own need first for a change and protecting his wife at the same time."

"That one I don't get," Aleta said.

"This is their special place. None of their children are involved in this sport. With seven children, you need a place where you are just a couple."

"And Evelyn," Stanley added, "knowing her own limits and trusting us all to help her. That takes courage."

"Which is what you came over to speak with me about," Martha commented.

"Evelyn?" Stanley queried.

Martha smiled, "No, her request to Aleta, couched in unbelievable gentle terms, to show her beloved Topaz."

"She was only asking Aleta's opinion. "It was a polite gesture."

"She was asking Aleta to show Topaz," Martha said firmly. "And Aleta knows it and she looked inside and found she wants to do it; but, you want Aleta to say here. Am I correct?"

"Well, if you're on my side, I'll say yes, but if you're not, I'll argue."

"Don't bother," Martha said. "Aleta has decided."

"That's it?"

"You expected more?"

"I expected you to persuade her it would be foolhardy for her to leave this camp."

"I'm not convinced it would be. That's where her heart wants to be."

"And if she doesn't go she'll be unhappy," Stanley countered. "I get that. But if she goes, she could also wind up dead."

"Look around," Martha said. "How safe is this place?"

Stanley looked around. In back of their circle of RV's and cars lay an open field. In front across the grassy roadway sat West's rig and beyond that the woods lining the creek. A man with a silencer could hide in the woods and take Aleta out with one shot and then disappear before anyone realized what had happened.

"It's only a semblance of safety, isn't it?" Stanley mused aloud.

"Pretty much," Martha agreed. "And it'll work for a while; but come the day's end, it won't matter where Aleta is; she'll be in danger."

Stanley's shoulders slumped. He knew the truth when he heard it. He turned to Aleta. "I'm coming with you. And nobody better try to send me to fetch anything."

Aleta giggled and Stanley found the sound ingratiating.

Chapter 18

"So now what do we do?" Junior asked Bill Pacheco as they walked away from the bridge toward the rings.

"Well, I didn't choose lunchtime just to eat," Bill explained. "I wanted to be here when Beatrice shows her mutts. If she wins, I'm gonna ask her to marry me. She'll be in a good mood."

"And if she loses?"

"I'm going to ask her to marry me," Bill said. "She'll be unhappy and a proposal will tell her I love her win or lose."

"So, you got it all figured out, but what about me? I'm supposed to persuade my mother to sign," Junior said. "And where the hell is Rimmel? He's supposed to try for Marge Tobias."

"No one said anything about Evelyn," Bill pondered.

"Doesn't that stuff take four hours to get a guy nutso?"

"Yeah, you're right. It's early."

"So once you propose, you think they'll let you in?"

Ed went into a funk when he heard Bill Pacheco was on the grounds. He moped around for almost an hour with only Martha Cook noticing.

When Ed passed, she called to him. "I need to ask you a question."

Ed immediately took the chair Stanley had vacated.

"You show dogs?" she asked.

"No. I just got Emma. She's a pet," he replied wondering where this was leading. Martha Cook didn't engage in small talk.

"You love her?" Martha asked knowing the question was redundant. He had her in the RV not tied up outside. The dog followed him everywhere and was currently lying at his feet. He'd even paid to fly her out when he came out here on business. In fact, he'd made her presence part of the contract. Harriet had told Martha this.

"Are you going to give me a pep talk about her being as good as any show dog?"

"Do I have to?" Martha asked coyly.

Ed blustered slightly. "Of course not. Hey, I know people love all kinds of dogs. I didn't need a dog show to tell me that. Heck, I sell snakes and toads and lizards… and I have a pet boa constrictor named Betty."

"Do you think Beatrice will like Betty?"

"I wouldn't ask her to," Ed said, then grinned. "Betty just might love her Scotties too much. I know Betty."

"But you don't know Beatrice?"

"I know she keeps picking losers."

"Ask her why?"

"Bill's here. Time's run out."

Martha took a diamond ring off her finger, and put it in Ed's hand and closed his fingers over it. "This is the ring my husband gave me. Now go."

Ed ran to Chief West. "You're a lawyer, right?"

"I'm a police chief."

"I mean you can answer questions about law stuff."

"I can't act as a lawyer or give counsel as one."

"Oh, heck," Ed said. "Just tell me this: Can I handwrite a pre-nup?"

"Yes," came the reply.

"Okay. Okay." Ed exclaimed. "If I do, will you witness it?"

"Yes," West said. He wanted to say more, but that would mean he would be giving legal counsel.

"Do you have a ring?" West asked.

"Martha gave me hers."

Shock registered on West's countenance and Ed ran into the RV. Beatrice and Evelyn were sitting having a cup of tea. Both looked at the excited little man.

"I figured it out," he said. "Martha helped me."

"Figured out what?" Beatrice asked.

"How to tell you I love you," Ed said. "Chief West says I can write it. You got paper?"

Both ladies shook their heads.

"A Bible?"

"You're going to write in my Bible?" Beatrice said.

"Yes," Ed said. "Do you trust me enough to let me?"

Evelyn looked over at Beatrice who was staring dumbfounded at the short man with the thinning hair, the man who made her feel good, the reason she could wear her yellow outfit again. She nodded.

"Stop me if you don't like the words," Ed said.

"This is a first," Evelyn observed.

Ed spoke as he wrote. "When we marry I promise that everything I have is yours, even Emma, and nothing you have is mine at any time, under any circumstances…"

"Wait," Beatrice said. "What if I want to give you something?"

"This is to prevent you from doing that," Ed said. "Otherwise, you might figure that's why I married you. Can I go on?"

"…circumstances even after you die. I love you. Ed Ornstein."

"But suppose I want to give you something," Beatrice protested.

"You can give me anything you want out of our money," Ed said.

"Our money?"

"Yeah, what we earn together."

"Earn?"

"Well, yes. You bake cakes and I sell them, I buy snakes, you sell them. Stuff like that," Ed grinned.

"You think my cakes are that good?"

"Lady I'm marrying you so I'll never run out of chocolate cake."

"This has got to be the weirdest proposal on record," Evelyn said.

"That's why you're the witness. No one will believe a word you say if you repeat anything."

Evelyn looked at Beatrice, "How can you refuse such honesty?"

"Wait!" Ed said. "I have one more thing."

He took Beatrice's hand and knelt down before her. Emma stood beside him and wagged her tail. Ed looked at Emma. "Please marry us."

Emma's tail wagged faster.

Ed slipped the ring on Beatrice's finger. It stopped at the knuckle.

"It's a loaner," he apologized. "Let me put it on your little finger."

"Who loaned it to you?" Evelyn asked. "Julia isn't awake. Marge wears only a wedding band."

"Martha Cook gave me her ring," Ed said.

"Wow!" Both women chorused.

"What's that mean?" Ed asked. "I didn't ask her. She gave it to me. Is that bad?"

"Wow!" Beatrice repeated.

"It's not bad," Evelyn said. "It's just unfathomable."

Beatrice looked at the ring on her finger. "It's a precious little ring," she said softly, folding her right hand over her left.

The door opened and West popped his head in. "Beatrice, show time."

"Get in here," Ed said. "Evelyn will tell you I wrote every word. I want both of you to sign it."

"You wrote it in a Bible!" West exclaimed.

"Yeah," Ed said.

"Show him the ring," Evelyn coached Beatrice.

Beatrice held out her hand. "It's a tiny bit small for the ring finger."

"Guess whose ring it is?" Evelyn said teasingly.

West scanned the words that were written. "To witness this I'm supposed to see you write it."

"Okay I'll sign again," Ed said and wrote "I wrote all of the above, Ed Ornstein."

"Date it," West said. Ed did so.

Lyle West and Evelyn Barnes added their signatures, and West handed the Bible to Beatrice. "I guess you're engaged.

Beatrice glanced at her hand and blushed, "I guess I am."

"It's a beautiful ring," West said. "Go show Martha. It'll make her day."

"You knew," Evelyn concluded aloud.

"You coming?" West asked.

"Aren't you staying here?" Evelyn asked Chief West.

"My men are. This is my day off."

"Have you ever shown a Scottie?" Beatrice asked as they left the RV.

"No."

"I'm taking my puppy in. Watch me and you'll know. You can take in Cassie."

"I thought Marge was going to help you."

"Marge only agreed so Aleta wouldn't feel pressured. She'd rather handle the camera."

"It could be fun."

"There's a bonus in it for you."

"What bonus?"

"I expect Tom Wilson to take winner's dog. He'll be going for the Breed for the major. I want you to take him on."

"Why not you?"

"He's at another level," Beatrice said. "That's why I was looking forward to having Aleta show Cassie."

"I'll give it a shot."

"Marge will help me bring the dogs," West said to Beatrice. "You go show off your ring."

A short time later, West approached Tom Wilson when Beatrice went in with her puppy.

"What are the judges looking for?" he asked.

"Fearlessness and a proud even gait," Tom said, then went on to explain the nuances involved in showing a Scottie.

Beatrice came out with her blue ribbon. "Your turn," she said to Lyle.

Tom raises a brow, "Since when…?"

Lyle just smiled as he took Cassie in. Beatrice watched him, grinning broadly.

"Why are you so happy?" Tom said.

A voice behind them said, "Because I'm here."

Bill Pacheco slipped his arm around Beatrice's waist and kissed her on the neck.

She didn't turn around. "Bill, go away. I'm busy."

"You're done. I want to talk."

"Not now!" Beatrice said frowning.

"Isn't that that police chief, West something or other, in the ring," Bill said putting his hand on Beatrice's shoulder and sliding it down her arm.

"Bill, leave me be," Beatrice said, shaking off his arm. "He's showing Cassie for me."

"He seems to know what he's doing, so come outside with me." The hand gripped the arm. "I want to talk with you now."

Beatrice shrugged his hand away and walked to the gate entrance. Bill followed her.

She stood waiting. The steward called her number and she entered the ring.

"Trouble?" Lyle asked.

"Under control," Beatrice smiled. "Thank God for ring ropes!"

"Take them around," the judge said.

Cassie took the points and Lyle exited with her. He told Bill Pacheco to wait outside.

"You aren't on duty," Bill snarled.

"I'm always on duty. And my orders are obeyed or jail time is involved."

"You can't order me not to talk to my girlfriend."

"I can't do that, but I can dictate that you keep the peace and move on out of here." He nodded at the cop who'd approached and Bill was quickly escorted outside.

The steward began calling numbers and Beatrice handed Marge the puppy and the striped ribbon and took Belle's lead, changed her arm band number and reentered the ring. Ed kept the video camera going as he had during the entire encounter between Bill and Beatrice.

He knew Beatrice hadn't told him about her engagement. She was just trying to enjoy her moment. He thought of interfering but decided Beatrice would know when to tell Bill so he hung back, his eyes waiting for any signal from her that he should help her.

Beatrice's face cleared when Bill left and he caught it on tape. Maybe if she saw it later, she'd see what his presence did to her.

Tom and Lyle vied for the Breed as they had in the Lab ring. Part way through the judging Tom's dog turned around to face the dogs that had been judged and he moved toward Cassie who stood her ground. The dog behind her moved too close and she spun and faced him until he took a step back. Cassie was taking no advances from males today.

When Lyle asked her to, she walked with him as if they two were alone in the ring. As she gaited, her coat seemed to float in a straight line. She took the Breed and the major that went with it. Because Tom's dog didn't back down, he took Best Opposite and also earned a major. Both handlers were delighted and Beatrice was beside herself.

When Ed joined her, Beatrice confided in him that a week ago she wouldn't have dared ask Lyle West to show her dog.

While the photos were being taken, Junior cornered his father. The argument began as it always did with Junior declaring that they should give him the money he needed to pay off his debts and his father saying that if they paid off his debts, he'd just pile up new ones.

"There's no end," Jason told his son. "I know. I've been there."

"This time I can pay off half myself," Junior claimed. "I only need to get Mom to sign a piece of paper."

"Saying she'll pay the other half?" Jason shot back.

"No, it's true. They'll forgive half what I owe them if she just signs a paper saying she wants the Trust to stay at the bank in California."

"Did you know that it was one of those bank officers that drugged your mother?"

"No. They wouldn't do that! It must have been... er someone else."

"The Ciccone Family in Nevada?"

"No! It wasn't them! They told us to lay off. They want all you guys alive."

"Who's the 'us'? And why did they tell you to lay off?"

"They need you guys alive to get the Tontine back to California. That's why they're after Harriet and Aleta because they're trying to move it out here."

Jason knew this. West had been clear in his explanation. What was new was his son's involvement other than owing money.

"What were you guys planning?"

"Well, if enough Tontine members died, we thought the money would be split up and distributed."

"Nathan poisoned himself?" Jason asked not able to make sense out of his son's tale.

"No," Junior objected. "That was a mistake. The pills were in Marge's bottle. She was supposed to take them."

"My Lord, Junior, what did you do?"

"Dad, they were going to kill me. Don't you see? These guys want what they want. No one can stand up to them. Before they wanted money; but, now they want this other thing. And all I gotta do is get Mom to sign. I don't gotta do anything more. And nothing will happen to me or to you."

"You leave your mother out of this," Jason ordered.

"But, Dad, it's only got to do with where she banks. They don't want no money."

"And you're just going to keep on spending your mother's money until it's all gone."

"Aw, Dad, I'm not gonna do that. Hell, I can promise you that wouldn't never ever happen."

"You can't make that promise," Jason replied. "And I think you've gone too far this time."

"You aren't going to turn me in. Tell me you aren't even thinking about it... Dad, please. They'll get to me anyway. They have ways. God, you can't mean you'd send me to jail."

"You made your own bed. I didn't."

"Mom won't let you do this," Junior said. "I'll tell her what you're planning, and she'll see I get a 'start over.'"

Jason scowled. What his son told him was true. Julia would never agree to her son going to jail. She'd want him to have a 'start over.' Junior was good at persuading her that this time he was serious. And Julia, who'd stuck with Jason himself until he'd finally broken the hold the addiction had on him, kept telling him Junior just needed the same kind of trust and he'd pull himself free just as his father had done.

But Jason didn't believe it would happen. Junior had gambled away his house, car, wedding silver and every toy of any value, he never saw the pain he was inflicting on his wife and children. Always he felt his parents could make it right if they wanted to, so he put the blame squarely on them.

And Julia accepted the guilt.

This deep sleep of Julia's was the door of opportunity. And his son's confession was the key.

Lyle West breezed out of the big, barn-like fair building talking animatedly with Tom Wilson.

"Congratulations!" Jason called to both of them. "Did the majors hold?"

"Yes, they did," Lyle said.

Jason put a hand on his son's arm. "Can I talk to you a minute. Junior wants to ask you if he can talk with his mother. I'm not sure it's a good idea."

West sensed something was wrong and excused himself. Tom walked on and West joined Jason and his son. "Let's walk back to the camp and talk about this," West said smoothly.

Junior suddenly began to perspire. It was a hot day, but West knew his sweating denoted increased nervousness.

"I just want to talk to my mother," he said. "I want to know she's okay. I want to know for myself."

"He's hoping she'll be awake so she can talk me out of having you arrest him for the attempted murder of Nathan Tobias."

"And how is she going to do that?"

Junior was completely bewildered by this odd conversation.

He stumbled over his answer. "By telling Dad not to say anything."

"There's got to be more."

"Don't I gotta be read my rights or something," Jason asked suddenly panicking.

"I guess we could do that," West said. He motioned to an officer near the bridge and the man approached.

"Cuff this man, arrest him for attempted murder, read him his rights and take him out the side road. Take him to Willow Glen. Tell Milani to question him personally. Today's my day off and I have to show my dog in Group. Tell Chief Milani that, please."

The young officer looked surprised. "I should really tell him all that?"

"Every last word."

"But I work for him. He's my chief."

"Well, then, be sure you're polite when you deliver my message," West said soberly.

Chapter 19

Upon exiting the building with her three Scotties, Beatrice insisted Bill and she move to an area of shade down by the creek.

"Why can't he take your dogs back and put them away?" Bill said. "I have something important to say."

"I asked Ed to come," Beatrice said firmly. "And that's all I'll say until we're out of the sun."

Ed walked silently beside Beatrice. She knows he'll explode and she wants privacy, Ed realized, and so he said not a word. When they reached the grove of trees, Bill asked Beatrice again to send Ed off.

When she refused, he grabbed her hand and he slid a large diamond ring on her finger. She took it off immediately and handed it back.

"I'm already engaged," she announced.

"There's no ring!" Bill protested.

"I have a pre-nup signed and witnessed," Beatrice countered.

"It's got holes in it. I guarantee it!" Bill declared.

"Yours would have had, wouldn't it?"

"All of them do unless they're drafted by a lot of really good lawyers. Who did the one you got?"

"Ed did it himself," Beatrice said. "But I won't be needing it."

"See, that's what he wants. You tear it up as a gesture of your love and then he walks away with everything."

"He knows I wouldn't ever tear it up," Beatrice said softly. "He made sure I wouldn't."

"A pre-nup scratched on a napkin and no ring. Some wedding proposal," Bill scoffed.

"Oh, I have a ring," Beatrice said. "A beautiful delicate ring worn for years by a happily married woman."

"He gave you his dead wife's ring?"

"Is that what you're giving me? A ring stolen from someone else. Or maybe its cost is on my charge card."

Bill softened is approach. "What difference does it make who bought it? You deserve the best."

"And you can't afford it."

"So I used your money to give you a present. Is that so horrible?"

"Ed won't do that. After we're married we can only give each other gifts out of money we earn." She giggled at the thought. "Snakes and cakes."

Bill ignored her seemingly meaningless quip.

"You earn money. How? You have no skills. And you have expensive hobbies."

"Oh, I can pay for my hobbies, my house, my cars, my dogs and my trips, but I have to earn money to give Ed a gift."

"That's the stupidest idea I ever heard of."

"I think it's romantic."

"But he gets one of your cars to drive, right?"

Beatrice looked at Ed. "Do I need a third car?"

"I've got a car. You need one to go shopping in and the RV for dog shows. If you want a van to drive the dogs around town, you can trade your car in for one."

"So he gets an allowance?"

Again Beatrice looked at Ed. "Do you want an allowance? I'm rich enough. Bill gets one."

"I work. And I own a pet shop," Ed said.

"Where are you going to live them? You can't run your pet store from here."

"I could open a store here. I think kids here buy snakes too."

Bill gasped.

"You sell snakes?"

"This is so stupid, Beatrice," Bill said. "You don't know this man."

"It's you I don't know," Beatrice said with amazing calm. "Ed has the finest references possible."

"They're fake!" Bill said. "You're being conned and you don't know it. Who are these so-called references?

Beatrice smiled enigmatically.

"Let's go," she said to Ed. "Bye Bill. Have your things out of the house by the time I get home on Sunday."

"You trust me?"

"I have nothing of value in the house. Everything I value is here," Beatrice said. "Oh, and call Chief Milani. He'll send over a man to supervise your moving out. I don't want you arrested for robbing the place."

As they walked away, Beatrice asked Ed, "Have we heard the end of him?"

"Not yet."

Chapter 20

Alfonso Mariana was close enough to the bridge to see yet another man cuffed and led away. Never had he seen so many arrests at a public affair full, as far as he could tell, of ordinary people.

The man chased down in the bushes, he figured, was his counterpart, probably the sharpshooter who'd missed his target the first time. He'd watched carefully as the girl emerged from the woods with the Bulldog, the police chief, and another man and it occurred to him that if the attacker was the sharpshooter, he'd actually seen the target.

Alfonso studied the girl. She did indeed match the sketchy description he'd been given: young, slender, red-haired, attractive, but with short hair.

When she lowered her head he saw a hairless stripe down her scalp. So she had been hit. That meant she'd survived two direct attempts.

Did this woman lead a charmed life, he wondered. How had she escaped in the woods? Whatever mistakes had been made, he wouldn't repeat them. He wouldn't strike until he was certain he'd be successful.

Harriet Locke woke midday, refreshed.

"Where are we?" she asked.

Ron Maxwell glanced back. "In Idaho."

"We went north?"

"Less travelled road. I thought it'd be safer. Seems there are three brothers. You killed Haze. Clay got burned pretty bad. There's one left—Fogg Spader. I figure he'll try to come after you."

"You want me to take over?"

"Why don't you wait until after we stop and air the dogs?"

Harriet walked back and dialed her granddaughter's number. Aleta picked up the phone immediately.

"I thought you'd be in the ring," Harriet said.

"Later," Aleta rasped.

"What's wrong? You sound hoarse."

Suddenly, the voice on the other end was masculine, "Stanley Praetzel here, Mrs. Locke. Aleta's lost her voice pretty much.

"How are things?"

"Hairy," Stanley replied and brought her up to date.

"Is Rimmel in camp?"

"He tried to get in, but Chief West turned him away. After he arrested Jason Junior, West got even more cautious."

"I think we need as many transfer requests as possible signed right away."

"We can't fax them anywhere until Monday."

"We need to get a couple signed immediately," Harriet said. "Who's not busy?"

"Julia's still sleeping; but Jason isn't sure she'll sign anything that could hurt her son."

"So you've talked with him."

"He talked to me. He says Julia may start campaigning to keep the trust where it is. She's blind to reality when it comes to Jason Junior."

"Let me talk with Marge."

"Marge is nervous because she's going into Group. Aleta won the Breed with her puppy."

"Why isn't Aleta taking Anya in?"

"You know the name of her pup," Stanley observed as an afterthought."

"Why wouldn't I? Now why isn't Aleta taking Anya into the Group competition?"

"West won't let her. It's too dangerous. His men have rounded up all but one that we know about."

"Let me talk to her," Harriet said. "Do you have a transfer order with you?"

"Yes."

Harriet first congratulated Marge on her win and listened while she relived the win. Then Harriet asked her about Nathan and as Marge completed her report, Harriet said, "You know his hospital bill has been pre-paid. Aleta did that the minute he was hospitalized."

"Can she do that?"

"She has my power of attorney," Harriet said. "But she's not spending anything the Trust doesn't normally cover."

"I really like her," Marge said. "And that detective you sent, he knew I hadn't harmed Nathan. He knew it and he persuaded Chief West I wouldn't, still West wouldn't let anyone see him, but then I understand that now more than before. I would have taken Jason Junior in to see him without a second thought. I still can't believe he would do such a thing, but Chief West said he confessed, and Jason agreed that his son did do that. It's that gambling addiction of his, but I never thought he'd go so far…"

A sudden sob caught in her throat and her words stopped.

"Marge, you must listen to me," Harriet said earnestly. "We have to see that this transfer is completed immediately. The bank is holding it up because they want the trust back. I've heard from reliable sources that the Ciccone Family is going to use the trust to launder money. If they're caught, and I think they will be, the Trust monies could be tied up for years."

"I don't want to fight Julia on this. Couldn't we move it more slowly?"

"I've already set up a fund with M&W Development to begin work on the hospital wing you want. Next week the architects will start working on the plans."

"Well, if my money's already in a fund, then they can't stop the project, can they?"

"No, they can't. But, don't you want everyone to be able to invest in their dreams?"

"Of course, but if Julia…"

"I have a plan that may help Julia. But right now, we need to save the Trust from anyone using it illegally."

"It's pretty scary around here," Marge said. "And after this weekend, I'll be alone."

"Marge, if you don't help me stop them now, you'll live the rest of your life under a cloud of fear."

"I… I don't know what to do."

"Sign the form," Harriet said. "And if you've changed your mind when we meet, you can reverse your decision."

"I guess I could do that," Marge said. "That'll give me time to think."

"Just remember the mob made it easy for Junior to bet until he was in so deep he became desperate. They are clever at persuading people to do unthinkable things."

"Will Julia hate me?"

"No. Deep down inside she doesn't want to be tied to the mob. She doesn't want to go to jail as an accessory to a money laundering scheme."

"Go to jail?"

"Well, yes. We are all facing jail if we knowingly allow the mob to use our trust as a vehicle to launder money."

"I can't go to jail. Who would take care of Nathan?"

"Go sign the paper, Marge. Remember not only have I put my life on the line, but my granddaughter's as well. That's got to be worth something."

Marge was the first to sign the transfer order. Evelyn signed below her and Beatrice added her signature.

"What about Julia?"

"We don't ask her to sign," Marge said. "It would be too hard for her to do."

"I agree," Beatrice said. "Stanley, do you know if the properties we own near here were among the parcels that were transferred?"

"They were at the top of Harriet's list. She personally got the County Recorder to transfer your parcels first. Are your projects on those parcels?"

Beatrice nodded. "Mine is a Free Spay Clinic on land to the east of Arborville an Evelyn's is an Animal shelter west… you know, Evelyn, we could combine our projects. Why build two vet clinics when one would do. We could build one state of the art clinic and offer free spay and neuter services but also diagnosis and treat all kinds of ills in the strays we pick up. They don't come in healthy as a rule."

"What will we do with the other land?"

"Have you looked at it?"

"Yes, it's beautiful with a spring fed lake and everything. I wanted a park-like setting to encourage people to visit and adopt strays."

"We can still do that. Why not create a pretty artificial pond on the farm land. We could really landscape it cheaper than taking up two sites for what could be one project. There's that huge tree farm north of town. We can move in mature trees and everything."

Ed saw Beatrice's eyes shine as she spoke. He could tell Evelyn liked the idea of having a joint project.

"You could work on it together," Ed suggested. "Good ideas are just flowing out of you two."

Evelyn laughed. "They are, aren't they?"

"I think we should use the pond land for homes for all of us, a place where we can have room for our dogs to run."

"Harriet might retire here then," Evelyn said wistfully. "I miss her still."

"Nathan's always wanted to design his own house," Marge said, her enthusiasm rising. "He'll be so excited!"

Aleta and Stanley stayed perched on the crate after the ladies left. "Tell Grams her talk did it. How did she know to call Marge first?"

"She knows these ladies," Stanley said, punching in the number.

When Harriet responded, Stanley said, "It's signed."

"Witness it," Harriet said. "Note date and time."

Stanley smirked. As if he didn't know how to prepare a legal document that could wind up in court.

"The ladies are gung-ho to start their projects. Lots of enthusiasm. Beatrice and Evelyn are going to make theirs a joint project. They want to build houses on the land with the pond."

Harriet listened for a few more minutes then told Stanley that he should fax the document to the Atherton Bank immediately.

"Can't. Aleta's going to show in group. I can't dissuade her," Stanley said. "You want to talk her out of it. She has laryngitis so she can't argue for very long."

"She's a sensible girl," Harriet replied.

"Not at dog shows!" Stanley exclaimed, exasperated.

"Go before the Group starts. There's time."

Stanley sighed. "Give me the fax numbers."

Alfonso saw a patrol car drive up to the RV entry gate and wait there. He waited to see if there was going to be another arrest. Instead, to his surprise, Aleta Locke left with her lawyer friend, the one with the white patch on his ear.

The damned police chief was removing the target from the range. He cursed under his breath and then rushed toward his own car.

I still have a chance to catch them, he thought. If I follow them I'll know where the cops plan to stash them.

He ran across the lot as the police car was backing up the one lane drive. He kept his eye on the patrol car as it reached the lot, spun around and headed toward town. He clicked his remote to unlock his car door and was out of the lot and on the road leading to town in half a minute. A bit of speed brought him close enough to follow easily. It didn't hurt that it was a numbered black and white.

In downtown Willow Glen, the patrol car stopped and its two passengers exited and ducked under the yellow police tape covering a doorway and disappeared inside the building.

Mariana looked up and saw the broken window in the upstairs office.

They'll be alone, he reasoned. No staff.

He guessed there would be a back entrance and drove around the corner and into the alley. He backed his car into an empty space and got out.

What could be more perfect, he thought. No clients would interrupt them. Two of the back doors were marked with store names to facilitate deliveries. The one at the end of the section was unmarked.

It was also locked.

He slid a bank card down the slit between the door and the frame and pushed back the lock. He slipped quietly inside.

He heard voices upstairs. They were still here. He looked across the lobby and through the window in the front door. He spotted the nose of the patrol car. He was out of sight of the cop.

He screwed the silencer on his gun.

Upstairs Stanley leaned over and kissed Aleta on the neck and she giggled. He whispered in her ear. "Someone came in the back door. Follow my lead."

Shocked, she stiffened.

Unexpectedly, he kissed her on her mouth. It was a sweet, albeit short kiss and she relaxed a bit.

"Why are you in such a rush just to go back that dreary house of Evelyn's? What's there?"

"It's been a long day. I'm exhausted. I want to sleep in a regular bed tonight."

"It won't be much longer," Stanley announced.

"How much is not much?" she asked, taking her clue from him.

"Two and a half minutes," Stanley responded.

"I'm going to time you," Aleta said.

"Done!" Stanley exclaimed.

"All the faxes have been sent?"

"Yep."

"Put the copies in your safe," Aleta said. "Hey, where does this door lead?"

Now Stanley picked up his clue from her.

"To the adjoining office."

"Is it empty?"

"Why? Are you interested?"

"I could be."

"Lock up. We'll go out through that office."

Aleta closed the door and threw the bolt.

She leaned against the door white faced. Stanley was looking at the monitor. A small light flickered on.

"He took the bait," Stanley said. "Hurry!"

Back in the patrol car, Stanley said, "Get us out of here and radio a nearby unit to check out the lot behind my office. A man broke into my hall downstairs, but when he heard voices, he left. I think he went next door."

The officer radioed a break-in in progress and said the suspect was possibly in parking lot behind Stanley Praetzel's office.

"Tell them he's armed," Praetzel said.

"Are you sure?" the young cop asked.

"He was there to kill us."

"Why did he leave?"

"He heard us say we were going next door."

The young officer relayed the remaining information adding, "He's the last one guys. See if you can catch him."

"Why didn't you call 911?" the driver asked.

"He was too close," Stanley said.

Aleta broke in,

"Tell Milani about Evelyn's. He could go there looking for us."

Milani was told and set up a trap. He caught someone in it—a rabbit when he was trying for a fox.

Louie Barnes was restocking his aunt's refrigerator with fresh oranges. He and his oranges were taken into custody.

The stakeout group reset the trap, worried that the arrest of Louie, despite having been accomplished with plainclothesmen and unmarked car, might still have made the fox wary.

Stanley returned to the show grounds to share in the celebration over Marge Tobias having taken a Group 4 with Anya who had sparkled in the ring. Marge kept saying she hadn't shown well, but Beatrice said she had a new exuberance and it traveled right down the lead to Anya. She added that Jason's confession had done the trick. Marge hated being suspected of trying to harm Nathan.

Stanley and Aleta snuck out of camp to watch Lyle West show Beatrice's Scottie. The judge remembered Lyle and Cassie from the Scottie ring, and when Cassie was even showier in the Group ring, she was walked out with a Group 3 rosette.

The whole camp was excited over the upcoming Sporting Group with two of their own in the field.

Because the interior of the metal barn had become unbearably hot in the late afternoon, the Show Committee moved the last three groups outside. Clouds had moved in and a slight breeze had come up. Working, Herding and

Sporting were all dogs with heavy coats. The handlers welcomed the decision.

Stanley surveyed the crowd repeatedly. He was nervous about Aleta being so exposed. Stanley was still shaken by their close encounter at his office. Lyle hoped aloud that his presence might have a detrimental effect on a hit man's plans. He told Stanley that he had alerted his officers to be especially watchful. Still Stanley fretted. He'd finally found a woman he wanted to share the rest of his life with, and while other men worried over what kind of flowers to send, he worried over where the bullet would hit.

He saw Aleta look at him and wink. He smiled. It was the least he could do. She was obviously having such a good time.

Idly, he watched a family cross the grounds, the young boy was kicking a soccer ball along the ground in front of him. Topaz spotted the ball just as his turn came to be judged. The boy kicked the ball toward the ring and Topaz rose to full alert, his tail wagging furiously. He loved to play soccer. Evelyn played with him all the time.

The mother bent over and told the boy to pick up the ball. He did so, and ball in hand, he sauntered over toward the ring, pushed his way between a couple of adults and stood just beyond the rope.

Topaz spotted him as he gaited back toward the judge. Aleta turned him so he was facing the boy with the black and white ball. Topaz's ears perked, his mouth opened slightly and his eyes glistened in anticipation. He leaned slightly forward and his topline came into perfect alignment, the angulation of his rear legs was accentuated and his shoulder muscles rippled under his shimmering golden coat. The judge missed none of these changes and mentally placed Topaz in the top four.

After all the dogs had been evaluated the judge came back down the line. Lyle smiled and Morgan cocked his head and looked at him quizzically. When the judge came to Topaz, the ball slipped from the boy's hand and rolled into the ring. Topaz bolted and Aleta lost her grip on the thin lead. Topaz ran to the ball quickly and nosed it back to the boy then spun around and trotted back, a satisfied look on his face and pride in his stride. It was an unusual display and the judge decided not to fault the dog for his action. The dog was obviously a soccer player. Topaz took first. Morgan captured second. It was a stunning victory for the group outside the ring.

Everyone joshed with Lyle about having one of his kids toss a duck in the air when Morgan was in the ring and he smiled and said, "This is Topaz's day. He deserved the win!"

Stanley hugged Aleta when she emerged from the ring.

"You were marvelous!" he said.

He would have said more, but suddenly, she was spun out of his arms by her taller, handsomer ex-boyfriend, Conan Lloyd, who likewise hugged her. However, his hug was more a sexual embrace than a congratulatory hug and his kiss was proprietary. He was claiming her as his in front of the world.

"You beat everyone," he exalted.

"The dog did the winning," Aleta corrected. "He showed himself."

"Hey, don't you go telling me what's what," Conan said. "I saw you move around the ring. Hell, I couldn't take my eyes off you."

"You're embarrassing me," Aleta whispered. "Please don't say another word."

"I'm just being happy for you," Conan stated. "You've been wanting me to share in your hobby, so I'm sharing."

She pulled away and walked toward the ring where the photographer was waiting.

"Forget him," Lyle West said. "Time for pictures."

"Can't you arrest him again?" Aleta whispered half-seriously as they walked.

"For saying you were beautiful in the ring?" Lyle asked.

Aleta blushed. "But he's acting as if… well…"

"Hey, I'm going to cop to his argument. It's better than saying you out handled me."

When Topaz stood on the platform for his photo, he looked old and tired. Evelyn told the photographer to wait. She didn't want a bad picture. She ran over to the boy with the ball and bought his ball for a hundred bucks. The boy's mother told him he could get a new soccer ball and a baseball glove.

When she returned with the ball, Topaz came alive. She threw the ball in the air and the photographer caught Topaz's expectant look as his eyes followed the ball's trajectory.

The judge congratulated Evelyn. "You breed good dogs," he said, "and this old boy is in great shape. I was proud to put him up."

Evelyn's smile lasted for hours.

Stanley was waiting for her when the photo session was over. "Are we done?"

"Not yet," Aleta said. "Right now we need to cool Topaz down. He's pretty tired. I'm not sure he can handle one more competition."

As she spoke, Evelyn came over and took Topaz. "Lyle loaned me Morgan's cool coat."

"Where's Morgan?"

"Jason went back to wake Julia and took him."

"What can I do?"

"Stay with me," Aleta said her voice giving out again. All her clear speech had been garnered up for her confrontation with Conan. She dared not look around for fear of making eye contact. She headed for the shade of a large tree while the Working Group filed into the ring.

She and Stanley settled down together, their backs against the thick trunk of the ancient oak. Stanley poured water from his bottle onto his handkerchief and wrung it out. Aleta draped the cool wetness on her face and leaned her head back slightly, letting it rest on the tree.

The breeze was light but it felt good against her throat. The cool cloth coupled with the shade and inactivity was refreshing her when a familiar baritone voice spurted, "What happened to your neck?"

Aleta didn't remove the cloth.

"Tell him," she croaked.

Her hand reached for Stanley's arm and gripped it lightly. Stanley briefly recounted Aleta's second brush with an assassin.

Conan was incensed. "And you didn't take her away?"

"She wanted to show Topaz," Stanley responded coolly.

"Are you an idiot or a jackass or both!" Conan raved. "Who puts a... a friend in such danger. Well, this stops now."

He started toward her. Aleta sensed it and her mouth moved. Stanley leaned over, "If he touches me..."

He patted her hand.

"What did she say?" Conan demanded.

"That if you lay a hand on her, she'll have you arrested."

Furious, Conan glared at the man with the big nose and close set eyes.

"You've got your hand on hers!" he stormed.

It was a weak statement because he didn't know if the threat came from Aleta or Stanley.

"She has hers on mine as well," he replied. "You're too rough. You hurt her neck with that wild kiss of yours before. Now she can't speak again."

Stanley didn't know how much of what he was saying was true but when Aleta squeezed his hand lightly he knew she liked what he'd said.

"Sit down," Stanley said. "And be quiet. You're making a spectacle of yourself."

Conan's rage flared. "Caring about her is making a spectacle? Showing enthusiasm because she won is wrong?

That's illogical. No wonder you have to work as a children's advocate. You haven't the smarts to tackle grownup cases."

Aleta's hand squeezed Stanley's. She took in a deep breath through the wet cloth. Maybe the moisture would refresh her throat enough to speak.

Stanley realized only that Conan was upsetting her. He motioned to a nearby cop.

"Get West," he said.

He radioed West, who was talking with Martha Cook.

West appraised the situation as he walked over. He arrived with a message, "Mrs. Cook has invited Mr. Lloyd to join her to watch the rest of the show."

"Who the hell is that," Conan asked.

"A woman with a chair beside her," Stanley said. "You'll have a front row seat."

Conan saw the empty seat next to an extremely old lady. "Is she crazy? Why would I want to do that?"

"She thought since this was your first show, she could help you understand."

"So she's an expert, huh?" Conan's tone was derisive.

"No, it's her first show too," Stanley quipped, "But she listens."

West continued, "She's usually too busy working to take a day off so it's a rare treat to have her here."

"Working? At what? Baking cookies?"

"She has a cook to do that."

"Going to tea parties?"

"You saw the Cook Construction signs when you drove from the airport?"

"So?"

"She's Cook Construction."

"So she's rich," Conan said. "I know a lot of rich old ladies. They all take a shine to me, but you tell her I'm busy. I got to talk this girl here into leaving this damned place."

"Before she goes in the ring?"

"She's been. She's won twice. That should do her for a while. It's a lot of nonsense anyways, not something she should risk her life over."

"I must admit I agree with him there," Stanley said. "But it's her choice."

"Don't be stupid. It's not her choice. Not when she's being stupid!" He reached down and grabbed her arm and yanked her to her feet and announced, "We're leaving."

Aleta pulled her arm away. "No!"

"Don't be an ass, Aleta! You aren't thinking straight. You'll thank me after we get back home where it's safe," Conan said, grabbing her arm again.

She looked at Stanley.

"Arrest him for assault," Stanley said and West signaled his man to do it.

"You can't do this. It's harassment. It's false arrest. I'll have your job."

Aleta tried to speak when Stanley said, "West reads lips. He has a deaf brother and he went to deaf school with him."

Aleta's face relaxed and she mouthed. "I'll back you up. I told him not to touch me or I'd have him arrested. I'm keeping my promise. He hasn't the right to force me to comply with his wishes."

"Gotcha," West smiled. "Boy! Give you a lip reader, and you are very vocal."

"If she can't speak," Stanley put in, "can she show?"

"Judges don't want you to speak," West said.

As Conan was being led away, Aleta tapped West on the arm and mouthed, "Maybe if I keep having him arrested, he'll leave me alone."

"No chance," West said. "But he'll soon learn he has to restrain from getting physical with you. So how do you feel, are you ready for Best in Show?"

The Dane went in first, followed by the Afghan with Tom Wilson on him. Aleta followed Tom and wasn't too sure that had been a wise move; although if Topaz was on, he'd be faster than the Bearded Collie that fell in behind him. If he didn't move quickly enough, he'd lose in the first go around.

Unknown to Aleta, Topaz's nose had picked up the scent of a bitch in season. And she was long coated and moving right in front of him. He had no problem with prejudice. A bitch in season was fair game for any dog. The first dog to mount her won.

Topaz almost overran the hound that was flying around the ring; however, Aleta had a stronger grip on the leash this time and held him in check.

Standing in line, Topaz rose into his best stance. It was a natural act, meant to attract a female. The Afghan never turned around, but males are persistent and Topaz held the pose until the hound moved up to be examined individually. Aleta knew Topaz had caught the judge's eye. She didn't know why he was showing so well, but the Best in Show judging went relatively quickly. All the dogs were the best of their groups. The judge just looked for one with an extra spark, a display of confidence, a surge of energy that made him stand out on that day, at the moment the judge's eye was on him.

Aleta knew Topaz had made an impression twice but she was certain the hound had as well. And the Bichon was a big winner. His reputation preceded him into the ring as did the Pomeranian's.

When stacked for the individual examination, the Great Dane looked regal. Aleta's heart sank briefly. These dogs were too good, and their handlers too well known. She had an older dog, one who'd never won the top prize, one with no rep at all, being handled by an unknown.

When it came Topaz's turn, the judge smiled at Aleta and commented, "I guess an in-season bitch brings out the best in any dog," and Aleta knew why Topaz was so charged up. Nothing like a female ready to be bred to get a male's hormones racing.

The question was could she keep him showy with the bitch at the end of the line and him facing away from her. Aleta stacked him quickly and moved in front of him. The wound began to burn again, and she shook he head. Doing that had helped minutely when she'd done it before.

It woke Topaz up and he rose on his toes and stretched forward. His tail started to wag slowly, gracefully as he cocked his head and looked at Aleta quizzically. The judge approached in time to catch the look. Then he quickly went over the dog. Aleta relaxed and fed Topaz a bit of liver. He was in superb physical shape. The judge's hands measured the shoulder layback, ran down to feel the depth of barrel, lightly brushed the topline, checked the number of testicles which was perfunctory at this level and came to rest on the heavy musculature of the thigh.

When he stepped back, Aleta moved to get Topaz to move his head slightly toward the judge. It didn't work because behind Aleta, lying at Evelyn's feet was his beloved soccer ball. His ears perked and his tail wagged faster. His excitement fired up his muscles into a new state of tenseness. Aleta was delighted.

Topaz moved down and back with a smooth controlled gait and, upon the wave from the judge, was taken straight into circling the ring to the end of the line without a single break in his stride. It was done in a fluid motion, with both dog and handler in complete harmony like dancers waltzing across the floor.

Aleta took a deep breath when she stopped. The judge went over the remaining four dogs, checking the line occasionally. Unlike in the Group ring, the Best in Show judge needed someone who remained showy from beginning to end.

Aleta's scalp burned. The sun had come out from behind the clouds and while it was late and therefore not as hot as midday, Aleta's burned skin rebelled at even the hint of heat.

She shook her head several times to allay her discomfort. Topaz watched her with curiosity. He wagged his tail. This display was fascinating. And while he wasn't as charged as before, his joy was obvious.

After the last dog had been examined, the judge came down the line slowly. Aleta needed to pull one more bit of magic from her bag of tricks. She tried to say, "Soccer", believing the word would excite the dog one last time. Her voice, however, failed her and came out as a croak, the word unrecognizable.

Topaz, being a Golden Retriever, and naturally oriented to pleasing his person, cocked his head as he tried to figure out the command. His tail wagged harder to tell her he was ready to obey. It was a new look and the judge found himself again taken with the unknown dog and his unknown handler.

He pointed at Aleta and Topaz. It took Tom Wilson turning and congratulating her for her to realize that it was she and Topaz who'd won. Others crowded around and Aleta realized that the cheers had been for her.

Evelyn stood outside the ring and sobbed. It was a miracle. Her beloved Topaz had done it.

Chapter 21

Immediately after Aleta's big win, Martha Cook told the people sitting near her that she'd ordered a catered barbecue that evening. The announcement was greeted with enthusiasm. Martha Cook never spared any expense.

One hour earlier, in a large Winnebago crossing the border from Wyoming to South Dakota, Ron Maxwell commented, "He turned with us."

"I know he's following us," Harriet Locke said.

"Let's just test your theory," Ron said. "When we get to the park, I'll stop for information and see if he pulls in with us."

The information station, however, was too isolated and Ron, remembering the attack on Harriet back at this place, passed it explaining that he'd stop at the lodge near Legion Lake that had maps. He'd visited Custer National Park a number of years ago and he'd stayed in a cabin nestled in the pine-shaded hills that that dipped down toward small lakes.

He told Harriet he'd driven the eighteen-mile Wild Life Loop Road at sunset and seen bison and pronghorn, white tail and turkeys.

"No elk though. They are hard to spot I was told," Ron said.

Harriet was enamored with the beauty of the rock formations and couldn't help but exclaim at the sight of full grown pines that survived from seeds dropped in cracks between the huge boulders. She marveled aloud at their very existence in a spot where there seemed to be no soil.

The animals Ron talked about, however, were scarce. The road was too widely travelled. The day still too young.

When Ron pulled into the parking lot, the maroon Datsun that had been following them drove on. Harriet saw it turn onto the road leading to the cabins and disappear; however, a few minutes later it reappeared. The man had turned around. Now he was waiting.

Ron took a long time talking with several people gathered around the cashier in the souvenir shop. Harriet picked out a sweat shirt and a couple of tee shirts with buffalo heads on them. One was Aleta's size.

She was still upset that Aleta hadn't taken her warning not to go to Stanley's office seriously enough to stay away.

Harriet knew the first two had seemed to Aleta to be based on prior knowledge that something was wrong. After all, she'd talked with both women on the telephone earlier. However, her warnings were based on a strong presentiment that the danger was immediate. It was more than a guess.

But, her warning about the danger at the office had popped out of her mouth unbidden. The minute Aleta mentioned her plans Harriet saw the danger in her mind's eye and the warning gushed out without forethought. No matter how it came, Harriet expected Aleta to heed it.

That she almost died reinforced her feeling that God was giving her these premonitions. Somehow He was vested in what was going on with the Tontine Trust.

Only if that was true, why couldn't she see when and where the guy following them was going to attack. Why was her mind crowded with premonitions about Julia's future?"

Every time she thought of Julia she thought about Sodom and Gomorrah and Lot's family escaping the destruction because they listened to God's prophet and left their home.

Julia had to do the same thing. It was important that she leave her son without looking back.

She won't listen to me, Harriet argued silently as she plucked a soft buffalo plush toy from the open rack and walked over to the cashier.

And she'll hate me, she added in her silent argument. And if I say that you want me to tell her this, she and everyone else will think I'm crazy. Aleta didn't take her seriously enough before. And I thought she'd believe me for sure.

Gathering her purchases she joined Ron who was buying sandwiches, soup, coffee, milk and chips.

We're stocked, Harriet almost said; but, then Ron suggested they each buy an ice cream cone and Harriet kept still. Buying treats was fun. And they'd had little enough of that on this trip thus far.

When they climbed back in the RV, Harriet asked Ron, "Do you have a plan?"

"Yep."

"Are you going to tell me what it is?"

"We're going to see if we can see some buffalo."

"They told you about a road, didn't they?" Harriet asked. "You know he'll just follow us."

"Not if I play it right," Ron said enigmatically.

Several miles up the road, Ron pulled over to the side of the road and parked just past a road leading to the right. He told Harriet to get out and collect rocks. Harriet spotted several alabaster white rocks lying in the short grass and had a sudden urge to have one so she climbed out, uncharacteristically compliant.

Once on the ground, she picked up a white rock, turned it over, saw that it was stained on the underside and, spotting another a few feet further ahead, she went for it. On the way, she saw a rusty red rock and picked it up. A glint of metal led her to pick up the one that contained specks of shiny silver mixed in with a myriad of other bits of colorful rock. She turned the rock over and tucked it into her growing collection.

As she moved along the roadside, Ron followed her in the Winnebago whose huge broad side protected her from a possible assault by a passing car.

As Ron Maxwell had predicted, the car behind him, after a short period of hesitation, was forced to pass.

Ron figured that whoever he was he'd wait for them up ahead where either a group of white-tailed deer or a single male bison would cause cars to slow down while people shot pictures.

As soon as the maroon Datsun went up over the small rise and disappeared around a curve, Ron called to Harriet. Her arms loaded with her treasures, she hurriedly climbed back into the RV. Ron backed up and then turned onto the side road.

Harriet went to the rear and watched the road they had just left for any sign of the maroon car.

Soon they were into a section of rock and Ponderosa pine surrounding a string of small grassy plains. In the middle of a third such plain was a herd of buffalo, a dozen of which were crossing the road. Ron moved down the road slowly as one would when approaching a herd of cattle. However, buffalo aren't cattle. A large bull took offense and faced the RV and snorted. Ron stopped and turned off the engine.

"Where do they think they're going?" Harriet asked. "There's no room on the side of the road they're heading for."

"I think we'd better settle down and wait until they've figured that out," Ron said.

Harriet looked out the large front windshield at the slow moving animals. "How about backing out?"

"Papa here wouldn't like it if we ran over one of his young ones."

Harriet looked through the rear view mirror.

"We're surrounded!" she exclaimed.

"Yep," Ron said. "They've got us alright."

"Can't we just inch forward?"

"That big one there says no," Ron reminded her. "We're in their space. And big as we are, they have the advantage. They can tip us over. We have no hope of moving even one of them."

Curiosity forced Harriet to silently count how many there were.

"Forty," she announced.

"Too bad we don't have a camera. No one's going to believe this," Ron said.

"Did you know this would happen?"

"Never dreamed we'd be so lucky."

Twenty minutes later, Ron suggested they eat. As they sat watching the buffalo, they nibbled on sandwiches and sipped lukewarm soup. Harriet slowly relaxed.

"It's like we're alone in the world," she observed.

"Peaceful, ain't it?"

"It certainly is," she replied. "And safe."

Shortly after that exchange, Ron decided to take a nap. He told Harriet to wake him if there was any movement in the herd.

Alone in the front seat, Harriet watched the huge creatures. Inexplicably, the story of Jonah popped into her head.

She tried to think of something else; but, the harder she tried the more persistent the thoughts were.

"This is not the belly of a whale!" she exclaimed aloud. She looked behind her. Through the open door she saw Ron lying across the bed, breathing lightly. He hadn't heard her.

She was so grateful. Embarrassed, she felt impelled to do something. She moved over into the driver's seat and without thinking turned the key in the ignition. She saw the head of the big bull turn toward her.

"I'm not afraid of you!" she said boldly.

She heard a snort just outside her window and looked straight into the eyes of an even bigger buffalo. He lowered his head and snorted again.

Harriet's fingers shook as she reached for the keys. The big one nudged the RV and it shook. Frightened, Harriet turned the key and killed the engine.

The bull in front of her flicked his tail and Harriet realized, she'd stirred something inside the two beasts. She froze in place and held her breath.

The bull in front of her laid down completely blocking the roadway. They couldn't go around. Not only were there buffalo milling all around the RV as if it were a tree, on the one side huge rocks would have hampered even a four wheel drive vehicle. On the other the slight drop away from the road would tip an RV.

How long do buffalo sleep? Harriet wondered. Her reason told her that the bull could be down a long time.

"Okay, God, you've got me," she said aloud. Her voice was softer this time. "Do you remember how angry Jonah was when You forgave Nineveh? Of course, You do. He got angry. And do You know why...? Well, I guess You do. Only, I want to say it anyway. Being a prophet is a thankless job. Either people don't believe you or they incarcerate you, which I guess is better than being beaten, or they hate you. Nobody loves a prophet!"

Having said that, she leaned back and closed her eyes. Her mind immediately pictured Elijah being taken up into the heavens in a chariot. Her mother had told her it was one of her father's favorite stories. He wanted to go that way. He didn't, but he died in his sleep, so God granted the heart of his wish.

"You win," she murmured. "You love Your prophets."

She kept her eyes closed and let herself drift off into a dreamless sleep.

Later, she would protest that there was no way, even subconsciously, that she would have lowered her window. But open it was.

Her head lolled against the frame and slipped downwards slowly. The snort smote her ear and her eyes flew open. Immediately they looked into one eye of a massive buffalo bull just inches away.

Startled she whipped her head back inside the RV. She sat stiffly upright unable to move as her fingers played with a bit of fuzz. She stared down at it and realized it had come from a buffalo. Surely, she hadn't reached out and tried to pet him.

Fear made her quake. Her heart raced and her stomach tightened. Both hands were shaking violently.

Touch was not something that was allowed by a wild animal.

She sat as still as she could, not daring to power up the window for fear that any movement might anger the bull even further. How could she have done such a thing? Even in her dreams she didn't do wild things.

She dared not turn her head to look at him. She didn't need to look to know he hadn't moved. She could smell the rank odor of the massive body and hear the air travel down his nose and back again. It made a faint rumble as it came and went.

Her heart pounded in her chest. She glanced over at the passenger seat. There sat her cell phone. She didn't remembering having it up front with her.

She picked it up and dialed Julia Danielson's cell. Jason answered. She heard the frustration in his voice. She asked him about it and he told her that Jason Junior had confessed to putting arsenic into Nathan's pills. He thought they were Marge's.

Harriet didn't need any more of an explanation. She sensed that the husband and wife were at a crossroads.

"God forbids you to help Jason Junior anymore," Harriet said bluntly, a bit surprised at the boldness of her own statement.

"I'm with you," Jason said, "but Julia can't let go."

"Let me speak to her," Harriet said. Jason handed the phone to his wife.

"Now, now, Harriet," were Julia's first words.

Harriet's response shocked her. "Since you've stopped speaking with God about this matter, He chose me to tell you what He wants you to do."

Incensed, Julia bit back. "I talk to God about Junior all the time."

"You tell Him what to do," Harriet said. "Now He wants you to listen."

"Who appointed you God's spokesperson?" Julia demanded angrily. "You think your words will sway me just because you say you heard them from God?"

"He wants you to let Jason Junior go so he can be truly restored to you."

"I'm not to help my own son?"

"Correct."

Julia was ready to do battle. "Jesus told us about the shepherd who left his flock to rescue one last sheep."

"And He also told us about the father who let his son go and spend his inheritance without interference. Eventually, the prodigal son was restored to his family but first degradation had to happen."

"We can argue Bible passages all night," Julia countered. "I don't think that was the message in that parable at all."

"I guess that's why God told me to tell you directly what He wants."

"I don't believe you!" Julia stated heatedly. "That's not the way He works."

"Look at the Old testament," Harriet said. "God sent prophets to people all the time."

"I know you think that because you guessed right three times that you've been blessed somehow and that now your thoughts are God's thoughts and your words, His words; but, much as you'd like to think so, they aren't."

"What would it take to convince you?"

"A prediction, no, three predictions about stuff that no one here could possible know would happen."

Harriet didn't even pause before speaking. Her voice was firm and strong.

"Before an hour has passed, three events will occur. Someone will burst into tears and you will seek to comfort her. You will save the life of one of your children. And you will almost be killed by one of your children."

"Those are terrible predictions!" Julia shouted. "Why are you doing this?"

"I'm not doing it. I'm just telling you what's about to happen."

"Not that last one!" Julia protested. "I know my children."

"All these things will come to pass within the hour," Harriet said solemnly.

"And when they don't you'll have some weird explanation," Julia countered. "Well, I don't believe you. I think you need to see a shrink and get rid of that guilt you're carrying around for killing a man and stop trying to take the speck out of my eye when you're got a log in your own!"

The phone went dead.

"She thinks I'm crazy," Harriet muttered. "And maybe I am. Maybe this is Your plan. While I might be safe in an institution, I don't like that choice."

She tossed the phone onto the passenger seat and it bounced onto the floor. She folded her arms and looked at it.

"Pick yourself up," she dared it. "I've spent my whole life being reasonable and rational, a person of intelligence, someone with foresight and I'm going to be remembered as a crazy old lady."

The bull that'd moved away during her mutterings returned and snorted at her. Immediately she regretted not closing the window when she had a chance. It seemed to be glaring at her.

Exasperated, she exclaimed,

"What do you mean I'm not done!?! I made the call. I said the words you put in my head. Why couldn't you speak to me... oh, I know... then I'd be told I had had an auditory hallucination. And showing me would be a visual hallucination. So what am I having? A mental hallucination. I'm sure there's a psychiatric term for what's happening to me. And why am I talking to a buffalo about this?"

Harriet paused. "Of course, there is the fact that you are a real buffalo. And I even have this soft, curly, brown lock of your hair in my hand. And Ron did see the herd. So that much of all this is real."

She leaned over and fished the cell phone from the floor. When she sat back up, she looked the bull buffalo in the eye and said, "I need to call Aleta."

He snorted but didn't move.

"Glad I have your approval," she said punching in Aleta's number.

"I was hoping you'd call, Grams," Aleta said. "Julia's not making much sense."

"Tell me everything she's saying."

The whole conversation was repeated. Julia hadn't changed a word.

"How much of it is true?" Aleta asked.

"Except for the part about me being crazy, it all is," Harriet said.

"Oh, Grams," Aleta moaned. "Don't tell me you heard God speak or have a vision."

"No, I didn't," Harriet replied matter-of-factly. "Do you know anything about buffalo?"

"A buffalo talked to you?" Aleta gasped. "Wait a minute, where did you come up against a buffalo?"

"They are huge, Aleta. Absolutely huge. They have the most massive heads."

"What has that got to do with your vision of what's going to happen to Julia?"

"We're stuck in the middle of a herd of them."

"You have a cell phone. Call a tow truck."

"Not that kind of stuck. We're surrounded by them."

"Where's Ron?"

"Sleeping."

"Sleeping?" The question came out coated with incredulity.

"We ate lunch and then this big one lay down on the road in front of us and Ron said it could be there for hours so he decided to take a nap."

"What about you? Did you doze off?"

"As a matter of fact, I did. And, evidently, I pressed the power button for the window. I opened my eyes and found myself staring at a huge bull straight in one eye. Can't stare into both that close. Their heads are too big. He was inches from my nose."

"How did a bull inches from your nose…?" Aleta couldn't think how to phrase her query. This was too weird for a reasonable exchange of words.

"He scared me, Aleta. Like Jonah being swallowed by the big fish," her grandmother finished.

"But where'd the prophecy come from?"

"Oh, that. God just put it in my mind."

"That's crazy."

"Well, it is pretty abnormal, but He's been feeding me prophecies since I shot Haze Spader."

"That's what you think they were," Aleta said, "but I'm not sure your intuition wasn't heightened by your experience.

"They were prophecies, Aleta. Little ones. It seems I've graduated."

"What'll we do if it doesn't come to pass?" Aleta asked. "Your credibility will be shot."

Suddenly, Harriet's voice changed. It carried a level of excitement that came over the phone. "Aleta, guess what? The buffalo are moving. Aleta, they're moving!"

Harriet's voice rose with enthusiasm. "They're actually making an opening. They're not only clearing the road, they're standing alongside it waiting for me to pass!"

Aleta heard her grandmother shout, "Ron, wake up! Look out the window!"

Suddenly, she was back on the phone. "This is an unbelievable sight, Aleta."

In the background, Aleta heard a shocked male voice utter a loud, "Wow!"

Without another word, Aleta hung up. Her grandmother would understand. It was time for her to join the party to celebrate her own miracle.

Chapter 22

Aleta rejoined the party and someone handed her a glass of wine. There was a lot of buzz about Harriet's conversation with Julia and Aleta sat down near Martha Cook and asked her what she thought.

"You just spoke with your grandmother, didn't you?"

"Yes," Aleta said, then smiled. "She was surrounded by buffalo. I guess she's somewhere where there are buffalo."

"Real or imagined?"

"Oh, real. I heard Ron say, 'Wow!'"

"Then I guess we'll just have to wait and see."

"But what do I do if...," she began. Emma, who had sensed her distress, wandered over and put her nose under her arm and lifted it. Unfortunately, Emma picked the arm holding the wine and her nudge upset the wine glass. The wine splashed onto the front of Aleta's outfit.

Aleta began to cry. "My other outfit's muddy. I only brought two." Once the tears began, she couldn't seem to stop them.

Julia rushed toward her. "You can borrow one of mine."

Aleta shook her head and struggled to smile. She wasn't successful. Words came out haltingly. "I'm too tall."

"I've got it. Kim, my daughter," Julia responded enthusiastically. "She's your height. She looks about the same size."

"Aleta can't leave the camp," Chief West interjected. "Can Kim bring over a couple outfits?"

"I'll call," Julia said. "She was going to paint her new apartment tonight so she'll be home."

After her mother's phone call, Kim scrambled to change and then selected three of her favorite outfits and hurried to her car.

She backed out of the driveway and had just moved the gear shift into drive when the boiler in the basement of her house exploded. She sat stunned in her car as she saw the whole second floor apartment drop onto her apartment and then both levels drop into the basement.

Kim's mind shifted into top speed accepting images so quickly that it seemed as if time had slowed to a crawl. The world seemed devoid of all life. There was just her and the collapsing building.

It was an old building, but Kim had liked the space it afforded and the nooks that were missing in the newer apartments. The rooms were irregularly shaped but she had a large bay window in the front shaded by a huge elm.

It was her first apartment, having just graduated from college in June, and all of her possessions had been moved into it. Her books, her CD's, her jewelry, her clothes, her stuffed animal collection, her tiny glass animal collection, her photos and videos, Her whole life was crushed by the falling walls and roof.

It was only a matter of seconds before the first spark ignited the wood dust, and with a loud whoosh the debris was enveloped in flame.

The fire engines roared onto the street minutes later; but, Kim knew what hadn't been pulverized by the collapse had been destroyed by the fire.

A tap on her window roused her.

"Will you move, please," a fireman said. "It's not safe here."

Kim nodded mutely and moved down the street. She crossed through the red on several intersections. Brakes screeched and horns honked, but Kim was oblivious to their racket. Her house had just burned down. She'd lost everything.

She drove down the two lane road to the fairgrounds and took the single gravel lane leading along the creek to the RV parking.

Still in a daze, Kim spotted a woman waving at her. The woman was standing at the side of the road. As Kim's eyes turned toward her, she turned the steering wheel. Her headlights caught the woman's surprised look and Kim realized it was her mother waving at her.

Kim saw her mother hastily try to avoid the oncoming car by backing up. Kim didn't see her mother trip over a fallen tree trunk and tumbled backward out of sight. Kim slammed on her brakes and her head bumped the windshield.

Jolted awake, Kim sounded her horn. She then fell forward on her horn and began to cry.

Moments later, Jason pulled his daughter from the car and held her. The two officers guarding the bridge were already in the water retrieving a comatose Julia.

"She saved my life," Kim sobbed as Jason, his arm around his daughter, walked her close to the men working on Julia.

"She saved my life and I do this," Julia repeated. "Oh God, why did this happen?"

Julia coughed and water gushed from her mouth.

"She's alive?" Kim choked out. "Tell me she's alive."

West, who'd run to the accident on Jason's heels, answered the distraught young girl's query. "She's alive. Your sounding the horn probably saved her."

Kim's smile was twisted into a grimace, "Yeah, after I caused her to fall in the first place."

"What did happen?" West asked kindly. "You're not accident prone."

"I am now," Kim said. "First my house explodes and then I knock my mother into a creek and she almost drowns."

"Your house?" West asked. "The old house over on Beech? I was called, but the fire chief is handling the investigation."

"Mine was the first floor front apartment. It had a bay window... and... Oh, Dad, everything I owned was in that apartment. My life was in that apartment."

"Kim, you're alive," Jason said. "Nothing else matters."

"If Mom hadn't called, I'd have been killed. I was in my car on the street when it blew up and caught fire. Dad, I couldn't move."

"You weren't supposed to," Jason said. "Sometimes being afraid keeps us safe."

"They told me to drive away. I was blocking the street," Kim sobbed. "They told me to drive away. I shouldn't have. I should have known better."

"You will next time," Jason soothed.

"I've got the clothes," Kim added. "I did do that right, huh, Dad."

"Kim, you did everything right!"

Kim managed a weak smile.

"Come; let's go see your mother."

"I've got to move my car."

"I'd rather you didn't drive anymore tonight," West said. "Two wet officers is all I can handle right now."

"I'm so sorry," Kim said contritely. "I really am."

"Will she be charged?" Jason asked apprehensively.

"No. Her wheels never left the roadway. She didn't hit her mother. And that's what my report will say."

"Thank you," Jason said. "Come, Kim, you will stay with us tonight."

Dr. Cook had just finished his examination when father and daughter entered. Julia was sitting on the couch wrapped in a blanket.

"Slight concussion," he said. "I'll check back in half an hour. She needs to stay awake tonight. With two of you here, you can take turns watching her."

"Kim is painting her apartment," Julia protested. "She can't stay."

"There was an explosion, Mom," Kim said. She rushed over and threw her arms around her mother and told her what had happened ending with, "I would have been killed if I wasn't getting my car to come here."

While she was speaking, Julia's face registered shock, gratitude, dismay and finally comprehension.

Julia stared at her husband not able to talk.

"Harriet was right," Jason said simply.

"Right about what?" Kim asked.

As her parents explained the prophesy to their daughter, Marge was telling those gathered around Martha Cook about Harriet's uncanny predictions.

"Well, it's not as if she had an accomplice," Ed said. "Emma didn't get a phone call from Harriet telling her to bump Aleta's arm."

Aleta reached over and snagged a bit of roast beef and handed it to the little black Lab, "You are truly a gift from God, Emma."

Emma wagged her tail, licked her lips and nudged Aleta's arm asking for another tidbit.

"Interesting," Martha murmured. "Her prophetic powers seemed to have more acumen today than a couple days ago."

"She told you she could prophesy?" Marge asked, her camera still in her hand running.

"I've never been able to see things so specifically," Martha said. "And my ability never increased."

"Harriet Locke appears to have developed into a full-fledged prophet," Stanley said.

"A psychic?" Marge asked.

"More of a prophet, I think," Stanley responded. "She prophesied about events interlinked in a time-locked sequence. The complexity of that boggles the mind."

Inside the Danielson's RV, the phone rang. Those outside heard the ring.

"That's Harriet," Marge said. "I need to go be with Nathan now."

Abruptly, she turned off her camera.

"I'll have a patrol car take you to the hospital," West said. He walked her over to one of the men on the bridge and told him to escort her all the way to Nathan's room.

Beatrice hurried after her. "Will you be back?"

"You bet," she said forcing a smile, "Camera in hand."

"Don't take Julia's desire to help her son personally. You know how it is with firstborns. Not all of them turn out the way your Nathan Junior did.

"He wasn't my firstborn," Marge said sadly. "I had to let go my first born to raise him."

"What are you talking about?" Beatrice asked as Ed joined them.

"Nothing," Marge said. "We all have our secrets. When Harriet shares hers, I'll share mine."

Walking back to the camp, Ed asked Beatrice why Marge's statement bothered her.

"She's right about secrets," Beatrice said. "I have one."

"I don't need to know it," Ed said. "I love you as is."

"I wonder what Marge meant when she said Nathan wasn't her first child."

"Her first baby could have been stillborn," Ed suggested.

"If it had died, she would have said something. No, her secret has shame attached, same as mine."

"So you wanna know what she's hiding?" Ed asked. "I'm a P.I. you know. It's what I do."

"I don't know," Beatrice hedged. "It seems wrong somehow. People should be allowed their secrets."

"Anybody know yours?"

"Evelyn does," Beatrice said. "She's my best friend."

"Want me to find out what Harriet's is?"

"Yes," Beatrice decided. "If Marge knows, then I want to know."

Ed grinned. "You're a bundle of contradictions. I love it."

Then he squeezed her hand and, holding hands, they started back to the camp.

Chapter 23

Jason opened the door of the RV and emerged obviously distraught. Dr. Cook rose and went over to him. Aleta followed.

"Harriet called," he said. "Julia's upset, I'm not sure keeping her awake is a good idea."

"Let me talk with her," Aleta said.

"She's not being reasonable," Jason warned.

"Let me try."

Jason stood back and Aleta entered. She asked Kim to wait outside and, reluctantly, Kim rose. She hesitated at the door.

"I have the power to help," Aleta said.

Julia waved her daughter out.

Aleta sat down in the chair opposite the couch. "You're distraught, but I have a solution that you might find palatable."

Julia huddled in her blanket and stared at this young woman. Her eyes dared Aleta to say she understood; but, Aleta didn't say that.

"Your son is in a lot of trouble and you want to help, correct?"

"I won't abandon him!" Julia declared.

"That's not the action I'm going to propose," Aleta began.

"Harriet did."

"Well, as Harriet was passing on God's wishes and as you obviously have no interest in following His suggestion, wise as it might be, I've been sent in."

"And who are you?"

"Harriet's protégé; but more importantly, the person with the power. First, we take care of the mob threat. We pay off Junior's gambling debt. We use funds in the Atherton Bank to do that, okay so far?"

Julia nodded, and her head raised a smidgeon out of its blanket shell. Aleta saw a flicker of true interest in her eyes.

"Then you sign the paper saying you vote against the transfer."

Julia's eyes suddenly widened and her brows shot up. "Why on earth would you tell me to do that?"

"Because the other ladies have already agreed that you can."

"We aren't transferring?"

"Oh, we're transferring. I've already faxed the confirmation of the transfer to Atherton."

"You did it without me."

"You were sleeping. No one could wake you. On top of that, your friends, whom you are willing to have killed, didn't want to force you to have to make a difficult choice."

Julia brushed aside the sarcasm.

"So, if I give Jason the paper, the mob will let him go?"

"Hey, let's get real here. They just won't kill him today. We both know he'll fall right back in the pit, that is, unless you stop him."

"How?"

"First you change your will. This hundred thousand is his inheritance. Your other children will understand that. Then killing you won't profit him."

"He'd never do that."

"Yes, he will."

"You're wrong. I know my son."

"Did you know he was capable of murder?"

"He wouldn't have gone through with it," Julia said.

Aleta's eyes flashed and her voice deepened as she growled, "If I hadn't come, Nathan would have died. Junior didn't intervene. I did. And when Marge was denied access to her husband he took no pity on her suffering. It was Ed who recognized the symptoms of arsenic poisoning. Jason knew what it was. He never said a word. He let her suffer."

The anger in Aleta's voice pierced Julia's heart and her head withdrew back into her blanket. "You're being cruel," she whined.

"You're the one who's being cruel. Your best friend is suffering as a result of your son's action and you refused to help."

"You don't understand. He's my son."

"Marge understands what you're going through better than you think she does. Your attitude is rubbing salt in an old wound of hers."

Julia looked at Aleta questioningly.

"Back to your son," Aleta said. "The Trust will supply a lawyer for Jason Junior. You choose."

"Lyle West's father. He's the best criminal lawyer around here," Julia said, decisiveness taking over her demeanor.

"I will arrange for him to be retained immediately," Aleta said. "But no bail."

"But they'll put him back in jail," Julia wailed.

"Which is where you want him. Out of danger. Inhibited from gambling. At least until negotiations are completed."

"He's innocent!" Julia said.

"He confessed."

"Well, he can take it back. I'm sure there's a technicality…," Julia said, her voice becoming strident.

"I doubt West made a technical error," Aleta shot back.

"Then there are extenuating circumstances. The mob. He can say they forced him."

"They didn't even know what he was doing. And, in fact, they told him to stop; but, since he'd targeted the wrong person, they didn't do anything more." Aleta responded. "He did this on his own."

"His gambling addiction...," Julia offered.

"And what caused your husband to stop?"

"He saw what it was doing to me and the kids."

"That hasn't worked with Junior, has it?"

"No."

"So he needs to suffer personally. It's his last hope. God brought us here to make that possible, but you must step aside and let it happen."

"I need to help," Julia whined. And Aleta recognized that her need stemmed from some psychological problem she wasn't equipped to handle.

"Help by letting God take over. He has his own way of working and so far He's done what you couldn't. He saved your son from committing murder. You didn't do that."

"I didn't know.

"God did. He acted. Now let Him finish."

"But..."

"You are thinking of this addiction as a splinter the like of which any mother can handle; but, this is more like a smashed head needing the surgical skill of a neurosurgeon. If you don't get out of the operating room, your son will die. Not only that, but you will have to live with the fact that you killed him."

"Did Harriet prophesy that?"

"My common sense can make that prediction. Certain consequences are inevitable," Aleta said. "I can't help with your addiction right now, but let me warn you about where it will lead. "If you lift a finger to help Junior, you will automatically forfeit your membership in the Tontine. It's in the rules."

"You're not leaving me a choice," Julia said.

"Oh, you have a choice," Aleta responded. "Just not one you like. Before you make one, however, I suggest you talk with your family."

Stanley, who was talking with Lyle West when Aleta came out of the Danielson's RV commented, "You look like the cat that just swallowed the mouse."

"That's the canary."

"No, the mouse. There's no smugness in your smile, just satisfaction."

Aleta was impressed with Stanley's acuity, but brushed aside her desire to talk about her encounter. "We have a ton of work to do."

"I have to get ready for Evelyn's hearing tomorrow."

Lyle West interposed quietly. "We arrested Louie Barnes. We confiscated the oranges he was putting in her refrigerator. Forensics has yet to get back to me, but we have him on breaking and entering."

"Evelyn won't press charges," Aleta said knowingly.

"We're counting on the oranges to seal his fate."

"How'd you catch him?"

"Stakeout. Our net was cast for a bigger fish."

"So the guy aiming for me is still out there?"

"We'll catch him. Tomorrow we'll be watching every ring. He'll be hanging around. But you're not bait. With Dr. Cook's warning about the sun, I guess you've done showing this weekend."

"I have commitments," Aleta protested.

"They'll understand," West said. "Conflicts are a part of the game."

"You're right!" Aleta said. "I need to see Tom Wilson."

"Mariana will have learned from yesterday," West pointed out, "He'll be looking for you in the Bulldog ring tomorrow."

"Right," Aleta said. "I'm counting on it."

With that comment she disappeared toward Tom's rig.

"Now what is she doing?"

"Juggling, I imagine," West said.

"Can't you confine her to this area?" Stanley asked plaintively.

Chapter 24

Stanley drove Aleta to Beatrice's house for the night. There were two guest bedrooms and each had its own bath. Stanley brought his briefcase and he and Aleta settled in for a long night of work.

By three Stanley called a halt and the two went to bed for four hours. With separate bathrooms, dressing in the morning went smoothly and they arrived at the show site by quarter to eight.

"I have to hurry," Aleta said. "I show at eight."

"Eight. You've only got ten minutes. What am I saying? You aren't going to go into any rings you were in yesterday."

"Wanna come?" Aleta said starting off toward the bridge.

"Where's the dog?"

"Waiting at the ring," came the reply.

Aleta took a devious path to the huge barn ducking around large bushes and traipsed along a path littered with twigs and tiny stones. The entrance itself was hidden from the view of the main rings out in the large field.

Stanley noticed that Aleta stayed out of the sun the entire way. He thought that was the reason for the devious path. He didn't know that Tom Wilson had mapped out the circuitous route which his assistants didn't take with his dogs. They were purposely led to the ring across the field where the grass was close cut and carpet-like.

The assistant picked up the armbands and stood off to the side while the class dogs were judged. Aleta joined her there and quietly took the French Bulldog, a brindle with apricot colored striping. He was a showy little dog whom Tom warned would stretch out his rear and thus smooth out his roach. He'd told Aleta to set his rear legs on the table and back him up on the ground to keep the roach in evidence. "His ears need to be at 11 and 1 o'clock," Tom had added. "He lays them flat when he wants to be petted."

Aleta smiled at the little dog and then shook her head. Her hair flew sideways and the Frenchie stared at the phenomenon. A curious dog, he kept his eyes on her face to see if that would happen again.

When he was on the table and the judge came toward him, Aleta swirled her hair and his ears went up. The timing was perfect.

She moved immediately to the next ring where she picked up a young Skye Terrier bitch Tom had contracted to finish. Aleta like the long coat that covered the dog's ears, eyes and every inch of her body. The coat skimmed along the floor when Aleta gaited her and the back rose and dropped like the waves on an almost still sea. She took the points but nothing else. Skye's don't mature enough to win the Breed until they're three or four. Tom didn't expect more than the points. Aleta was satisfied.

The Wire Fox Terrier was next. She needed to take the Breed on this one because Tom wanted him to make it into Group. When she accepted the Best of Breed ribbon, the judge asked her where Tom was.

"Showing my Lab Special for me," Aleta said. "I can't go into the sun today."

The Goldens were still showing in the outside ring and Marge was taping Evelyn going into the ring with Carmel when Aleta took the first of Marge's Doxies into the ring. Beatrice had fetched Marge's dogs and taken them to the huge metal barn where Aleta waited. Beatrice brought a second video camera and handed it to Stanley who was just beginning to appreciate the complexity of the arrangements made so Aleta could show dogs in the only area the person hunting her hadn't seen her in the day before. Not only did Aleta not come and go, she never left the building. The dogs were brought to her.

The Tontine women had figured that Marge was the key. She had recorded the action of the group including Aleta all day the day before. She was the constant. Today she was the diversion.

Marge was willing to scratch her dogs; but, Beatrice wouldn't hear of it.

"Aleta and I can handle them," she assured her. "Ed's going to help me take dogs back and forth."

Aleta again won the two points with Anya only when Beatrice took over Anya and Aleta took Rufus' lead, there was no one to show Lisa.

"Let me try," Stanley said boldly. Aleta looked at him and noticed he'd put on his suit again even though it was going to be another hot day. She resolved to ask him why he did that later.

"If Anya takes the Breed or Best Opposite, it'll be a major only if Lisa's in the ring," Beatrice argued. "And Lisa is an old hand at this. He'll do fine."

"Okay," Aleta agreed. "Just relax, Stanley, and enjoy yourself. The judge will help you if you need it."

Beatrice had Stanley give the camera to Ed. "Nathan will get a charge out of this," she commented.

Aleta led the group into the ring and Rufus who was Anya's grandfather and Lisa's father outdid both of his progeny and took top honors. Anya did capture the Best Opposite spot for a second major in two days. She was lively and energetic and an outstanding puppy in the judge's eyes and was rewarded accordingly.

The judge stopped Stanley on his way out.

"First time in the ring?"

"Did I ruin the dog's chances?" Stanley asked.

"It was close. The pup had more zest and I like that," the judge said. "Next time will be your turn."

Stanley left smiling.

When the photos were taken, Stanley asked the judge if he could be in a picture with Lisa. "It was my first time in the ring. There'll never be another first time. I'd like to remember it."

Aleta faded back next to the wall to keep from giggling at the wrong time.

Beatrice went into the ring and tried to get Lisa to look at her. The judge stacked her while Stanley just stood behind the table holding the lead and smiling.

As Aleta was standing in the shadow of one of the metal supporting beams, a man came through the door. He stepped immediately into the shadow on the other side of the door and Aleta watched him look at Stanley being photographed. Beatrice was next with Anya and Ed was filming it all. He turned the camera to her and she pointed at the man on the other side of the door. Ed kept the camera moving, but the man, visibly upset, left at once.

"Did you get him?" Aleta asked afterward.

"Don't know. Where's West?"

Aleta glanced at her watch. "In the Lab ring I would guess. You can't interrupt him.

"Why not?

"Because then everybody would know where I am."

Ed grew thoughtful. She was making sense. He decided he'd look around as he travelled with Beatrice to exchange dogs.

Alfonso Mariana, upset because he'd been caught by the camcorder, headed for the nearest men's room and exited it immediately. It was too open. As he did so he spotted the stables and strolled past them to the far side. There was a half-filled trash barrel on the far side. He stepped behind the building and began discarding his disguise. He peeled off the gray wig and the goatee and jammed them under the trash.

The gold-rimmed glasses he stuck in his pocket. He was stuck with the paunch. It was foam-filled and held in place with straps. His cane held a thin strong blade that he could extract with a twist of the handle, so he kept it with him.

What he couldn't figure out was where Aleta Locke was.

He had found three of the group whose faces he had familiarized himself with yesterday. The man in the ring was the lawyer accompanying her to the office in Willow Glen yesterday. Considering the laughter he'd heard, he fully believed they were tight. Yet the man was in the ring and the woman encouraging the dog to pose was definitely not Aleta Locke.

She hadn't shown up at any of the rings she was at yesterday. He'd noticed her odd, unruly haircut only because it was reddish. The thought had crossed his mind that she might have cut her hair; but, he'd dismissed it. Women were loath to cut their hair.

If she was here, he decided, she'd show that dog she won with yesterday. The paper had carried a photo of her emerging from the woods and another of her winning later that day. An arrest had been made within minutes of the attack. No motive for the attack was known.

He'd seen the man carried away on a stretcher and wondered how he'd been injured. There was a rumor that a dog had bitten him; but, when the Bulldog had emerged from the woods, Mariana had thought it more likely that the dog had scared him and he'd stumbled and tripped trying to get away.

Thus, while Ed and Beatrice were leaving the barn with the Doxies, Alfonso Mariana passed them on his way toward the ring where the Golden Retrievers were scheduled to be shown. He'd searched his catalog for a dog named Topaz which he remembered from the news article and found it in the last section of the Golden Retriever listings. They were in Ring 10 right next to the Labs. He was walking swiftly because he knew the way.

Ed remembered that the mysterious stranger had a cane; but, he also recalled whitish hair and a goatee and glasses. This man had none of those.

As the man hurried toward the main rings, Ed relaxed and temporarily dismissed the suspicion that had crossed his mind.

Aleta and Stanley waited outside the side entrance and talked in low tones.

"I have something I want to give you," Stanley said partway through their conversation.

He took a handkerchief from his pocket and carefully unfolded it. Inside was a lovely ruby ring.

"It was my grandmother's. I'd like you to wear it on the third finger of your left hand."

"Why?" Aleta asked repressing a smile.

"Because I'd like you to marry me."

"Why?" Aleta asked.

"Because I love you."

"Okay," Aleta said and stuck out her hand. "I had to be sure that was the reason."

"You mean you thought I was after your vast fortune?"

"Well, are you?"

"I'll admit it does make you more desirable," Stanley joshed, finally aware that he was being teased. "That and your haircut."

Aleta sobered. "Suppose it never grows back?"

"Then it doesn't," Stanley said. "Louie's wife has a great plastic surgeon. Maybe he'll give us a group rate. Your scalp and my nose."

"I like your nose," Aleta said.

"Nobody likes my nose," Stanley countered. "Not even my parents."

"It's distinctive. You're distinctive. In fact, you're quite wonderful," Aleta said. "You want to know why I accepted so readily."

"Well, since you said 'yes,' it's got to be positive, so go ahead and tell me."

"You understood how important it was that Lisa be shown and you were willing to humiliate yourself to take her into the ring. But the topper was, you had a photo taken and you smiled as if you'd won something. And you had. You won me."

"Well, let's go in and show some more. I can't wait to see what I win next."

Tom Wilson was at ringside with the same male Scottie he'd shown the day before when Aleta and Stanley reentered the building.

"How'd you do with Drummer?" Aleta asked.

"A JAM again. I'm glad Lyle only shows that one dog," Tom said. "Oh, by the way, your boyfriend was there looking for you."

"Ex," Aleta said. She held up her hand. In the light streaming in from the open doorway the ruby sparkled.

"So Stanley did it!" Tom exclaimed. "Good for him!"

"Did you tell Conan where I was?"

"I told him to watch for Topaz and pointed to the Golden ring. I left him paging through his catalog.

"I owe you!"

"Enough to show the Bulldog in Group. George Sciretta is adamant about it. He says since the Group will be indoors, there won't be any sun."

So intense was everyone on what was happening in the Scottie ring that no one saw Alfonso Mariana enter the building. He'd remembered yesterday that Tom Wilson and Aleta were somehow connected. He didn't understand how; but, when Tom directed Conan to the ring where the Goldens were showing, Mariana got suspicious. So far no one had hinted they had any idea where Aleta was. So when Tom pointed one way and went another, Mariana followed Tom.

He watched Aleta in the ring in her bright pink outfit with its close fitting skirt, long enough to be modest, short enough to allow long strides and its waist high jacket which rose up when she bent over to show a bare slender waist. When Cassie stood on the table, Aleta stood behind her and the black Scottie had a contrasting wall of pink so her profile was highly visible.

Alfonso Mariana watched as Aleta's dog appeared to challenge any who came too close. The tail went rigid, the muscles tensed and the little dog stared her competitors into backing away.

Feisty, Mariana thought.

He thought that would cause her defeat, but he was wrong. Aleta and her Scottie won.

Mariana stayed hidden in the shadows along the wall and surveyed the area. There were three exits, not two. He wandered over to the little side door and looked down the shaded dirt path. He guessed it was little used and realized it was the path Aleta used which is why he hadn't spotted her earlier. He had wondered how he could have missed a redhead in a bright pink outfit.

His pager vibrated and he backed out the way he had entered the building and made his call. No one ever beeped him unless plans had been changed.

"Al here," he said.

"The Ciccones are arriving at O'Hare in thirty minutes," said the voice. "I want it done."

"Can't rush it."

"Thirty minutes!" the voice demanded before the phone went dead.

Mariana wished he didn't have the padded paunch to contend with. Slender and agile, he knew ordinarily he could slip in and out of the bushes with ease.

Well, what was, was, he thought as he walked along the little used side of the big building.

His escape was quickly conceived. He would run back to the stable area, retrieve his hair and whiskers, put on his gold-rimmed glasses, throw the cane onto the stable roof and walk out of the fairgrounds. He was certain that Aleta would not have a contingent of friends accompanying her. She would sneak away just as unobtrusively as she had slipped into the barn.

He glanced through the door before ducking behind a large bush near the side entrance. He glimpsed the pink suit near the photographer setting up the shoot and knew Aleta and her dog were the subjects. He sunk back into the bushes.

Through the leaves he caught a bit of brown passing by. He was glad Aleta wore pink. The minute he spotted the color, he could simply spring out of the bush, stab her, and run.

He donned plastic gloves and wiped the handle of the cane and the sheath that held it. He knew he had time. He'd watched a few photography sessions.

Aleta was all smiles when she came out of the ring. She showed her ring to George Sciretta who'd showed up personally to ask her to show his Bulldog.

"I'm not sure I can do any better than Tom can," she said.

Beatrice took off with two of her Scotties, and Ed followed, his filming duties over.

"He's got a French Bulldog to show in Group today," George said. "His assistant would need to show Maggie. Please."

"If Chief West says it's okay," Aleta said.

"Where do I find him?"

"Either by the main rings or at camp."

George hurried off, a determined look on his chubby face. Aleta looked around. "Where's Beatrice?"

"They left," Stanley said.

"I can't let Cassie walk on the dirt path. Too much debris."

"I'll carry her," Stanley offered, but when he reached down Cassie backed away.

"Let me," Aleta said, swooping her up. "Just to the grass. It's not that far."

Stanley walked on Aleta's right which put Cassie closest to the bush row in which Alfonso Mariana was hiding.

Cassie's nose caught the man's scent. It had a mixture of adrenaline and sweat combined. Cassie didn't like it. He was too close to her space.

She tried to leap from Aleta's arms; but, Aleta held her first attempt in check. The man tensed.

Cassie grew more desperate. She pushed against Aleta's shoulder and dug into her stomach with her back paws. Then she twisted and pushed on Aleta's arm with her front paws while shoving away from Aleta's body with her rear legs. Her movement was quick and she managed to get free. Aleta stumbled as she tried to catch her.

Ed and Beatrice heard a man yell just as they reached the bridge. They turned in time to see Cassie running toward them.

Ed caught the little dog and handed the leash to Beatrice and ran toward the exit he knew Stanley and Aleta had used.

West was already on the scene when he got there. He listened to Aleta saying she hadn't seen her attacker at all but she'd felt his fat soft belly when he fell on her. It was like a cushion, she said.

Ed lifted the camera in his hand and began to scroll back on the roll. "I think I took a picture of him."

West came over and looked at the video of the man hovering in the shadow.

"I punched him in the eye," Stanley said as an officer applied a tourniquet to stem the bleeding. "I know I connected because his nose spouted blood."

West looked at Aleta. "If he fell on you, your jacket might have some of his blood."

"You can have it, but not yet," Aleta said. "I don't have a blouse on."

At that moment, Conan tried to burst through the gathering crowd, insisting he was Aleta's fiancé.

West looked at Aleta. It was her call. She held up the hand with the ruby ring on the third finger. "It's from Stanley. I'm his fiancé."

"Aleta, you can't!" Conan cried. "We haven't talked. I was planning to ask you to marry me!"

The crowd parted. This was as interesting as the stabbing.

Conan stepped forward. "You don't have to settle for second best." He nodded toward Stanley.

"You are so right!" Aleta countered. "I realized that when Stanley proposed. I almost settled for you."

The crowd murmured.

"She's not thinking straight," Conan said weakly, moving away. "Trauma can do that."

Slowly, he inched his way back through the crowd murmuring, "I can wait."

The paramedics drove across the field to where Stanley lay on the far side of the building.

West showed Stanley the tiny video picture after they'd loaded him onto the stretcher.

"The man I saw didn't have gray hair or glasses. He was young with dark hair," Stanley said.

"The gray hair and glasses could have been a disguise," Ed suggested.

"Well, what do my men look for?"

"A man with a shiner," Stanley said.

Aleta went to him and took his hand. She couldn't speak. There were tears in her eyes.

He smiled. "I want to see a video of you winning with Maggie."

Chapter 25

Ed went to the main gate to aid the officers stationed there. West had one of his men accompany Aleta to her RV to change. He and another officer scoured the grounds around the barn. West thought of bringing out Morgan to track the man but that would take a while and the attacker might easily slip away as he was pursuing where he had been.

Ed remembered the man's height and body configuration. He reasoned that since he was still wearing the padding that it was strapped on beneath his clothes. He would want a disguise to leave the grounds. All exits were guarded. The only way out was through the main gate.

The stream of people leaving the show grounds was steady as the judging in the rings finished and the people and their dogs were done. Mariana joined a large group of people heading toward the exit.

At the entrance, Mariana recognized the short balding man as the one who had video trapped him earlier; but, he kept his pace steady until he'd passed the two cops.

Suddenly, he heard a voice shout, "Mariana, stop!"

He kept going.

"That's him!" Ed shouted.

Mariana leaped away from the group and sprinted down the parking lot. He was surprised to find two policemen not only running after him; but gaining on him.

Damn! He thought. These yokels were fit.

When a squad came at him from the far end of the lot, its lights flashing and siren blasting his ear drums, he stopped and put his hands in the air. They would have to say they arrested a gray-haired man with whiskers and glasses. He knew the lawyer had caught a glimpse of him. He'd have to say he wasn't gray-haired. And that man who took the video had him in the building in his disguise. They couldn't prove he took it off.

He'd be free in a day.

Aleta called her grandmother and told her the good news and the bad news.

"Didn't you know I was going to be attacked?" Aleta asked straightforwardly.

"No, my dear, I didn't. I'm so sorry about Stanley."

"Why didn't you know?"

"I have no idea. I can't see the future except in isolated instances."

"So people can die and you wouldn't be able to foretell it?"

"Afraid that's true," Harriet said. "I'm not God. Just a most reluctant prophet."

"So what's your next prophesy?"

"It has nothing to do with you."

"Grams, I need Stanley. I can't get this task finished within the time constraints by myself. Please don't leave me in the dark."

The old voice hesitated but a brief second. "It's Julia's family. They are in grave danger."

"Julia's? She signed the retraction."

"Her grandchildren and children are the targets."

"Targets of what?"

"All I can say is they are going to be systematically terrorized. Everything is such a jumble I don't know who the exact targets are. I see houses burning down, children dragged from their beds, bombs planted under cars."

"Why pick on her? She's done what was asked of her.

"She's the weakest link."

"The terror arrived in Chicago a few minutes ago. It will soon spread your way within hours."

"Did you tell her?"

"Yes, but I'm sensing reluctance on her part to leave Junior."

"Let me try. I think I know someone who can help."

In the Danielson's RV, Aleta got straight to the point. "The transfer is still hanging by a thread. The Ciccone Family has flown in from Vegas. Grams says you're the first target."

"Why me?" Julia asked looking at Chief West who had come in with Aleta.

"You're the most vulnerable and the one that's the hardest to protect. Your family is scattered all over the county."

"I can't leave Junior without telling him what's happening," Julia cried.

"He's the reason we're all in this mess," Jason said.

"No, he's not," Julia protested. The scowls made her back off. "Well, not the whole reason."

"Dad, I vote we take the family somewhere safe," Kim said.

"Your mother has the money."

"You think we care about that!" Kim exclaimed. "Our lives are more important than money to all of us but Junior."

"He can't help it," Julia said defensively.

"He doesn't want to help it!" Kim exploded. "And you're addicted to helping Junior. If I had any sense, I'd give up trying to reason with you too."

"Those are harsh words,' Julia scolded. "I know you didn't mean them."

"I've never meant anything more in my life," Kim insisted. "Jason's got a hold on you as strong as gambling has on him. No wonder he can't break free. He sees that you can't."

Julia scowled at her daughter.

"Now is no time for a family fight," she declared.

Kim's vice shook as she tried to get through to her mother. "We're talking about my life, Mother. I want to live. Doesn't that mean anything to you?"

"Junior is my child too. I have an obligation to him," Julia insisted. "He needs to know I love him."

Kim broke down and cried. Her father gathered her into his arms.

"The worst part is," Aleta broke in, "is that they'll start with your dogs."

Julia blanched.

"Drummer will be first. He'll be tortured and left dying on your doorstep. And he won't understand what he did wrong."

Tears welled up in Julia's eyes and spilled out down her cheeks. Soon she was crying. The vision was too horrible to handle. Everyone waited and after a few minutes, she gulped and wiped her eyes.

"Why would they do that?" she choked.

"Because it's no risk for big gain," Aleta said. "Animals are expendable. Your grandchildren would be next. They'll just disappear. Kidnapping's too risky. But there's a black market for small children. They'll wind up in a warehouse somewhere chained to a poster bed until they're sold. Should I go on?"

"No, don't," Julia said. "You're right. Jason is safe. It's time to protect the others."

"We have a plan," Aleta said.

An hour later, Jason, Julia and their daughter Kim drove Evelyn's van through the RV gate and onto the road leading away from the fairgrounds. Evelyn had agreed to the exchange and dogs and clothes were quickly transferred.

Lyle West called Tom Milani who had his officers round up all the Danielson offspring and lead them in their vehicles to a gas station ten miles west of Willow Glen where they filled up on gas, snacks and drinks and tried to guess what was happening while they waited for their parents and an explanation.

It came along with the Chief of Police who confiscated every cell phone after he explained that the police received a reliable tip that the entire Danielson family was in danger, and as a result, the entire family was being put under protective custody and being moved to a safe location.

The loudest protests flowed nonstop from the three eldest sons. They had jobs. Milani told them no one had a choice. No one could contact anyone. All calls would be relayed to a special phone at police headquarters, and worried friends and family would be reassured. Everyone's place of business would be contacted on Monday and told a family emergency took them out of town.

Once at the site, the police officers accompanying them would do all the shopping. The family would be confined to the house and fenced grounds. The dogs would be confined to the kennels on the grounds. The small pets, cats, hamsters and fish left behind would be gathered that afternoon and spend their days cared for at a vet clinic. The houses would be watched, mail and papers picked up, outside gardens cared for by professional house sitters. Valuables would be boxed and stored at police headquarters.

Instructions on the everything from the whereabouts of jewelry to the names of cats were hastily gathered from the families.

Jason with Julia and Kim and the three Labs led the caravan in Evelyn's van. An unmarked police car carrying two officers and the youngest of the Danielson children, both college students, followed. Three more vehicles lined up. A second unmarked car took up the rear. The two police cars were in constant radio communications. Chief Milani had sent a lieutenant.

Chief Lyle West had told the group remaining that it was important no one outside the group be aware of the Danielson's departure. They all agreed to enjoy the show.

Harriet had only predicted bad news for Jason and Julia's family. The rest of them had a respite.

Ed manned the barbecue, flipping hamburgers which smelled so tempting everyone had one including the police officers guarding the camp. Lauren and Lyle came over and a few other neighbors joined in. From a distance, Dennis Rimmel surveyed the group. He mistook Lauren West for Julia and so reported that everyone was there except the lawyer that had been knifed.

Chapter 26

Forty miles away, in Chicago the Ciccone brothers huddled over the round oak table in the library of the Chicago boss Frank Catalano. Hearty roast beef sandwiches and fine wine had been served and the doors closed as the men deliberated their first move.

Rimmel had secured only one letter of opposition to the transfer thus far. He hadn't been allowed into the camp and had to limit his activities to the times the principals exited to show their dogs and they had told him repeatedly they wouldn't talk business until after the show was over.

"Think they're stalling?" Big Mike asked.

"No," Ray said. "Only Julia was motivated to act. We had Junior by the balls and we were squeezing hard. He was the key."

"Do the others have children?" Big Mike asked.

"The Tobias' have a son," Tony Ciccone, the middle brother, reported. "The husband's the one in the hospital half dead. Be easier to take him out than the son."

"The other two have no kids, just dogs," Ray added, adroitly dashing cold water on Tony's suggestion. "And that's the easiest way to begin."

"What? Snatch their mutts?" Big Mike asked.

"Show dogs. According to Rimmel these people are really hung up on their dogs," Ray pointed out. "And the beauty of this is that we can kidnap a dog and it can't identify us and if we kill it, we can toss the body anywhere."

"Just doing in dogs ain't strong enough," Big Mike declared.. "We got one night. We gotta make a really strong statement."

"We could go after Julia's children," Ray suggested.

"What for?" Tony asked belligerently.

"Because we don't have a motive. Nothing terrorizes a person more than to hit a target for no reason," Ray said.

"Then how do they get scared into doing what we ask?" Tony charged. The middle brother, Tony was the shortest of the three and developed a chip on his shoulder early on.

"We get Junior to tell them," Ray said. "I hear he's got a great lawyer; but no one is putting up his bail."

"How do you know that?" Tony pressed.

"When the lawyer handed over the hundred grand, he said that was the end. The family was done."

Big Mike took out a cigar and lit it. That quieted the brothers. He did this when he wanted to think.

After a couple of puffs, he said, "We should send someone to see if she puts up the bail. If she don't, we do."

"You want one of us to go?" Tony asked.

"No, Frank's got someone who can do the job."

Frank nodded agreeably. "No problem."

"You also got a guy what can let Junior know we need him to deliver a message to his mother, right?"

"Sure, Big Mike. No problem."

"Have him punctuate it a little, huh, Frank."

"No problem, Big Mike."

Big Mike continued laying out his plan.

"We hit the houses at night three hours apart," he decided. "Each hit is harder than the last."

"I say we hit the others at the same time," Tony proposed.

"They don't have children," Ray pointed out.

"They got dogs," Tony said. "Take the Tobias broad."

"What about her?"

"She'll be in the hospital with her husband," Tony said. "Seems to me her dogs will be easy to grab. I can do that."

"Dumb idea," Ray said annoyed. "It'll put us right in the mix."

"Naw. I'll do it same time the first of the Danielson's houses goes up. Give me a perfect alibi," Tony said. "It says we ain't doing the bad shit, just the little shit."

"He may have a point, Ray," Big Mike reasoned.

"I don't like it!" Ray shot back.

"So, he's caught. So what?" Big Mike said. "Tony, you do the wiener dogs."

Tony smirked. He'd won over Ray. The guy was all talk and no action and sometimes that pissed off Big Mike.

"Louie Barnes messed up this afternoon," Frank Catalano reported. "He got caught filling his aunt's refrigerator with spiked oranges. No judge is gonna give him power of attorney after that shit."

"So we do her dogs too," Tony said. "And we get Pacheco to snatch Beatrice's mutts."

"I'll go along with using Pacheco," Ray said. "But I can take care of Evelyn in court. The Tontine Trust has power of attorney already on file. But here's where it gets interesting. Harriet Locke has been hiring attorneys for the Trust on her own. It takes three to agree on an attorney for the Trust. Stanley Praetzel probably wasn't properly hired. And Aleta Locke can't practice in Illinois so she can't represent the Tontine either."

"So what are you saying?"

"I'm saying we can lock Evelyn Barnes back up unless she agrees to sign our paper renouncing the transfer," Ray said. "And Stanley Praetzel can't stop us."

"I like it," Mike said.

Chapter 27

At the Fairgrounds, Ed Ornstein took Chief West aside just as the first group started.

"I didn't want to say nothing in front of the ladies, but I think Emma just came in season and I want her to have puppies."

"Are they sold?"

"Seven of them are. Two want boys, three want girls and two don't care," Ed said. "I got a hundred dollars up front. They all want a black Lab like Emma. Now that I'm going with Beatrice, I thought I'd like to try for one of us to keep to show if you think Emma's good enough."

Lyle didn't answer that question, but rather asked several more about what genetic testing had been done and Ed told him he'd done all that because the lady with the stud asked for it.

"She lives in Illinois," he said. "Sandy Parker. You know her?"

"She has good Labs."

"As good as Morgan and Drummer."

"She bred Morgan."

"I thought you did that."

"I owned Morgan's father."

"That counts then, huh?"

"In a different way."

"So does she own studs as good as Morgan?"

"She owns his brother, Casper."

"That's who I'm getting."

"Go for it," Lyle said warmly. "And do think about keeping a show bitch for yourself. Emma could produce one with Morgan's brother as the father. He has a lot of bone. Your pups should be very nice."

"You won't get offended?"

"No," Lyle said matter-of-factly, "you made a commitment before we even met; I believe you should honor it."

"I'd like to see Casper first. Is that okay?"

"I can't see why it wouldn't be," Lyle said. "But if I were you, I'd go out there soon."

"How soon?"

"Well, you're staying with Evelyn and she has a stud dog. You could wind up with an accidental breeding. I'd go right after the show. It's only a couple hours west of here. You should probably leave Emma there."

"I can't do that."

"Talk to Beatrice. She'll help you figure out your options."

Ed did just that.

"Sure," Beatrice said when he told her. "We'll go right away; but how about tomorrow morning after a good night's sleep."

"Tomorrow's fine," Ed said.

"How long's Emma been in season?"

"Don't really know," Ed said. "She's so clean."

"We'll check her at Sandy's place and go from there," Beatrice said. "Will Aleta mind that you're gone?"

"It'll only be for half a day," Ed said.

The Toy Group was first at two. The barn was hot, but livable. Terriers were next and Aleta took in Cassie whose temper hadn't completely cooled from the encounter at the door. The barn was a place full of enemies according to the little Scottie bitch.

Cassie was young and inexperienced. After a few more shows, she might calm down a bit. But even though this was her second time in Group and the dog behind her was the same Westie male that was there yesterday, she still spun around and told him to back off which he did. Satisfied, she walked beautifully for Aleta after keeping her stack on the table.

Beatrice had groomed her perfectly. There wasn't a hair out of place. She'd been bathed for a second time that morning and her coat glistened and flowed evenly as she moved.

The judge moved her up into second place in front of a Wire Fox Terrier. Cassie paused before she entered the line, and stared at the Wire Fox Terrier who took a step back to make room. The Norwich Terrier spun around and Cassie jumped forward slightly and he made way as well. Cassie required lots of space. The judge noticed the interplay. There was something special about the Scottie. She was moved up to the head of the line and led the group around the ring. The first was hers.

Beatrice was ecstatic. She hugged Ed and then cried on his shoulder.

Aleta handed her the leash. "I'm in the next group with Maggie. Photos will have to wait."

Tom Wilson went in with the French Bulldog, Aleta followed with Maggie. The bulky pied bitch came into the ring, her rolling gait causing her back to sway at every step. She began to pant almost immediately. The heat inside the barn had risen. Too many people. Too many dogs. Too much sun too long on a metal roof. Too little fresh air coming through the huge wide open doors.

Tom shared his spray with Aleta but it did little good. Maggie was hot. After the first run, she lay down and rolled over, her ears lying splayed out from the side of her head, her feet in the air. Rather than urge her to rise, Aleta took the spray bottle and rubbed her belly, spraying her feet lightly.

The water was barely cool, but it helped. Maggie's panting became less labored.

As each dog was examined and came to the end of the line, they moved past Maggie, smiling at the only dog that'd made herself comfortable in the heat.

Aleta kept her eye on the line. The Frenchie was her bookmark. By now Tom had a new spray bottle for him.

When Tom was getting ready for the table, Aleta coaxed Maggie into a stand, quickly wiped her back and ears with a damp cloth, and moved to the front of the line.

The judge smiled at her, "Had a good nap, did we?"

"Yes, thank you, we did," Aleta replied grinning. Her scalp was as usual causing her a problem. The heat caused perspiration to rise between the hairs on her head. Aleta was sure it would drip down her face any second. She refused to wipe her face with the cloth she used to wipe the saliva from Maggie's jowl. She shook her head slightly. The burning stopped.

Maggie, who's been waiting for this wonderful perk, lifted her head. Her profile was perfect and natural. The judge liked what he saw.

Despite the heat, Maggie moved in a lively fashion, the rolls on her back gently rolling as she trotted.

Back in line, the judge walked past the posed dogs selecting those he wanted a second look at. Maggie made the cut. The judge came down the shorter line and Maggie stepped out of her stack and faced the judge. Her front was her best feature, but Maggie wasn't thinking about that. She'd stepped out because the Chow in front of her was blocking her view.

Maggie took a group one and George Sciretta, true to his nature, screeched his utter happiness and clapped his hands. The French Bulldog took third and Tom leaned past the second place Dalmatian and congratulated Aleta.

"Good day for Bulldogs," he grinned.

"Wash and wear dogs took the day," said the handler of the fourth place dog, a Chinese SharPei.

"Are they going to move the Groups outside again," Aleta asked. "It's like an oven in here."

"They're talking about it," Tom said. "That's the Superintendent and the Show Chairman huddled in the corner."

The announcement came a few minutes later.

"Good news for me," Tom said. "I'm showing my Afghan."

Aleta turned to one of Tom's assistants. "I'm keeping Maggie with me. Bring me a cool coat and an umbrella and we'll park at ringside and wait."

The assistant rushed off.

"Will you take Maggie in?" Tom asked.

"I was assuming you would," Aleta said.

"I have my Afghan. He's apt to make Group, but even if he doesn't, George will want you."

"I need to talk with Beatrice," Aleta said. "I did win in Group with Cassie."

But Beatrice surprised her, "I was planning to take Cassie in. I thought you weren't supposed to expose that head of yours to sunlight."

"I'm not," Aleta said. "And if Tom's Afghan doesn't win Group, he'll take Maggie in."

"Even if he does, he has assistants," Beatrice scolded.

"I know. I know," Aleta said. Her heart was pounding. She had an opportunity to go into 'Best in Show' again. How could she not do it? The sun would be lower in the sky by five. Surely, it wouldn't be serious to be in the ring for twenty minutes with her head exposed when the sun was low in the sky.

After the photographs, Tom's assistant fastened the cool coat on Maggie and handed Aleta an umbrella. Ed was fetching chairs for them. While she waited next to the building Aleta wished Stanley was there. He had made the weekend so much more fun.

The Herding Group was already in the ring by the time Beatrice came to fetch her.

"Someone's sitting in our chairs," Aleta said.

"You mean you don't recognize him without a shirt and tie? My, you two have had a circumspect relationship."

Aleta's first reaction was shock. "What's he doing here?"

"Waiting for you would be my guess," Beatrice snickered.

But Aleta wasn't amused.

"I mean what's he doing out of the hospital?"

"Recovering, I guess. Having a bit of fun. Checking up on you. Take your pick."

But Aleta had dropped her sense of humor back at the spot where the shock of seeing him had hit her.

"What are you doing here?" she demanded as she sat down. Maggie settled at her feet.

"Waiting for you," he grinned. "Aren't you glad to see me?"

"Shouldn't you be in the hospital recovering?"

"Did that," he replied evenly with a small smile. He recognized her anger as springing from concern and he was touched.

"It looked bad."

"It was," Stanley said. "They operated right away."

"It takes a long time to recover from an anesthetic. I know."

"I had a local."

"And they agreed?" Aleta gasped.

"I wanted to watch," Stanley grinned, knowing her imagination would make her gag. He was right.

"I heard you won twice in a row!" Stanley said.

Aleta wasn't so easily switched. "Did the doctor okay this or are you here against doctor's orders?"

"Let's say we compromised."

"What did you promise?"

"You aren't going to let me off the hook, are you?"

"No."

"No driving. And no helping at camp. I'm to sit and watch for the rest of the day. Oh yes, and you have to cut my food."

"If I give you any after such a stunt," Aleta snapped. "And who is going to monitor your behavior?"

"My doctor," Stanley grinned. "He's standing behind us, so I'm glad you arrived with an umbrella over your head."

"He can't be here," Aleta wailed.

"When we heard you'd won, we both figured you'd not be able to resist going in for Best of Show."

"What is he going to do?"

"He's going to watch you."

"That's it?"

"He said I need to learn early that redheads can't be stopped once they've decided to do something. You see, I said you were reasonable. And he laughed."

"So he's here to collect his bet?"

"Oh, I think he wanted to come. I was a good excuse."

Aleta reached over and took his right hand and squeezed it. "I'm glad you're here."

"We're also here to watch Lyle in the Sporting Group. It's nice to finish this as an ordinary day."

Marge won a Group Two with Rufus who outdid himself in the ring. The same judge had judged him earlier and remembered him. Ed followed her with the camera, knowing Nathan would enjoy watching his dog being photographed more than watching the Working Group.

Seeing Ed move off, Aleta said to Stanley, "He's going to breed Emma. You want a Lab?"

"Two dogs?" Stanley queried.

"Maggie's breeding could be over a year away," Aleta said. "Don't you like Emma?"

"I like Morgan better."

"So you want a male Lab and a female Bulldog," Aleta said. "That would work."

"So, who's Ed breeding Emma to?"

"Morgan's half-brother. Same father."

"So the pup might look like Morgan?"

"Good chance.

"Okay then," Stanley said.

"You'll need a house."

"I have a house."

"Why did we stay at Beatrice's then?"

"My house only has one bedroom," Stanley said. "It's a work in progress."

"How much progress?"

"It has a bedroom."

"You said that," Aleta pressed. "What else."

"A nice bath."

"What else?"

"A fireplace."

Aleta gasped. "That's it? A bedroom, bath and fireplace?"

"A couple other rooms but they don't have names yet."

"How can you have rooms without names?" Aleta queried. "Do you have a place where you watch TV?"

"My bedroom."

"Where do you cook?"

"That's yet to be decided. Either to the left or right of the front door."

"Didn't your house have a kitchen when you bought it?"

"I put the bedroom there. I liked the view."

"Where'd you move the kitchen?"

"I didn't. Just tore it out."

"Boy, you'd never sell the place without a kitchen."

"I don't want to sell it. I like working on it."

"How long have you been working on it?"

"Five years."

"One room in five years," Aleta mused. "That means we won't have a nursery until our twenty-fifth wedding anniversary."

"I could work on that next."

"Kitchen first, then a study. We are lawyers after all. Then a family room to relax in with our dogs. A dining room for dinners and a living room to entertain in."

"Have to hurry up the process some, won't I?" Stanley asked.

"Oh, yes, and we need a grooming room for the dogs." Aleta responded lightly.

"I guess it's a good thing I have room to expand."

"How much room are we talking about?"

"Seventy six acres."

"That's practically a farm!"

"I have an orchard. Apple trees."

Aleta settled back. "I love apples."

Ray and Tony Ciccone came through the show entrance unobserved. The show was winding down. Catalog sales had closed up. A few vendors were beginning to pack up while keeping an eye out for last minute buyers. People were pulling carts loaded with crates and equipment through the main entrance to the parking lot.

"This was a mistake," Ray said.

"There's Rimmel," Tony said waving.

"Hey, play it cool. We don't want the cops to notice us."

Tony looked around. "Boy, these cops are good. They sorta stand in the shady spots."

"It's a hot day," Ray sneered. "Where would you stand?"

"Usually, they're out where you can see them. It keeps the order."

"They aren't here to keep order. They're here to catch us."

Dennis Rimmel walked up and shook the hands of both men.

"One of the Tontine members, Marge Tobias, is going to that big building to get her picture taken," Rimmel said. "I thought I'd follow her."

"Tell us who else is here," Ray said.

Rimmel pointed out others as they walked.

Rimmel approached Marge Tobias and congratulated her. Ed videotaped the exchange then turned his camera and caught the Ciccone brothers unawares.

"Is it possible we could get together later?" Rimmel asked politely.

"I need to go see my husband as soon as this is over."

"Perhaps I can take the dogs home for you and wait until you come home, and we can talk then."

"Oh my," Marge said. "I forgot about the dogs. Julia was going to take them but..."

Ed interrupted her. "Beatrice and I will take care of your dogs. Don't you worry. Perhaps Mr. Rimmel would be kind enough to drive you to the hospital. We'll have a lot to do to air all those little guys."

Rimmel stepped in. "It would be my pleasure."

"Okay," Marge agreed. "I'll meet you at the bridge after Best in Show."

"You're next," Ed said, stepping back and turning on the camcorder.

Dennis retreated and joined the Ciccone brothers. "I'm driving her to the hospital to see her husband. We'll be alone in the car."

After Rimmel left, Ed warned Marge not to refer to Julia again.

"I almost gave it away, didn't I?" Marge sighed.

"I don't think they caught on," Ed replied.

"I wish I could stay at the hospital overnight," Marge mused. "I hate going home to an empty house."

"Do it," Ed agreed. He pocketed the tape with the Ciccone brothers on it and inserted a fresh one.

The video camera recorded every moment of the Sporting Group competition. Evelyn was energized and her energy flowed through her hands and infused equal excitement to Topaz with every touch. The Irish Setter was grace in motion. The tiny pasty-colored Cocker kicked his longhaired shirt with every step. His back stayed straight as the legs moved the body along. The German Shorthaired Pointer held a regal stack and moved true. But it was Lyle West and his black Lab Morgan who matched them all. Morgan moved with easy grace, both front and rear parallel, stacked with his thick otter tail held straight behind his short-coupled body. He was a beautifully balanced dog and in the end, the judge rewarded him with a Group One.

Ed caught up to Lyle when he exited the ring.

"We need to talk," he said.

Lyle handed Morgan to his wife and asked her to cool him down, then he walked away with Ed.

"The Ciccones are here," Ed announced. "I got them on tape."

"How many?"

"Two. They're hanging with Dennis Rimmel."

"Is Aleta in danger?"

"Actually, we're all safe right now. When whatever is going to happen, happens, they will be somewhere else with and alibi."

"Good! I've never taken a Best in Show and today's judge started out in Labs."

"And that's good?"

"Not if your dog has faults."

The Best in Show contenders lined up outside the ring. Tom Wilson was the first with his Afghan hound. The Doberman and Collie were next followed by Lyle with

Morgan. Beatrice followed Lyle with her Scottie, Cassie, and then came the two dogs with rolling gaits, the Bulldog and the slow-moving Pekingese.

Every dog in the ring was a breed that had frequently won the top prize except for the Labrador. He was an everyman's dog, a regular dog, one common around any town in the country. He was the number one dog in the nation, but not in the eyes of many show judges.

Some dogs don't present as well in the breed ring as others. The Lab was one of those dogs.

Yet, here was Morgan, resplendent in his shiny black coat wagging his thick tail and enjoying the extra treats another ring session meant. Lyle was an exacting master. One foot wrong, and the liver was held back. Morgan tested him every time they walked in the ring. Lyle never expected less than perfect.

A Lab is not made for precision as a Golden is. Goldens love to train and do it right every time. Topaz put every foot down right. He showed with almost the same perfection as the day before, still this time Morgan came out on top. Topaz took a Group Four and Evelyn was happy. It had been a great weekend for her.

But for Lyle, the top prize was still beckoning him. Morgan sensed his master's excitement and stepped forward. Lyle put up a finger and he put his paw back. Evidently, they weren't going to play.

He wagged his tail. What were they going to do? He was in a ring with some really strange dogs. There was a big ball of fluff at the end of the line and a feisty little black dog dancing around behind him telling him to move. Lyle's poised finger told him to stay. He ignored the little dog and lifted his nose.

There was a bitch in season somewhere. His nose told him the dog directly in front was a male. The bitch was in front of him somewhere. Both of the dogs had long coats. Morgan didn't care. He preferred black to yellow dogs but one was gray and the other had a partially black coat. They'd do.

The judge took his time with Morgan. The coat was thick, a harsh outer coat with a soft inner coat. The tail felt good in his hands. He loved a good otter tail. He felt the muscles in the rear legs and they matched the rest of the powerful body. The judge stepped back and looked at Morgan's head again. The soft expression in the eyes, the strong thick muzzle, and the broad head matched the standard, but more than that. The whole head was in beautiful balance. No doubt about it, he was one handsome dog.

His heart was won at that moment, and yet Morgan had not done anything but be himself.

Lyle circled and then took his place at the back of the line and watched Beatrice. Cassie was lively and yet walked like a little lady, letting her black skirt sway gently as she moved.

"Good job!" Lyle told Beatrice when she came back into the line behind him. They both watched the Bulldog who was next.

Aleta had managed to restore Maggie's spirit and she was a happy hunk of dog that most spectators found appealing. Her gentle nature was obvious. She kept her eye on Aleta. Lyle waited for Aleta to shake her head. He wasn't disappointed. The hair twirled and Maggie wagged her stub of a tail and then followed Aleta up and back in that slow rolling gait peculiar to the Bulldog. She was excited and happy and the judge looked at her a long time. Here's another winner, he thought.

The Peke was last. He was a multiple Best in Show winner and going over him the judge understood why. There was a solid dog under all that hair.

While the Peke was moving to the end of the line, the judge walked down the line one more time. He paused in front of the Lab and again in front of the Bulldog. They were brief pauses but the crowd knew who was in contention.

When the judge pointed to Morgan, it was Ed whose shout matched Lauren's, although others were quick to join in. Claps also came from the officers close enough to see the win.

This would be a topic of conversation around the police station for a long time.

Chapter 28

George Sciretta rushed up to Aleta. "Did you see the judge look at Maggie?"

"He really liked her," Aleta said. "You have a prize bitch here Mr. Sciretta. You'll do well with her."

"Do you realize she got half her points this weekend thanks to you?"

"Tom got some of those points," Aleta said.

"Are you staying in the area? I mean, can you be her handler?"

"She has one of the best handlers in the country now."

"But I'd be your first client. So Maggie and I would always be special to you."

"Mr. Sciretta, I'm a lawyer. Tom's a professional handler."

"You could be too," the little rotund man said eagerly. "Here's my card. Think about it. Please. I'll give you one of her puppies when I breed her."

"That's the best offer I've ever had," Aleta said. "Stanley was saying he wanted a Bulldog puppy. He fell in love with Maggie."

"Heck, as a thank you for today, you can count on one," George said.

Aleta handed George his dog's leash and went over to where Stanley was sitting and leaned over and whispered, "I just earned a Bulldog puppy for you. It's my engagement gift to you."

"And what am I supposed to give you?"

"You mean besides the most beautiful ring in the world?" Aleta smiled. She loved besting him in a verbal exchange.

"How about a kitchen?"

"Where?"

"In our house."

"I'm not sure I should say yes. It may not be the most important thing the house needs."

"What would be more important?"

"A roof. A floor. Windows. Heating. Stuff like that…"

"The roof doesn't leak, the floor is solid and the windows have glass in them. Some of them you can even see through."

"I want heating!" Aleta declared.

"Okay anything else?"

"I can't think of anything."

"How about a front door?"

Aleta's shocked expression delighted Stanley. "Come on. I'm teasing you. It's very unfinished, but it's livable."

Dennis Rimmel walked Marge Tobias back to the bridge and waited for her to gather that day's video cartridges to show her husband. He watched as her friends crowded around with messages for Nathan.

It's a close-knit group, he thought, one Harriet Locke is nowhere near at the moment. He needed to make a strong, succinct pitch.

As they walked back to the car, he asked how her husband was doing. She talked about how sick he'd been and that he'd just finished the Dimercaprol treatment which she explained was used to bind the arsenic so it could be flushed out of his system. His recovery had been complicated by a bout with pulmonary edema. He wasn't out of the woods yet.

Tonight they were starting him on Penicillamine to bring arsenic level down even further.

"It might not work," she finished.

"If it doesn't, what's next?"

"Kidney dialysis."

"Sounds like there are some precarious days ahead for him," Rimmel said sympathetically. "We at the bank want to ease your burden a bit."

"I think everything's being done," Marge replied, not quite ready to discuss the transfer. They were ten minutes from the hospital.

"I was thinking of facilitating the payment of his hospital bill," Rimmel said. "I can see that the medical bills are paid promptly if you'll just sign to reverse the transfer. Otherwise there's no telling when you'll get the money."

"The hospital bill has been prepaid," Marge said. "And Dr. Cook will wait."

"Who did that? Harriet's not here."

"Aleta took care of it."

"Well, what about calling in a specialist?" Rimmel pressed. "She didn't offer that, did she?"

"No," Marge admitted, a worried frown creasing her forehead. "Do you think Nathan needs a specialist?"

"I'd want one if it were my wife," Rimmel said.

Now that he had her on shaky ground, Rimmel decided to press for a more aggressive treatment. "And I'd insist that they move ahead and do the dialysis right away."

"I'll ask Dr. Cook," Marge said.

"Now's a time for a second opinion. Dr. Cook won't want you to do it; but, I'll stand behind you."

"I think he will."

"Well, Aleta won't agree to it."

"She will if I ask for it."

"She can't," Rimmel said. "She may have been able to prepay the hospital; but, all movement of funds from the Trust is frozen."

Marge felt vulnerable and scared. Rimmel continued talking; but, she heard very little of what he said. All she could think about was Nathan. Was everything possible being done?

They found Dr. Cook at the nurse's station. He turned when he spotted them and came toward Marge smiling. "You'll have to wait for a few minutes before you see Nathan."

Marge paled and Dr. Cook helped her into a nearby seat and assured her that asking for a second opinion didn't mean Nathan was worse, but Aleta had insisted that it be done.

Marge's mouth dropped open as she listened. Aleta had ordered a second opinion without telling her. She knew Marge would be hesitant, fearful of insulting the doctor. She flushed with embarrassment.

"He's actually getting better," Dr. Cook said taking her hand and patting it. "Don't worry so. We aren't going to lose him. And if Dr. Robbins agrees, I'd like to jump ahead to dialysis. We need to be a bit more aggressive in our treatment."

"Whatever you say," Marge said. "Mr. Rimmel had worried that you weren't doing enough. But he was wrong."

"The Trust won't pay for a specialist," Rimmel charged, at a loss at what else to say.

Cook smiled enigmatically. "It already has."

"That's not possible," Rimmel sputtered, his smoothness disappearing as frustration took the lead.

Dr. Cook left to check on Nathan. Dennis decided he'd best apologize and he did so with a sincerity that touched Marge.

"You just don't know how good our Dr. Cook is," she said.

"I was wrong about him," Dennis admitted humbly, "but I'm not wrong about the best place for the Trust. We've been doing a good job for years, why switch now?"

"Because you're getting in bed with the mob," Marge responded with a cool certainty.

Dennis felt as if he'd touched a hot wire. The shock was almost physical. Where did this steel backbone come from? It wasn't there just moments ago.

"Whatever gave you that idea?"

"The attempts on Aleta's life."

"We had nothing to do with those."

"Isn't Melissa one of your officers?"

"She's been fired," Rimmel responded, growing increasingly uncomfortable. He wanted the fearful, hesitant woman back.

Marge didn't let go. "She was selected to come here and represent you. I figure she was one of your best."

"As a matter of fact…," Rimmel began.

Marge cut him off.

"And if she wasn't, your boss lacks good judgment. He sent a fool to talk us out of trusting a genius."

"Harriet's not here," Rimmel said feeling as if he had a toehold again.

"Her representative was expertly chosen. She understands dogs at an expert's level and so could bond with us. She is a lawyer and so could advise us. And she is kind and honorable and so is someone we could trust."

"I'm sure you have things you want…," Rimmel ran on. He couldn't give up. This was too important. "Things denied you as a member of a group. I can make sure you get what you want."

"You have no idea what I want."

"Well, I know you want your fair share. And Julia has put seven children through college."

"Just six," Marge retorted. "Junior didn't go to college."

"But he's cost the Trust a fortune."

"Not the Trust. Jason and Julia have footed that bill themselves."

"Still six through college against one. You came out on the short end."

"You couldn't be more wrong," Marge declared. "Go home, Mr. Rimmel. We like the way things are going."

"We can tie the Trust up in court for years," Rimmel declared. "We can freeze the funds."

"So that's what you plan to do if any of us makes a demand you don't like," Marge charged. There was fire in her eyes, fury in her tone. It did not fit the muddy complexioned, brown-haired woman of middle age.

Again Dennis Rimmel, the suave man about town sensed that he was unevenly matched. She was overpowering him with her passion and reason. He could not understand what was driving her. He didn't know about the hospital wing, her way to atone for what she perceived to be an unforgivable act of cowardice.

"No! No! Of course not!" he exclaimed. "We are reasonable people."

"That's the last thing I need," Marge finished with a flourish, "a reasonable banker. They know neither how to make money nor how to spend it."

Rimmel sunk into a chair, clenching his fists. He wanted to spit out a series of devastating comments that would bring her to her knees but he held his tongue. His time would come. He had to be careful if he were to capitalize on it.

He'd lost this battle. He wouldn't lose the next one.

Chapter 29

Back in the RV section, everyone was packing up. Dogs were loaded into their crates; equipment was torn down, folded up and stacked. Every item had a place.

This is when the group was the most vulnerable. Chief West had alerted his men.

Lauren came across the bridge alone.

"Lyle," she said, "is still accepting congratulations."

"Ever heard of a 'silent season' in Labs?" Aleta asked.

"Sure. Why?"

"I think that Emma is ready to be bred. She's flagging," Aleta said. "But almost no color."

Lauren came over and checked Emma by brushing her rear lightly. The tail went straight up and the end bent to one side.

"Full flag," Lauren said.

"I think tomorrow might be too late," Aleta said.

"I agree."

"But I was gonna check out the dog," Ed protested.

"You'll like Casper," Lauren said. "Go tonight."

Ed looked at Beatrice. "You up for a two hour ride?"

"I'm too excited to sleep." Beatrice said.

"What about Marge's Doxies?" Aleta asked.

"They'll fit in my RV," Beatrice said. "Their crates are small."

"Sandy has a kennel. She can house the dogs overnight," Lauren said. "Lyle will tell Marge when he checks in at the hospital tonight."

Evelyn waited until Ed and Beatrice drove off before mentioning her dilemma. "I was going to ask Beatrice to pick me up at the hospital and drive me to court tomorrow."

Lauren walked over as Aleta responded, "We can do that."

"I just called Sandy Parker. She has a bitch in season at her place. Casper bred her not an hour ago. She's going to repeat it tomorrow night."

"So Ed's in for a huge disappointment," Aleta said. "And here Morgan stands ready and eager."

Morgan is a BB. Casper is a BY," Lauren said. "If Ed breeds to Morgan he won't get any yellow pups."

"He doesn't want any. He's sold only blacks," Aleta responded. "Morgan would be perfect. In fact, Morgan would be better. Lyle had to talk him into Casper being as good as Morgan."

Lauren nodded. "Prior commitment. Lyle honors those."

Aleta opened her cell phone.

"Can't reach him. He might have turned off his phone," Aleta said. "I hate to have them try to drive back tonight."

"I could drive Morgan to Sandy's," Lauren said.

"What about your family?"

"Lyle's mom would love to watch the kids for one more day. Lyle will be working 24/7 until the crisis is over so he won't even know I'm gone. And, I'd get to visit with Sandy and see her new litter. It's a win-win situation," Lauren said enthusiastically.

She looked around. "All I need is Morgan."

"We'll help you pack up," Aleta offered.

Stanley joined them ready to help, but Aleta made him go back and sit down in a chair. Lyle and Morgan arrived shortly afterward.

Lyle went over to Stanley and spoke to him first, "Wouldn't let you help, huh?"

"All three of them ganged up on me," Stanley commented.

"You didn't try to argue with two redheads, did you?"

"I tried."

"Foolish man. Now, tell me why Aleta and Evelyn are helping me load up."

So, Stanley brought Lyle up to date.

Lyle's response was odd.

"You can't park the Danielson's RV in Beatrice's driveway. I was going to have one of my men hide it."

"Evelyn has her dogs inside. The Danielsons took her van."

"I forgot about that," Lyle said.

"We could hide it at my place, behind the orchard."

"And Evelyn and her dogs will stay with you?"

"I had another scenario in mind; but, as I reflect on it, your suggestion is the only viable solution," Stanley said. "Evelyn can't be alone even for a short time until after the hearing tomorrow."

"Watch her carefully. Harriet predicted a disastrous night for the group," Lyle said.

Morgan wagged his tail and Lyle petted him on his head. "Not for you, old man. Tonight you're going to get the ultimate reward."

"Okay, Morgan," Lauren called. "Let's go make babies."

Once Lauren left, Lyle helped the two women complete the loading process.

The Ciccone brothers watched from beyond the bridge.

"It must be Julia Danielson with that lawyer and Aleta," Ray commented. "Rimmel said that was her RV. And she put three dogs in it. Rimmel said Julia had three retrievers and that's what went into the RV."

"Maybe it's Evelyn Barnes," Tony said.

Something wasn't right.

"Rimmel said Evelyn drove a van. Evelyn left before we got here."

"I don't like not seeing the mister," Tony said. "My gut tells me something's going on."

"You trust your gut too much," Ray scoffed. "I trust facts."

"Facts? Hell, you're working hard to fit what we see into your facts. And you're trying to fit a screw into a nut what's the wrong size. It almost fits, but it don't."

"We're done here. Everyone went home, so we can begin."

"What about that sports car?" Tony asked.

As he spoke Chief West got in and drove it away.

"The chief's got two cars," Ray said. "Now you satisfied?"

"No, I ain't," Tony said. "You'll see."

Stanley rode with Evelyn, and Aleta followed in Stanley's car. The evening was young and the RV moved slowly. Aleta dropped back a bit so she could take in the countryside. She'd never been to the Midwest before and while it had been described as the "flattest land in the world," she found the area around Willow Glen replete with slightly rolling hills, a little less rolling than the Napa Valley vineyards, but not outright flat like the marshlands. Of course, water was the great evener there, filling in the depression and presenting a smooth even surface. Reeds grew up in the shallow spots and hunting dogs frequently headed for them hoping they meant land underfoot.

Here she passed by huge trees. Evidently Illinoisans didn't fear trees falling as much as Californians did. The latter lopped off tree tops with the same careless abandonment as Midwesterners trimmed hedges.

The warm air blowing in the window was refreshing after a day half of which was spent inside a stuffy metal barn and the other half of which was spent sitting in the sun under an umbrella. No cooling breeze wafted in as the day wore down as in the Bay Area. Here night didn't mean automatic relief from heat. There were no ocean breezes here to cool the earth; but somehow the gentle warm air was pleasant brushing her cheek.

The RV skirted the main part of Willow Glen and drove into an area of large estates. It was not the type of place one would expect to find a rough shell of an old house.

This land is too high priced, Aleta thought, unless Stanley got an unwanted sliver of it bordering a dump or a quarry. Aleta didn't know which would be worse. One would be smelly, the other noisy. Neither appealed to her.

She saw the orchard up ahead on the right. It was a real orchard, smaller than the ones in California's central valley, but still substantial. The house was to the right of the orchard with the unpaved driveway cutting between the two. Evelyn turned left where the row of trees ended. Aleta pulled in behind her.

"I need to call Grams," she said as Stanley got out of the RV. "I'm worried about her. She said she was going to be here in time to catch the end of the show."

The phone was answered on the first ring.

"Engine trouble," Harriet said in response to Aleta's question. "Where are you?"

"Stanley's house. Evelyn is with us. She has a hearing at ten tomorrow morning."

"We'll come straight there," Harriet said.

"I'll have Stanley give you directions."

"No need," Harriet said. "Stanley gave them to Ron when he hired him to drive me to Illinois. He promised him a hefty sum to do it. Said he was rich enough."

"He hired Ron?" Aleta queried. "The Trust could have… oh, wait a minute… you wouldn't have charged the Trust. You would have driven yourself… Gotta go kiss that man. Bye."

"See you soon," Harriet said into the disconnected phone. "My, my… things have really progressed."

Aleta turned and hugged Stanley and kissed him. "You wonderful man! You took care of my grandmother. How did you know she wouldn't ask for help?"

"I figured she was probably like you. She shot a man and then warded off a second attacker by herself. Ron said she was pretty shaken up; but was planning to drive here anyway. I didn't want her to die before I thanked her for sending you out here."

"I didn't even tell her I was engaged," Aleta said.

"You told her you were going to kiss me," Stanley chuckled. "I'm guessing she won't be surprised."

Evelyn joined them. "Are we going in? I'm dying to see the inside."

"What about the dogs?"

"They've been aired," Evelyn said. "They'll be okay."

"Stanley, just bite the bullet and lead the way," Aleta said. "The orchard is beautiful and you aren't next to the dump."

Stanley looked surprised. "Whatever gave you the idea my house was next to the dump?"

"I don't know," Aleta grinned, "maybe your description of your shack."

"I never said it was a shack. I just said it didn't have a kitchen."

"You know what you led me to believe."

"Well, what was I supposed to do? I didn't want you to marry me thinking I was wealthy."

"But you are, aren't you?"

"Sorta," Stanley hedged. "Aren't we getting a bit personal here?"

"Hey, you're talking to the granddaughter, the favorite granddaughter, of a very wealthy lady."

"Third-hand wealth isn't like firsthand wealth."

"Oh, heck! Just show me the house."

Evelyn, who'd been listening to the verbal exchange with amusement, exclaimed, "It's about time."

The entry was through a beautiful hand carved oak door flanked by two stained glass panels. Stanley opened the door.

"Don't you lock it?" Aleta gasped.

He pressed a few numbers in an unobtrusive panel in the corner behind a potted fern as he replied, "And have the burglar break my stained glass window?"

"So just opening the door activates the alarm?" Evelyn asked.

"Only when I set it."

"I like that," Evelyn said and then looked around. "Whoa!"

"You have a stone fireplace!" Aleta breathed. "A huge stone fireplace."

"It's two sided," Stanley said, "So either room could be the living room."

Aleta looked out the huge window overlooking the orchard. "This is the living room. There's no question... Is this a real hardwood floor?"

Stanley nodded. "I designed the pattern myself."

"You put a hardwood floor in the kitchen?"

"I like hardwood floors," Stanley said without a modicum of defensiveness. "And until this moment it wasn't the kitchen."

"What was it?"

"Dining room? Family room? Study?"

"Were you going to do without a kitchen forever?"

"I don't cook."

"I cook."

"Well, then let's figure out where you want the kitchen."

Evelyn, who'd disappeared during this exchange, reappeared. "Aleta, wait until you see the master bedroom and bath. You'll understand why he can be so casual about finishing the rest of the house."

Aleta hurried toward the door leading to the bedrooms and looked left. The window overlooked the orchard and the fields beyond. Were the two vehicles not there it would have been an unobstructed view of a grassy field bounded by a woods at the far end. Off to the right was the edge of the old barn she'd barely glanced at on the way in. Now framed by the window, it added interest to the natural painting. She could see the seasons changing the view. She envisioned the fiery foliage of autumn replaced by a bare deadness which would take on a splendor come the first snowfall. Then as the snow gave way to the rain of spring, the apple trees would blossom and the grass would send up shoots of green and the cycle would begin again.

The rest of the room was lost on Aleta who was fascinated by the picture of her future she saw in that window. Behind her Evelyn was commenting about everything.

Stanley found Aleta's reaction particularly gratifying.

"How do you survive without a kitchen?" Evelyn asked.

"I order out."

"Isn't that expensive?"

"I don't have many indulgences. When I want a home cooked meal, I invite myself over to my parents' house."

"You have parents?" Aleta burst out; then laughed at herself. "I mean, around here?"

"Yes. They own the woods over there," Stanley said.

"You going to introduce me?"

"When I heal," Stanley said.

Aleta nodded. "And maybe when my hair grows back."

"Not that long," Stanley shot back. "They read the papers. They already know about your head."

"You made the papers too," Aleta countered.

"Well, I think the headline was 'Lawyer Shot'. They wouldn't have read that story."

"Why not?"

"Too close to home."

Aleta leaped to a quick conclusion. "Your parents are lawyers too?"

280 • SUSAN DAVIS SANDBERG

"Of course. That's why you and I are so much alike. Lawyers spawn rebel lawyers."

"They do not! I am not!"

Evelyn cut in. "Whatever you are, how about supper?"

"I'll order it. American? Chinese? Mexican?"

"Roast beef," Aleta said.

Harriet arrived before the food was delivered, and Stanley immediately called and increased the order. "Just double it," he said.

The restaurant cashier took the call. Bill Pacheco was paying his bill at the time and was impatient at the phone call.

He waggled his fingers indicating that the cashier should hurry with his change.

The cashier, however, wouldn't be rushed. He waved at a nearby waiter and said, "Go tell the kitchen to double Praetzel's order."

Bill's ears alerted to the name. How many Pretzels could there be?

"Is that the Praetzel over on Oak?" he asked.

"No," said the cashier as he counted out Pacheco's change. He didn't add anything and Bill decided not to press.

He climbed in his car and parked near the kitchen exit. He didn't have long to wait. The man exiting carried two plastic bags loaded with Styrofoam boxes.

He's got company, Pacheco thought. Maybe that's where Beatrice is.

Bill followed the delivery van at a distance. When the delivery truck left, Bill drove up the driveway. He saw an old woman dressed in jeans and a work shirt out in the field with a giant pale brown dog.

The RV he spotted in the back of the orchard was brand new. Beatrice's was a different make and older. The second RV parked there was brown. Beatrice's was lime green and white.

A hefty man emerged from the house and Bill waved and backed up down the long driveway.

Bill headed back to Evelyn's. He was now ready to wait all night if he had to.

At midnight, two masked men entered Gary Danielson's house through the window to the nursery where the baby's crib was. They found it empty and would have headed for the living room had not they heard a noise at the front of the house. That coupled with distant sirens made both men nervous.

"Do it here! The one growled and his companion splashed gasoline over the crib, the dresser, the stuffed animals and the pile of blankets.

The leader backed out the window through which they'd come.

"Hurry!" he hissed at his companion.

The man inside dropped the can and ran to the window. His companion pulled him out, lit a match and threw it inside. Flames roared up and swept through the gasoline-soaked room.

The two men spun around and came face to face with the business ends of two guns in the hands of two grim faced Sheriff's deputies. A fire engine roared to a halt on the grass near the fire and hoses were pulled to both sides of the nursery addition.

The arsonists, now unmasked, were handcuffed as they lay on the ground and watched the firemen get ready to let go their spray.

The leader smirked. Water would only spread the fire further. But the hoses spewed foam on the fire and thus contained it before it spread to the main house.

"The nursery's a mess," the chief reported over his radio. "But we saved the house… Yeah, the deputies caught them coming out of the window. Thanks for the heads up."

"I wanna lawyer!" the leader insisted. "I want my phone call."

It was morning before he got either. But he wasn't questioned either, just booked and thrown in a holding cell.

Tony Ciccone broke into Marge Tobias' house at exactly midnight. The house was empty.

Cursing, he sat down and set the cardboard animal carriers on the floor.

The phone rang and Tony realized he'd set off an alarm. He rushed out the back door as a squad car screeched to a halt in front of the house. He managed to scale the four foot fence and run down the street.

"Damn alarm!" he muttered, and then thought about how fast the cop had gotten there. He dismissed the fast arrival as being anything other than his own bad luck that a cop was nearby.

A radio call reported the break in.

"I'm sending forensics," West said.

"Don't think they had time to get anything," the rookie reported, "Brought the strangest boxes to haul stuff away in."

"What kind of boxes?"

"The kind you carry cats to the vet in."

"Don't touch anything. I want prints."

Bill knew how to deactivate Beatrice's alarm. He entered the house and was surprised that not a single of Beatrice's mutts greeted him. He'd noticed that the RV wasn't parked in its usual place; but Bill wasn't one for puzzles. If the RV was gone, she was at Evelyn's. Where else would she be?

He took the spare RV keys from the rack and left. He'd get those dogs and wring a couple of necks. He only needed to return one for her to be grateful.

He headed for Evelyn's.

"I didn't hear from my guys," Frank Catalano reported. "The house was torched. I just saw it on the news."

"Any arrests?" Big Mike Ciccone asked.

"None on the news."

"Weren't they supposed to fix themselves up with an alibi?" Ray asked.

"Yeah, but usually they call."

"Be glad they didn't. It would connect them to you," Ray assured him. The lawyer in him was trying to anticipate what the investigation might turn up.

"Guess you're right," Frank replied. "The lawyer hasn't been called neither."

"Who's next?" Big Mike asked.

"Mike Danielson. He lives in Willow Glen," Frank said. "It's not in the Sheriff's jurisdiction. Some local small time police chief will be in charge so he won't make the connection."

"I think we ought a move up the last hit."

Ray objected.

"We were going to make a contact in between the two hits."

"We can still do that after the third hit," Big Mike decided. "We do the two together. Aren't they in the same town?"

"Yes."

"And they got one fire department, don't they?"

"Yes."

"So at least one house will be burned to the ground, won't it?"

"Guess so."

"We call the Danielson's after that. We need to make a strong statement right away."

In the wee hours of the morning, two men entered Mike Danielson's house and snuck up the stairs. The house was dark and deadly quiet. The stairs creaked under their footfall and they moved faster. One checked the bedrooms. The first had two beds in it. It was too dark to see anything more. The second door led to the nursery. A ticking clock was the only sound.

One man stood guard while the other entered and went over to the crib.

"It's empty!" he hissed. "Just some toys."

The two men checked the other rooms upstairs.

Suddenly, something crashed through the downstairs window.

"We're late!" the leader cried. "Run!"

They made it to the staircase when the bomb exploded. They were thrown backward by the force of it. They scrambled to their feet and raced down the stairs as the fire spread rapidly through the living room. The men dove through the front door rolling on the grass to put out the fire. When they stopped they were hauled to their feet and cuffed.

A fire engine rolled in and hoses were unrolled. Firemen hurried toward the house.

Up the street a patrol car intercepted the car speeding from the scene. Four arrests were made.

Across town a similar scene took place. Milani called West, "Think that's it?"

"Well, Kim's place went up already and Bruce and Jenny were staying with their parents. I don't think they plan to torch the parent's house. Harriet didn't... um... say anything about that."

"Is she moving back here, this Harriet person?"

"Could be. Wouldn't it be something if we both had our own Martha Cook?"

"Something else happened," West said. "We had a break in. The guy didn't steal anything because one of my men was on the scene. He left boxes."

"That's a bit odd."

"Animal boxes," West said. "I think they plan to do a bit of dognapping. You've got three of the group in your jurisdiction. Beatrice is out of town. She's got Marge's Doxies with her as well as her own dogs. I'm giving them a heads up. That leaves only Evelyn. I think she went to Stanley's place but I'm not sure."

"I'm stretched to the limit," Chief Milani said.

"I can loan you some men." Chief West offered.

"Send two. I'll check out Evelyn's place myself and then send them to Stanley's house if she's not here."

Chapter 30

Bill Pacheco was asleep. His head had slipped down and was lying on the passenger's seat which is why Chief Milani didn't spot him when he parked at the end of the cul-de-sac.

The lights from the chief's car woke the neighbor's terrier who barked through his window at the moving car. Bill woke up. He almost raised his head when a second set of lights shone in his rear view mirror. He waited until they passed before inching his head high enough to peer through the space under the steering wheel.

The street light shed enough light for him to recognize the Willow Glen police chief. Two uniformed police officers emerged from the other patrol car and conferred with the chief.

Bill crouched down as they left with the police chief's car leading the Arborville police car.

Weird, he thought.

Bill pulled out without lights, turned around in the cul-de-sac and sped down the street.

He caught up to the two cars on a road leading out of town. He slowed down to a crawl and was relieved to find the cars easy to follow. The cars parted at Praetzel's driveway.

Bill waited a few minutes, and then drove casually past the Praetzel driveway. The porch lights went on and the door opened.

He knew where Evelyn was.

With two cops standing guard, Harriet's driver Ron Maxwell, retired and left the guarding of Evelyn to them. Evelyn slept through the switch. In the house, Aleta and Harriet were deeply involved in dividing the Tontine monies while Stanley poured over the Tontine document.

It was shortly after 3 AM that Stanley found the loophole.

"I passed right over it," he explained to Aleta and Harriet, "because it only came into effect if you, Harriet, assigned power of attorney while still alive and capable of making financial decisions. Then your assignment overrode the clause in which the trustee for the Trust has a blanket power of attorney. Once you gave Aleta power of attorney, other rules came into effect. She could do everything with the Trust except transfer it. That would take the signature of all members of the trust."

Stanley stopped for a breath. He had the full attention of both women.

"But I already transferred it," Harriet said.

"That would be okay if you were still Trustee, but you made Aleta trustee before more than three-quarters of the assets were transferred. And Atherton Bank stopped the transfer because you had resigned as Trustee. And they did it in time."

"Now what?" Harriet asked.

"I've been listening to you going over the value of the assets that have already been transferred. And I realize how we get around this loophole. For the transfer to be considered completed, Signet Bank simply needs to hold three-quarters of the assets duly transferred from Atherton Bank. You are three million short of that mark."

"So what are our options?"

"We have to either get Julia Danielson to reverse herself…"

"She won't," Aleta declared. "She's afraid for her son's life."

"You said 'either-or'," Harriet said. "What's our other option?"

"If Atherton Bank transfers another three million, then the transfer is, by their action, completed. And they will have no legal recourse but to send the rest of the assets."

"Do they know this?" Aleta asked. "Because Dr. Cook is prepared to buy two million in art from the Trust."

"Garding has instituted a stop order on the transfer," Harriet said.

"This wouldn't be a transfer. This would be a sale," Aleta said.

"The money would still have to go back to them," Harriet said. "They would still retain more than a quarter of the assets.

"So we lose."

Harriet grew thoughtful. "Right now Atherton has no liquid assets, so they'd welcome a sale that would bring them some."

"How will that help?"

Harriet brushed off her query and went on excitedly. "We get Dr. Cook to buy three million in art. Have him wire the whole amount to Atherton in the morning. We're two hours ahead so the money will be there when the bank opens."

"Now at least the numbers match but how do we get the Bank to transfer the cash."

"We don't," Harriet declared. "Instead we get Julia to demand half a million each for the damage done to her children's houses."

"That was why West called you," Aleta guessed. "It wasn't just to tell you he was sending cops to guard us. What you predicted came true, didn't it?"

"Yes, it did."

"They were insured," Aleta commented. "Why would the Trust step in?"

"This was arson. The insurance company is going to investigate. Meanwhile, they need their houses fixed. And this wards off a lawsuit against the Trust. Garding will see that."

"Why Julia?"

"Because she's the only holdout on the transfer. If they've read that part of the Trust document, then they know how valuable she is. Even if they don't know about that, they would expect her to go through them and not us in light of her written note not to transfer."

"That's still not enough," Aleta said. "We'd be short by one and a half million."

"I'm hoping that's what they think too," Harriet said.

"How am I wrong?"

"A distribution lowers the total amount of the Trust. What we have at Signet bank will constitute three-quarters after that distribution."

"I prepaid the hospital for Nathan and Evelyn," Aleta said. "Will that mess up your numbers?"

"All that is figured in," Harriet said. "Stanley, you go to bed. You're going to court tomorrow. We have to wake up some people, so we're pulling an all-nighter. Ron will drive you to the courthouse tomorrow. Aleta and I will need to sleep in."

Before the night was over, Harriet had arranged for the wire of the monies to Atherton and had talked to Julia about asking for compensation, for the damage to her children's houses. She agreed.

West had roused Rimmel from a sound sleep and told him. "I have a very angry woman on my hands. She doesn't understand why she was targeted when she stood alone in agreeing to keep the Trust with your Bank."

"You know about the Trust?" Rimmel had stammered.

"It's my job to know," West said coolly.

"I'll be glad to talk with her," Rimmel said.

"She's in protective custody," West said indignantly. "Your friends made that necessary."

Rimmel stumbled. "They aren't my friends."

"Get dressed."

"What for?"

"You're going on a tour."

The tour was brief, the destruction at each site was vivid and the police chief's voice demanding. Rimmel faxed Julia's written request and copies of photos to Garding at Atherton Bank. He added a note saying that they might lose her vote if they didn't come through.

As soon as West returned Rimmel to his hotel room, Rimmel called Garding at home and demanded an explanation. Garding called Big Mike Ciccone.

"Where is Julia Danielson?" Mike demanded not bothering to explain the action."

"Rimmel doesn't know," Garding stated flatly. "The police have the whole family squirreled away somewhere."

"Why are the cops messing around in this?"

"You burn down houses and you don't expect them to investigate?"

"Look," Ciccone said, "these Tontine people are stubborn. They needed to be scared a little."

"Why pick on Julia?"

"She's the one with the kids," Big Mike said. "We want her to persuade the others we mean business. What happens to one happens to all. No one is safe unless everyone agrees to climb on board."

"Suppose she jumps off."

"After what we did? There's only one way she can go," Big Mike responded angrily.

He slammed down the phone, "Stupid jerk! What was he expecting us to do?"

"What about the others?" Ray asked. "We may have to be more direct."

"Tony says he can't find nobody home nowheres," Big Mike grumbled.

"Well, we know Evelyn has a court hearing in the morning," Ray said. "I'm going to be there."

Big Mike nodded absently. "What about that Pacheco dude. Did he pull off his end?"

"He says Beatrice is gone. He knows where Evelyn is though. Says the cops are guarding the place."

"What's with those yokels? Why guard Evelyn?" Big Mike said screwing his brows together. "In fact, why not just tuck her back in the hospital? They already got a cop on that husband. Seems to me it's pretty dumb considering the size of the force."

"These guys aren't territorial," Ray said, "which means they got enough cops to go around."

"Okay. So's they share," Big Mike acknowledged. "But why guard Evelyn?"

"You mean that even if there was a leak, she wasn't a target."

"Yeah. And there's gotta be a leak. Them cops was waiting for our guys."

"Maybe the phones are bugged," Ray offered.

"Frank checked them out," Big Mike said, then left that topic and went back to an earlier question. "Maybe the cops were guarding someone else."

"Not the Danielsons," Ray insisted. "Not enough cars. Pacheco said there were just two RV's and one car."

"What about the RV's?"

"One was new and he saw a man and old lady taking a big dusty brown dog for a walk. The other RV was dark brown...," Ray reported, and then paused. "...like the Danielson's RV."

"You said..."

Ray cut in. "I know what I said. The cops wouldn't have hauled the RV outta there in the middle of the show. I watched Beatrice and that new boyfriend of hers leave in her RV. Didn't see Jason Danielson. The lawyer was nursing that arm of his, so the chief helped the two women load Julia's RV."

"And if it wasn't Julia helping Aleta, then who?"

"Evelyn. And she went home with the lawyer and Aleta is there too."

"Who's the odd couple?" Big Mike asked.

"Someone Pacheco doesn't know," Ray replied.

"He knows everyone, except…," Big Mike began. "Quick, get that list of dogs. What kind of dogs does Harriet Locke have?"

Ray pulled out the list. "Chesapeake Bay Retrievers. What do they look like?"

"Don't you remember Fogg Spader cussing out Harriet Locke and that big, brown dog of hers?"

"Harriet's here?" Ray asked.

"Yeah."

"If we take her and Aleta out while the transfer is not three-quarters done, then the order is cancelled," Ray told his brother.

"Can't they redo it?" Big Mike asked.

"Only with everyone that's left voting for it," Ray said.

"So all we gotta do is take out Harriet and her granddaughter?" Big Mike asked. He didn't expect an answer.

He was already planning the hit.

"This time," he said, "we don't tell nobody. You go to court, Ray. Tony and me will take care of it."

"Fogg Spader's in Chicago."

"He don't come on this one," Big Mike said.

Chapter 31

At nine in the morning when Stanley and Evelyn were dressing for their day in court, across the country to the west, Doug Lim was sitting at his desk on the second floor of the Atherton Investment Bank preparing the paperwork for the sale of one painting and one small sculpture. Both would be packed and shipped today.

Operations would handle the insuring and shipping. He would personally authorize the sale. He would report it at the nine o'clock meeting for the section heads. While Garding would be annoyed he wasn't consulted, he would eventually agree it was the decision he would have made.

Lim had put the other faxes on the table in order to let others deal with those. Harriet had told him to keep hands off the distribution.

It didn't work out as he envisioned. Sprattley picked up the fax that had the three signatures backing Harriet's decision to transfer and he holed himself in his office. Doug Lim worried. If Sprattley studied the rules too thoroughly, he might get worried and run the numbers.

However, what Roger Sprattley did was call Ray Ciccone who told him that if Harriet and Aleta were dead, the one hundred percent rule would come into effect.

Sprattley didn't know that J.G. Garding had called Big Mike several hours ago, so as soon as he hung up, he made a beeline for Garding's office and unloaded the mob's intentions.

Garding took it with a good deal of aplomb. "Who did you think we were bedding with? The Mormon Tabernacle Choir?"

"Well, no... But knowing the plan in advance. That makes us accessories."

"And how's that different from what we were yesterday?"

"Yesterday, we had suspicions, but I can live with those. They don't make us liable."

"So, we act like we don't know. Who's going to accuse us?"

"We're walking a tightrope here. I'm uncomfortable."

"We're being paid to be uncomfortable."

Later, at the meeting Sprattley opened with the fax from the three Tontine members supporting the transfer.

"Is Harriet still alive?" Garding asked. The question shocked Doug Lim.

"Have you heard something?" Lim stammered thinking about his conversation with her only a few hours before. The plump man's jowls waggled when he shook his head. "No one seems to know where she is or if she's still alive. We're holding off until we're sure."

"What about this request from Julia Danielson?" Sprattley asked. "Rimmel personally verified the damage."

"How much of a buffer do we have?"

"About three million."

"Any of it liquid?"

"A hundred thousand and change," Sprattley said looking over his pince-nez glasses at his boss.

"So we'd have to liquidate property or one of the hard assets," Garding mused. "I don't like it."

"Excuse me," Doug Lim said. "We sold a painting and a statue this morning."

"Who did that!?!" Garding charged staring hard at the group sitting in a semicircle around his desk. Garding wanted no one to forget he was the head of the Trust Department.

"That would be me," Doug Lim replied politely. There was no apology in his tone. "We made a nice profit."

"I forbid all transfers."

"This was a sale."

"It's a scam!" Garding declared. "That granddaughter of Harriet's conjured up this whole thing to get around my order to halt the transfer."

"I don't think so," Doug ventured. "We have the money."

"By us, do you mean our bank?"

"The three million came in by wire to Atherton this morning. I didn't cut the order until I saw the wire," Doug Lim said. "It's a clean sale."

"Three million?" Garding mused. "What are they thinking?"

"It's the best offer we could have received for those pieces. We got the full appraised value for the painting and the statue," Doug reported.

"Now we have even more of an edge," Sprattley gloated. "And we can satisfy Julia Danielson's claim right away."

"You're sure of your figures?" Garding asked.

"Checked them this morning," Sprattley replied.

"Do it again."

Doug Lim left with a somber look. Neil Willis stuck his head in Lim's office.

"You look down."

Lim shrugged off the comment.

"We'll see," he said enigmatically.

"Anything I can do?"

"If Sprattley asks you to check numbers, just check the ones he gives you. No more."

"Can you tell me what's going on?"

"Sorry," Lim said sorrowfully. "Later."

"Just check the figures? That's all?"

"Yes," came the reply.

Neil walked over to Valerie's desk. "Something weird's going on."

"Any idea what?"

"Nope."

Sprattley, however, didn't ask Neil to check his figures. He asked Valerie. Lim hadn't taken into account Sprattley's prejudices which is why he didn't ask Lim either. Valerie may be a woman but, at least, she was Caucasian.

Chapter 32

At the courthouse, Stanley Praetzel and Evelyn Barnes were still waiting. They were fifth on the docket all of which were scheduled for ten.

In a courtroom downstairs Lyle West's father appeared in front of the judge with his client Jason Danielson, Junior.

The D.A. wanted no bail, West Senior asked for remand. The judge set the bail at five hundred thousand. West Senior objected; but didn't prevail.

"Next case," the judge said.

"I'll post the bail," came a voice from the rear. Junior turned, startled.

The lawyer saw his jaw muscles tighten.

Within thirty minutes, Junior was on the street.

He hitched a ride to his house. It was empty, but his truck was there. Someone must've picked up his wife, he thought. He tried his parent's house next. No one home there either.

They're all somewhere, he thought. Maybe one of the kids was having a birthday party. He drove to Gary's house and was shocked to find the nursery burned to the ground. A plastic covering over the side of the house told him that the damage didn't stop there.

He headed for Mike's house wondering what had happened and if the baby was okay. He liked little Richard. He hoped nothing had happened to him.

His anger over his parents not being in court was fading. He didn't care what they said. He expected them to be there. They always were.

Mike's house had been even more devastated by a fire. The living room was a blackened shell. He parked the truck and walked up to the yellow police tape and stared. Someone took a picture. He was incensed. They were invading his family's privacy.

Now he was certain he knew where everyone was. As he drove to Ross's house, he hoped that Mike's family hadn't been hurt.

Everyone could be at the hospital, he thought, but I'll check out Ross's place first.

No wonder no one was at his arraignment. Well, at least the mob appreciated his paying them in full. They put up his bail.

Ross's house was the final shock. He sat in his car stunned. What was going on? His mother had paid them off. She had signed their damn paper. Why had they done this?"

This was why he'd pressured his mother to sign. This was what he'd been afraid might happen. And it did. But it made no sense.

He'd try one more place. Kim had just moved into her new apartment. Almost no one had her address yet. She'd asked him to help her paint it so she'd given it to him. He'd promised he would. She'd be there and tell him what was going on.

When he saw the burned out shell of Kim's apartment building, his heart began to beat so fast he couldn't breathe. His chest tightened and he jammed on the brakes.

He gasped for air. His head was pounding.

Serve me right to die from a heart attack, he thought. Then another thought climbed on top of that one. What are the odds of that happening?

He grimaced, If I bet on my own death, I won't live to collect. It would be the ultimate irony.

The thought made him laugh and the laughter relaxed him. His breathing became easier and slowly his headache faded.

"Nerves," he muttered. "Just nerves. I need a drink."

As Junior entered the bar where he placed many of his bets, he began to relax. Whatever happened had not been his fault. And he was out of jail.

He ordered a drink and placed a bet. He felt lucky.

The night before, back at Sandy Parker's Kennels, Ed had watched Lauren and Sandy breed Emma. However, when they had wanted to put her in a kennel, he had objected. He promised to keep her in the RV with him and only let her walk with a leash on.

The little dogs were another matter. Beatrice put her Scotties in one kennel and Marge's Doxies in another and stayed inside to talk dogs with the two Lab breeders. She was a rapt listener now that she was about to add a show Lab to her menagerie. Both breeders love talking to a newcomer who started at a level that allowed her to understand the nuances of breeding and showing Labradors.

Ed excused himself and borrowing Sandy's computer, with Emma at his feet, began his search for the secrets that Beatrice wanted to know.

He found Marge's secret first. She had had a child a year before her son. It was a daughter. There was no death certificate. That meant she was still alive.

As he was searching the birth records he came across a Beatrice Olson. He stopped. Beatrice's maiden name was Olson. She had joked with him about only marrying Swedes before him.

"Olson to Carlson to Jacobson to Johnson," she had joked. "I was in such a rut."

Beatrice had given birth to a baby girl at age sixteen. The father was not listed. That happened at a time when illegitimate children were almost automatically put up for adoption. Open adoptions were a recent phenomenon. He wondered if Beatrice knew where her daughter was.

He checked Evelyn Barnes' name in the birth records, but didn't find it. Her secret wasn't a child whose birth had some shame connected with it.

What else would a decent woman be ashamed of? A criminal record? Prostitution? Porn movies? Mental illness?

He voted for the latter. Were he at home, he might be able to find out if she were ever institutionalized, but even that wouldn't tell him what had gone on inside the institution or what effect that had on her. It would, however, explain many things about her. No wonder she never married. No wonder she had no children. Then he considered her style in the dog show ring. There was a place where she could be confident. Her beloved dogs never judged her and somehow she'd managed to handle losing. What a complicated lady! No wonder she was Beatrice's best friend.

When Beatrice came to check on him, Ed shut off the computer and suggested they walk Emma. The driveway ran alongside a field of summer wheat and Emma strained to get free; but Ed held on wrapping the end of the leash around his wrist. Beatrice warned him that Emma could pull him off his feet if she leaped after a rabbit. He shrugged off the possibility as unlikely and added that she wouldn't get very far with him as an anchor.

"I made a promise," he ended.

Beatrice took his arm and hugged it. "Now what did you want to talk with me about?"

"I know Marge's secret. Well, at least part of it."

"Tell me!"

"I know yours too," he said softly.

"Mine?"

"I didn't look for it. It just popped out at me when I was searching for Marge's."

"Why would you search through birth records for...? Never mind."

Neither spoke for a few minutes, and then Beatrice said softly. "I was only sixteen."

"Yes, I know," Ed responded gently.

"I didn't know what else to do."

"You did the brave and loving thing," Ed said. "I'm proud of you."

"I didn't even know…"

"Hush," Ed murmured. "It's not important. What is important is that you gave your child a chance at a normal, happy life."

"Things went wrong," Beatrice said. "I often wonder if I should have kept her."

"Did you ever want to find her?"

"I know where she is," Beatrice replied. "She thinks I'm her aunt. I told her my sister, her mother, died shortly after giving her up."

"Didn't she ever ask for a photo?"

"I gave her one of Evelyn and me as young girls."

"So Evelyn knows?"

"Yes, she knows."

"I will need longer to discover Evelyn's secret."

"Don't," Beatrice said. "I want you to stop. People should be allowed to keep their secrets."

Frank Catalano had two of his enforcers at the bar Junior frequented. A limit had been set. It took Junior just two hours to blow past it. He was betting on everything, absolutely fixated on the idea that this was his lucky day. He used the losses as incentive to double and redouble his bets. He was meant to win big today.

Catalano's enforcers had been told to more in fast. Information was needed and needed quickly. They were to squeeze it out of him.

Junior was surprised when he was dragged into the alley behind the bar after he couldn't pay up.

"Hey, I'm good for it. Check with your boss," he said. "I just paid off a hundred grand. You're making a big mistake; but, hey let me go and I'll forget this ever happened."

A quick clip under the chin by a closed fist sent Junior reeling back into the garbage cans. They kept him from falling to the ground. He leaned over and spit out a mouthful of blood.

'No need to get rough," he said. "I tell you I'm good for it."

"Where you gonna get it?" one asked. The man had a long thick stick in one hand.

"My mom," Junior sputtered hastily. "She'll come through for me."

"How soon can you get the money?"

Junior hesitated. "I ain't too sure. Some bad shit went down last night. I figure someone got hurt and she's at the hospital."

The stick came down and hit the knee lightly.

"What'd you do that for?" Junior blubbered. "I can get the money. All's I gotta do is…"

The stick knocked the knee again.

"Hey that hurt!"

"She's not at the hospital," the man with the stick growled. "So where is she?"

"Hell, how should I know? Someone took out four places where my brothers and sisters were and my wife and kids was took. And I don't know where. That's the honest truth."

"Last chance for the knee," the man warned.

Junior began to sweat. "Listen, guys, if I had any idea, I'd tell you."

This time the wooden stick cracked his kneecap. Junior howled in agony as his leg gave way.

The partner grabbed Junior as he started to collapse and held him up.

"One down, one to go," the hitter said.

"Wait. Wait," Junior whined through gritted teeth. Tears were streaming down his face. "I can't tell you what I don't know."

"Oh, you know. You just ain't thinking hard enough."

"No! No!" Junior screeched. "I don't know. Please, please don't... Maybe I can find out. Gimme a chance, please."

The man holding Junior up let go. Junior collapsed and howled as his injured leg folded under him.

"You still owe the money," the hitter said as the pair walked away.

When the ambulance brought Junior into the emergency section, Chief West was there. Junior heard someone ask him who they should call.

"No one," he said. "He has no family."

"I do too," Junior protested. "Get my mom down here. She'll take care of things."

"Not this time. She's in protective custody."

"Well, get her out."

"It could mean her life," West said.

"She'll be okay. They ain't gonna kill her. They're just gonna talk to her."

"So you know who attacked your family last night?"

Junior whitened. "It weren't nobody I owed. Them debts was paid in full."

"So who was it?"

"Don't know. Honest. Now, please, tell her I been hurt," Junior begged.

"I'm guessing you were hurt to bring her out of hiding."

"Naw. That weren't the reason. I had a damned cold streak and couldn't pay up."

"How much?"

"Five grand."

West raised an eyebrow.

"They let you slide on a hundred and broke your kneecaps over five?"

"Yeah, go figure."

"I did," West commented. "And I figured they wanted you to tell them where your family is. Did you know they planned to kidnap Gary's baby, Richard?"

Jason paled, but recovered quickly.

"Well, mom can fix it. All she's gotta do is come out of hiding."

"And get her family killed?"

"Hell, I'm her family too. And right now I need her. She's gotta stop being such a chicken."

West swallowed hard and left abruptly.

Chapter 33

Ray called his brother from the courthouse. "We're the case after this one. We're going to be heard before noon, so go ahead."

Big Mike turned to Tony who was seated next to him and said, "We have a green light."

"By the way, Charlie called," Ray said.

"Not now!" Big Mike shot back abruptly.

"Charlie says the Bank has a million liquid right now. He wants to ship the stones."

"Sure," Big Mike said. "Go ahead."

"Tell me we ain't jumping the gun," Tony said.

"It's a test run. If they screw up, they lose and we got a million for our trouble."

"I don't like doing more'n one thing at a time. We need to fix our brains on this job."

"My brain's where it's supposed to be," Big Mike snapped. "Are our guys here?"

"Yeah, here they come."

Aleta knocked on the door of the blue and white RV and then went in. Stoney greeted her with a tail wag. She petted him absently.

"You left the door unlocked," she accused, her brow furrowed. "And what's with the guns?"

"Stoney's out," her grandmother said and Aleta knew the dog would protect her better than a flimsy lock. Suddenly, her mind made a quantum leap.

"Did you get some kind of warning?"

"Two men set the barn on fire while you're inside."

"What about our guards?"

"They were in a heap outside this trailer."

"What else?"

"I was surrounded by four gunmen. They shot Stoney right in front of me! And then they turned their guns on the trailers and..."

Harriet began to cry.

"Call Milani," Aleta ordered.

"I did, but he's not going to make it."

"Give me a gun. I'm taking Stoney with me."

"What are you going to do?"

"Stop them from burning down Stanley's barn," Aleta said. "Obviously, they saw me go in there and that made them split up. I can surprise two with Stoney. Can you, Joe and Terry handle four?"

"Go!" Harriet said. "I've got an idea."

Aleta shoved the rifle under her shirt and left the trailer. Harriet followed her, rifle in hand. She waved the two officers over to the space between the two RV's.

"Joe, boost me up on top," she said. "Terry, hold my rifle."

"What do you think you're doing?" Terry asked.

"Trying to stay alive until Milani gets here with the cavalry," she answered.

Joe laced his fingers together and Harriet put her foot on his cupped hands and stepped up. He lifted her up and she scrambled on top as Babe and Keeper set off a cacophony of barking that spread to the three Goldens in the other trailer. Their racket masked the noise Harriet was making scrambling on top of the RV.

Terry handed her the rifle. "This is our job, you know."

"There are four with automatic weapons coming after me. Aleta has a plan. Don't interfere."

Both looked around nervously.

"Separate," she hissed. "Or you'll die."

Her words shook Joe and he immediately dropped down and rolled under the same RV that Harriet lay on top of.

Terry glanced around again. He didn't like his vulnerability. The increase of the noise from inside the trailer told him the enemy was closing in. He snuck around the back of the other trailer and the scooted underneath. He drew his gun.

Joe saw Aleta disappear inside the barn. Two men dashed across the field on the other side of the barn. It was two against one.

"Shit!" Joe muttered. Then he remembered that West said Harriet Locke was Milani's Martha Cook. He hoped that meant she was more than just rich. He hoped she'd sense if her granddaughter was in danger. He hoped he'd live to see his kids again.

Terry was lying under the other RV thinking, we're outnumbered, outgunned and in a stupid place to get off a good shot, on top of which, I'm lying on my bulletproof vest. I'm gonna die. I know it. I haven't even gotten good on the shooting range. Oh, God, if you get me through this, I'll practice. I promise. Just let me be lucky this once.

Shoes appeared and stopped in front of the bumper of the blue and white RV. Terry shrank back a few inches even though the shoes were next to Joe's nose and not his.

A second pair joined the first and then Terry got his own pair of shoes as two men squeezed between the two RV's. Terry wondered who was going to shoot first. If I see a gun pointing at my face, he decided, I'll shout 'Police' and shoot. He put both hands on his gun. They were shaking. Cops hands weren't supposed to shake. He rested the butt on the ground and that helped some.

He didn't dare take his eyes from the shoes to look at Joe. Joe's hands weren't shaking, he knew. Joe was experienced. He was glad Joe was here. He never would have crawled under the RV if Joe hadn't done so first.

That first dive told him that he should try to survive. Just like the old lady said, he thought. Survive until the others got here.

The shoes moved toward the door of the blue and white RV. The two cops stayed still in their hiding places. Harriet watched the men approaching the barn from her place on the top of the RV.

She remembered what Aleta had said about saving the barn. She looked up at the loft opening. There, framed in the A made by the roof and the loft floor, standing motionless in the center of the large opening meant to receive bales of hay, stood her granddaughter, rifle in hand.

Don't Aleta! Harriet commanded mentally. If you do you'll draw everyone to you.

Please, God, let her know, the grandmother prayed.

Aleta had left Stoney by the back door, out of gun range she hoped. She had no intention of involving him in her plan. All she could think about the moment she announced she'd take him was to relieve her grandmother of the mental anguish the thought of seeing her beloved dog executed had visited upon her.

Stoney would stay put. The fact that she climbed the ladder near the rear of the barn guaranteed it. Not being able to follow her, he would wait at the foot of the ladder for her return. He wouldn't leave without her.

Aleta had moved carefully but speedily across the loft floor. She was surprised at how solid the floor was. This old barn had a lot of life left in it.

When she reached the far end, she squatted low to survey the area. She saw several men slowly moving around the RV. Her grandmother was lying on its top. She wondered where the cops were. At least they weren't lying dead by the vehicle. So far the men hadn't seen her, they were watching the field. She looked in the direction they were looking and saw two men coming across the field, heading straight for the barn. One was carrying a red gasoline can. Grams was right, she thought. They mean to burn down the barn.

She stood up, raised her rifle and realized that the first shot would focus everyone's attention on her. Both of the men in the field were carrying guns. Her first two shots had to be quickly made and pinpoint accurate.

They came one after the other, both hitting their mark. The gasoline can flew from the carrier's hand with holes front and back. The second hit the man's shoulder and he dropped his gun.

The head of the second man in the field located her by the time hers second bullet hit his partner. His look of surprise was short lived. Anger replaced it as he swung his gun upward and began firing.

As with many who use assault guns, the shooter counted on the spray of bullets to hit his target. Aleta dropped to one knee and hit the second shooter in the shoulder. Spun by the shot, he nevertheless managed to switch his gun to his other hand and continue to shoot.

The bullets hit the rafters above Aleta's head bringing down a shower of dry wood and long undisturbed dust and bird droppings.

Aleta saw the men outside the RV turn and begin to run toward her.

A new spray of bullets peppered the side of the barn and Aleta fell to the ground and lay flat behind the board framing the opening. She stopped shooting as she slithered back along the floor to an opening in the floor boards.

Harriet was the first to drop the man heading for the barn. She hit him in the back and he dropped like a stone straight down.

Joe fired his gun at the same time and hit another in the leg. His position didn't leave him a choice. Terry, understanding that this was the time to shoot, aimed and, surprised that his hand was suddenly steady, shot. His bullet went wild. He took better aim and his next shot hit its mark. The man fell, his heel shattered.

The fourth man, seeing his companions fall, turned toward the orchard and ran. He never made it. Harriet's bullet hit his shoulder and travelled straight to his heart.

The men in the field kept firing at Aleta. Then suddenly they stopped. Aleta crawled back and peered over the edge. The men were lying sprawled out on the grass face up with two guns leveled at their heads. The guns were being retrieved by a third cop as the men lay helpless.

Aleta looked over at the RV's. Her grandmother was being helped off the roof as two of the shooters were being handcuffed. She saw Joe and Terry crawl out from under the RV's. Then she noticed that neither handcuffed man could stand.

She assumed the two lying motionless were dead. She hoped it wasn't her grandmother who had shot them. She was having trouble enough dealing with the first man she shot.

Once on the ground, her grandmother raced toward the barn.

"I'm fine, Grams!" Aleta shouted down from the loft. "Okay, Stoney, go say hi."

The big dog raced toward Harriet, but slowed down when he reached her and pranced in front of her expectantly. She squatted down and threw her arms around his massive shoulders and hugged him. Her tears began to flow.

Aleta bounced down the stairs and asked gaily, "We did okay, didn't we?"

Harriet rose, her countenance switching rapidly from relief to anger. "How dare you take such a risk?"

"Grams…"

"You could have been killed! How would I have explained that to your father?"

"They were coming for both of us. We could have both have been killed," Aleta pointed out.

"That I wouldn't have had to explain," Harriet said.

"Just think," Aleta reasoned. "Now you don't have to do any explaining."

Harriet softened. "Well, there is that."

"And I saved Stanley's barn," Aleta said gleefully. "It's a nice old building. I have plans for it."

"You're going to renovate it?"

"No, just let it be. Wouldn't you have loved to have a barn like this to play in when you were a kid?"

"It's not safe."

"Stanley can fix that," Aleta said. "Isn't it just great?"

When the two approached the RV's, West who'd come late on the scene took them aside.

"You were lucky," he said. "You didn't kill either Big Mike Ciccone or his brother Tony. Actually it was my men who shot them and the mob expects cops to do their job, so there won't be a vendetta."

"They came gunning for us," Aleta retorted. "Doesn't that factor in?"

"Legally, yes," West said. "It means you and your grandmother had just cause. But, on the street, the killing of a mob boss calls for vengeance of some kind."

"And killing his men doesn't?"

"They weren't his men. They were Frank Catalano's."

Harriet looked worried. "One of them wasn't Fogg Spader?"

"Who's he?"

"The brother of the man I killed."

"You think he's here?"

"Yes," Harriet replied suddenly looking weary. "I do. And he has revenge driving him. The Ciccones won't stop him."

"I'll see that Tom posts men here," West promised. "By the way, Hawk is going to dig out the bullets in your barn and match them to the guns.

"They were all shooting," Harriet said.

West smiled. "We want proof they were actually shooting at Aleta. These guys have good lawyers."

Milani joined the threesome. "We'll be here a while. We've got a lot of evidence to gather. We need your guns."

"But then we won't have any," Harriet protested.

"Men were killed," West said.

Milani added a note of assurance. "I'm leaving protection and I promise they will follow your instructions as well as West's men did."

"I killed two more men," Harriet said. "I may no longer be favored with any prophetic powers."

"Don't worry about that," West said. "We'll track down this Fogg Spader and keep an eye on him."

But Harriet was worried. The Trust still wasn't secure. And one lone vengeful man could wreck everything.

Chapter 34

It was just before noon when Judge Plackett decided to take one more case and thus complete the cases on his morning docket. Both lawyers looked pleased at his decision.

Ray Ciccone looked at the man seated next to Evelyn and judged him to be every inch a small town lawyer and, by that token, no match for him.

Stanley didn't make the mistake of questioning his being a member of the Illinois Bar. He had checked. Ray Ciccone could practice in a number of states besides Nevada, Illinois and California being two of them.

"Okay, Gentlemen, what's this about?" Judge Plackett asked.

Ray Ciccone replied first. That Stanley Praetzel let him as far as he was concerned was the mark on an uncertain, non-aggressive attorney.

Ciccone was succinct and simple in his presentation.

"Evelyn Barnes was hospitalized last Thursday and the medical report indicates that she was hallucinating and behaving irrationally. She is a drug addict and her nephew wants her put in a treatment center. He would like to be granted power of attorney to take care of her affairs until her release."

During his entire speech, Stanley had been patting Evelyn's hand and this helped her retain some semblance of balance even though she'd blanched at every suggestion she needed to be institutionalized. Her greatest fear was in front of her. She wanted to scream and run; but, she didn't.

Stanley rose. "Mr. Ciccone has presented two issues. One is whether Miss Barnes needs to be institutionalized and the second is who should make financial decisions for her. With the court's permission I would like to focus on only the first of these. Should the court decide that Miss Barnes needs hospitalization then I would ask for a continuance in order to prepare to argue as to who should be given power of attorney over her medical and financial affairs."

"Point of order," Ciccone interjected. "Mr. Praetzel is not Miss Barnes' attorney. He is here representing the Trust that wishes to retain power of attorney over Miss Barnes."

Stanley Praetzel stood up. He was a much less impressive figure than Ray Ciccone; but Judge Plackett had found him to be a formidable advocate. He liked having him in his courtroom.

He looked at Praetzel who stated, "I am both, which is why I asked for the matters to be separated."

"So ordered," Judge Plackett said. "Miss Barnes, take the stand."

"But, Your Honor," I have medical reports to present," Ray said.

Praetzel popped up. "We stipulate as to the accuracy of those reports. Miss Barnes was hospitalized suffering from hallucinations and erratic behavior as a result of ingesting mescaline."

Stanley helped Evelyn to her feet. "Be completely honest and you will walk out a free woman," he said quietly.

The judge asked the first question. "Did you hire Mr. Praetzel to represent you?"

"Yes, I did."

"And how much did you pay him?"

"One dollar," Evelyn said. "I wanted to pay him more, but he said it wasn't necessary."

Ray Ciccone cut in.

"Ask her where she got the dollar."

The judge smiled at her. "You may answer."

"Ron Maxwell loaned it to me. You see my purse is still at the hospital and I didn't have any money," Evelyn said. "But I plan to pay him more. He charges a hundred dollars an hour and so waiting in court this morning, interesting as it was cost me two hundred; but, if you don't mind my saying so, Judge Plackett, you made a smart decision for me moneywise not holding us over until after lunch."

Judge Plackett moved abruptly to the reason for her hospitalization. "Do you think your nephew made a wise decision to have you hospitalized?"

"It was a good decision, but the place he chose was wrong."

"Wrong? How?"

"He was sending me to a treatment center for drug addicts. I'm not a drug addict. I was being poisoned by him so he could get his hands on my money."

Judge Plackett looked askance at the frail woman in the flimsy dress.

"You believe you have money?" he asked gently.

Evelyn looked at him squarely and asked, "Can a lawyer lie in court? I mean, aren't they bound by some oath or other to tell the truth."

"You want me to ask your lawyer, Mr. Praetzel, if you are rich?"

"Heavens no!" Evelyn blurted out. "That would be breaking his oath, wouldn't it?" She didn't wait for an answer but rushed on. "I want you to ask Mr. Ciccone if I have money. He knows I do."

Judge Plackett looked over at Ray who said with all the aplomb he could muster, "The lady is correct. She has money."

The judge wasn't satisfied. The reply was too vague.

"Is she wealthy?" he pressed.

Ciccone swallowed hard. This wasn't going well. "Yes, she is wealthy."

The judge appeared satisfied.

"Are you a drug addict?"

"No," Evelyn said. "I didn't know Louie had put mescaline in my orange juice although I wondered why it was so bitter. He assured me it was okay and, well, why wouldn't I believe my own nephew. But, being gullible is no reason to be stuck in an institution."

"You took drugs," the judge insisted.

"Not willingly," Evelyn said. "And mescaline isn't physically addictive. It's psychologically addictive but all I ever had was 'bad trips'. Why would I want to repeat that?"

"Mr. Praetzel, have you anything to add?"

Stanley stood up. "I was with her at a dog show for two days. She repeatedly made sound decisions, refusing, for example, to take her own dogs into competition until she was physically able. Most people, fired up by competition, would not have shown that much restraint. When she did enter the ring, she won under two different judges. After two days of attendance, I found that showing a dog requires physical skill as well as mental acuity at the higher levels which is where she entered the competition."

When his turn came, Ray Ciccone moved to another aspect of the recovery period.

"For those two days, you felt you were still recovering from the effects of the mescaline, correct?"

Evelyn sensed a trap; but, she could see no way out.

"Yes," she responded.

"Do you think you should have been making significant financial decisions at that time?"

"The only financial decision I made had to do with voting in favor of a decision that had already been made by someone more astute financially than I am. Two others voted at the same time. Two attorneys were present and affirmed our decision. If we cannot trust longtime friends and professionals in such matters, then we are all lost."

"But, Judge," Ray Ciccone said, not used to having to plead his case this way, "Mescaline could have long term effects. One slip and she could lapse into a permanent psychotic state."

"Do you agree she is not there now?"

"Yes, Your Honor, Miss Barnes appears to be rational at the present time."

The judge turned to Evelyn, "Have you selected a person to give your power of attorney to should such a tragedy befall you?"

"I have, Your Honor," Evelyn said. "The Trustee of the Tontine Trust who is currently Aleta Locke is soon to be Mrs. Stanley Praetzel. Isn't that wonderful! He gave her a gorgeous ruby ring yesterday and she's already decided where the living room is going to be."

The judge's face went from delight to confusion.

"If Your Honor would allow me to suggest that only the first sentence of that tirade is applicable," Stanley offered politely.

"Tirade?" Evelyn spouted. "What tirade?"

"You departed from the subject of the question. You departed a long way."

"Did what she said make sense to you?" Plackett asked soberly.

"Yes, Your Honor. My house is unfinished. Aleta did decide where we were going to put the living room."

"Well, I'm glad you cleared that up," Judge Plackett said, cupping his hand over the microphone. "And congratulations."

Minutes later Evelyn walked out of the courtroom relieved, smiling and crying. Stanley put his arm around her. "You won the day, dear. All by yourself. And I think John likes you."

"John?"

"Judge Plackett."

"Really?"

"Bet he comes to the next dog show."

Evelyn blushed.

Chapter 35

The police were still swarming all over Stanley's land and barn when he returned. His first thought was Aleta. The car was not completely stopped when he opened the door and swung out a leg. He stopped when Aleta opened the front door and ran out to meet him. Harriet came out on her heels and Stanley relaxed with one foot out the door until Ron, following the uniformed cop's directions, had pulled to a stop away from the center of activity.

Stanley stood up and surveyed the scene. Two ambulances rolled out and the coroner arrived. Officers were on ladders propped against the sides of the barn. Other officers were working in the field beyond.

When the officers around the RV parted to make way for the coroner, Stanley saw the body of a man sprawled face down on the ground half-way between the RV's and the barn. He was still clutching an automatic weapon. The coroner, however, headed into the apple orchard.

How many were there, Stanley wondered.

Aleta slipped her arm around his waist. "Grams and I had some excitement while you were gone."

"Anyone killed?" Stanley asked. It sounded like a dumb question, but he was having trouble wrapping his mind around the fact that there appeared to be two dead men lying near his orchard.

"Just the dead guys," Aleta said pointing to the two in street clothes. "Grams is deadly with a rifle. I'd marry that granddaughter of hers."

"What are the cops doing crawling all over the barn?"

"Digging for bullets."

"Why were they shooting at the barn?"

"I was standing there shooting at them."

"What on earth possessed you to do that?" Stanley gasped, his composure barely intact.

"They were going to burn down your barn."

"You risked your neck to save a rundown old barn?" His tone was replete with disapproving overtones.

Aleta smiled. "That and Grams. It was all part of my plan. You want me to tell you every detail? You have to say yes because I might say something in my statement that could be incriminating."

"You just want to gloat," Stanley said.

Aleta saw the lines leave his face and led him to the house.

"You have to order lunch, you know. There's not a thing to eat in the house."

"Food? You can think of food with corpses lying in the... on the... next to... I'm not hungry."

"Sandwiches. Lots of sandwiches. Ron can go get them for us. Can't have a stranger coming and going. There's still someone out there gunning for Grams."

"Who?" Stanley was forced to ask.

"The brother of the men she killed in Mill Valley."

"There's another Spader?"

"Yep. Fogg Spader. And he's in the area."

Stanley drew his lovely bride-to-be to him.

"Aleta, promise me you won't try to save my barn again."

She knew what he meant.

West and Milani joined the group for lunch.

"There's still danger," Harriet said. "The transfer isn't complete. I have a plan in the works; but, Sprattley is studying the numbers. If he doesn't ask any of my people to help, the transaction we've engineered will pass muster."

West spoke up, "I'll tell Lauren to keep Beatrice and her dogs and Marge's dogs at Sandy's for an extra day."

"And the Danielsons?" Harriet asked.

"The families will stay put until either Milani or I give the all clear," West replied. "I'll get Marge Tobias to stay at the hospital with her husband under guard. Have I forgotten anyone?"

"Don't you think, after all this that the Ciccone brothers will give up trying to snag your trust?" Chief Tom Milani asked.

"They've already got their first transaction in the works," Harriet replied. "They must think they are going to be successful or they wouldn't have…"

Aleta cut in. "When?"

"This morning. A million has already been wired. The rubies are coming in this afternoon."

"Before the attack?" Aleta pressed.

"During it, probably," Harriet replied. "I got the call just a bit ago."

"Has anyone made a phone call?" Aleta asked Chief West.

"We wanted to book them all first," Chief Milani replied.

"So, their order to proceed must have been made on the assumption that six armed men could surprise and take out two cops and the two women they were guarding."

"What does that have to do with the transfer?" Harriet asked.

"They assumed our deaths," Aleta explained.

Harriet immediately knew where Aleta was heading. "They jumped the gun. They can be caught."

"We need you two to delay the processing for a couple of hours," Aleta said. "And no phone calls."

"What do you plan to do?" West asked but Aleta had turned to her grandmother.

"What do you want to bet that these guys couldn't do a straight transaction if their lives depended on it?"

"It would take time to get them on money laundering," West put in.

"The rubies," Harriet said. "If they supply their own appraiser, then we'll know."

"Won't the Bank accept them if Sprattley says so?"

"He'd want an appraiser's report for the record."

"Doesn't the bank always use the same appraiser?"

"I broke precedent when I had Wendy Oshiro bring in a relative to get the transfer moving."

"So Sprattley could do the same to speed up the Bank accepting the stones."

"Why would the Ciccones use fake gems in the first place?" Chief Milani asked.

"Because gangsters are paranoid," Aleta said. "And dishonest."

Back at Atherton Investment Bank, a power blackout of the area had taken out the air conditioning system as well as the lights. The closed second floor soon became stifling hot. Garding refused to let anyone go home.

Doug Lim called Neil Willis and Wendy Oshiro into his office and told them about Harriet's plan. He noticed that Neil had shed his coat and had beads of perspiration forming on his forehead. Wendy Oshiro had calmed herself to ward off any unseemly physical reaction. She looked cool.

He explained the plan.

"I get it," Neil said. "Wendy comes to me because she has a problem because the appraiser finished in one-third the time it usually takes. I come to you and you say a second appraisal is in order and I order one."

"I will call my uncle. He will come quickly as a favor to me," Wendy said.

"What I don't understand," Neil said. "is why am I writing a check for the fee of the first appraiser?"

"Proof," Lim replied.

While J.G. Garding sat in his office letting his huge battery operated fan keep him relatively comfortable, Doug Lim quietly sent his people home one by one, beginning with Valerie who was red-faced and perspiring heavily.

"Go across the street," he said. "Get yourself some ice tea. They have power."

Valerie was the first of the section to sit down and order ice tea. She was soon joined by Neil and Janis Thai.

"Wendy must stay with her uncle," Janis reported. "But so far all gems are bogus."

"Lim's going into the lion's den alone," Neil said.

"More like the fiery furnace," Valerie quipped.

"He's got more guts than me," Neil confessed. "Boy, it was hot as hell in there!"

"We could call him," Valerie suggested. "You know... tell him we're with him."

Back in his office in the bank, Lim called Harriet Locke.

"Just as you thought," he said.

"I alerted the Chairman of the Board. He's on his way over. Wait for him."

Lim did as he was told. He waited in his office and the Chairman approached him directly. "Where is everyone?" the Chairman asked.

"It is too hot to work," Lim said politely. "I sent them home."

"Why are those people over there working?"

"They are not members of my section."

"Just a minute," he said. He walked over to the other section, spoke with one man and then came back. Lim saw everyone grabbing coats and heading for the elevators. They crowded around the door and stood there for a few minutes punching the buttons before it dawned on them that the power outage meant the elevators weren't working. Laughing, they headed for the stairs.

Sprattley emerged from Garding's office, started at the group, singling out one and looking directly the man asked sternly, "Who gave you permission to leave?"

He pointed to the chairman sauntering toward him with Doug Lim at his side. Sprattley decided he should give Garding a heads up and ducked back in the office.

"The chairman is here," he said shutting down one of the fans.

"Don't do that," Garding said. "You want him to swelter?"

Sprattley turned the fan back on.

The chairman smiled as he entered. "Cooler in here. Glad it's not as hot as out there."

Garding rose, "Mr. Gillis, I didn't expect you. What a nice surprise."

"Mr. Lim tells me you've hung onto the Tontine Trust that wanted to leave us."

"The Tontine is big. We can't afford to lose it," Garding explained wiping his brow. "We felt that Harriet Locke was being vindictive because we didn't promote her people fast enough and wanted to appeal to the other members of the Group."

"But we still have it legally, right?" Gillis asked.

"Yes," Sprattley answered him, happy with the way this meeting appeared to be going. "Three-quarters of the assets must be transferred before the transfer is considered final. It's a peculiarity of the Trust documents."

"And your sale of the painting and sculpture wasn't risky," Gillis inquired.

"We had the money in hand before we transferred the art," Sprattley reported happily. "We were careful."

Garding beamed.

"You bought rubies today, correct?" Gillis questioned.

"Yes, we did," Sprattley answered, smiling.

"Did Mr. Lim suggest this buy?" Gillis asked pointedly.

"No, he had nothing to do with it," Garding declared. "Mr. Sprattley and I made this deal. We already have a buyer lined up. We will realize a handsome profit for the Tontine."

"It will come out to ten percent," Sprattley boasted.

"Were the rubies appraised by our regular appraiser?"

"Well, no. We had to move quickly on this deal," Sprattley said. "I substituted a qualified appraiser."

"How did you find him?"

"The seller suggested him," Sprattley said.

"Mr. Lim ordered a second appraisal," Gillis said.

"You didn't pass that by me," Sprattley said staring down his long nose at the mild-mannered protégé of Harriet Locke.

"It's standard protocol if there is a doubt," Lim stated.

"And you're an expert on gems?" Sprattley scoffed.

"No, I'm not," Lim said.

"And who's paying for the second appraisal?" Sprattley charged.

"The Trust," Lim replied.

Sprattley looked at Garding.

"You cost the Tontine money," Garding dictated. "You will personally reimburse them."

"The stones are worthless," Gillis said. "I have the second report here. You were duped. Had you followed standard bank protocol, they never would have made it into our vault."

"The sale's tomorrow," Garding said, now sweating profusely. "The buyer is expecting the gems."

"Surely, you aren't suggesting we perpetuate this fraud," Gillis charged.

"No, no, of course not," Sprattley blurted out. "We would never suggest that. We were just overwhelmed by the second report."

"We thought we could trust the man we were dealing with," Garding put in hastily, wiping his brow.

"We'll call the police and you can file a report," Gillis decided. "We've got the sellers on fraud."

"No, we can't... I mean, we shouldn't. It's just a mistake," Garding stammered. "We can straighten it out. I only need to make a phone call."

Gillis pointed at the phone. "Do it."

"What happened?" Harriet asked.

"The power is back on. The air conditioner is working. I can breathe again."

"Lim, don't tease. Tell me what happened."

"The remainder of the Tontine will begin to be transferred tomorrow. Everyone is gone now but me."

"And Garding and Sprattley?"

"Garding wanted to buy the rubies. Gillis said no. He said the bank would not defraud an ex-employee, even one such as he."

"So the Tontine Trust is out one million?" Harriet asked.

"Not so. Garding and Sprattley did an illegal trade. The Bank Commissioner will be called. My guess is that he will require restitution to the Trust."

"What about Rimmel?"

"With the Tontine gone, we're downsizing," Doug replied. "He's at the top of my list."

Chapter 36

Junior, his cast reaching from his ankle to his upper thigh, was lying in his hospital bed when two men entered his room.

The sight of the pair terrified him. He began to beg for another chance. Once he got out, he'd find his family, he promised. All they needed to do was give him a chance.

They pressed for details and Junior babbled on about this gigantic summer place his parents went to every year for a week. Every one of the Tontine members went there, he told them. He didn't have an address but he remembered a postcard from the place his mom had sent his sons last year. They'd tacked it up on the bulletin board in the kitchen.

"I'm sure I could recognize the place," he said. "And I can talk my mother into anything. I got the paper signed, didn't I?"

"Why didn't ya go find 'em?"

"I looked everywhere. I couldn't find them."

"And now you can?"

"Hell, I was out of jail, so I really didn't need 'em."

"You wasn't worried?"

"About what?"

"You seen their houses."

"Yeah, so?" Junior sloughed off any concern he might have had as immaterial. "I knew I could find them when I needed them."

"Your mother must be some psycho broad to love a shit like you."

Junior pushed himself up on his elbows. "Hey! Hold on. She's a good woman!"

"She's your mother, ain't she?" the bigger one said. "Come on let's go."

"You can't find her without me," Junior insisted.

"You wanna watch us off your mother?"

"I thought you was just gonna talk to her," Junior cried, his fear constricting his throat. "Nobody said nothing about killing."

"We got her note. We don't want her to change her mind."

"I can be sure she doesn't," Junior croaked, the fear causing beads of perspiration to emerge from the pores on his forehead.

"Our way is surer," came the reply.

The two men found the postcard pinned to the bulletin board in Junior's kitchen. They began driving north immediately. Four hours later they arrived at the town on the postcard. It was evening, but when they inquired at the general store they were told about the large cabin overflowing with families.

A twenty bought them the phone number at the cabin.

A man answered. The leader of the pair asked politely to speak with Julia Danielson. He was asked his name.

"It's about her son," the man said.

"Which one?" the voice at the cabin asked.

"Junior," came the reply. "He's in the hospital."

"We know."

"I was just with him. He sent me with a message."

"Asking for money?" the voice asked.

"It's personal."

"She's not here," the voice said. Abruptly the phone went dead. "He said she wasn't there," the man said returning the receiver to the hook. He frowned.

"And you believe him?"

"I dunno."

"We should check."

"How?"

His partner pointed at a boat rental place. "We go fishing. They bite really good in the evening."

"We won't be able to see soon."

"So they won't see us neither."

"Great plan," was the sarcastic reply.

"We use our listening stuff. It can pick up sound."

"Not from inside the house you dummy."

"It's a hot night."

"So what?"

"Look it where we is. It's hot. Now where's someone gonna cook?"

"Let's go get us a boat."

At Sandy Parker's farm and kennel, Ed balked when Beatrice said she wanted to leave for Praetzel's house right away. Lauren had delayed the second breeding until the next morning; but, she said she was flexible.

"But Harriet isn't?" Beatrice said. "She says we gotta complete our business now before..."

"Before what?" Ed persisted, then seeing the distressed look in his love's face, guessed. "Her life's in danger."

Beatrice nodded. "You stay here with Emma. This is important."

Ed grew somber. "I don't want you waltzing into danger."

"Harriet's afraid the dogs will be shot. She says both times, Stoney saved her. So that's why I have to leave the dogs here."

"Your Scotties don't look anything like a Chessie," Ed argued.

Lauren popped in with a bit of news. "Someone broke into Marge's house with three cardboard dog carriers. Lyle believes they were going to kidnap her dogs. He wants her dogs to stay here."

"Did they catch the guy?"

"No, he got away."

"Does Lyle think my dogs are a target?" Beatrice asked, her voice trembling.

"Stanley doesn't have kennels. Evelyn is sending her Goldens here," Lauren reported.

"I won't leave Emma," Ed declared. "She comes with us."

"She can't," Lauren said. "They're depending on Stoney as a warning device. Emma's ripe. Stoney wouldn't be able to do his job with her around. You could cost Stoney his life."

Ed's countenance fell. "Sometimes we gotta do hard stuff."

"So I'm going alone?" Beatrice asked. "It's okay Ed. Just pet my little guys once in a while."

"Sandy'll have to do that," Ed said. "I'm coming with you. You do know I won't be worth much without Emma."

"Don't underestimate yourself, Ed Ornstein," Beatrice said. She threw her arms around him and kissed him.

Fogg Spader had tagged along after the two Ciccone brothers. His car was parked several fields away. He kept track of the activity from the second floor window of Praetzel's nearest neighbor to the east, tying up and gagging the maid.

He saw Harriet climb on top of the RV. He saw her shoot two men, neither of which were the Ciccone brothers.

He stayed planted next to the window with his binoculars, watching the cops and other people come and go all afternoon. Three dogs with long coats were loaded into a van and driven off the premises. He waited for the brown dogs to be likewise transported but they weren't.

Instead, he watched Harriet leave the house with the big dog. She entered her RV and emerged with two more dogs. All stayed with her while she walked toward the barn.

First she waited for each to relieve itself and then she played a game of fetch with them. It was late in the day but the sun hadn't set yet.

Dogs were creatures of habit. People were creatures of habit. The barn was the perfect place to wait.

Chapter 37

Fogg Spader waited until the dark had settled over the land and only a scattering of lights were visible through the trees. He snuck down the far edge of the property using only the faint moonlight to make his way. He moved stealthily to the rear of the property and then snuck back in toward the barn.

There was almost no breeze; however, he had been told by his brother in the burn unit that Harriet's big dog could hear the crack of a twig at a hundred yards and smell him even with no breeze.

There were so many scents left by the myriad of police milling around all afternoon that Fogg hoped that his scent would mix with those and the dogs wouldn't realize he was there. He didn't realize dogs could distinguish between new scents and old ones.

But that wasn't as important as the proximity of a live scent as opposed to an old scent. A dog would know immediately that there was a strange man in the barn.

Still Fogg climbed up into the loft confident that being high meant he was beyond detection. He loaded his rifle and the tranquilizer dart gun and lay down to wait.

His plan was only half-formed in his mind, but it seemed like a good one. He planned to shoot Harriet Locke when she came out to walk her dogs and then set the barn on fire to keep everyone busy while he escaped across the field in back.

The darts weren't for the dogs. He planned to shoot them too. The darts were for the cop that accompanied her.

He wasn't a cop killer.

Earlier that evening the members of the Tontine arrived. Beatrice and Ed were the first and a fire was started in the barbecue pit outside, benches were dragged over and conversation dwelt on the recent happenings. Marge was brought in by police escort and shortly afterward Julia and Jason drove in. Harriet's three dogs, being the only ones now on the property were given free rein of the area.

Had Fogg Spader come at that time, he would have been immediately singled out by the dogs and apprehended.

The men stayed outside and talked, except for Stanley, who according to Harriet, because he was the Tontine's lawyer, needed to be privy to that evening's discussions.

The women gathered around the huge fireplace, sitting on patio furniture dragged from Stanley's storeroom and canvas armchairs plucked from the RV's. A folding table served as Stanley's desk with his right arm still useable, he dug out several large yellow legal pads and set them on the table along with a cup full of pens. Stanley was used to working at home.

Harriet began with a declaration that it was time to share secrets. She could sense that guards were being raised. "I've almost been killed three times and I have a foreboding. I sense more death. I don't know whose; but, it is vital that what I know not die with me."

The women blanched.

Aleta spoke first. "Do you foresee your own death?"

"Not clearly, but I have a strange foreboding."

She looked meaningfully at Marge who blurted out, "You want me to start, don't you?"

"If something should happen to me, don't you want someone to know why the Tontine has been making regular payments to the Brookfield Home in Wisconsin?"

"I thought it was for her mother," Beatrice put in.

Harriet was silent.

"It's for my daughter," Marge said quietly. "She was born with Down's Syndrome and a bad heart. We didn't expect her to live. Nathan and I talked about keeping her but I was pregnant with Nathan Junior by the time she was ready to leave the hospital and the care she needed was too much, so we put her in an institution. After the baby came, Nathan had his accident and I knew I couldn't handle a paraplegic and a baby and a child needing twenty-four hour care, so we left her in the institution."

Murmurs of sympathy greeted her revelation.

"I still feel so guilty," Marge confessed. "I have time for dog shows and volunteering but not time for my own child."

"You are talking bits of time spent here and there as opposed to a twenty-four hour commitment. How would you feel if you'd fallen asleep from exhaustion and she'd died while you were sleeping," Beatrice said, then asked, "Is she happy?"

Marge smiled. "She loves her home."

"Does she have friends?" Evelyn asked.

"Oh, yes. She has two best friends who are in similar situations. They enjoy things together. And the Home provides lots of good activities. She and her friends make lunch for the whole house sometimes. I told her about sliced bananas in peanut butter sandwiches and they were such a hit, she keeps asking me for new ideas."

"So she knows you're her mother?" Julia asked.

"I cry every time I leave her; but, then I think about how protected she is. And how happy. And I remember that my visits add to her life. She doesn't know anything else. It would be cruel to remove her now."

Beatrice cleared her throat. "My secret isn't as noble as Marge's..."

Marge sputtered, "Noble?"

"Well, at least your baby was legitimate," Beatrice said.

Evelyn moved over and put her arm around her friend's shoulder. She could tell she was getting ready to cry.

"Is that why you couldn't have children?" Marge asked gently. Sometimes it was easier to open up indirectly.

"That was God's punishment for my transgression," Beatrice said tears streaming down her face.

"Why tell us now?" Julia asked.

Marge spoke up. "Because she has someone she wants the Tontine to care for should anything happen to her.

Beatrice nodded.

"But you'll have money," Julia said. "We all will."

"I have grandchildren," Beatrice said. "I want the Trust to be there for them just in case, you know, like it will be for your grandchildren, Julia, like it will be for Marge's little girl. That's why Harriet has given her power of attorney over to Aleta, who's young enough to carry on the purpose of the Trust."

The women nodded with understanding. Beatrice knew that she didn't need to say another word.

"I think by now you've a good idea what I'm concerned about," Evelyn declared. "And it's more immediate than Marge's and Beatrice's. Harriet promised me if ever my eccentricities fall into the category of needing constant care, I would not be placed in a mental institution."

"I did promise that!" Harriet affirmed, turning to Aleta. "Private care. With her dogs around her. But I don't think it will come to that. Evelyn and I are going to build new homes on the small rolling acreage with the pond. She will be too busy with that and her other project to fall apart for a long time."

"Well, that's a relief," Aleta said. "I plan on spending the next few years teaching Stanley how to show dogs and fixing up my kitchen."

"Are we going to have a wedding?" Harriet asked impishly, "Or are we going straight into domestic bliss Aleta-style."

"Straight into domestic bliss unless your secret will dissuade Stanley from his chosen path."

Harriet Locke gasped. She hadn't planned to share hers now with Stanley present.

"This isn't a good time," Harriet said, her words coming out stilted.

"It's nothing to be ashamed of," Marge said kindly.

"You know?" Beatrice asked.

"I found out by accident," Marge said. "We were talking about Elyria. Ohio and my family, it seems, knew her father."

"I thought Harriet's father died before she was born," Beatrice said.

"He didn't," Marge said simply. "But my family remembers him as a gentle, exceptionally knowledgeable man who, but for his color, would have been a university professor."

"His color?" Aleta breathed softly.

The room was quiet for a long minute. Eyes left Aleta's ashen face and wandered over to Stanley's.

He spoke softly, but soberly, "Well, of course we have a few family secrets; but, I'm not sharing. I bound by law to keep your secrets. Lawyer-client privilege. But, you aren't sworn to keep mine and my mother would be furious. And my mother is a formidable woman. I have no intention of angering her."

"So are you going to marry Aleta or not?" Beatrice asked. She knew Aleta needed an answer.

"Why would there be any question?" Stanley responded. "I was hoping Harriet would have a family secret I could hold over Aleta's head at critical moments. This isn't as horrible as I'd hoped for; but it will have to do."

Two of the women tittered.

"Now," Stanley said, "Harriet brought this up for a reason."

"She didn't bring it up. Aleta did," Evelyn remarked.

"Aleta knows her grandmother," Stanley observed astutely. "So the question is who does Harriet want the Tontine to take care of?"

Harriet nodded. Stanley's conclusion was correct.

"I was the youngest by twelve years," she said. "I have an older brother and two older sisters who are well past retirement age. I've been able to send them all monthly stipends following their retirement so their income is slightly better than when they were working; but, my sons don't know. My father's family understands this. If I should die, I want the Tontine to care for them. I've already paid for the college education of their children and I want their grandchildren to have scholarships as well. Most of my nieces and nephews became teachers so they aren't rich people."

Julia began to smile. "I've been feeling so guilty all these years because each of you had been so supportive of my having so many needs with my big family. I couldn't understand it. This is such a relief! You have no idea how big a relief."

"It was important that this come out now, Julia," Harriet said. "Because as a group we need to tell you that the Tontine will not allow you to support Junior anymore."

To everyone's surprise Julia smiled. Inquiring looks bade her to explain.

"Aleta told me," Julia said. "She pulled out all stops, Harriet. Did you know that when she sent our family off to the lodge to hide, she sent a psychologist along with us?"

"No, she didn't tell me."

"He finished the job."

"So now what?"

"Jason Junior is on his own. His lawyer warned him. If he didn't believe him, that's his problem. This time he starts off with a broken kneecap, a hospital bill and five thousand in gambling debt. He's also out of our wills."

"He won't understand," Marge said.

"He'll get a glimmer when we mortgage our house to pay back that hundred thousand the Tontine put out."

Marge's face reflected her distress.

"Does she have to do that?" she asked Harriet.

Before Harriet could answer, Julia did. "Yes, I do. We can't undo the terrible thing our son did to you, Marge; but, at least we don't have to ask you to foot the bill."

"Well at least this year's distribution will help," Marge commented.

"I'm not taking a distribution this year," Julia said. "Jason and I decided we need to do this on our own. My three sons are returning the money the Tontine gave them too."

"That's not necessary," Aleta said. "It's reasonable compensation. They were innocents in our war with the mob."

"I vote with Aleta," Marge said. "The kids keep the money."

"Me too," Beatrice said. "And we keep supporting the two still in college. They shouldn't have the rug pulled out from under them either."

"Yes," Evelyn said. "And Julia's project gets funded just like the others."

"What about Junior's wife? What is she going to do?" Marge asked.

"My sons decided to help her pay for nursing school. She wants to be a nurse," Julia said. "That won't break any rules will it?"

"If it does," Marge said, "we need to change the rules."

"It doesn't," Aleta said. "But it could be a problem. Jason's creditors may come after her for Jason's debts."

"She's not ready to divorce him," Julia said. "Would a legal separation help? She's willing to do that."

"I'll look into it," Stanley said. "Meanwhile we need to stop the bleeding. Julia, you need to go see Jason and tell him yourself that he's on his own. Take a tape recorder. I may need to use his comments when talking with his wife."

Junior was surprised to see his parents when they arrived in his room at the hospital. His face lit up with happiness. His mom was here. Now everything was okay.

His father was the first to speak, however. Jason told his son what he and Julia had decided.

"So what's it mean?" Junior asked not fully comprehending.

"That your slate was cleaned for the last time yesterday. Your lawyer gave you a heads-up."

"But you're going to pay him, right?" Junior asked.

"He's expensive," his father commented.

"He's the best," Junior bragged.

"We decided to mortgage the house to pay him and that hundred thousand dollar debt you owed."

"The Trust will do that," Jason burst out angrily. "Don't try to con me."

"Actually, when you went after a member of the group, your mother lost her place in the group."

"She didn't have nothing to do with that!" Junior declared. "Did you tell them?"

"They know."

Junior pondered this for a minute. His mind raced toward a new argument.

"So what! You don't need them! You got money. You got a house and a shop. You can mortgage something," he said. "I ain't got no income so you gotta loan me some money."

"That's why we're here," Jason said. "If you'll promise to quit gambling, your wife can get a loan and pay off your hospital bill. Debbie can't afford to do more. She doesn't make enough money."

"Screw the hospital," Junior said. "Tell her to pay off my bookie. He's the one connected to the guys that done this." He tapped his cast as if having it suspended on ropes didn't make it obvious enough.

"What about the hospital?" his father asked.

"Debbie can get another job."

"Then she won't have time for your children."

"There's stuff like foster homes, ain't there?"

Julia blanched but remained mute.

Junior spotted her reaction. "Look, mom, it ain't as if I gotta choice. I gotta pay my bookie what I owe. But you gotta choice. You can help Debbie and me too. It ain't right your grandkids should starve when you got enough money to bail me outta this jam."

"Sorry, Junior," his father said. "We did that and you didn't take advantage of it."

"Look, I will this time. Honest," Junior begged. "I wasn't thinking."

"And you weren't thinking when you sent the mob to the lodge to kill your mother?" Jason asked.

"I didn't know they was planning that, honest! I found out after I told them where she was that they were planning that."

"And you didn't call and warn us?"

"They would a killed me," Junior wailed.

"Better your mother than you, huh?" Jason said, his anger barely in check.

"I didn't have no choice."

"You always have a choice," his father said. "And you've been getting away with making the wrong ones for too long."

"What's that mean?"

Jason turned and went to the door and waved at a man standing nearby. "Chief West, he's all yours."

West entered the room and arrested Jason Junior on conspiracy to commit murder.

"I want my lawyer," Junior cried as West handcuffed him to the bed.

A guard was posted outside the room and Jason took Julia's arm and left. Julia clicked off the tape recorder in her pocket.

Back at Stanley's house, the women took a break.

Stanley went outside and asked the man if there was any coffee left and the man checked the RV's and reported that they'd put on two new pots. Stanley stayed outside and sat by the fire. He told them he'd wait.

"Don't they need you?" Ed asked.

"They're taking a break. Nobody's going to say anything important for the next half hour," he replied.

Twenty minutes passed before Aleta noticed he wasn't nearby.

"He went for coffee," Harriet responded to her query.

Suddenly, Aleta was frightened. "You don't think anything happened to him?"

The anxiety in her voice roused the dogs. Stoney came over and pushed his muzzle against Harriet.

"He wants to go out," Harriet said.

"It's too dark out," Aleta said. "Go lay down, Stoney. You too, Babe. Keeper, just stay put."

The dogs reluctantly settled down.

Stanley returned and the women settled down to the business of funding each one's special projects.

Two hours later there was a knock on the door. The women exchanged glances. Ed and Ron had long ago given in to fatigue and retired. The door was opened by the officer on duty.

Julia and Jason stood outside. "May Jason join us? There's no one left out here. And I want to share what happened at the hospital, okay?"

The two were welcomed warmly and Julia began the tale with the end. "He's under arrest for conspiracy."

"How'd that come about?"

"We called West on our way over," Julia said. "We were worried about Jason's wife and the mob coming after her. We wanted Junior back in jail while we sorted things out. I'd like you to hear the tape. I'm so proud of Jason."

Murmurs of assent were quickly given.

The room was silent while the tape ran.

"I don't know if the judge will allow this as evidence," Stanley said.

"West told us that," Jason responded. "However, I can testify."

"And so can I," Julia said.

"And you're going to be okay doing that?" Marge asked.

"People were coming to kill me and he did nothing. That's what I'm not okay about," Julia replied somberly.

Stoney nudged Harriet and whined.

Harriet stood up. "You'll have to excuse me. Stoney needs to go out. Meanwhile, go on Beatrice, make your offer. Stanley can keep it legal.

Beatrice cleared her throat. "Marge and I want to hold the mortgage on your house."

Harriet slipped out the door.

After the door closed, Aleta glanced at the fireplace where the rifles were. She had gone out in the dark without a gun.

A sinking feeling in the pit of Aleta's stomach told her that this wasn't good.

"How low can we go on interest?" Beatrice asked Stanley. Aleta heard the question, but her worry shoved the response out of her mind.

Her grandmother wasn't safe. She shouldn't be out alone with just Stoney. The other Spader brothers both struck in the wee hours of the morning when the world slept. Why shouldn't the third brother have the same preference? The only difference would be that he'd be prepared for Stoney.

Aleta went over to the fireplace and took the rifle from the mantle and opened it to check its load. She grabbed some shells from the box and stuffed them into her jeans pocket.

"Aleta, what are you doing?" Stanley gasped.

"I'm just going to bring Grams her gun," Aleta responded as she clicked the gun closed. She moved quickly toward the door. "Go on with your discussion. I'll be right back."

Stanley heard her speak to the cop outside the door and instantly relaxed. They'd take care of her. He went back to explaining to the women that the interest had to be close to the current rate.

Aleta walked swiftly from the first guard to the second one who was posted next to the RV's. She spoke to him briefly. He nodded an acceptance of her order. She trotted with her rifle held barrel up toward her grandmother who was a hundred feet ahead of her. Stoney romped ahead of the seventy-year-old who's step was spritely enough to keep the distance between her and her dog less than fifty feet.

Despite her quick pace, Harriet was enjoying the stillness and the myriad of earthy smells. The night air was balmy, not even raising one goose bump on her bare arms. The lights in the house behind her were less helpful as she approached the barn. She knew the area was free of debris that would cause her to fall. The men had left nothing behind. Still she slowed her step.

In the loft, Fogg Spader watched her approach. Behind her he saw a young woman with a rifle hurrying to catch up.

She didn't have a flashlight either. He couldn't believe his luck.

Slowly, he rose because the dog was coming close and the angle was wrong. He reached for his gun in the darkness and cursed because the two had the same feel. He'd forgotten which was which.

Harriet had envisioned the total darkness she was now in. She sensed that terror waited in the dark. That was all. Nothing more. She wondered if her prophetic powers had been taken from her.

After the last shootings where she'd killed two men, she'd experienced a lessening in her ability to prophesy with clarity.

She was back to vague feelings of uneasiness and a fleeting sense that she was supposed to be here at this moment. Whatever God had in store, she was ready. Her friends were eagerly discussing how to help Jason and Julia and do it properly. She'd clued them into her other family's needs. Her work was done. Aleta could take over now. She was glad that this time Aleta was out of harm's way.

Harriet had sensed that somehow Aleta was going to be embraced by the same darkness that awaited her. There was no way she could have told her to stay behind. Aleta had to feel that she was just going for a bit of air where the policemen were stationed which is why she left her gun behind.

Then she heard the footsteps coming up behind her. She recognized Aleta's light footfall and spun around.

Stoney, who had loped all the way to the barn, stopped dead just outside the huge yawning opening beyond which was total darkness. His nose told him a man was lurking there. He looked up. The scent was above him. He growled. It was not a loud growl so Harriet and Aleta didn't hear it. The man in the loft, however, did.

Harriet, with her back to the barn, shouted at her granddaughter. "Go back to the house! Now!"

As if to punctuate her yell, a gunshot pierced the night air. The two women jumped at the unexpected sound. Stoney's yipe of pain followed the report. Electrified, Harriet rushed toward her fallen dog.

Aleta swung the rifle to her shoulder and shot at the area in the loft where she'd stood earlier that afternoon. She heard a yell. She'd hit him.

She began to run toward her grandmother. She heard two sets of running footsteps behind her. Flashlights swung thin beams around. They weren't yet close enough to light up the loft.

She couldn't see the man, but she knew her grandmother who was kneeling over her dog, cradling him in her arms was too easy a target.

Aleta fired another round into the loft. There was no answering yell this time. The man had either moved or was lying injured, possibly dead on the floor.

The beam from the flashlight of the cop coming up behind Aleta caught the glint of a rifle barrel. It was pointing down. Aleta realized she was wrong. He was still there and ready to fire.

Harriet, looking up, saw the man aiming a rifle at her. She quickly fell on her dog to protect him. Her movement, quick as it was, didn't take her out of his line of sight. Fogg Spader pulled the trigger.

The rifle bullet hit its target. Harriet collapsed over her dog.

Aleta's rifle was up and aimed at the man in the loft a fraction of a second too late to prevent him from squeezing the trigger. Her shot, however, caught him before he could move back out of the flashlight's beam.

He doubled over and fell back out of the flashlight's range.

Aleta ran to her grandmother, knelt down, and called to the cop behind her. "Call for an ambulance!"

The man in the loft saw men spilling out of the RV's and the house with guns in their hands. A pair of large dogs raced alongside them.

Fear of getting caught or killed quelled his sudden desire to put a bullet in the woman who had shot him. His gut was on fire and the men were coming too fast. He needed to get out of there.

Hastily he lit the string of firecrackers with his lighter and tossed them onto the dry wisp of straw on the barn floor. Tiny fires started up as the firecrackers lit up the dry fodder.

At the first pop, the running men dropped to the ground. The quick little pops and the small fires allayed their fears and they hurriedly scrambled to their feet and ran toward the barn.

Old bales of hay had been stacked against the barn walls by the forensic team who had found only one useable ladder in the barn. The falling firecrackers missed the bales, but one of the wisps of straw pushed away by a tiny explosion landed on the corner of a bale near the door and set it on fire.

"Let's get that bale away from the barn!" Ron Maxwell shouted. "Or the whole place will go up."

Jason and Ed diverted to help him while two cops, guns in hand, entered the barn. The cops proceeded cautiously.

Babe and Keeper circled the melee confused by the smell of gunpowder, the fire and a myriad of human scent. They followed Stanley over to Aleta.

Shielding her with his back, Stanley persuaded Aleta to let him look at the woman and dog she was shielding. Babe stuck her nose in with his hands that ran down the back of the fallen dog. Babe whined at Stoney to get up. Stanley's fingers touched the tranquilizer dart. He yanked it out.

"Stoney was tranquilized," he told Aleta as he gently turned her grandmother over. More blood was oozing out from the exit wound then from the entrance wound.

"Grams was shot," Aleta announced superfluously. "I've got blood on my hands."

She held them up and Keeper licked them.

A siren's wail could be heard. It was coming fast.

"She's still breathing," Stanley said, "Give me your shirt."

Aleta pulled off her tee shirt and Stanley pressed it against Harriet's shoulder. He told Aleta to keep the pressure on the wound while he directed the ambulance. Aleta pressed on the wound and prayed.

Babe and Keeper crowded around licking Harriet's face and Aleta's hand. They whined softly.

Harriet opened her eyes.

"Stoney?" The question was an almost unintelligible croak. The woman gasped for air.

"Tranquillized," Aleta replied. "He'll be okay."

Her thank you came out wordlessly. There was not enough air in her lungs to speak. She took a deep breath.

"Don't talk," Aleta said feeling the on rush of blood.

"Death in barn," she wheezed.

"You mean I killed the man who shot you?"

The head moved slightly side to side.

"Don't talk," Aleta said. "I'll ask the questions."

But before she could ask her first one, Harriet coughed out one word, "Explosion."

"In the barn?" Aleta asked, her mind racing. Two cops had gone into the barn. The other men were busy stomping out the small fires as the bale burned off to the side. Shouts were being hurled back and forth as sparks ignited new bits of dried grass. She couldn't even see the two policemen; but the others were moving through the doorway.

She realized that her voice even if it carried might not dissuade the men from their task.

She grabbed her rifle with one hand and, pointing it toward the field to the side of the barn, toward the empty dark field, and fired one round. The men paused, bewildered. She fired a second shot.

"There he is!" she shouted.

The cops emerged from the barn and began moving where the rifle was pointing. The other men went back to their self-appointed task of stomping out new sparks of fire.

She remembered what Stanley had said about not sacrificing herself to save his barn. She had no idea whether it was only the cops deep inside the barn who were in danger or whether it was anyone near the barn.

Harriet struggled to speak again. "Use senses you don't have."

She pulled the trigger on her rifle. The report cut through the noise and the man paused for a split second.

Her scream brought all three to her side.

"Are you hit?" Ron asked.

"Let me do that?" Ed said putting his hand on hers and allowing her to lean back. The two Chessies crowded close and Jason gently pushed them away. "Tell us where he shot you."

The explosion wasn't huge. It was from an old hand grenade tossed by Fogg Spader just before he descended the stairs. He'd heard the rifle shots and the shout. He had no idea whether the woman had seen him moving across the loft or not.

It didn't matter. The grenade would give him a few precious seconds.

Aleta, whose eyes were fixed on the barn, saw a shadow after the blaze of light. It slipped out the door in back into the dark field beyond.

The grenade set the barn on fire. She decided not to tell the men where the shooter had gone. If they gave chase, the light from the burning barn would make them easy targets.

She explained to the worried men that she hadn't been shot, but that Grams had told her that there would be an explosion.

"So you sent the cops on a wild goose chase?" Ron asked.

The ambulance rolled to a stop within a few feet of the group. The loud horn of the fire engine turning toward the barn cut into her answer.

"Can you carry Stoney someplace safe?" she shouted and Ron and Jason lifted the comatose dog while Ed kept his hand on Harriet's chest.

"Come on, Babe, Keeper, let's go back to the house," Aleta said, picking up her rifle. She walked off and the two dogs followed. She opened the rifle and reloaded as she was walking.

"Where's she going?" Stanley asked Ed as the paramedics took over.

"Taking the dogs back to the house."

"Good," Stanley said. Half of him recognized that that was a reasonable action considering that she was almost shirtless, but half of him knew Aleta would use that as an excuse if she had something else in mind. So, he didn't take his eyes off her until she was almost at the front door and the paramedic asked him a question.

He turned to answer. When he turned back Aleta was gone.

Suddenly, he realized she was going after the shooter. She knew where the man was.

He turned to Ed, "She knows where the man is. She's going after him with the dogs."

"Are you sure she didn't go into the house?" Jason asked.

Stanley only half heard him as he broke into a run. Ed and Jason followed.

Aleta, meanwhile, skirted around the backside of the house and entered the field where the darkness still was king. She could barely see a few feet in front of her but she walked straight out from the house a hundred yards before giving the two dogs beside her the command to quarter. They moved back and forth in front of her never moving beyond shooting range.

It was dark but their noses described in detail what their eyes saw vaguely. Neither dog knew that Aleta could see less well than either of them and had a worthless nose for hunting as well. How could a dog know that their scenting ability was forty times more powerful than a human's? It was the human brain that gave a number to the difference. The animal brain didn't concern itself with such matters. These two were on a mission. There was game in the field. They were to find it.

Being bird dogs they were ignoring the rabbit trails and concentrating on the scent of pheasant. They flushed two, but Aleta didn't shoot. Still she encouraged them to hunt so they kept going. They caught the scent of the man crouched in the grass and moved fearlessly toward him. Hunters frequently hid in blinds waiting for birds to be flushed by their dogs.

This man, however, didn't have the scent of excitement with which they were familiar. This man smelled of fear.

Keeper hesitated as did Babe. Aleta called both dogs to heel. She moved ahead slowly, one dog on each side.

She could see nothing which means her quarry could see nothing. She paused periodically and looked to see where her dog's noses were pointing.

Fogg Spader stayed crouched like a rabbit when a fox is hunting the field. Whoever it was couldn't see him, Fogg reasoned. After the man passed, Fogg figured, the light from the fire would outline the person's body and he'd nail him.

What he didn't realize was that while he was crouched so low that he blended in with the grass, the dog's noses pinpointed his location.

"Put the gun down," came the voice of a woman. It surprised the man hunched down in the wheat. The tone wasn't soft, but firm and commanding.

He raised his gun and aimed it at the voice and squeezed the trigger.

An answering shot hit his shoulder.

He reeled from the impact, but held his ground, determined to take out this woman. A third brother couldn't be beaten by a woman. The resolve overwhelmed his reason. If he died, she would die too.

Aleta saw the gun raised.

"Down!" she yelled. Babe and Keeper dropped to the ground as a third shot sailed over Keeper's head. Fog Spader keyed in on her voice and got off another round while she was reloading.

She answered his fire and again hit him. It was only a graze on his arm, but it fueled his fury. Rising he aimed downward. She had to be crouching as he had been. He fired both guns simultaneously. The tranquillizer dart hit Keeper and she yiped.

Aleta took careful aim at the shadow lurching toward her and squeezed the trigger. She hit Fogg Spader in the chest and he fell face forward only twenty feet from where she was.

She heard his death rattle and turned to check out Keeper. The dog was breathing but comatose.

Men came running, flashlights in their hands. She was surprised that it took them so long. She didn't realize that once the battle began, only a few minutes had passed. Without the dogs to guide them, the men had moved through the field at half her speed.

Ed checked the fallen man and ascertained that he was dead. Jason picked up the fallen dog and carried her toward the house. Stanley led Aleta away.

"You told me not to save the barn," she said.

"And this is what you thought I meant?" Stanley queried. "Obviously, I need to work on my communication skills."

"Or you could just add, 'and don't chase the bad guys'."

"Would you obey?"

"I didn't save the barn did I?"

Chapter 38

The entire group went to the hospital with Aleta. They were alone in the waiting room on the third floor. Chief Lyle West posted men at the doors. Chief Milani called him earlier just as the ambulance was departing with Harriet to the hospital. Milani wasn't too optimistic. West called Martha Cook who immediately called in a specialist.

By the time Aleta arrived, the specialist had already arrived by helicopter from Cook County Hospital. Aleta pushed to have her grandmother flown to a larger hospital; but, Stanley told her that the Tri City Hospital was well-equipped.

"Martha Cook lives here," he said. "Her grandson practices here."

"I want the best," Aleta said, her voice near breaking. "I let her go out alone. What was I thinking?"

Stanley put his arm around his betrothed. "Ask yourself what was she thinking?"

"If she'd taken her gun, I'd have gone with her," Aleta confessed. "She didn't want me to come. She was angry when she saw me."

"So she knew something was going to happen?"

"I think so."

"So she chose to save you."

Aleta's eyes blazed. "She doesn't have the right."

"You mean you have the right to sacrifice yourself for her and she doesn't have the right to do the same."

Aleta refused to back down. "Absolutely!"

"You love her that much?"

Aleta's tone softened, "Absolutely."

"Do I get to sacrifice myself for you?"

"Absolutely not!"

"Why not?"

"I don't want to live without you," Aleta said.

Stanley grinned, "Now we're back on a page I like."

"I should call my dad," Aleta said.

"Let's hear the prognosis first," Stanley advised. "It'll only be a matter of minutes and you don't want to be on the phone when they come to tell us."

Aleta managed to sit still for four minutes. She looked at her watch seven times and complained three times.

"When we have children," Stanley said, "I hope they realize you are the impatient sort and don't take too much time being born."

"I'm not impatient," Aleta snapped. "I have lots of patience."

"Did you tuck all of it in your other pants," Stanley asked, "because you didn't bring any with you."

"This is different! Grams could die."

Stanley gathered her to him with his one good arm. "Use my good shoulder," he said softly.

Aleta leaned on him and began to cry.

In the corner of the room the women joined hands and quietly began to pray. Dr. Cook opened the door and entered and they stopped to listen.

"We're going to operate," he said simply. "We had to replace some of the blood loss first."

"I thought the bullet went through," Aleta said.

"She's bleeding internally," the doctor explained.

"Is she going to live?"

"I hope so," Dr. Cook said.

He left the room as Aleta protested, "That's not an answer!"

She turned toward Stanley and asked in an anguished voice, "What am I going to tell my father?"

"The truth," Stanley replied.

"He'll be asleep," Aleta said.

"Well, the news will put an end to that," Stanley said. "I guarantee he'll be wide awake when he flies out here. Sprinkle a bit of good news in with the bad."

"Good news?"

"Your grandmother is still alive and a specialist is working on her. That's the good news."

"Oh," Aleta said only half hearing him. "Good news with the bad. Good news with the bad."

She dialed her parents' home. "Dad, are you sitting down…? Well, of course I know what time it is… Grams has been shot… Yes, shot… with a gun… I'm at the hospital… No, I haven't been shot. Well, at least not today. I was shot a few days ago… Yes, I'm fine; but, Grams could die… The doctors didn't give me any idea what her chances were… It's bad, Dad. She was shot in the back. There's a lot of internal bleeding… No, it wasn't a hunting accident… She was shot on purpose… Well, not exactly…"

She turned to Stanley. "He wants to know if the man was caught."

"Tell him."

"He wasn't actually caught. I shot him. I killed him, Dad… He wouldn't stop shooting at me, Dad… He wouldn't stop. I had to…"

Stanley took the phone from Aleta's hand and introduced himself and gave his future father-in-law several phone numbers before he hung up. He then turned to Aleta.

"He'll be on the next flight. Your mother's coming too, as well as your uncle."

"Why's my mother coming?"

"To take you home," Stanley said. "It seems your ex-boyfriend made quite a deal about this being a dangerous place for his future bride."

"He didn't tell them about us?"

"Guess not."

Four hours later, Dr. Cook came through the door and his smile told the group what they longed to hear. Two hours later, Harriet was moved out of intensive care.

"Five minutes," Dr. Cook said when they all crowded into the room after promising that only one would talk.

Aleta cleared her throat and began by telling her grandmother that her two sons were flying out.

"What for?"

"I need to see my dad," Aleta said simply.

"Oh, okay then."

"Mom's coming to take me home," Aleta went on.

"Are you going?"

"I'm going to introduce her to Stanley," Aleta said, "and show her our house and tell her she can plan the wedding."

Harriet grinned, "You do know your mother, don't you?"

"Your secret is yours to share with the rest of the family," Aleta commented. "But only if you want to. Stanley and I intend to get to know that side of the family. We thought we'd be married a second time in their church. Would they like that?"

Tears sprang into Harriet's eyes. "I'm the one who would like that. Your great grandfather would be so proud."

"Stanley wants his parents there too, but it's up to you," Aleta went on. Her hesitant voice told her grandmother that she was afraid.

"I'll leave that decision up to you," Harriet said. "What about your own parents?"

"One wedding will be enough for them," Aleta responded firmly and Harriet knew she didn't want to tell her mother or sisters. Furthermore, she didn't want to burden her father with having to keep such a secret.

"How are your parents getting here? And who's watching my dogs?"

"Ron's taking care of the dogs," Aleta replied smiling. This part of her life was under control. "Stanley hired a limousine service to pick up Mom and Dad and Uncle Paul."

"Your mother will be so impressed," her grandmother said.

"It was Stanley's idea," Aleta said. "He thinks like a rich man."

"I am rich," Stanley said casually.

"Yeah," Aleta scoffed lightly. "Remember, I've been in your house."

"I've been busy working," Stanley said.

"A rich man would have had the work done."

"If he chose to."

"Nobody chooses not to have a kitchen!" Aleta declared.

"You're really fixated on having a kitchen, aren't you?"

"I'm not moving in without one!"

"When are we getting married?"

"When it's done."

"In a month then," Stanley decided, "unless you insist on doors on all the cabinets."

"I won't even go into contractor-type delays which are legendary because I want to know why the doors are a problem."

"They're going to be hand crafted."

"By you?"

"Me? No, of course not. I'm not a skilled carpenter. Besides we have a huge task ahead of us setting up the Funds. I wouldn't have the time."

"So who's this miracle contractor?"

"Martha Cook, of course," Stanley said.

Harriet laughed and, for the first time, Aleta realized exactly where the discussion was taking place.

She blushed and said hurriedly, "We should not be squabbling in here."

Harriet laughed again. "Don't deprive me of a good floor show. Go on, Aleta, tell Stanley how you plan to pull off a formal wedding with the mound of legal work you have in front of the two of you."

Stanley let the corners of his mouth turn up. Aleta spotted the smug look. Her response was quick and decisive.

"That's what mothers are for," she declared. "My mother buys all my clothes now. She is certainly capable of picking out a wedding dress."

"There's more to a wedding than a dress," Stanley put in casually.

"I know that. I've been watching Mom fussing over the details of my sister's wedding for months now. She's got plenty of experience. No sense letting that go to waste."

Harriet laughed just as Dr. Cook walked in.

"I was going to tell you all that your time's up, but seeing as how you have our patient laughing, you can stay a few more minutes."

Aleta turned to Dr. Cook and challenged him. "Stanley says that your grandmother can complete his kitchen in a month, can she?"

"With or without the cabinet doors?" he asked.

Aleta met her parents and uncle at the hospital entrance. She was alone. Her happy face confirmed her earlier phone conversation telling them that Harriet had come through the operation successfully.

Her mother's first words were, "You're coming home with us. Conan is waiting. The firm won't hold your position much longer. And, good heavens, what happened to your head?"

"I told you I got shot," Aleta said. "I know it looks awful but Stanley doesn't care."

"Well, I do. I'll take you to the best plastic surgeon in the city when we get home."

Aleta scowled as the group entered the elevator. "It might heal."

"Well, we'll get you a wig," her mother went on. "San Francisco has good wig makers."

"Wigs are hot."

"You can't just go around in public looking like that!" her mother declared.

"Why not? I've nothing to be ashamed of. Besides the skin is sunburned and Dr. Cook says to keep it uncovered."

Aleta's dad gave her a hug. "Doesn't bother me any. A battle scar is rather an interesting additive to a pretty woman."

"That's what Stanley said," Aleta responded, holding out her hand. "We're engaged."

"Is that real?" her mother asked. "Conan said he gave you a piece of used junk."

Before Aleta could defend her ring, her father said hurriedly, "It's lovely, Aleta. A family heirloom, isn't it? He must really be smitten. No one parts with a family heirloom lightly."

Aleta giggled. "Smitten. Yes, Dad. That's the word."

"I'd like to meet him. Is he here?"

"His parents have invited us for lunch. We'll pick him up at his place on the way."

"So you're here to stay, are you?"

"Grams is going to build a house here near her friends so I'll have some family here. Her friends have been great. They all let me show their dogs and Stanley and I have already ordered two puppies. I'm going to teach him to show. And he has an empty office next to his where I can hang my own shingle.

"Sounds great!" her dad said enthusiastically. "I haven't seen you this excited since you graduated from law school."

Paul Locke picked up the conversation as they headed down the hall, "What kind of dogs?"

"A black Lab male out of two really nice dogs. And a Bulldog bitch, probably in a year."

Paul laughed. "Does my mother know you've left her favorite breed in the dust?"

"We've been too busy…," Aleta started as she pushed open the door.

Paul and Robert hurried over to their mother's bedside. They were shocked at how wan and lifeless she appeared. Aleta quickly assured them that she was doing well.

"Is the doctor available? We want to speak with him," both demanded in unison.

Aleta glanced at her watch. "He's still at the clinic; but, we could go over there and wait."

"Why isn't he here?"

"He's just next door. It's the free clinic. You saw it on your way in."

Aleta's mother cut in. "You mean you had the doctor of a free clinic operate on Harriet?"

"He called in a specialist," Aleta said. "And he checks on her more than most doctors would."

But Marian Locke wasn't through with her daughter. "We have money. You know that. Why didn't you have her transported to one of the city hospitals?"

"Stanley said this was better," Aleta said.

"Better?" Marian scoffed. "How can a small town hospital be better?"

"Because Martha Cook lives here," Aleta said. "That's how Stanley explains it. You really have to be from here to understand."

A light rap was heard and a man in a white coat stepped into the room and went straight to the woman in the bed. "Harriet, how are you?"

He took her hand and felt her pulse after which he turned to her two sons. "The nurse told me you'd arrived. I'm certain you have questions. Let's step outside. Mrs. Locke, why don't you come as well."

The three followed the doctor outside and Aleta looked hard at her grandmother. "You don't look well." She took her hand and it was cold.

"Keep your mother out of here," Harriet whispered.

"Done!" Aleta stated staunchly.

She saw the lines in her grandmother's forehead fade. She rubbed the thin hand gently.

"Did I upset you?" she asked. "I won't be insulted if I'm too… too… much for you right now. Please tell me."

"You?" Harriet smiled weakly. "You are my life, my enthusiasm, my light."

"But Stanley and I argued in front of you."

"And that was more fun than a hundred TV shows."

Color began to come into the old woman's cheeks. "And Stanley is welcome anytime too."

Outside Robert was telling Dr. Cook that he and Paul would take care of all Harriet's medical expenses.

"Aleta has already done that," Dr. Cook said.

"Aleta?" Robert inquired. "She has no access to any money."

"Did she charge it?" Marian asked. "She has my card."

"She paid it from the Trust."

"What Trust?"

"Your mother is part of a Trust. Aleta has her power of attorney. She just signed the bills. The Trust always pays immediately upon receipt of the bill."

"What Trust?" Robert repeated.

"Your mother must have set one up for her," Marian said. "But why not for her sisters? That's so unfair."

"Marian, hush," Robert said. "Doctor, can we talk with her about this Trust?"

"No," Dr. Cook stated flatly. "One of the three of you has upset her. Either that or whatever you were discussing. I'm afraid until I find out which, you can't visit her. She's not even a day post-op. We could still lose her."

"Why is Aleta in there?" Marian challenged.

"She makes her laugh and relaxes her," Dr. Cook replied.

"We are very powerful people!" Marian declared. "We will go to court if we have to. We didn't fly two thousand miles to be insulted."

"I'm not insulting you. I'm stating a fact. The three of you together with Aleta upset her."

"Then we'll tell Aleta to sit out on our visits," Marian said. "She's too young to be dealing with this."

"Believe me, Aleta spared no expense. Your mother had the best cardiac specialist in the whole Chicago area on her case."

"She didn't order a private duty nurse," Marian pointed out.

"Discuss it with your daughter. If she agrees, she'll arrange it. She has power of attorney to make decisions against Harriet's wishes. You don't."

Inside the room, Harriet patted Aleta's hand. "Even though you and your mother don't think alike, she loves you."

Aleta frowned. She didn't want to discuss her mother.

"Paul asked me if I told you what dogs Stanley and I were getting. He thought you would be upset if they weren't Chessies."

"The fact that you chose to bring up the topic means you know it wouldn't."

"One's a Lab."

"Out of whom?"

"Lyle's Morgan and Ed's Emma. You met her didn't you?"

"A lovely bitch. Almost made me want to change breeds."

"We also put in a bid for one of Maggie's pups. She's the Bulldog I showed."

"A Bulldog?"

"Stanley wants a Bulldog," Aleta responded happiness returning to her tone. "He went into the ring cold with one of Beatrice's Scotties. He saved the major, and, grams, he knew it! He is such a quick study. He says he enjoyed it. He even had a photo taken. He said he wanted to remember the first time he showed a dog."

Harriet put her hand on Aleta's arm. Aleta stopped talking and waited for her grandmother to speak.

"Aleta, when you go to Stanley's house, take your father to the barn and walk him through what happened. Be sure to take him up to the loft."

"It's been destroyed."

"No it hasn't. Stay close to the wall and go to the front. It's safe enough."

"Then what?"

"Then tell him why you were there."

Marian Locke complained all the way to Stanley's house about Dr. Cook.

When Marian wound down, Paul asked, "What kind of lawyer is Stanley... what's his last name?"

"Praetzel," Aleta said.

"I hope you don't plan on taking that name," her mother commented. "Modern girls frequently keep their maiden name."

"I haven't decided. Stanley's mother kept her maiden name, but that's because she was an established lawyer by the time she married. I'll be married when I set up my practice here."

"It's still a good idea to keep Locke," her mother insisted.

Aleta smiled inwardly. She was prepared for this one. "Perhaps you're right. Stanley has such a great reputation; I'd hate to tarnish it."

In the rear view mirror, Aleta saw her father smile.

When they drove down the driveway, Aleta grew uneasy.

"What are all these trucks doing here?" she asked.

Stanley came out of the house accompanied by several young men.

"There's Stanley," Aleta said. "Everything's okay."

"Why wouldn't it be?" Marian Locke asked glancing out the window at the men pouring out of the house. "Which one is Stanley?"

"The one with his arm in the sling," Aleta said.

"I wonder what's going on," her father said quickly to cover his wife's gasp of surprise. He leaned forward to shield Aleta from the frown of disapproval on his wife's face. He jumped out of the car first, and with his hand extended walked briskly up to Stanley and introduced himself and then his brother.

Marian lingered back in the car. "Aleta, you could have had your pick. Why him?"

Aleta remembered her father's smile, and it bolstered her spirit.

"The construction crew is here," Stanley said walking over to the car. "Where do you want the kitchen window and the sink?"

"Sink under the window," her mother said making the decision without being asked. She stepped out of the car and added, "Window facing a view."

Aleta nodded. "Mom knows what I like. Grams wants me to talk to Dad."

"That's your total input?" Stanley asked aghast.

"Mom's got great taste," Aleta said. "I've got to steal Dad away before he gets involved."

"But I don't know what kind of window you want," Stanley pleaded but Aleta took her father's arm and walked away.

Stanley turned to her mother and asked, "Do you know anything about windows?"

"Show me the ones you're considering."

"Come on inside. The architect drew up several versions of that wall."

"That must have cost a fortune," Marian commented as the two walked toward the house.

"Well, Aleta doesn't seem to like to delve into detail unless it's in the law. Then she's a sticker for it." Stanley held open the door. "Come on in Paul, I can use all the help I can get. I understand you're an architect."

"Well, yes, but…"

"So if Mrs. Locke has a question you can probably answer it."

"Well, yes, I guess but…"

"The plans are a bit complex because they include a lot of future expansion," Stanley explained.

Paul surveyed the large room. "What a wonderful beginning! This house looks so modest from the outside."

"Deliberately," Stanley said succinctly.

Stanley introduced Paul to Hammond Carter, his architect, and the next few minutes were spent while Paul and Hammond exchanged respectful comments about each other's work.

Hammond unrolled the blueprint and Paul studied it then commented, "You have quite an addition planned. "When's this work being done?"

"I'm just here about the kitchen today," the architect said. "Stanley insists we do that part immediately."

Paul pointed at the blueprint. "You can't do it without the family room."

Stanley took Mrs. Locke aside and explained how the two rooms would be connected.

"Sounds nice," she said disinterestedly.

This was happening too fast. She comforted herself with the thought that the plans had been drawn up pre-Aleta.

Paul rushed over. "Aleta will love this. I know it."

"So should I go ahead," Stanley said. "Or wait for Aleta?"

"She likes what you've done so far," Paul said.

Marian looked at him askance.

"Oh, Marian, go with the flow. You aren't going to win this time."

"Win?" Stanley queried.

"She's determined that Aleta should return to California where it's safe."

"I'll tell the crew to start digging," Stanley said.

"Don't you have to survey and mark the area?" Paul asked.

"We did that this morning. Your niece gave me a deadline. I've got to use the crew when Martha sends them," Stanley said. "The plumber and electrician are coming at one to talk with the architect. The cabinet maker is coming at two and we have to select the wood before then. The carpenters are coming at four to set up the framing for the foundation."

"I'm going outside with Hammond," Paul said. "Marian, you help Stanley pick out the wood."

Aleta walked to the barn with her father. Stoney accompanied them. She told Stoney to sit while she climbed the ladder. Her dad, despite cautioning her that it looked dangerous, followed. At the front edge, he stood beside her and looked out over the orchard which spread from the driveway to the field where the wheat had been crushed by numerous tire tracks and countless footsteps.

"Why are we here?" Robert asked his daughter.

"Grams said to explain to you why I climbed up here and shot two men."

Robert sat down near the edge of the loft and said, "I have all day."

And Aleta began with her desire to save Stanley's barn which she knew it was important to him when she looked through the picture window in the bedroom and saw the barn included in the view. She told her dad about Gram's prophecy and when he appeared skeptical she told him about the events that Gram's had prophesied concerning Julia Danielson's family.

Slowly, Aleta saw a flicker of openness in her father's face.

"So why did you take Stoney with you?"

"Grams prophesied his being killed in front of her, and I was determined to change that part of the prophecy; so I took Stoney and the gun and came up here."

Aleta watched her father's eyes reflect a growing interest in Aleta's tale. She described the scene in detail and when she finished, he asked, "You were up here alone?"

Aleta rose. "Standing. Right here."

"That was foolish! You made yourself a target!"

"Look at the distance between here and the RV's. There were four men armed with automatic weapons after Grams. I had to draw them away. I couldn't let her die!"

Her father pulled her down and hugged her. "Oh, Aleta, don't you know how much I would miss you if you died? You are my most wonderful treasure."

"Dad, I didn't intend to die. No one was expecting me to be up here. I had the element of surprise. And…"

"Don't ever try to save a barn again!"

"I already promised Stanley that I wouldn't. That's why this barn is half gone."

"I thought you shot the can."

"And the man. That time I shot two men," Aleta explained. "It was Fogg Spader who set the fire that burned this barn after he shot Grams right down there."

"She was shot in the chest," her father said bewildered.

"She was bending over Stoney trying to protect him. The bullet went through her lung."

Then Aleta walked him through that night. They wound up in the field with Stoney quartering as Babe had the night before. Her father envisioned a soldier in a heavy pack and helmet moving cautiously across an open field at night and then he put his daughter, shirtless, doing the same thing.

How clever she was not to come directly from the burning barn where she would have been silhouetted against the fire's light.

His mind saw the picture as vividly as if he'd been there.

"Daddy," Aleta said suddenly in a small girl's voice, "I killed him. I tried wounding him but he just kept shooting."

"It seems justified to me."

"Daddy, you don't understand. I wounded him when he was in the barn; but I was too angry to give him any slack. I was so angry I hunted him down and killed him."

"I don't know if I would have had the guts to do that, especially shirtless and in a white bra."

"Dad, this is serious."

"And I'm being serious. Did you ever wonder why men darken their faces and wear camouflaged clothing in combat?"

"Oh," Aleta said in a small voice.

"Don't ever chase a bad man again," her father said, "or did Stanley already say that."

Aleta chuckled, "More or less."

"I gather he doesn't try to control you."

"No, he doesn't."

"He makes you happy?"

"We have so many great plans, Dad," Aleta said. "We have this grand house and he's a great lawyer."

At this point, Robert Locke sobered as a new thought entered his thinking.

"This Trust your grandmother is involved with, is it big?"

"Yes, it is," Aleta responded, slightly taken aback by the switch in topic. "Why?"

"Fogg Spader's family may file a wrongful death suit."

Aleta's jaw dropped. "On what basis?"

"Well, you were justified in returning fire when he was firing on your from the barn; but, afterward you said you personally hunted him down."

"Well, if they do, they won't get much. I'm just the Tontine's lawyer.

"Give Stanley and me time alone to have a long talk about your statement. I understand you haven't given it yet."

"Why can't I just tell the truth?"

"Is there a good criminal attorney in the area?"

"Chief West's father is the best."

"Hire him."

"But, Dad, I shot in self-defense."

"Hiring a lawyer doesn't mean you're guilty of any wrong doing. But civil actions are a nuisance. And, when it comes to the kind of wealth Stanley has, some lawyer may give it a shot."

"Stanley is wealthy?" Aleta asked her eyes opening wide.

"Well, I didn't tell your mother because sometimes a person's being rich outweighs all else, but Stanley is very wealthy."

"How wealthy?"

"Very."

"He gave me a pre-nup," Aleta said.

"And didn't ask you to sign one?" her father asked.

"No."

"Now I am impressed," her dad said. "Let's go and let Stanley's family impress your mother."

"You sound like Grams."

Her father laughed, "Well, she did raise me."

Chapter 39

When they got back to the house, Robert Locke took Stanley into the bedroom and closed the door.

"Now what?" asked Marian.

"Dad's going to talk with Stanley about a pre-nup," Aleta replied slyly.

Her mother's fact lit up. "Good idea. I knew your father would protect your interests."

Rather than snap back, Aleta affirmed her mother's statement. "I think that's why Grams insisted I talk with him."

"Well, good for her," Marian said. "Who are these people coming out of those RV's?"

"Friends," Aleta said. "My guess is that Stanley asked his parents to invite them for lunch too."

"Can't they cook inside those trailers?"

"Yes, but they're Stanley's guests," Aleta said. "And Stanley's parents can handle throwing an extra hot dog on the barbecue."

"We're eating outside?"

"They have a pretty yard I'm told."

"I'm not the hot dog type, Aleta. You know that."

"Mother, be nice. These are Gram's best friends from years ago."

"I have nothing in common with them," Marian sniffed.

"Then don't say anything," Aleta suggested.

But after introduction, the talk turned to where Stanley was.

Marian usurped Aleta's answer with one of her own.

"He and my husband are talking about a pre-nup."

"I thought you already had one," Ed said.

"There was trouble with the last shoot," Aleta said. "Stanley's getting hold of Mr. West."

"Chief West?" Ed asked.

"His father."

"Let me go talk with them," Ed said.

Marian objected and moved to block the way. "I'm sorry. But the matter is private."

"I was there," Ed said. "And I'm the detective for the Trust."

"Let him pass, Mother," Aleta ordered in a tone her mother hadn't heard before. It was authoritative and decisive. Marian stepped back.

"Ed is a good detective," Beatrice said. "He may have seen something."

Marian glared at the plump lady with the bleached hair in the wild strawberry-colored suit thinking that the pair just wanted to pry. Why didn't Aleta see that?

Aleta broke in. "He's the man who accompanied me out here. And he and Beatrice are engaged. He gave her one heck of a pre-nup."

Beatrice blushed. "And a ring."

She offered her hand and Marian saw the tiny diamond on her little finger.

"It was Martha Cook's engagement ring," Beatrice said. "She is smaller than me. He said he'd get it resized but I said no."

Aleta could almost see her mother's mind at work. She decided that she needed to redeem Ed's reputation. "Ed bought Beatrice a painting for over her fireplace."

"Cost him a fortune, too," Beatrice said. "He planned to give it to me whether I said yes or no. He said I deserved to be surrounded by the best."

"Does he make a good living as a private investigator?" Marian asked pointedly.

"He only does that part time. He owns a pet store in California."

"Will you be moving back there then?" Marian asked with forced politeness.

"He's moving here," Beatrice said joyfully. "We're going to build a new house on some land we own. So's Marge and her husband and Evelyn. Harriet's going to build there too. It's a pretty piece of land complete with trees and a pond."

"Beatrice and Evelyn are planning to fund a dog shelter and a free spay clinic," Aleta said. "Stanley and I are setting up the fund's operation."

Marian only half-listened. She was glancing repeatedly at the closed bedroom door.

"Mom's not into dogs," Aleta explained, and then said. "Marge is funding a new physical therapy wing for the hospital."

Marian's head snapped around. She looked at the plainly dressed brown-haired woman and wondered if she'd heard Aleta correctly. She decided she hadn't.

"That's nice," she said vaguely.

"Aleta's a brave young lady," Jason commented. "Going after an armed man alone in the field with only a rifle."

Suddenly, Marion's attention was captured. "She did what?"

Aleta stepped in. "That's why it's taking so long mother. Daddy's afraid the man's family might sue."

"Sue? For what?"

"I shot him and I killed him, Mom."

Jason coughed. "After he'd shot Harriet and set the barn on fire. Come on, Aleta, it was a righteous act."

Marian, however, was stuck on the word that frightened her. "It evidently wasn't so righteous if the man's family can sue. That finishes it. You're coming home with me."

"And you don't think the suit will follow us there?" Aleta argued forgetting her resolve not to fight with her mother.

"Your father knows topflight attorneys at home. You need someone better than the police chief's father!" Marian exclaimed and then rushed on angrily. "No wonder you took your dad off to the barn alone. He's a soft touch. He'd do whatever you asked. Well, I'm your mother and this time I dictate what's going to happen."

The men emerged from the bedroom, smiling.

Aleta's father took her in his arms. "It's going to be okay. Ed was there, you remember."

"Vaguely," Aleta said.

"He said your last shot hit him in the chest and knocked him off his feet but it was your first shot, the one you fired into the barn that killed him."

"My first shot?" Aleta mouthed.

"So we don't need a pre-nup," Stanley said.

"Oh, yes, you do!" Marian shot back. "I won't let her get married without one. I can't believe you're being stubborn about this."

Aleta interrupted. "Of course, I'll sign one."

"Aleta, don't be silly. He signs it, not you."

"Let's not argue," her father said. "Let's go to lunch. Mr. West will come over this afternoon and counsel you on your statement. Stanley agrees that you need to be careful."

"Why are we hiring a lawyer?" Marian asked. "You're a lawyer, Robert."

"A tax lawyer," her husband replied.

"What about Stanley?"

"A child advocate? We need a criminal lawyer on this one especially as the brother of this man is still alive. We know he's vengeful."

"I don't like any of this!" Marian exclaimed. "Aleta will be safe at home with us."

Her husband scowled at her, "My mother was almost killed just five miles from us."

Marian was silent during the short drive. Her daughter had almost been killed. She'd actually shot a man. Nobody was making any sense. Why wasn't Robert backing her up? She knew he wanted the best for his favorite daughter. Conan Lloyd was a man she approved of. How did Conan lose to this man? Well, she could be as polite as the next person. She certainly wasn't going to say anything derogatory to the man's parents. She would keep her mouth shut.

Stanley called his mother as they left the driveway. "We are actually on our way, Mother… Well, it's your fault for starting early… I told you I'd call. No I didn't show them every inch of the place a dozen times. We had other business… No, I can't tell you… Well, yes I can… It's about signing a pre-nup. Aleta wants one. I don't… Yes, okay… I'll tell her."

"Tell me what?" Aleta said.

Marian leaned forward in the back seat.

"She says no. She never had to sign one and neither should you."

"You signed one!" Aleta said. Her mother raised her eyebrows and glanced at her husband who was watching her, smiling.

"It was a gesture," Stanley said. "Ed did it and it seemed like a good idea. I didn't know if you had money or not."

"My dad told me about you. We need another pre-nup!"

"You told her, Sir?" Stanley asked. "When did you know?"

"I asked my mother," Robert smiled. "Aleta insisted Mother call me when she was hiding out to let me know she was okay."

Stanley smiled, "So, how involved was your mother?"

"Well, I know she didn't like Conan."

"Neither did I," Stanley responded, and both men laughed.

The car turned into a wide driveway leading to a large two story house with lovely tall Corinthian pillars holding a roof that shaded the portico.

"Mother is from the south," Stanley said. "She brought a bit of it with her."

Marian's awed expression lasted long enough for Aleta to see it. She watched her struggle to recover.

"I thought your mother worked."

"She does," Stanley replied kindly. "She took the day off which I must admit made her a bit testy about our delay in arriving; but, mostly, I believe she was nervous about meeting you. She wanted everything to be perfect."

Aleta leaned over and kissed him on the cheek.

"What's that for?"

"Tell you later," Aleta said.

He drove to the side of the house and the other cars followed him. Stanley's father came out to greet them. It was instantly obvious whom Stanley took after. Hubert Praetzel shook Robert Locke's hand and smiled warmly. "We thought you'd be comfortable on the patio. A dining room is so formal."

He ushered the group through the gate down a hedge-lined path to a lovely, expansive garden area. Tables were set up with white linen cloths and fresh flowers.

A tall woman came to greet them. She had on a soft flowing, pale green print dress.

"Judge Davis," Beatrice said, "it's a pleasure. Please allow me to introduce everyone."

"Call me Lydia," she said and Beatrice then introduced the group.

"I've set the men at that table and we women at this one," Lydia said.

"Still sorting, huh, Mother," Stanley commented.

"You men will want to talk about all the shootings and we women will want to discuss the wedding," Lydia replied. "Do you want to argue for an alternate plan?"

"Mother, you know I never argue with a judge."

"That'll be the day!" Lydia quipped. "Come let's sit down. I want to hear all about Marge's project."

The women began to settle as did the men.

Stanley called over, "That's not talking about the wedding, Mother."

"Well, you have my permission not to talk about the shootings," his mother retorted.

Marian sat, her mouth open in amazement, as Lydia drew out each woman at the table about their projects.

Beatrice looked at Aleta's mother who was as tastefully dressed as her daughter and came up with an idea.

"Mrs. Locke, I need a special dress for my wedding. Would you help me select one, I mean, as long as you'll be shopping for Aleta's wedding gown and trousseau. I can show you the best stores in the city. I don't use them much because I have a local shop I like."

"Jean Perrie's?" Lydia asked. "I shop there too."

Marian's surprise was evident. The women didn't dress at all alike. Aleta caught her look and commented, "You know, Mom, Jean Perrie seems to have a knack for figuring out what people want.

"That would be a place to start," Marian Locke admitted. Aleta smiled, satisfied.

"Have you seen Stanley's fish?" Lydia asked abruptly. "He has quite an aquarium."

"No," Marian said. "Is it here?"

"Heaven no," Lydia laughed. "I made him put it in his office. By the way, Aleta, thanks for helping him save them."

"Sorry I didn't save Judge Davis."

"Well, at least you didn't lose Martha Cook."

Marian puzzled aloud, "Martha Cook is a fish."

"He's very fond of those Koi," Lydia went on. "I've never been enthralled with animals; but I want you to know, Aleta, that your dogs will be welcome here anytime."

"What dogs?" Marian asked. "I thought you'd left that part of your childhood behind."

"Well, it's back, Mom," Aleta said gaily. "I've been promised one of Emma's pups. She's Ed's Lab. And Mr. Sciretta told me I could have pick bitch for Stanley. He wants to show her."

"A Bulldog!" Lydia gasped. "Stanley wants a Bulldog?"

Marian felt an immediate connection with Stanley's mother.

"When I said Maggie was cute, Stanley looked at her face and decided I had a skewed idea of cute," Aleta commented.

"And what do you think of Stanley's looks?"

It was a loaded question.

"I see him as you do," Aleta said. "And I wouldn't change a thing. And, if I'm very, very lucky, I'll have a son that looks just like him."

Marian looked at her daughter with new respect.

Aleta leaned back and eavesdropped on the conversation at the men's table. Her father was speaking.

"You know you can offer to buy the wood from some old barn that's being torn down and rebuild your barn with the lumber. I'd be glad to help."

"I'm not much of a carpenter," Stanley said.

"I'll teach you," Robert Locke said. "I can stay awhile. This is the slack time for tax attorneys and Marian won't want to leave even the tiniest bit of the wedding planning to Aleta."

"I'll be pretty busy," Stanley said apologetically.

"I can help," Ed said. "I'm pretty handy."

"It's a big project," Stanley said.

Robert Locke brushed Stanley's remark aside and addressed Ed directly.

"We've got to match the wood," Robert said.

"PI's are good at finding stuff," Ed said.

Aleta looked over at Stanley to see if he was upset. He smiled and winked.

Chapter 40

Two weeks later, Aleta entered the hospital just after dawn.

"Tell me why I'm here," Aleta said. "And why is Chief West downstairs?"

"You do know I'm checking out today," Harriet said, putting her robe in her suitcase and closing it.

"I know."

"Well, I'm leaving a little early."

"I thought you weren't having any more... um... whatever it is you have.

"Prophecies, Aleta. They're called prophecies. And I'm a prophet."

"Okay. Prophecies. I thought you weren't having any more."

"Whatever gave you that idea?"

"You said you only had a premonition the night you were shot."

"That's true."

"And you haven't prophesied since then."

"Haven't I?"

"You mean you didn't share?" Aleta asked angrily. Then a thought struck her. "It was about me, wasn't it?"

"I took care of it."

"How?"

"I asked you to talk with your father and you did."

"And if I hadn't...?"

"I would have taken other steps."

"You aren't going to tell me the prophesy are you?"

"You died! Now are you happy?"

"How? The Ciccones?"

"Car accident," Harriet said. "Here's my ride."

An orderly appeared with a wheelchair which cut off all further communication instantly.

"Has my furniture arrived?" Harriet asked settling into the chair.

"Just the living room stuff. It's nicely set up in Stanley's house. Robert and Ed moved it half a dozen times before Mother was satisfied. I kept telling them it was a temporary arrangement. It is temporary, isn't it?"

"Until my house is built," Harriet responded.

"But I'm going to be married in two weeks," Aleta wailed softly.

"And I'm going to house sit comfortably while you're gone."

"You're going with us."

"Only to Ohio," Harriet grinned. "Then I'm going to enjoy your house until you return."

"I'm glad you realize we're coming back."

"Then I'm moving into my RV. I'll be quite comfortable."

"We can't impose on Stanley's hospitality forever."

"Of course, I can," Harriet said. " After you're married I'll be family. Besides I'm going to enjoy popping in on you at odd hours."

"Grams!" Aleta exclaimed.

Harriet laughed.

"Stop worrying. Stanley and I already set the rules."

Only after they were driving away did Aleta dare ask, "Why this early morning ride?"

"There's a sniper waiting for me. West has set a trap."

"But the Tontine Trust is completely transferred."

"Clay Spader is still out for vengeance."

"But he's still in the hospital. In fact, I heard he wasn't expected to live."

"He isn't. This is his last hurrah. He hired a shooter," Harriet said. "Turn here. Take the long way home. We can talk on the way."

"About what?"

"About your nightmares."

"How did you know about them?" Aleta charged.

"I have them too."

"Oh," she responded in a small voice, "I thought you could..."

"What? Read your mind?"

"Something like that."

"I can't even see the future. My prophetic powers are very circumscribed. God, it seems, likes our plans."

"So, you can't help me with the nightmares?"

"I didn't say that."

"Stanley says it was a righteous shoot."

"But we know better."

"What do you mean 'we'? Yours was," Aleta insisted.

"The cops wounded the two they aimed for," Harriet responded. "You , my dear Aleta, wounded the two in the field. I, on the other hand, shot to kill."

"Still, they were attacking. You were saving me." Aleta argued. "But when I went after Fogg Spader I wanted him dead. I was so furious I actually hunted down a wounded man to kill him. It doesn't matter that my first wild shot actually did the trick. I acted out of pure rage. Evil rage!"

"Rage isn't evil" Harriet said. "It's just an emotion. We can't help our emotions."

Aleta scowled. Before she could respond, Harriet went on.

"Our emotions are triggered by events, people, things. We can't control what makes us react. All we can do is control what we do when the emotion hits us."

"I think some emotions are evil."

"Like rage?"

"Well, yes, like rage."

"Jesus felt rage. He acted upon it when he attacked the moneychangers outside the temple. Rage is an emotion. You can't control feelings. They come unbidden. God never told us to control our feelings, just to choose what to do when we had them. Jesus said, 'Do unto others.' The emphasis is on action."

"I remember reading about thinking pure thoughts."

"Well, of course. Reveling in vengeful thoughts will only destroy you."

"So what has this to do with my nightmares?"

"Your conscience is struggling with what you did. God, you and I know what drove you to kill a man. It is difficult for us to accept that we choose both good and evil knowingly."

"The rage was so strong."

"Rage is a powerful emotion," Harriet said. "But you chose what to do, didn't you?"

"I did. I chose. I chose to kill a man. I brushed aside the alternatives. I wanted him dead."

"That's what you need to ask forgiveness for your choice to do evil."

"Will He forgive me?"

"He did me."

"How do you know?"

"I can still prophesy. Much as I hate it because people expect me to know what the future holds, and I only get glimpses when God wants it changed, and I don't know how to explain that."

"Why does that tell you you're forgiven?"

"Because we're still connected, He and I."

"Will my nightmares go away?"

"Probably not. They're a consequence of your action. Forgiveness doesn't erase consequences. Remember the prayer Jesus taught his disciples?"

"Of course."

"Now you know what 'deliver us from evil' means."

Chapter 41

The wedding would be the main topic of conversation for years to come. It wasn't that it was replete with mishaps which did occur; but, they didn't seem to affect either the bride or groom and therefore didn't mar the singular feeling that this had been a perfect wedding.

Just moments before the ceremony was to start, Aleta's mother had tried for the third time to persuade Aleta that she needed to wear the veil with its tiara for her wedding outfit to be complete.

"The scar is still sensitive," Aleta said referring to the path the bullet had made less than a month prior down the center of her scalp.

"Surely, you can stand a little discomfort for fifteen minutes," her mother reasoned.

"No, I can't," Aleta said. "And Stanley wouldn't want me to.

"The look will be ruined!" her mother wailed.

Aleta kissed her mother lightly. "No, it won't. It'll be different but not ruined."

A tap on the door interrupted the pair. Lauren West, the matron of honor, opened the door. A man handed her a flat florist's box. The card on it read, "For my beloved bride."

The argument was put on hold and Aleta opened the box. Inside was a lovely crown of white lilies."

Aleta touched the delicate petals.

"So soft," she observed.

Lauren tucked her fingers under the crown expecting to find a circular rim of wire. She uttered a soft surprised exclamation. "It's held together by a silk ribbon."

Aleta put her hand next to Lauren's.

Her mother looked at the flower crown thoughtfully then said, "We could probably attach the veil to that."

Aleta shook her head. "Too much weight."

She set the crown on her head.

"Lovely!" Lauren said. "I should have real flowers too, shouldn't I?"

Aleta took a lily from her bouquet and handed it to Lauren who removed her cap and fastened the flower in its place.

Harriet slipped in through the door.

"Everyone's here," she said. "My, don't you look lovely, Aleta."

She turned to her daughter-in-law. "Marian, you outdid yourself. Everything is perfect."

"Too bad there are so few people on the bride's side," Marian said sadly.

"Few?" Harriet scoffed. "It's overflowing."

Aleta grinned knowingly, "What did Stanley do? Instruct the ushers not to sort people?"

Harriet smiled, "He's cleverer than that. He instructed his ushers to ask guests if they'd met you. If they had, he said the ushers were to then assume they were friends of the bride."

"I've met a lot of Stanley's friends," Aleta said.

"And they'll be beaming at you from your side of the aisle."

"What did Stanley's mother think about that?"

"I think she wanted to join them."

Aleta watched as her mother's face brightened. Aleta hadn't realized until that moment how important that was to her. Stanley had.

Lauren preceded Aleta down the aisle while her two sisters sat with her parents. Her mother had first insisted her sisters be bridesmaids but Aleta had wanted a simpler wedding.

While Chief Lyle West was Stanley's best man, the entire Arborville police force plus the entire Willow Glen force was seated on Aleta's side of the aisle. The police from nearby Oakwood, the third police force in the tri-city area, were on loan for the day to police the streets of Arborville and Willow Glen.

The church itself was resplendent with flowers. Only the huge wooden cross in front of the stained glass window was left unadorned.

All this beauty, even though awe-inspiring, was nevertheless expected. The Praetzel's were among the community's wealthiest families.

The bride was as beautiful as Stanley's relatives had been told she was. She moved down the aisle on the arm of her father with surefooted grace. Absent a veil, her even features balanced into a pleasing whole were hardly noticed, so beautiful was her smile intended only for Stanley. No one could remember seeing a happier bride.

At the altar, Aleta leaned over and kissed Stanley lightly on his cheek.

"Glad you could make it," she whispered.

"I had to. West is already married," Stanley retorted in a soft voice.

The minister cleared his throat and the two, still grinning, faced him. He couldn't help but smile back.

"Dearly Beloved," he began. He barely managed to finish his first sentence before Stanley took over. Aleta's father quietly slipped into the seat next to her mother who hissed at him that he was to give the bride away.

"Not today," he whispered. "Stanley has his own agenda."

"In the presence of God and this company," Stanley said in a voice just loud enough to be heard by the entire congregation. "I promise to love you wholly and forever, to endow you with all my worldly possessions and to be utterly truthful from this day forward. With this ring, I promise to cherish you and care for you above all others."

Stanley took Aleta's hand and deftly slipped the ring on her finger.

"I knew you would be doing this," Aleta said in a voice as clear as Stanley's. "You wanted me to know you'd considered your promise carefully, didn't you? Don't answer that. It was rhetorical. Well, I thought about our vows as well. You didn't think you were going to upstage me, did you?"

Stanley smiled. Here was his bride at her best.

"Here's what I promise. Not my eternal love. You already have that. Not my respect. You earned that weeks ago. There is only one thing left. I'm about to promise you something I have never promised another person nor will I ever promise again. It is my singular gift to you alone."

The silence in the church deepened as people held back their very breath so they could hear.

Aleta turned and took the ring from Lauren's hand. "With this ring, I accept your promises and offer mine. From this moment forward, I promise to obey you."

Aleta smiled at the surprise she saw in Stanley's eyes. More than that he understood how profound that promise was for her.

As the two gazed at each other the minister pronounced them husband and wife.

Instead of turning toward the congregation, Aleta and Stanley turned toward the cross and knelt without benefit of a padded stool. The organ began to play the opening strains of the Lord's Prayer and the soloist began to sing almost at a whisper. After the crescendo, the minister spoke the final words, "Whom God hath joined together, let no man put asunder."

The bride and groom rose and kissed tenderly.

Harriet squeezed Martha's hand and the two smiled at each other. With lace trimmed handkerchiefs both ladies dabbed the tears threatening to spill down their cheeks. But the next moment was to surprise and delight both. The bride and groom, hands clasped, moved down the aisle past both mothers and stopped in front of Harriet Locke and Martha Cook.

"Thank you," they said in unison as each presented a rose to the flabbergasted old ladies.

Aleta leaned over and whispered in Stanley's ear, "We surprised two prophets! Can you believe it?"

Stanley kissed her lightly on the cheek and, laughing lightly, the two trotted gaily up the aisle.

"Did you see that coming?" Martha asked Harriet.

"It seems God allows me happy surprises," Harriet replied. "I'm asking Him to find another prophet to replace me."

"I think being a prophet is a lot like a marriage. You're in it for the duration."

"But in a marriage you get to agree to the union somewhere along the line."

"Think of it this way," Martha counseled. "Thanks to your warnings, this came about.